Back Track

Detective Mahoney Series

Julie Hiner

Killers and Demons

Final Track © 2022 Julie Hiner

First Printing in 2022

Publisher: Julie Hiner

KillersAndDemons.com

Editing by: Taija Morgan

Bio Photo by: Aune Photo

Cover Design: 100 Covers

ISBN: 978-1-7781424-2-0

First Edition

To all those who feel the energy coursing through their veins when the moon is full.

To all those who had their bodies taken, emptied of minds and souls, and used as vessels.

To all those who must live out a fantasy pulsing through their cells, or face a death within.

To all those who spiral down a black vortex, trying to save the souls in empty vessels.

Most of all, to all gothic metal lovers.

Contents

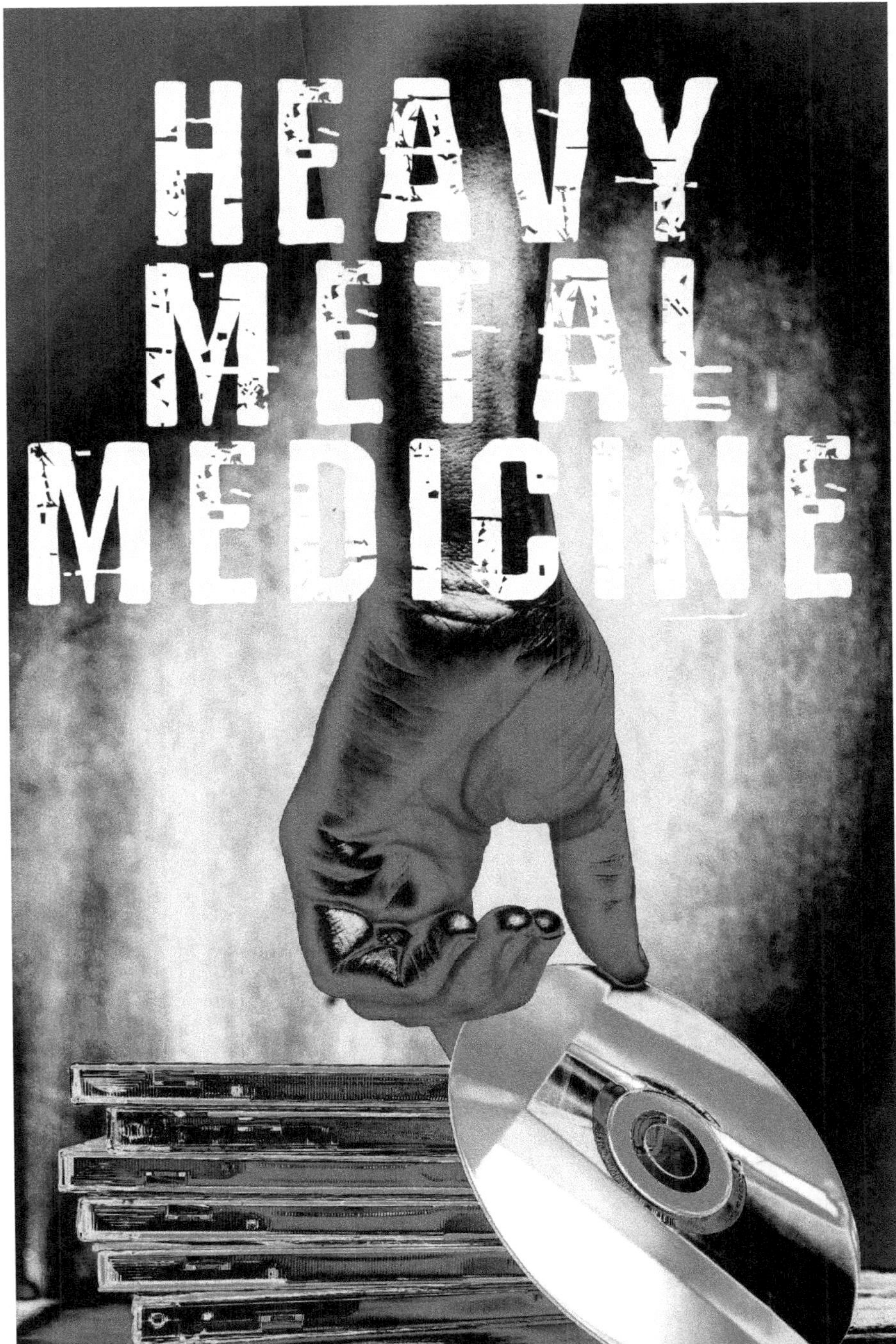
HEAVY
METAL
MEDICINE

Chapter 1

Suitcases

October 15, 1987

The door on Detective Mahoney's '69 vintage orange Pony creaked as he flung it open. He reached over to the passenger seat, scooped up his tattered derby, and slid out of the car. A gust of wind threatened to steal his beloved hat. He clamped it to his head with one hand and slammed the door shut with the other.

Pulling the sides of his tweed herringbone coat close together, he strode straight into the cold headwind, across the parking lot. It wasn't even Halloween, yet the Canadian winter was already wrapping its icy claws around the city. Half a dozen rusty beaters were scattered over the lot, reflecting the income level of the residents of the low-budget apartment complex in Calgary's northeast. It wasn't exactly anybody's dream home.

A familiar brown-and-black Jeep Wrangler caught his eye. His shoulders relaxed. He was more than a little relieved that Terra Blackwood was the medical examiner on scene. If he had to face another murder, he was happy it would be with her.

A flash of yellow tape stretched across a half-open door on the second level of the complex. Mahoney headed over to a staircase crumbling with time and climbed up. At the top, shielded by the row of apartments, he released his hold on his hat and strode to the front door of the crime scene.

Cold hands crawled through his insides. He shook them off. He'd hoped he wouldn't have to see another corpse. An unrealistic wish for a homicide detective.

He didn't know what was wrong with him. He used to be able to walk away from a dead body, focus on the facts, and find the killer. Case after case, he breezed through dozens of dead bodies, no problem. The last two cases he'd been on still haunted him. Both killers were dead. So were a lot of innocent boys.

He halted at the door, staring at the crime scene tape. He swallowed.

The door flung open. A lanky man with a thin moustache and round spectacles stared at him, his eyes wide. "Sorry. Didn't know there was someone here." The young man's jacket revealed his crime scene tech status.

"No problem." Mahoney stepped aside and let the techie by.

His stomach clenched as he thrust himself into the apartment. *Just another case. Just another body.* Yet, he knew it wasn't. The images haunting him night and day had been clamping down hard lately. Seeping into his every thought. Clutching their dead hands around his aging heart.

The room was small and cluttered. Several crime scene techs flashed cameras and combed through the mess with gloved hands. Long, black hair shone under bright bulbs. A silver streak caught his eye. *Blackwood.* She was crouched by a closet in the far corner of the room.

He took several long strides, catapulting himself away from the busy work and over to Blackwood.

A lavender cloud seeped around him as he approached. He smiled to himself. She wasn't in his realm, but he couldn't help it if things inside of him stirred up in her presence.

He took a glance at the core of the scene. No body. A row of six suitcases lined the floor of the open closet. The door hung crooked from bent hinges.

Blackwood looked up over her shoulder. "Mahoney." She smiled. "You're just in time for the show. Look." She pointed at the corner of one of the suitcases. Thick, scarlet shapes stained the rough material. "We think there are bodies inside."

Six suitcases. Did that mean six bodies? *Dammit.*

"Mahoney. You OK?" Blackwood's almond-shaped eyes seeped concern. "You look pale."

He cleared his throat. "Yeah. Fine. Didn't get much sleep."

"We need to open one of these." She looked back at the row of suitcases. She called across the room, summoning a techie to perform the gruesome photoshoot she was about to unfold.

The walls of the small apartment closed in around Mahoney, as if they were breathing. He gritted his teeth and stared at the first suitcase in the lineup as Blackwood eased it onto its side. Camera flashes electrified the dim room. The lanky techie with the thin moustache crouched over the suitcase, positioning his camera to follow Blackwood's every move.

Flash. The room lit up, sizzling Mahoney's eyeballs. A flicker of a corpse invaded his mind, shooting him back in time. A college boy. Dead. Painted up like a glam rock god about to put on the performance of his life. A shimmering cloak half covering his lifeless body. His lips painted pink, pulled into an enunciated shape, unreal and grotesque.

Blackwood pulled the zipper on the side of the suitcase, causing a *zzz* to clip through the still air of the stuffy room.

Flash. Another photo. Another corpse scintillating through his mind. A young boy, decayed and skeletal, dough-white skin filling in the contours of the face he once had. Empty eye sockets staring into Mahoney's soul like black caverns, seeking an answer to his demise.

Blackwood flipped open the top of the suitcase. A mess of limbs were cluttered together, bloody flesh dripping from severed bones, torn tendons hanging like gory tentacles, weaving over the pile of body parts.

Mahoney's stomach roiled as the smell spilled out. Acid clawed up the back of his throat. Sweat sprouted across his brow. The room tilted sideways. The walls closed in.

He swallowed hard and shook his head. His derby slid off, thudding against the crusty carpet.

A voice from far away ebbed through the thick space, searching for him. "Hey...ey...ey...you...ou...ou...ooo...kaaay?"

He tried to respond. Hot air pushed down against his voice, forcing it to bulge in the pit of his throat.

The room swayed back and forth. The bloody limbs crawled out of the suitcase. Writhing over the crusty floor, their bloody fingers reached for him.

The room spun wildly, all the way around. Blackness followed. Pain shot through Mahoney's skull as his head hit the ground.

Chapter 2

Glaring Suns

April 5, 1989

Detective Mahoney stared at two sunny-side ups sizzling in a pan. His eyes burned. Grease flew through the air, searing his cheeks. Rust crawled over the sides of the old pan. He wondered if he would ever buy anything new for his empty apartment. Old and empty. Just like him.

His early—and sudden—retirement hadn't helped him. After back-to-back cases, two serial killers were dead. Seth and Sid. One had created the other. Seth had left a trail of college boys painted up like glam rock gods scattered across city parks in elaborate displays. Sid had wrapped young boys like mummies, took their eyes as trophies, and collected them in his underground desert sanctuary.

It used to be that Detective Mahoney could compile a murder scene, purge the images, and focus on the facts. After the *Glam Boys* case followed by the *Mummy Boys* case, his mind refused to clear. Like shots from an old horror flick, images of corpse faces flashed sporadically inside his head between fuzzy glitches of darkness. The *Suitcase Slaughters* had put him over the edge.

He forced himself to look at the bulbous golden eggs, willing them to shine like suns through the darkness piercing every corner of his brain. The slew of gory pictures grew stronger every day, despite the time and distance that had been forced between him and murder. His mind buzzed. He blinked hard and stared into the frying pan.

A young boy's ghastly face overtook the golden spheres. A shiny black cloak engulfed his thoughts, tassels fluttering. Mahoney shook his head.

He forced the image of the ghost face out of his mind. He exhaled. Long and hard. He took a sip of coffee, picked up a rusty metal flipper, and poked at the crusty, white edges swimming in grease. He blinked, feeling the next image surging inside his head.

No. No more.

He glared at the tomato-sauce-dotted tile lining the wall behind the stove. When was the last time he cooked spaghetti? He forced his eyes across the red-spattered black tiles, running his mind across last week's dinners, searching for pasta and tomato sauce. All he found was a sudden, clear image of a child wrapped like a mummy. Fake black nothing eyes stared back at him. His shoulders shook. His arms tingled.

He yanked the knob on the stove and shoved the rusty pan to the back burner. *Screw this.* Looking at the ground and rubbing the back of his neck, he sauntered to the bedroom. He lay down on his bed with a thump.

He had all the time in the world now. But what was he good for? He had pried himself away from the slew of dead bodies invading his every thought. He had tried to escape all the corpses that had piled up. They wouldn't leave him alone. They cluttered his mind, every second of every day. What good was all this time when he couldn't even function?

Function? What the hell did that even mean?

His body was old and tired. His mind was rotten with ghastly and horrific images. His brain was an overstuffed photo album, with pictures falling from the pages and the binding splitting in all directions.

He lay hard against the bed, closed his eyes, and tried to see nothing. *What had Doctor Sherry said? Clear all the bad images. See them floating away into nothing. Replace them with good ones.*

He took a deep breath. In. Out. He tried to imagine the sounds of his daughter, Stella, giggling and calling his name. He tried to feel the ocean breeze on his face and the soft, warm sand sliding through his toes, reliving that last visit he'd had with her.

How long ago had that been? She was already twelve. He grasped for a drop of happiness. A sense of *normal.* The word sounded like it belonged to a foreign language, one he had never spoken. Taking a deep breath, he willed his mind to hear the laughter, crashing waves, and squawking seagulls.

Bam. A ghost face slammed against his skull. Every happy, normal image disintegrated. Dark, nothing eyes stared at him. He bolted up in his bed, his eyes flung open. Nothing worked anymore. Nothing.

He walked to the bathroom and stared in the mirror. Circular shadows wove around each eye. Day-old bristle had built into week-old bristle, threatening to become a full-on beard.

Ha. When's the last time you had a beard, old man?

He laughed. It felt good. But it sounded like a crazy man's laugh. Pulling open the cabinet with a snap, he scanned the rows of bottles.

He grabbed the sleeping pills Doctor Sherry had prescribed to him. She was actually quite stingy with the medication. Probably a good thing.

The tiny letters on the back of the bottle told him to take one at a time, not to mix with alcohol, and not to operate any machinery. He popped the cap and tilted the bottle to his lips, letting a couple of pills slide onto his tongue.

He swallowed hard against the desert in his throat and felt the two capsules forcing their way down his insides. Placing the bottle back in the cabinet, he clicked the mirror closed.

Shuffling across the bedroom, he found himself at the makeshift bar in his living room, wondering how he got there. He stared at the bottle of Woodford. The black nothing eyes pierced his brain.

"Get the hell out of my life!" He lifted his shaking hands to the bottle. He unscrewed the lid. The sweet aroma permeated his nose as the rich brown liquid flowed into crystal.

He steadied his hand, lifted the glass to his lips, closed his eyes, and shot back his poison in one swift movement. Before a single thought could enter his mind, he poured another and shot it back.

His throat stung. A slight numbness slithered down his arms and legs. His mind halted. Then it swirled. Long, fuzzy swirls of nothing. No ghost faces. No black nothing eyes. The swirling, he could handle.

He walked his body to his bed and flopped down face first into the pillow. He closed his eyes and willed himself to sleep.

Chapter 3

Beer-Soaked Bar

The cold air sliced at Detective Mahoney's cheeks. He planted his shiny dress shoes against the icy pavement, staring at the black door. Faded red letters were scratched in the concrete; time and weather had washed away whole letters, leaving *on's oint,* where once *Don* had declared that this was his *Joint.*

What are you doing, Detective? You've lost your badge. What else you looking to lose?

He stared at the washed-out entrance. He almost decided to spin on his heel and go home. But he'd been home, alone, for days, weeks, even months. There wasn't anything at home. Just sleeping pills, bourbon, and horrifying images that refused to leave him alone.

It was too late. He'd chosen to chase sick, sadistic monsters who killed as their vocation. He'd left his family behind, not wanting to taint them with his darkness.

A tingle crawled down his arms and through his insides. His flesh was a mere shell clinging to a vacant being.

The wind picked up. His cheeks prickled against the icy wave cutting across them. It was *supposed* to be spring, but a damn cold front had blown in. He pulled at the black door. It didn't budge. The top of the door had been smashed in at the corner.

He yanked hard. It gave way, creaking open toward him. A long, steep staircase shot down into the unknown.

The wind pushed an icy hand against his back. He stepped through the door. He jumped as it slammed behind him. Chattering voices floated up the stairs. Warm air soothed his cold, chapped face. *One beer. I'm already here. And it's cold as fuck out there.*

People kept asking him why he didn't go south, now that he was retired. He didn't know. He couldn't wrap his mind around *retirement*. He didn't know what it meant. Not for him.

Shaking the cold off his shoulders, he descended the stairs. It was even steeper than it looked. He snickered. *I'll tumble to my doom.* He grabbed the railing with a gloved hand. The glove stuck as he tried to slide it along. The leather stretched as he pulled his hand away. It released with a snap. *Sign of a dive.*

Focusing on each step, he descended without the help of the sticky railing. A cloud of body-odour-drenched warm air engulfed him as he stepped from the last stair. The room opened up, a bar on the left, a stage on the right, and vast space filled with cracking wooden tables and chairs in between. A few handfuls of scruffy, homeless-looking patrons sat holding beers and chatting it up.

Mahoney walked across the room. A sticky coating on the floor grabbed at the bottoms of his shoes. This was the type of place you didn't look into the corners of. He hoisted himself up onto a high chair at the bar.

A young woman wrapped in tight, black leather spattered in silver buckles slithered toward him. "What can I get ya?" Her blood-red lips moved, exposing bright-white teeth.

"Beer."

"Well, you'll have to be more specific than that. We've got choices." She ran her obsidian-coated fingernail along a series of taps.

"Pint of Club, please."

Urine-like liquid filled the glass, bubbling at the top. She slid the glass over the bar. "Three-fifty. Cash only. Pay as you go."

Pulling his tattered wallet from his back pocket, he slid several bills across the counter. They caught on a slimy, pink gob. He pulled them up, pink goo stretching along. It snapped as it let go. He handed her the bills and retreated his hand with haste, avoiding the countertop.

A deep rumble vibrated behind him and across the dirt-smeared wooden floor. The stool he was perched on shook.

He twisted to face the stage behind him. Several leather and chain clad young men had taken the stage and were setting up drums and guitars. A thick man with the beard of an unkempt mountain beast leaned over the cords at the back of the stage, exposing more crack than Mahoney had planned on seeing through the course of the evening.

A man with dark locks approached the microphone at the centre of the stage. His black-painted lips caressed the metal bulb. "Check, check." His smooth voice eased into Mahoney's ears.

"Satan's Sorrow."

Mahoney turned to face the bar.

"The band. Satan's Sorrow. They start in fifteen." The blood-red-lipped bartender picked up a tall glass and sipped from an orange straw. "You seen them before?"

"Uh, no. First time here."

"They're good. Raw. Rough. Real guttural." She ran her tongue over her top lip. "You need anything else before the show starts?" Red lips glared under the purple and blue lights dotting the bar.

Hell, I'm already here. Why not have the full dive-bar experience? Maybe he could lose himself in another world.

"Uh, yeah. You got bourbon?"

She slithered closer and leaned over the bar. "Oh, you're a bourbon guy? Nice. Yeah. We've got a few choices." She turned, leaning against the bar and pointing up at a line of bottles. The leather stretching across her back had several ornately-shaped cut-outs exposing her milky skin. A dark birthmark dotted the top right corner, just below her shoulder.

A milky breast pushing against tight pleather, a chocolate-brown birthmark, flickered across his mind. He hadn't thought of Sasha in a while. She was his last regular bartender. She'd had such a sweet spot for him. He'd soured it quickly.

Mahoney scanned the bourbon collection. "Maker's Mark. That'll do."

She tilted up onto the tips of her toes and wrapped her fingers around the bottle. Turning back to the bar, she settled the bottle and grabbed a glass. "Ice?"

"Straight up."

Her black eyebrow raised. Her blood-red lips stretched into a smile.

She poured the caramel liquid and slid it toward him. "Enjoy." She turned to walk away.

"Wait. What about pay as you go?"

"Oh, that one's on me." The silver shadow over her eye glimmered as she winked. She walked to the corner of the bar to tend to a patron in tattered jeans and a black t-shirt, the words *Tainted Death* scrolled across in heavy letters.

Mahoney downed the bourbon in three shots. Then he finished his water-beer. He scanned the dingy room. It was filling up. People clustered in groups at the wooden tables. The smell of sweaty bodies had stepped up several notches. The temperature had followed. Mahoney removed his tweed coat and hung it over the back of his chair.

He turned and watched the band putting the final touches on their setup. A man in leather pants, chains hanging in semi-circles on each of his thighs, planted his heavy black boots against the stage and strummed at his bright-red guitar tattooed in skulls and devil horns. A deep riff vibrated through the entire stuffy, beer-soaked joint. The tattered looking patrons turned their chairs, gulping their beers.

"Another round?" Purple lights blended with red lips.

"Yes, please."

She smiled. "You're polite. Not used to that around here."

Mahoney's cheeks flared.

Leather-clad red lips went to work on his order. She slid a cold, bubbly beer and a short glass of sweet brown liquid his way. "Eight-fifty."

"Oh, so we're back to pay as you go?"

Red lips twisted into a half smile. "A girl's gotta make a living. And I don't even know you."

He slid a small stack of bills her way, avoiding the pink glob his last payment had discovered. "No change."

"Well, you are quite the gentleman." She leaned against the bar. Her breasts pressed against the tight black leather caging them in. "You don't seem like you belong here."

"Let's just say I'm trying new things."

The room vibrated with an electric riff. A deep, smooth voice took over the room. "Hey, fuckers. We're Satan's Sorrow. Let's get this show on the road."

The riff deepened, taking over every corner of the room. The guitarist rooted his black boots hard against the stage. He stood in a half squat. His arm swung in furious circles, filling the room with an electric rawness.

"Told you. Rough. Raw," red lips informed, then vanished.

The room had filled up. A line of patrons perched along the bar. Most of the tables were cluttered with groups of leather-clad, jean-wearing, chained and buckled riffraff looking for an escape from life. At least for the night.

Mahoney decided he wasn't going anywhere. He shot back a gulp of bourbon. His throat stung. The sweetness clung to the back of his tongue. The constant buzzing in his brain had faded to a low hum. His mind was image free. Maybe he could escape the corpse show for a few hours.

Chapter 4

Black-Pleather Bourbon Bath

A pair of crystal glasses clinked as Mahoney set them on the glass table in the centre of his living space. Peeling the wax off the top of a Maker's Mark bottle, he stole a glance at the black-leather-clad server, now his guest. She sprawled leisurely across the tattered couch in his desolate living space. She stretched her arms over her head, leaning into the stuffing protruding from the head rest.

"Mahoney. That's your last name, right?"

"Yeah." He pulled the cork. It released with a pop. Sweet bourbon taunted him.

"What's your first name?"

He looked at her with a sideways smile.

She shot him a sly grin. "Oh. Secretive, are we? So why the last name thing?"

He tilted the bottle. Rich brown liquid splashed against crystal. "It's a detective thing."

She licked her lips. "Mmm. Sexy."

He handed her a glass. Her obsidian-tipped fingers wrapped around the crystal as she lifted it to her lips. She paused, breathing in and closing her eyes. The silver shadow on her eyelids shimmered under the bright light. He looked up at the exposed bulb glaring at him through a hole in the broken lampshade. As she took a slow sip, she let out a soft sigh. He looked back at her. The rich liquid touched her lips as they parted slightly. She moaned as the sweet treat filled her mouth.

His insides tingled. Fuck, she was sexy. Pale. Yes. Clad in leather and chains. Yes. But he found it hot.

She lowered the glass. Her eyes had a glazed look. "You know your bourbon."

"How did a metal head working in a dive bar get into high-end bourbon?"

"My dad had good taste. And he treated me like a man."

Mahoney's brain contorted over the statement. She didn't look like she had played with Barbies. He left it at that. Better things to tend to. She called to him like a delicious crisp apple. He wanted to lick her, bite her…taste her.

She leaned toward the table, placed her glass down with a clink, her breasts pushing hard against the tight black leather holding them captive. She stood. Two steps in and she was leaning into him, pressing her breasts against his chest, running her fingers along his arm. A tingling followed her obsidian fingernail up his arm and across the side of his face.

"I love a little bristle. I'll show you what you can do with that." She ran the tip of her tongue across his bottom lip.

He licked the sweet residue she left behind.

"You got any good tracks?"

He paused. "In my car."

"That won't do, *Detective*." The last word dripped from her candy-apple lips.

His loins groaned for attention. He probed his brain. The old blaster, in his room. "I have an old boom box, in the bedroom."

"Sweet." She snatched the crystal and vanished into the disaster of a room he slept in.

She danced across the worn carpet, missing every pile of soiled clothes, landing by a small set of shelves. Running her hand along the top of a cracked tape deck, she turned to him with a McIntosh smile. Pointing her finger toward the ceiling, she giggled at the ball of dust perched atop her fingertip.

Tilting the glass to her Honey Crisp lips, the remaining liquid slid into her mouth. She handed the glass to him. "Fill me up, *Detective*. I'm gonna rifle through your cassette collection."

He followed his orders. Rattling plastic against plastic echoed through his ears as he headed back to the living space.

As he emptied his own glass, then poured them both another round, he heard faint giggles from the bedroom. He could still feel her fingernails on his skin. The tingle returned and rippled down his insides. Perching the glasses in one hand, grabbing the bottle with the other, he swiftly returned to the bedroom.

"So, you're a blues guy?"

"Who doesn't love the blues?" He pleaded with his eyes.

"Love the blues. Everything came from the blues. Rock. Even my metal."

His heart seized. Was he dreaming? Hallucinating again?

He handed her a glass, which she took eagerly. She sipped rich bourbon as she held up her hand, a dusty cassette clamped between her pointer and middle finger.

Skid Row stared back at him in jagged, blood-red letters. Wow. He'd forgotten he had that. Did one of his other tasty treats leave it behind?

"This is perfect for my mood." She spun, slid the cassette into the open door of the boom box and clicked it closed. She pushed a button. Wheels spun, catching briefly, then finding momentum.

The riff hit him right in the gut, pumping aggression into his veins. She turned to face him, crystal in one hand, the other hand reaching for the ceiling. Silver chains jangled as she swayed her hips to the beat. Her breasts heaved against the tight leather top, begging to break free. She slithered toward him. Blood pulsed through his veins in anticipation.

She opened the buttons on his shirt and slid her soft hand over his chest. Her tongue ran across her top lip, pulling the red gloss into a thick smear. He wished it was his tongue. He longed to know what flavour she was. Brown sugar? The gooey cooked apple part of a freshly baked crisp? Bourbon-coated saliva dripped down his throat. He swallowed.

A rough voice violated the room, wailing of subways, stilettos, candy canes, and loaded guns.

Bourbon slipped through apple lips. He took his own long swallow, the rich liquid burning its way down his throat, the sweet aftertaste lingering at the back of his tongue, like he hoped she would.

The room swirled in a slow spin around him. Sweet bourbon-coated apple intoxicated him as she leaned hard against him. Her mouth moved in sync with the voice of the rock god vibrating from the boom box speakers, screaming of wet lips and dropping bombs. He closed his eyes and breathed her in. Her sweet caramel-apple breath wove over his face as she touched his lips with her soft mouth. Her candy-apple tongue was like sugar against his, dissolving in a slow sweetness, coating his entire mouth. He swallowed back her sweet nectar.

She pulled away, shot back the rest of her bourbon, and set the glass down with purpose. Her eyes bore into his. He could feel her looking into him. He didn't shy away. He let her in. She shoved him onto the bed.

She lowered herself to her knees and unzipped his pants. He downed the last splash of bourbon, then dropped the glass on the floor with a soft thud. He settled back onto the bed. She moved toward him. He stopped her. He looked into her eyes.

"I want to taste you first."

She blinked. "Well, a lady can't say no to that."

Sliding up to standing, she slid her tight leather pants over her curvaceous hips, exposing her milky skin. A black snake wove its way down her right thigh. Its fangs loomed toward her pleasure spot.

Lucky snake.

Hooking her fingers into black lace lined with a thin silver chain, she slipped her panties down to her heels, leaning into him. Shaking one foot, then the other, she released the intriguing combination of lace and chain to the worn carpet.

His veins pulsed with fresh blood.

Her perfect curves lured him in. He was Adam. She was the apple.

He pulled her to the bed. She landed beside him, then lay back into the mess of blankets. Her arms reached over her head, her back arched, and her legs spread slightly. He slipped his shirt off and slid off the bed, resting his knees against the carpet, and made his way to her. To his treat.

His mouth wet, he leaned in to taste her. A sweet mix of Amaretto and cherry slid down his throat like a Sicilian Kiss.

He lost himself in her sweet juices and soft moans. Her back arched higher. Her toes dug into the tangled sheets. Ample breasts pushed hard against stretching black leather. Silver chains jingled. Out of the corner of his eye, a scaly black snake slithered, its fangs threatening to steal his treat.

Her body quivered. She sunk into the bed. Her eyes glazed in pleasure.

She rolled off the bed and slithered across the room. Her milky ass taunted him. The openings in her black leather revealed her back, the soft flesh as milky as her arms and ass. The dark birthmark pierced his eyes, reaching into his mind. A soft, circular brown spot on a creamy breast sprung from his memory bank. A tight corset hoisted it closer. Cotton-candy lips whispered into his ear. Bubblegum wafted through the air. Sasha. How sweet she had been. Apple lips was different. Would he poison her, too?

Click. She pressed the *'on'* button again. He was soothed by a sultry riff. Hendrix told him an angel was in his midst. *Oh, Jimmy, you have no idea.*

The reptile slithered its way toward him with every move of her sexy thigh. He didn't resist when she pushed him back against the bed.

His entire being tingled. Images of Candy-Apple lips, snake fangs, and creamy skin swirled into each other, forming a lustful collage. He succumbed to the spinning world wrapping itself around him.

BACK
TRACK

Chapter 5

Back Track

Bzzt. Bzzt. Bzzzzt.

Mahoney's eyes flung open. He looked around the fuzzy room.

Bzzt. His clunky cell phone rattled like a plastic brick across the chipped end table next to his bed. Mahoney sat up and grabbed it. He could fake alertness. He'd been practising for two decades.

"Det...uh...Mahoney here." His voice was gruff. His throat was parched.

"Bug." Sweetness seeped through the phone. "Takes time to get used to answering as plain old Mahoney."

"Pegs." The room swirled around him. Milky skin and black lace stirred on the other side of the bed. He lay back against the pillow and closed his eyes, pressing the phone to his ear.

"Bug. How are you? We miss you around here." He could see her smile. "*I* miss you around here."

"I know, Pegs. I miss you, too." He did. He looked across the bed. The dive joint bartender rolled over, opened her eyes, and smiled at him with deep-red lips. The scent of sweet cherry and Amaretto seeped across the bed.

"I know the Sarge told you to retire. But something has happened."

His mind whirled. He closed his eyes. Black lace, silver chains, and a slithering snake tattoo flashed across his mind. He sat up, rolled his shoulders a couple times, and opened his eyes. The room steadied.

He slid his feet onto the floor and stood. His legs wobbled. He sat back down.

"Bug? You still there?"

"Yeah. I'm all yours." The bartender's fingers crawled up his back, tingling his skin.

"Listen, I hate to call you up like this. There wasn't any other choice."

"Pegs. Spit it out."

"You know, sometimes I hate my job."

He could hear tears in her voice. "It's fine. You need to separate your orders from your feelings." *Yeah. Just like you do, Bug?* Tingling followed the fingers creeping around his back, up his chest. He stood up, turned, pressed his finger to his lips to signal the need for quiet. Candy-apple lips pouted.

"Well, I know."

"It's me. It will be fine. I promise." He walked across the bedroom and into the living space.

"Like I said...something *happened.* A body was found. Not here."

The line went silent. "You still there?"

"Yes." She cleared her throat. "Teenaged girl...out east."

Cold sliced through his gut. His body went rigid. He sat down on the worn couch, sinking into the dip in the middle cushion.

"Bug?"

"Yeah. Go on."

"I'd tell you where, but I think you already know."

"Yeah."

"She was wearing a black dress. Her face was...all painted up," Peggy's voice wavered. She sniffled.

A rush of images flooded Mahoney's mind. The body of a teenaged girl materialized. She lay on the green grass of a city park in an elaborate display. She was dressed for the fanciest dinner of her life. A deadly dinner. Blood-red circles wove around her eyes. Enunciated, black lips popped against her blanched face.

The case he'd been on, sixteen years ago. The one that went cold.

"Bug."

Mahoney jumped. *Dammit.* "Sorry. I'm here." He cleared his throat. "What's my instruction?"

"Sergeant requested you. Said you'd understand."

"Got it."

"They're convening in an hour." Her voice was strained. He wondered if she was holding back a tear or two.

"Tell the Sarge I'll be there."

"Are you sure? I mean...look...I know I had to call you, but there must be some way you don't have to do this."

"No. I have to do this."

"Why, Bug?"

"You know." He pushed hard on the off button and set the plastic brick on the coffee table. He looked around the room—piles of black leather on the floor, circular caramel stains on the glass table. *You've got to get yourself together, Bug. You have no choice.*

First he had to deal with the sweet, leather-clad red apple he'd dug his teeth into. He stood. The room swirled. He closed his eyes, steadied his mind, then walked toward the bedroom.

He had to get himself together. Now.

Who else would care enough to hunt down a killer who'd resurfaced after sixteen years?

Chapter 6

The Best Ingredients

Chester eyeballed the cart as he pushed it down an aisle of the brightly lit grocery store. He preferred the high-end small grocers to the massive, big-box stores. High-end ingredients made for high-quality baked goods. Everyone who got a bite of Chester's baking delighted in the taste. They became addicted, begging him for more.

The items in the cart, lined up in perfect rows by category, dried goods—flour, sugar, salt—dairy—butter, milk, eggs—and all the extras for specific recipes in their own corner. He looked down his list, ticking off the items with a pen. Yes. He had everything. Oh, except the coconut. Dina would want some macaroons. He didn't want to disappoint Dina.

He guided the cart further down the baking aisle toward the specialty items. He looked over the rows of chocolates, nuts, and candies. *Coconut. Coconut. Oh, there.* He decided to grab three packages. That way, he could make enough for the whole cul-de-sac. He didn't want anyone feeling left out. He needed them all on his good side. His public persona side, as he liked to think of it.

He doubted he was any different than anyone else. Didn't everyone put on a slightly altered face when they left their house? He was sure they did.

Satisfied with the contents in his cart, he wheeled it over to the cash register. It was Donald behind the counter. Good. He didn't mind Donald. Donald was less nosy than some of the others. Especially Liza. Liza always asked too many questions.

"Hello. Did you find everything you were looking for?"

"Yes, I did. Thank you, Donald."

"You're welcome. Say, I've seen you in here before. You like this store?" Donald's pudgy, red cheeks rippled as he spoke.

"Yes, I do. You carry good-quality items here."

"The owner, Ronald, he's all about top-notch products." Donald swiped three large bags of Italian flour over the scanner—*blip, blip, blip.*

Ronald? You're kidding. Ronald and Donald. Ridiculous. Chester smiled. "Well, I'm happy he is. It's all I buy."

"Wow. It looks like you're up to some serious baking here." Donald pushed his glasses against his sweaty face. "What are you making?"

"Cookies, mostly. They're my specialty."

"I would love to have homemade cookies. I miss my mom's cookies." Donald pouted.

"Oh? She used to bake for you?" *Whiney kid. Why doesn't he learn to bake his own cookies?*

"Yeah. But, well, she had to move into a home. She can't bake there."

"How about I bring you a batch the next time I need supplies?"

"Really?" The chubby half-kid, half-adult looked far too excited about a batch of cookies. His shaking belly indicated that he didn't need them. Chester didn't understand how adults let themselves become doughy. He spent two hours every morning in his gym sweating out fat and shaping his muscular physique.

Oh well. If he brought cookies to this kid-adult, it would help him be more...amiable...wouldn't it? "Yes. Of course. It would be my pleasure."

"That'd be swell. That'll be eighty-nine ninety-nine." Donald moved over to the groceries and started stacking the items into heavy paper bags with the *Ronald's Regal Grocery* logo printed on the side.

Chester flipped open his wallet, counted out the required cash, and placed it on the counter. "Thank you, Donald."

Donald took the bills, handed Chester his change, then picked up several bags. "I'll help you out."

"Well, that's nice of you. Thank you." *Look how good I'm getting at being polite.* He grabbed the remaining bags and followed Donald out of Ronald's store.

Chapter 7

HQ, I Miss You

The golden nameplate on Sergeant Jackson's door hung crooked. The 'son' tilted downward to the right. Detective Mahoney raised his hand to knock on the door. It swung open before his knuckles made contact. Sergeant Jackson's brick of a frame blocked the doorway. He scanned Mahoney from head to toe.

"You look awful." The sergeant pursed his lips in a thin line.

"Yeah. I do."

The sergeant turned his back to Mahoney and walked over to his desk. He sat down in his chair, bathed in sunlight flooding in through the large window. Stretching his arms up in the air, he bent his elbows and placed both palms against the back of his head.

"Mahoney."

"Sarge."

"Haven't seen you since Sutton's shindig."

"How's he doing?"

"That gut of yours was right, per usual. Sutton makes one hell of a Prime Investigator."

A smile pulled at Mahoney's mouth.

"Good kid. You taught him well." Sergeant Jackson smiled, wrinkles of time relaxing around his mouth.

"It's all him. He works hard. He's got instinct."

"Yeah." Sergeant Jackson leaned his broad shoulders toward the desk, plucked the phone from its cradle and pushed a button. "Tiffany. Be a dear. Get us some coffee in here." He clicked the receiver back in place. "You been seeing the doctor they assigned?"

Doctor Sherry's sweet smile floated through Mahoney's mind. "Yeah."

"And?"

"She wants to talk about things that are done. Deep dive, she calls it."

"So. Are you?"

"They're done. Nothing to say."

"You know that's a lie." The sergeant frowned.

Mahoney leaned forward, resting his elbows on his knees.

"Mahoney. You've seen a lot of shit. At the front line. A man needs to purge that stuff, or it'll drive him crazy."

A knock at the door prevented Mahoney from having to respond. A young woman in a red suit entered, pushing a tray. She wheeled it to the corner then turned to leave.

"Thank you, Tiffany."

She nodded. "Sir." The door clicked shut.

"I'm an old man, Mahoney. I know a thing or two. You sleeping?"

"Sure."

"Another lie."

"No. Not a lie. I'm sleeping, thanks to Doctor Sherry."

Sergeant Jackson snorted. "Fine. For now. You can't stay on those things too long. Trust me." He stood and walked over to the coffee tray. Returning with two mugs, he handed one to Mahoney.

Smoky spice wafted from the shiny porcelain mug. The mug was chip free and painted in a lovely scene by a lake. "I leave and you get new mugs and better coffee?"

Sergeant Jackson laughed. "Yeah." He put the mug on his desk. Placing each of his hands on the top of the desk, he leaned over and glared at Mahoney. "Look. I think it's opposite of my best judgment to call you in here. But certain higher-ranking officers think it's *procedure* to send you out east to join the investigation. In case this body is linked to those girls from sixteen years back. You'll be working with one of their sub-ordinates, Sergeant Tomlinson. He's leading the case. I need to go along with this to cover my department's ass." He sighed and ran his fingers through his short, stiff hair peppered with silver. He stared across the desk.

Mahoney took a sip of the upgraded homicide department coffee. He lowered the mug and glowered across the desk. "It's fine."

"That's what I told myself. But then you come walking in here, pale and sickly looking. And that eye…you're scarred for life."

An image of Sid, the last killer he'd hunted, loomed in his mind. Sid had slid a knife right into Mahoney's eye, leaving the so-called *scar for life*. "It's a reminder. I wasn't much to look at to begin with."

The crow's feet crowding Sergeant Jackson's eyes deepened. His eyes bulged. "This isn't a goddamn joke, Mahoney. I remember, too well, the toll those back-to-back cases took on you. Seth and Sid. Then that damn Suitcase Slaughters scene did you in. You don't look much better now than you did when I sent you home that day."

Mahoney sat up straight, his lips a thin line. "Boss. I hear you. I say it's fine, it's fine."

The sergeant's eyes bored into him. "OK." He took a sip from his mug. "I have no choice but to trust you, anyway. But…*this* case. *This* perp."

"Yeah." Mahoney took a deep breath and exhaled loudly. "I have no choice, either."

The sergeant's eyes protruded further from their sockets. He swallowed. "You *need* to get him. Don't you?"

Mahoney nodded, took a swig of coffee, then stood. "Sarge. My gut says it'll be fine." He stared at his sergeant for a moment.

The sergeant sighed. "Let's be clear here. My main motivation for putting you on this case was to follow required procedure." He paused. "My secondary motivation is that I understand, all too well, how much you might need this. The possibility of closure."

Mahoney nodded. "Thanks, Sarge." He took a swig of coffee. "I assume we're convening in that hot, sticky war room?"

"Yeah. In ten."

"Stop worrying. See you in there." He sauntered to the door, pulled it open, and walked into the dimly lit hallway. Good old headquarters still smelled the same—a perfect blend of cold coffee, detective sweat, and anxiety. He walked down the hallway, nodding hellos to familiar faces. His mind thrust forward, scanning and re-scanning his brain for every scrap of memory related to the case that went cold. *Yeah, boss. It'll be fine. Doesn't have to end like it usually does. Just has to end.*

Chapter 8

Bake Time

A little egg timer blipped. Chester wiped his hands on the floral apron covering his dress pants. Sliding a sunny yellow oven mitt over his manicured hand, he opened the oven and pulled out a hot baking sheet. He looked at the twelve perfectly positioned cookies. The tops were golden. Piercing one with a fork, he smiled. *Nice.* Crispy on top, soft in the middle. *Margery will be pleased that I reached an excellent execution of her recipe on the first try.*

Humming to himself, he slid a silver flipper under each cookie in turn and placed them on a bright-blue cooling rack.

Eyeballing the next batch, making sure they were evenly spaced, he slid another pan into the oven. The heat wafted over his face. He jolted back and closed the door. Turning the egg timer to ten minutes, he moved over to the centre island. Dozens of cookies, baked golden, were stacked in neat rows on silver platters. *Old Pete will be pleased as punch. For the two minutes it takes him to wolf down a batch of my cookies, he's actually happy. Or as close to happy as he'll ever be. Old wart.*

Chester pulled on a pair of latex gloves, releasing each with a snap. With the utmost precision, he placed twelve cookies in three meticulous rows of four, in a parchment-lined pastel-blue box. He repeated the process, layering another three rows on top. Each row was now two cookies high. He crouched down, narrowing his eyes, to make sure the cookies were perfectly placed. He closed the box, wrapped it with a matching blue ribbon, then set it aside. *Blue on blue for old Pete.*

Chester's insides tingled. Baking was fun. It was easy. It was...normal. It was his way of earning the role as the star neighbour on the secluded cul-de-sac of Roches Point. The upscale community overlooked a lake, was close enough to a freeway shooting straight into the massive metropolis of Toronto for easy access to supplies, yet far enough away to escape the filth and rot seeping from its core. His

Victorian mansion perched at the top of a u-shaped drive, the houses spawning down each side were well spaced from each other, separated by large plots of land, and guarded by wrought iron fences. Every gate opened when Chester's voice announced a cookie delivery over the intercom.

The mansion had belonged to his grandfather. When Chester was fourteen, his older sister had perished. He'd been dumped into a home for deviant juveniles. A couple of years later, his mother, drowning in sorrow, took her own life. He'd never had a father. Thus, when he turned eighteen, he was released, his slate wiped clean, and the mansion landed in his hands. A decent trust fund came with the mansion, gifting Chester with plenty of time for his activities.

With gloved fingers, Chester placed three rows of four cookies into a peach-coloured box. The egg timer interrupted his work with a happy chime. He snapped off the gloves, tossed them on the counter and slid on the oven mitt. *Oh yes, perfectly golden.*

He returned to humming as he placed each cookie onto the cooling rack. Another inspection of cookie placing followed. Once the next batch was in the oven and the timer set, he returned to wrapping. First, he snapped on a fresh pair of gloves. Then, he finished the perfectly packed twelve by adding another layer of three rows of four. He crouched down, inspecting the cookie placement, making sure they were carefully placed in their parchment-lined home. The finishing touch, a bright-pink ribbon, he tied with care. Dina would love the peach and pink combination. His cookies were the only dessert she allowed to enter her perfectly carved body.

Ding. The egg timer. *Dammit.* His timing was off. He needed to wrap one box each for the four neighbours. Two dozen cookies per box. Eight dozen total. Plus the six dozen he needed to bake and wrap for the *MGSG—Missing Girl's Support Group.* He'd been spending more time at the support meetings since more girls had gone missing.

He placed the next batch of cookies in the oven and set the timer. Leaning against the centre island, he counted the cookies on the silver platters. His process needed to be perfect. If it wasn't, that damn twitch tugged at the corner of his lip. He didn't want to be some sort of twitchy freak.

Ding. Dammit. How long had he been standing there counting? The egg timer told him ten minutes.

He snapped the gloves off, yanked on the oven mitt and pulled the hot pan out. The heat blasted his face. A bead of sweat trickled down his cheek. His stomach clenched. His lip twitched. Once.

He paused, took a deep breath, then looked at the perfect golden cookies. His stomach settled. His lip stilled.

He slid the last batch in and placed the hot ones on the cooling rack.

Two more boxes to wrap for the neighbours. *Good.* He settled into the wrapping, first snapping a fresh pair of gloves into place, then choosing a mint-green box for Mindy. *Oh, Mindy will love it.* She loved all things mint—in taste and in colour. Minty Mindy, he called her.

After aligning another three rows wide, four cookies long, and two rows deep, he closed the mint-coloured box and wrapped it with a red ribbon. Mindy's own pastel Christmas.

Ding. Retrieving the last batch of cookies, he turned the oven off. Sweat trickled down his back. He wiped his forehead with a thick blue tea towel and tossed it into the sink.

He needed to catch up. Get this done. The deliveries had to be complete in exactly two hours. Four o'clock on the dot. And some of his customers would be chatty. He needed to get back home in time to prepare and spend time with his girls.

He chose a bright-yellow box for Margery. Placing the two layers of three rows by four cookies, he aligned them and closed the box. He tied it with a matching yellow ribbon. Margery liked matching colour on colour. At least he suspected so by the ridiculous colour-on-colour outfits she wore. The way the bright material pulled over her plump body, she looked like a human marshmallow. The way she squealed with delight at the boxes he brought to her, he wasn't sure if she was more excited about the colour co-ordination of his wrapping job, or the thought of the sugary contents inside.

He looked at the calendar on the fridge. In perfect penmanship, *girls' club meeting* was written on the square for tomorrow. The cookies for the meeting could be wrapped in a single large box. The rest of the afternoon would be eaten up with cookie deliveries on the cul-de-sac. The evening was to be dedicated to his girls. Tomorrow, he would need to recover from the evening activities.

The baking complete, he set to work filling and wrapping the large box for the meeting. The box was pink, in honour of the missing girls.

Chapter 9

War Room Love

Mahoney pushed open the war room door. A hot, sweaty cloud engulfed him. He coughed, then plunged into the sauna. No one was in the room yet. His old team must have just come off a case, or had their hands deep into a new one.

The door opened. Dara, the top-notch analyst he used to rely on, scampered to the corner and set down her notebook. She looked the same as the last time he'd seen her, decked in a pristine navy-blue suit, her silver hair back in a tight bun. "Bug. Good to see you." She smiled. "It's a nightmare in here."

She grabbed a can from the table and walked up to the front. Pressing her finger against the red button on the top of the can, a mist erupted from the tiny hole. She waved the can back and forth in a zigzag pattern, bending her knees and crouching, then rising again. The mist disintegrated the smell of sweat, leaving a fake coat of fresh mountain air. Dara walked back over to the door, pushed it open and wedged a stopper in place.

"That'll do." She nodded at Mahoney then made her way back to the corner.

"You still have a magic touch."

She humphed. "It's something." She looked at him. "Are you all right?"

"Yeah. I'll be fine."

"You don't look...well."

"I know. Don't worry."

"You need some good TLC. You eating?"

"Yeah." A pizza in a to-go box popped into his mind, greasy circles of processed meat sinking into the gooey cheese.

"You need a good home-cooked meal, and a good night's sleep." Dara shot him a concerned smile.

The door swung open. Chatter pierced the room. Detectives Sutton and Hayes, deep in conversation, walked across the room. Sutton's boots clamped to the tattered rug when he saw Mahoney.

"Boss."

"Sutton."

They both stared, lips shut.

"Hayes. Good to see you both." Mahoney nodded.

"Hi, boss," Hayes spoke.

Hayes, leaner than ever, sported the same buzzcut he'd had the last time Mahoney saw him. Sutton's brown curls still framed his face, though his muscles had swelled up a few sizes. They both held Styrofoam cups with long straws poking from the top.

"Hayes, you still running?" Mahoney asked.

"Every day."

"Sutton, looks like you're pumping like a madman." Mahoney smirked.

"Sure am. Doing a competition."

"Where's the Big Gulp?"

"You won't believe it, boss. Hayes got me onto these smoothies. They work. Helping me with my competition prep." Sutton's face relaxed. He smiled, raising the Styrofoam cup.

Mahoney chuckled. His shoulders relaxed.

Sutton's eyes widened, his voice lunging up an octave. "You leading this, boss?"

"You're the PI now. I'm just here for kicks."

"Yeah, but you were on this thing, when it started." Sutton's forehead furrowed.

"That was a long time ago. Not sure how much good I'll do here now," Mahoney responded.

"Nah. You still remember every detail. Don't you?" Hayes inquired.

Mahoney shook his head. "Old-man brain. Not sure what's still in there." Three dead girls flashed through his mind. They still lurched in the corners of his brain. *They're still in there. Every last one of them.*

Sergeant Jackson strode through the door to the front of the room, his boots hitting the floor with thumps. He looked up from a file he had been scanning.

"OK, team. Let's get moving." He snapped the folder onto the long centre table, flipped it open, and picked up a stack of photos.

Mahoney's insides froze. He stared at the stack of photos in Sergeant Jackson's hand. Watching in paralyzed silence, he saw each picture removed from the stack, plastered against the cream-coloured crime scene wall and stuck into place with a bright tack. A sickening scene built itself over the creamy, chipped paint. Several angles of a lifeless body were captured, showing every bit of torturous ritual that had been executed upon her.

Mahoney's eyes were glued to the photos. His stomach surged, shooting a hot stream of bile up to his throat. He drowned it back down with a gulp of cold coffee.

A tingling spread through his gut. A cold hand wrapped around his heart and squeezed. There were no rules this time. The intended outcome wasn't the same. His gut spoke and he listened. He knew that he wouldn't step back from this case. *Nothing* would stop him from finishing what had to be done.

Chapter 10

Sugar-Free Lemonade

Chester walked down the cul-de-sac toward the bright-yellow house at the bottom. He liked to start with the furthest house and work his way up. He only ever carried one box at a time, enough for one delivery. It was too risky to carry more. He could drop one.

Besides, arriving at a house with just enough for the neighbour living there also gave the impression that he only baked for them. He suspected they knew. Margery was a gossip. The impression was what mattered, wasn't it?

He trotted up the cobblestone driveway and buzzed the intercom.

"Hello?" Dina's high-pitched voice rang through the wired speaker. Only someone filled with a million endorphins could sound that happy.

"Dina, dear. It's Chester." He coated his voice with a sugary tone.

"Chester. Come in," Dina shrieked.

The intercom buzzed. The large iron gates opened with an electric whiz.

Chester walked up to the front door. Dina was already standing on the porch with a big smile on her face. Every day she executed hours of fake exercise on some sort of machine, creating a million forged endorphins, and causing a phony glow over her skin.

"Is that what I think it is?"

"Yes, it is. One of your favourites, I believe."

"Those will go right to my thighs, you know." She wagged her pointer at him.

"Don't be silly." He applied a second coat of sugar over his words. "You'll work it right off. Is that a new dress?" God awful shade of green. He couldn't deny her figure could make anything look good. But she wasn't his type.

"Oh, Chester. Do come in. I made sugar-free lemonade. And we can share the cookies."

"I'll take the lemonade. I've had too many cookies." A lie. He never touched sugar. Turned right to fat. Made him weak.

He followed her into the front hall, blasting a dose of positive energy through his veins in preparation for the torturous chat he was about to endure. He had to put on the perfect neighbourly front. It was part of his public-world persona.

Chester followed Dina into the modern sitting area. White walls, stainless-steel coffee table, and space-aged-looking chairs circled the room. All the furniture faced a massive bay window that looked out onto a perfectly manicured, jungle-like garden. You couldn't see the street through the tangle of greenery.

Dina motioned for Chester to sit. He sat awkwardly on one of the funny-shaped chairs. Fashion took precedence over function in Dina's house.

"I'll be right back, Chester. I'll get us that lemonade." She slipped away, into the kitchen.

Chester looked at the jungle scene. Urgency shot through his veins. He was anxious to get back home, to prepare for his time with his girls. *Easy. You need to maintain this impression.*

Dina returned, her blonde hair shining under the pot lights. She leaned over and placed a silver tray on the stainless-steel coffee table. It all looked so sterile. Just like her. She shone and glowed like she'd been scrubbed with expensive disinfectants and rubbed with lotions that weren't tested on animals.

She poured two glasses of lemonade and handed one to Chester. "Sugar free." She smiled.

Well, at least she got something right. He didn't need any sugar tainting his body. He needed to be top notch tonight.

She sat in a practised pose on the edge of the chair.

"So, what've you been up to?"

He wondered what it would be like to dye that perfect blonde a raven black. "Oh, the usual. Baking. Volunteering."

"Oh, you are so admirable. You give so many hours to the families of those poor girls." She fake pouted.

It wouldn't be worth the effort to dye her hair. Her carcass wouldn't be worth anything. And her blood wasn't pure.

"It's the least I can do. Those girls might never be found."

"Oh my. You really think so?" She sipped her lemonade in a practised, precise motion. Her bright lipstick remained in tact.

"Well, we need to hope they will be." But they won't. "But, after the first forty-eight hours without a solid lead, the odds of finding them decrease drastically."

"Oh my." She deepened her fake pout, careful not to wrinkle her forehead. He suspected Dina avoided wrinkling motions of any kind.

"Enough about me. Dina, I'm dying to hear about what *you've* been up to." He smiled. It hurt his lips, but he forced it to stick.

He listened to her drone on about her fake exercise, salon appointments, and the latest healthy recipes. *Blah, blah, blah.* He forced the smile to stick through it all. His mind wandered. He thought of his girls. He could bear this. They made all this worth it.

He needed to endure her nonsensical chatter. Then three more visits, working his way up the cul-de-sac, with a final arc back up to his house. It was only a couple of hours. He could do it. Then he'd be free for his transformation.

Chapter 11

Horrific Scrapbook

Detective Mahoney burst through the door to his apartment and tossed his keys onto the table of the claustrophobic front entrance. He had to pack. Sarge had told him to be ready to hop on a flight first thing tomorrow to join the investigation in Toronto. First, he had some reading to do.

He walked past the kitchen and across the living room. He stopped at the single bookcase and eyeballed the half-dozen books scattered haphazardly along the top shelf.

Casebook of a Crime Psychologist
The Evidence of Things Not Seen
Criminal Behaviour: A Psychological Analysis

He never had been a reader. The only books he seemed to be able to digest pumped his head full of ideas about how killers like Seth and Sid could exist and slip under a detective's radar. A chill washed through him.

Seth. The killer at the end of the trail on the Glam Boys case. Seth had been sadistic and insane, transforming college boys into rock god corpses.

Sid. The killer at the end of the Mummy Boys case. Sid had been demented. He'd turned boys into afterlife dolls, wrapped like mummies, and taken their eyes as trophies.

Seth and Sid were both dead. It was time to flush the memories away and plunge further back in time. It was time to review the frames from sixteen years ago, still lurching in the back corners of his mind like a horror flick that he couldn't unsee.

He pulled an old binder from the bottom shelf, walked over to the small table in the adjacent kitchen, and placed it on one of the chairs. Grabbing a fresh dish cloth from a drawer beside the sink, he gave the table a thorough wipe down.

Sliding his feet across the cold linoleum, he entered the tiny pantry and emerged with a bag of whole, dark-roast beans. He plunged a scoop into the bag, dropped the beans into a grinder, and pushed down on the top. The grinder whirred; the beans crunched. A smoky aroma seeped from the beans as they were crushed by the sharp blades. His nostrils flared.

After preparing himself the first real cup of coffee he'd had in a while, he sat down at the table and stared at the binder. A tingling crept up his back, like an imaginary daddy long legs, pricking his skin one step at a time as it crawled up his spine.

The book didn't contain anything that could be used as hard evidence. Its contents, a myriad of grisly photos and newspaper clippings, had haunted him ever since he'd closed it and put it on the shelf. He'd shoved the replicated images shimmering in his mind into a back room and slammed the door shut. Sixteen years ago.

He took a big swig of coffee, savouring the spicy notes and letting the warm liquid soothe his throat as he swallowed. He placed the mug on the table tenderly and stared at the bright-yellow letters reminding him of his biggest failure. *Best Dad.*

He'd let people down. Seemed the only ones giving him a second chance were the dead ones. *Fine, then.* Another order of corpses, coming up.

The book sat, waiting to be opened. He swallowed hard against the pulsing ball of fear forming in his throat. He lifted the binder from the chair, plunked it onto the table, and swung it open. A ragged-edged square of newspaper clung to the first page. Yellowing, curled strips of tape barely held it in place.

Toronto Gazette

April 20, 1973

The body of a sixteen-year-old girl was discovered by a local jogger in Gairloch Gardens at 8:00 AM on April 18. The body has striking similarities to two others found in the past two weeks. Susie Lawrie was found on Wednesday, April 4 in Waterfront Park. Alison Parrott was found on Tuesday, April 10 in Cedarvale Park. It is suspected that all three girls were killed the day prior to being found. The identity of the latest victim has been confirmed as Stella Stearne.

Some pieces of information have been obtained by witnesses strolling through the park shortly after the body was found, prior to the scene being secured. The girl was said to have long, dark hair and to have been wearing a black dress. Her face was painted white, red rings circled her eyes, and her lips were thick with black lipstick.

Witnesses say the victim's face looked demonic and horrifying. The previous two victims had similar makeup, and they also had long, dark hair.

All three victims were slit from the heart to the pelvis, and exsanguinated—drained of all blood. No evidence of sexual assault was found.

Prior to disappearance, all three victims were living in foster care centres, located in smaller areas on the outskirts of the Greater Toronto area. Susie, gone the longest, was missing seven weeks. Alison had been missing for five weeks, and Stella for three. All victims had been declared as runaways on their missing persons reports.

The killer has been tagged as the Killer Vampire, and the Blood Demon, amongst other informal titles. The most common name for the case is the Susie Slaughters, due to the name of the first victim.

It appears that a serial killer is preying on orphaned teenagers on the outskirts of Toronto. As to what the killer is doing with the blood drained from the bodies, one can only speculate.

The ball of fear swelled, choking Mahoney. He coughed, grabbed for his mug, and washed rising bile away with warm dark roast. He recalled how the press has been on high alert after the second body was found, lurching in vans by the parks in the wee hours of the morning, ready to pounce. It had been hard to stave them off. The imaginary spider returned, crawling up his neck and over his skull, the tingling following each slow step.

He closed his eyes, rolled his head in slow circles, and took a few deep breaths. Opening this binder was the last thing he'd wanted to do. But he had to.

He had led the investigations that ultimately hunted down two of the worst serial killers he'd ever encountered. Here, in his own beloved city of Calgary. Both of the sadistic monsters were dead. This was deemed a success. All the ghost faces swirling through his mind in a constant collage deemed otherwise. So many bodies had been left behind, and the families left grieving, or forever wondering.

The case hiding within the binder had never been solved. He had been part of that team, a long time ago when he was fresh and eager. And naïve. It had gone cold. Until now.

The article had summarized the facts that had been released by the homicide department, with a twist of sensationalism. Re-reading it now, after all this time, the facts on the page still aligned to perfection with those filed in his memory.

What wasn't printed were the details that were not released. The details that were deemed better kept secret to identify an authentic confession, and to prevent the killer from thinking they were too close to him.

What wasn't printed was that each of the girls had the same blood type. Type O negative. That each girl had a symbol branded into her back. A circle with an intersecting V. These were the things glaring in his mind. The things he remembered, but that weren't printed, and that the binder didn't contain. Was his memory accurate? Would he find this information in old case files when he got to Toronto? Would the latest victim align with his memory of the old ones?

His gut pulsed. He had no choice but to help. He had no choice but to look through this entire binder. They needed him. *Do they? Do they really, Bug? Or do you need this?*

He opened his eyes, took a sip of coffee, and looked back at the article. He flipped the page. The first scene came alive, leaping from the paper clippings, back into his life. Scanning the words, the details came rushing back to him. The way the body was displayed. The clothing she had been dressed in. Her black lips. The blood-red circles around her eyes. A young woman turned into a devil corpse.

Flipping through the pages over several cups of coffee, Mahoney relived every scene. All three. The more he read, the more focused he became. The black nothing eyes made no appearances. Neither did the ghost faces of boys wrapped like mummies. His brain buzzed as he put together the pieces he had abandoned.

Dead women seeped from the pages, begging with black lips to tell him their story. He listened. Susie, Alison...*Stella.* The last one had stuck hard in his mind, having the same name as his own daughter.

The same details repeated themselves on every page of the scrapbook. Sixteen-year-old girls. Thin and pale. Long, dark hair. Killed and left on display. Slit from their heart to the top of their pelvis. Bled out. Painted up like hell's demons. They never did figure out where all the blood went.

Three bodies. The second girl was killed six days after the first. The third girl was killed eight days after the second. The case went cold.

Hours passed. Finally, he turned the last page. Mahoney reached for the several-day-old bristle on his chin and gave it a scratch.

A distinct and clear image stuck in his mind—an image not reflected in his binder, only in his memory. A strange symbol, comprised of a crude circle intersected with a V. Branded into the backs of each of the girls.

Standing up, he snapped the book shut and kicked himself into gear. He needed to get himself together. Whether he was doing it to respond to some ultimate call for help, or because he had been calling for help, didn't even know it, and this was the answer—well, he wasn't sure. All he was sure of was that he needed to catch the killer that got away.

Chapter 12

One Beer, Two Bourbon, Three Pills

Mahoney slammed the binder shut and pushed his palm hard against the stiff cover. He closed his eyes and hung his head. No more ghost faces of young boys. No more child mummies. No more black, nothing eyes. *That was good, right?* No. Now the images were replaced with the new, horrifying collage of the faces of young, dead women, pale and ghastly, blood circles weaving around their black orb eyes. A barrage of midnight lips moved, whispering in his ears.

'*Bug. You never saved us.*'

"Sshhh!"

'*Bug. There were more to come.*'

"Enough."

'*Bug. There were so many of us. So many more.*'

He balled his hand into a fist and slammed it against the table. Pain shot through his knuckles. He stood suddenly. The chair screeched back and toppled over with a bang. Wood crackled and split.

Dammit. He looked down at the chair.

The clock on the tomato-spattered stove told him it was 2:45 a.m. *Shit.* He had to be back at HQ in a handful of hours. How had he lost so much time in that damn book? *Because, Bug. Because you can't let go. You never did let go.* It's like his body fed on pictures of corpses and scattered pieces of a horrifying puzzle. He couldn't put it away until the last segment was clicked into place.

He picked up the glass on the table and downed the last spit of sweet bourbon. The bottle looked half empty. Hadn't he just opened it? *Dammit.*

Sliding his feet across the cold linoleum, he shuffled into the bedroom, kicked at the piles of clothes on the floor clinging to his feet, and went straight to the bathroom. Whipping open the medicine cabinet, he grabbed the gift from Doctor Sherry, popped the cap, and pressed it against his lips. He leaned his head back. Several pills landed on his tongue. He swallowed them down his dry throat. Replacing the container on the shelf, he snapped the mirrored door shut, avoided his reflection, and shuffled over to the bed. He flopped down, face first, and squeezed his eyes shut.

His mind fought against the barrage of ghosts. Doctor Sherry's white-capsuled donation released their contents into his bloodstream. The sleeping power took over his mind, numbing his body.

A shield cloaked his buzzing brain, slowing his thoughts. His eyelids grew heavy as his shoulders slumped against the soft blankets. Numbness wove down his arms and legs. His breathing slowed. Something like sleep, but more like a nightmare-infested paralysis, took over him.

FRESH
START

Chapter 13

Purge

Pulling clothes from the bottom drawer, throwing them haphazardly across the floor, Mahoney searched deep into the bottom. He was sure he still had at least one pair. He pulled an old, brown-wool sweater out. Grey sweatpants appeared. *Yes. I knew it.*

He stood up, pulled on the soft sweats, and walked over to the closet. Did he still have a pair of running shoes? After a full rummage through the closet, he concluded that he no longer owned any type of athletic shoe. Had it really been that long since he'd engaged in physical activity for the purpose of fun or to *be healthy?* He knew the answer.

He stared at his shiny black work shoes. Was that really all he had now? A tall woman dressed like she was ready for a safari flashed into his mind. *Ah, yes. The hiking boots.* When the Glam Boys case had hit, when he had first met Medical Examiner Blackwood, he had purchased the hiking boots that became a staple at every crime scene. Since this early retirement thing, he hadn't worn them. He bolted to the front hall, opened the closet, and looked down at the sturdy boots. *Better than dress shoes. You need all the grip you can get, old man.*

Donned in grey sweats, a tattered t-shirt, and hiking boots, he hit the pavement running. After two hours of restless sleep, tops, he'd given up. He hoped the fresh air would breathe new life into him. A warm Chinook wind had blown in over Alberta's Rocky Mountains, bringing spring back with it.

Within minutes, he was coated in a layer of thick sweat. His t-shirt stuck to his back. He gasped for air. Forcing several deep breaths of fresh oxygen into his lungs, he steadied his breathing, keeping the pace. The toxic mix of sweet bourbon and white-capsuled sleep seeped from his pores and drizzled down his arms. He bent over, looking down at the pavement.

Taking several big gulps of air, he stood and ran. He ran for a while. He sweated. He purged. The memories of Sid and Seth, the evil pair that tried to take over his city, poured out of him. Every white ghost-boy face. Every pair of dark nothing eyes. The shimmering cloak. The mummy wrappings. An arctic-ice pendant, swinging on a long, silver chain. Each image flashed before his eyes, then vanished.

Every single image escaped from his mind, his body, his soul. Ridding himself of every horrific memory, every gory image, every bad feeling. He let it all go.

The horizon opened up in front of him. The downtown view of Calgary, the city he grew up in, came into view. The sun hung low, casting a pink-orange hue along the skyline. Lights shimmered across the city streets, brightening the deep-blue sky. He stopped at the edge of the path and took it all in. A warm hand wrapped around his heart. *Pretty place. Prettier without serial killers.*

Seth and Sid. Both gone. Forever. An anomaly in this city. Never to happen again. At least, he hoped.

Mahoney slipped his hand into the soft pocket of his sweats. He stroked the polished stone resting inside. He pulled it out. It rolled into the palm of his hand. He stretched his fingers out and stared at the shining, pink rock. Rose quartz. Given to him by a woman in flowing scarves in a basement gem shop, one of his stops during the Glam Boys case. He imagined an aura of warm energy pulsing around the stone, seeping into his pores, weaving through his body. The warmth around his heart surged, migrating inside of him, up his throat and down into his stomach.

He looked out at the pink horizon, now tinged with tangerine. This was it. The turning point. Maybe he wasn't made for retirement. *Maybe? Bad images. Pills. Bourbon. No maybe about it.*

He knew he needed this case. He hoped it needed him. Turning back the way he came, he started running into a second round of purge.

Chapter 14

Bug is Back

A red-horned man—his hand forming a claw, his black fingernails threatening to puncture anyone in his way—stared at Mahoney from the plastic case. An equally threatening series of bold, red letters glared at him. *Satan's Sorrow.* He turned the key. The engine rumbled. *Old. But still good.*

Mahoney flipped the case open, clicked the CD from the plastic, and slipped it into the thin line in the dashboard. The CD disappeared with a *whssst.* He stroked the steering wheel a couple times, listening to the grumble of the engine.

Kicking his car into gear, he drove through the belly of the city, losing himself in the soothing voice of the metal god from *on's oint.* The deep crooning of the dramatic voice wove through the cab and into the back seat, filling the corners of the car that felt like home to him.

Black lips moved through his mind. The words penetrated him.

The car rolled to a stop. He gazed up at the red light. Scanning the streets, here in the deepest part of the downtown core, he watched the early-morning homeless combing through garbage cans, looking for collectibles to add to the bulging garbage bags hoisted on their backs or tied to the handlebars of the shifty-looking bikes they had 'found' somewhere.

He cracked the driver's side window. The crisp air hit his face. The black-lipped rock god reminded him some people sought abuse. He believed it. His self-abuse had escalated to new heights recently.

The light flashed green. The engine rumbled again as he hit the gas. An easy cruise through town, early enough to beat rush-hour traffic jams, he arrived at HQ only three tracks into his newly purchased album.

Putting his car into park, he let it idle. He picked up the red-horned devil case and flipped it over. He scanned the track list scrawled in heavy lettering.

1. Tortured Soul 3:45

2. Beyond Satan 4:42

3. Hell's Core 3:23

4. Fire of Death 4:13

5. Raging Rant 2:30

Huh. Only takes two and a half minutes to rage a rant. Ha.

6. Sick Poison 3:23

7. Satan's Drink 5:13

8. Heat and Love 2:45

9. Six Six Six 6:66

10. Filthy Lining 3:12

Guess he'd have to wait for a dose of sick poison until he was on the road to the airport. That would be a nice farewell.

The driver's side door creaked as he pushed it open. He shoved his tattered grey derby onto the top of his head, straightened his tweed coat, and slammed the door shut. A few brisk strides took him to the tall glass doors.

He felt like an entirely different man than he had when he walked through these doors yesterday. It was amazing what a sweaty purge could do for the soul. Not to mention his new repertoire of Satan's Sorrow. Candy-apple lips and tight leather flashed into his mind. What had the bartender at the beer-soaked joint said? *Heavy metal soothes the soul.*

He picked up his pace, waking the man he had once been. He paused at the front desk.

"Morning, Pegs."

"Good morning, Bug." She smiled. Her blonde bob shone under the bright lights. Her cherry lipstick accentuated her full lips. "You look...better." Her cheeks flushed pink.

"Thanks." He smiled. "You heard anything about where this case is going?"

"It's all very hush-hush."

"C'mon. You heard nothing?" He tried to charm her with his smile.

"Well." She looked at her desk, then raised her gaze back to him. "Seems the Sarge may be arguing with the guys out east. Thing is, they were the ones who contacted him. But he's got some conditions. And it doesn't seem like they're too happy about it."

"How's Sutton handling this?"

"Oh, he's right on top of it. You know, you groomed him well."

Mahoney snorted. "He always had it in him. I've heard he's been working his ass off around here."

"True. But good leadership provides the path to success."

"What? Where'd you read that? Some poster or something?" The heat rising in his cheeks wasn't welcome.

"No." She placed a small desk calendar on the counter and turned it to face him.

He read the caption out loud. "*You can be whatever you want.* Oh, really?"

She flipped pages. "Here is it. Last Monday. I know it's just a calendar, Bug, but it's true. Sutton was inexperienced. You boosted his way to his promotion. But I know you aren't good at taking compliments."

Oh man. "Fine. Thanks, Pegs. Gotta get to work." He turned before the blazing fire building in his cheeks and down his neck could be spotted. He bolted down the hallway.

"Let me know if you need fresh coffee in there," her voice chased after him.

"Thanks, Pegs," he called back.

Chapter 15

Pre-Flight War Room

Heat swelled in the stuffy room. Dara's mountain-fresh canned air struggled beneath a coat of hot body odour.

Back here. Again. Mahoney wished he could be at home, wrapped in his soft, white robe, un-showered, drinking dark roast from his liar of a mug. Sleeping pills and a bottle of bourbon popped into his head. Then again, maybe this was the best thing. He shrugged off the doubt in his gut, building like a fire eating through fresh logs.

His mind was clear. The horrific scrapbook of images past had taken a break. He had sweat them out. At the end of the second purge, the second round of his run, he'd felt cleansed. Most of the bourbon and the sleeping pills had worn off after the deep, troubled sleep he'd had. The run rid him of whatever remnants had been clinging. He'd cleaned himself up real good, found a suit, shined his shoes, and put on his tattered, grey derby for the first time in a while.

Grab that cleansed feeling. Cling to this fresh start. He grasped the end of the thread that could unravel his whole 'Bug is back' coating he'd painted over himself.

The thick aroma of dark roast called to him. He strode over to the corner table.

Dara was occupied with her typewriter. Sutton and Hayes sat at the long centre table, sipping from large Styrofoam cups. He smirked to himself. *Hayes really got Sutton into those smoothies.* He pictured Sutton devouring a juicy, thick burger, the way he had almost every day in this room during their last case together. The *Mummy Boys* case, compliments of Sid. Apparently even well-trained detectives could develop new habits.

The door opened with a *whoosh*. Sergeant Jackson adjusted his glasses and stared at an open folder in his thick hand as he walked up to the front of the room.

"OK, everyone. We need to get moving." He looked up from the file. "Sutton, Mahoney, you're on a flight in three hours. You'll be met by Sergeant Tomlinson. He's the head of homicide in Toronto."

Hayes whistled. "Good luck with that."

Sutton slipped the straw from his mouth. "You know him?"

"Yeah. He was in charge when I did my rookie training out there. Real piece of work."

The Sarge glared at Hayes. "He doesn't mess around. Gets things done."

"Glad I'm not going," Hayes said.

"I wanted to send all of you. Keep you a cohesive unit. Budget is tight on our end. The guys out east were specific about how much they're throwing in."

"Cheap bugger. He always was." Hayes smirked.

"Enough." The Sarge glowered. "Hayes, I need you on this here, with me. We've got to make sure everything is by the book from our end. We'll keep on top of where Sutton and Mahoney are. Every single thing they do, we need to log. We'll keep a tight record on this end."

"Tight paper work to cover your ass." Hayes smirked again.

The glower on Sarge's face deepened. "No one's covering anyone's ass. We need to avoid any *glitches*. I don't have to ask if you all remember the *Mummy Boys* case." The Sarge shifted from one foot to the other. "You recall the first scene was out in K-Country. The RCMP owned that scene. You boys had built quite a team on the Glam Boy murders. The red coats wanted our expertise. They wouldn't let go of owning the scene, but it was a real bitch getting them to process it right. Hayes, you were the one out there dealing with that shit."

The smirk vanished from Hayes' face. "Yeah. It *was* a bitch dealing with them."

"We need to avoid the same issues we dealt with then. There are certain things we can do to ensure a smoother ride. Dara was here most of the night, wading through a stack of policies with me."

Mahoney shot a smile back at Dara. Her suit was perfectly pressed. Her smooth bun didn't allow any stray strands. How did she do it?

Dara chimed in, "Sometimes the best way to easy communication is to follow the rules. Dot your I's and cross your T's. When something does come up, you just follow your paper trail. Takes all the emotion out of it, boys. Eases tempers."

"Back to the plan," the sergeant said. "Sutton, Mahoney, you boys need to head to the airport in a half hour. Make sure you aren't late. I can't afford to buy another pair of tickets."

Mahoney nodded. Sutton tipped his Styrofoam cup.

"Hayes, we're spending the day reviewing this process that Dara and I worked on—making sure it's airtight."

"Got it." Hayes' mouth was a thin line.

"When you two touch down, Tomlinson will meet you. You'll go straight into debrief. He'll be running the show. You'll need to follow orders. Check your egos. Play it cool. For now." The sergeant shot them each a stern stare.

Sutton agreed, "Got it, boss."

Mahoney tipped his pointer as he nodded.

"We'll touch base at the end of the day. Just us. We'll go from there." The sergeant took a deep breath. "OK. So let's do a quick review of this scene before you go."

The sergeant walked up to the cream-coloured crime scene wall. Mahoney watched him, from the back of the room, as he pointed at each photo pinned to the chipping paint. The sergeant's lips moved, spouting the details of the new scene, laid out on the wall. The body. Sharin Lane. Sixteen years old. Found on Thursday, April 6, in Tommy Thomson Park. Suspected time of death was April 5. The black dress. Slit from heart to pelvis. The blood-red circles around the eyes. The painted black lips. A young woman staged like a demon doll.

Sergeant Jackson's lips moved, but Mahoney didn't hear a word he said. He already knew it all. The horrific scrapbook he'd absorbed through the night came to life again. The images flashed from one murder scene to the next. Three bodies, sixteen years ago. Painted up like hell's demons. Slit open. Bled out. Left on display.

Just as quickly as the killings began, they halted. They never had found the knife that made the incision from heart to pelvis on three girls. The quarts of blood drained from the bodies had never been found.

There were so many strange things about the carnage left behind. When the bodies stopped appearing, resources ran thin. Toronto Homicide lost something. It might have been interest. Or focus. Mahoney had suspected they lost their appetite for such gruesome work. Or the lack of parents breathing down their necks let the case trickle to a stop. When the bodies stopped, time passed, and the general public went back to their safe world. The girls were forgotten.

He never forgot. The images he'd kept locked away in the back of his mind for all those years came to life again as he stared at the crime scene wall. Every scene he had reviewed at his kitchen table with a bourbon in his hand presented itself in his mind. The reels on the horror flick turned, the lights dimmed, and he was faced with a fresh viewing of an old film.

Chapter 16

Pre-Flight Bourbon

A tumbler sat on the counter of a crowded bar tucked in the corner of the Calgary airport. The smell of sweet caramel wafted from the rich, brown liquid, floating around his face. His hand twitched. It was still morning, but he wanted to pick up the glass.

Bug. Get yourself together.

He stared at the glass.

One drink. Take the edge off. You heard Hayes. King of the show we're joining is a real dick.

His hand twitched again. He continued staring at the glass.

Fuck it.

In a single, swift motion, he picked up the glass and downed half the liquid. It delivered. The sweetness lingered over his tongue. A slight burn followed as the bourbon slithered down his throat.

It's just bourbon.

Doctor Sherry's prescription for sleep was back home in the medicine cabinet.

It's just one drink.

His homicide, or rather, his ex-homicide department was on a tight budget. He would be seated next to Sutton in cozy economy. He'd be reverting back to good ol' ginger ale in the air—just like the old days when he was in the trenches of a never-ending series of murders.

The rest of the bourbon vanished in one fell swoop.

"Another?" A young man, dressed in a bright-red vest, smiled at him eagerly. His shiny gold nametag labelled him *Kenneth*.

"No. Thank you, Kenneth." He smiled.

Snapping a couple bills on the counter beside the empty glass, he twisted his wrist and looked at his watch. Ten minutes to boarding time. *Better find Sutton.*

Sutton was easy to spot with his broad shoulders and soft brown waves of hair. He looked like he belonged in a Head and Shoulders commercial.

"Hey, boss...I mean, Detective."

"You're the boss now, kid."

"Yeah, well, it's uh..."

"Get used to it. You're the kingpin now."

Sutton's cheeks flushed.

"So, you know anything about this Tomlinson guy? Mahoney rubbed the bristle on his chin. He didn't recall any Tomlinson from the one time he'd worked in Toronto.

"Only what Hayes said. Sarge didn't spill any details."

"I'm getting the sense he's a real a-hole," Mahoney said.

"Nothing we haven't dealt with. What about the red coats, on your last case?"

"Nah. They were a pain in my ass, but only for about two seconds. A little rough talk and they complied."

"You don't think that approach will work here?" Sutton asked.

"Nope. I think we're in for a real ride, *boss*." Mahoney tipped his derby.

Sutton chuckled.

"Say, tell me something about those Suitcase Slaughters." Mahoney hated thinking about the body parts crumpled in a bloody pile. After his episode at the scene, he'd been off the case. He'd been off every case. No-one ever brought it up. He'd read what he could find, but he knew that not everything was printed for public consumption.

Sutton raised an eyebrow. "What?"

"Why wasn't there more stink coming out of those suitcases? You'd think someone in the apartment above or below would have noticed."

Sutton snickered. "The suitcases were lined in plastic. Held in the stink."

"Really? How can you be sure?"

"I did an experiment. With a bunch of suitcases, garbage bags, and a pile of hams. Left them in my garage."

"Wow." Mahoney smirked. Once in a while, you learned something somewhat amusing on a murder case.

Sutton stood. "We gotta get to the gate. We're boarding now."

Mahoney followed Sutton down the long hall lined with boarding gates. They passed one, two, three bars. They all had Maker's Mark. It was gonna be a long flight.

Chapter 17

Missing Girls Support Group

A stainless-steel coffee pot perked in the corner of the room, shooting out spouts of brown water over the chipped wooden table. Middle-aged men and women, mostly in couples, wandered aimlessly around the room, thin Styrofoam cups in their hands.

Joe and Joanne chatted with Tom and Laverne. Joe held a half-eaten cookie in one hand, nibbling at it between dribbles of conversations. The trauma over his missing daughter hadn't affected his appetite. Joanne looked at him with disgust, eyeballing the cookie like she couldn't understand how he could *eat* at a time like *this.*

Laverne looked at Joe with her wide eyes, hanging on to his every word. Was he spouting that hope crap again? Chester sure hoped not. Or, maybe he did. It seemed to keep them...calmer.

Laverne wrung her hands around a blue handkerchief. Was that the same one she'd been holding at the last meeting? Handkerchiefs were unsanitary at the best of times. Chester didn't even want to imagine what germs were festering on the crumpled blue cloth sticking to Laverne's dirty hands.

Tom stood, nodding, sipping cheap coffee from cheap Styrofoam. His eyes scanned the room between focused moments on whoever in their small group was blabbering on. As usual, Tom didn't speak. He just stood and listened. Chester wondered what he was thinking. Tom was the only one he had trouble reading.

Gloria, one the newer members of the group, waddled up to the table of refreshments, her floral frock swaying back and forth. She was the most fascinating attendee. The raw grief of the other parents was expected. Their daughters had been their own flesh and blood. Gloria was a foster parent. The girl that she had called her own had belonged to someone else, at one time. Yet, Gloria grieved as openly as the others. Chester was drawn to her emotional pouring for a girl that she had received, something like a gift. He understood it. Too well.

The room rose several degrees as the couples filed in, their heat and stink wafting through the stuffy space. Chester walked over to the percolating coffee machine to check on its progress. The fluorescent tube lights glared down on him. He lifted the lid off the coffee pot and peered inside.

The pot, three-quarters full of thin black liquid, was nearing the end of the percolation cycle. He replaced the lid and walked over to Tina. She was focused on lining up the homemade cupcakes she had brought on a cheap plastic tray.

"Tina. The coffee's almost done."

"Oh, Chester, great. Thank you. I hope they like the cupcakes. I'm not the accomplished baker you are."

"I'm sure they'll love them. It was thoughtful of you." He placed a hand on her shoulder. He'd have to sanitize it later.

She melted under his gesture. "Oh, you think so? Oh, good." She placed the last cupcake on the tacky orange tray, next to the shining silver platter housing Chester's cookie creations.

"We can start the meeting now."

"OK." She grabbed a thin paper napkin and wiped sticky icing off her fingers. "I hope I do all right. You know, George usually runs the meetings. But, you might have heard, he can't this evening."

"You'll be great." Chester plastered a wide smile on his face.

"Thanks." Her cheeks blazed red.

She was too easy to play.

He watched her walk to the front of the room. Making a meek attempt at raising her voice, she somehow got the attention of the sorry-looking people milling about the room, sipping free coffee. They moved like cattle, herding themselves to the front of the room and sitting on cracked plastic chairs.

Tina started reading through her prepared script. In a less-than-convincing voice, she told them not to lose hope, that they were in this together, and that they needed to believe their girls would be found.

Chester stood in the corner, watching the pathetic play re-running itself again. He'd seen the same gathering unfold too many times. Yet, he couldn't stay away.

He couldn't understand why they clung to hope when the facts told them after forty-eight hours a missing child was unlikely to be found. At least not alive. Hope was their death, stringing them along, giving them something to grasp on to. Another sleepless night. Another day without their spawn. Another corpse-less day to cling to. Day after day, until they were mere shells, a coat of human flesh over empty frames.

He looked over the people clinging to Tina's weak words. Their eyes filling with tears, the women pulling tissues from overstuffed purses and grasping the arms of their husbands. Such sorrow. It drew Chester in. Week after week, he felt compelled to come here, to submerge himself in this sea of sadness, to share in their loss.

He figured it was the least he could do. He knew their girls were never coming home. He knew their girls didn't belong to them anymore. Besides, the ultimate boost to the quality of his public-world persona was giving so generously of his time and patience to comfort those he had *taken* from.

The scripted speech came to a halt. A weak applause pattered through the room. A fluorescent tube buzzed, blasting a shot of bright light through the room, then burned out, leaving the corner dimly lit. The people sitting in the chairs stirred, some rising, some moving the chairs into awkward positions to continue a conversation they had started mid-applause. Chester challenged himself to put on the best performance he could. He walked toward a small group milling by the coffee machine—the eager ones looking for a refill on the free coffee before it ran out.

"Joe, Tom, Gloria. Nice to see you," he greeted them with a wide pasted-on smile.

"Chester. So nice of you to come. You give so much of your time here," Joe chattered away.

Tom took a sip from his Styrofoam cup. Droplets of cheap coffee clung to his bushy, black moustache.

Gloria forced a smile as she clung to her half-empty Styrofoam cup.

"Volunteering is good for the soul," Chester said.

"Your cookies are amazing." Joe's gut jiggled as he chuckled.

"Don't forget about Tina's cupcakes. She went to such an effort." Chester lifted the cheap plastic tray toward Joe's belly.

Joe grabbed for the cupcake with the most icing. Just what he needed, more sugar to make him weaker.

Gloria shook her head. "No, thank you. My appetite has been, well, non-existent." She looked at the floor.

Chester put his hand on Gloria's shoulder. "I'm so sorry for what you are going through." *But your girl is home now. She's been re-purposed.* Chester put the tray back on the table.

Gloria shook her head. Her body quivered. Cheap coffee leaped from the Styrofoam cup. She put it on the table. Covering her eyes with her hands, she wept.

Chester rubbed her back. "It's okay. What you are feeling is to be expected." *You must mourn your loss. She's where she belongs.*

Gloria's shoulders settled. She looked up, the skin puffy and red around her eyes. "I'm sorry."

"It's all right." Joe looked at his half-eaten cupcake in disgust. "Oh hell, I just keep eating. I feel like a pig. It's the only thing that gives me a moment of happiness." His mouth turned down in a twisted pout.

Chester kept his hand on Gloria's shoulder and put his other hand on Joe's shoulder. "Listen, what you are all feeling is normal. You need to go through the proper cycles. You're experiencing shock and denial at the same time."

They nodded. Joe took another bite of his cupcake, icing sticking to his thin lips. He licked it off.

"I feel awkward. Some people say that my daughter wasn't really mine. They don't understand my grief." Gloria wiped her eyes with a balled up tissue.

"You love your daughter." *I love her now.* "You want her to come home." *She is home.* "You wish the best for her." *She will get the best.*

Gloria nodded. Joe looked back at the cupcake sticking to his fingers. The disgust returned. He threw it in the trash bin next to the coffee maker. Grabbing a napkin, he wiped at the icing sticking to his fingers.

"Give yourselves time. The path forward will become clear."

They looked at Chester, eating up his words. Letting him guide them through their life, one meeting at a time.

Just like their girls, they would find their salvation.

THE
CIRCUS
IS IN
TOWN

Chapter 18

Circus

Mahoney stared at the hot-pink lips moving in rapid bursts, repeating and confirming orders back to Sergeant Tomlinson. The pink lips belonged to Barbie.

The sergeant's wiry moustache twitched erratically. It reminded Mahoney of Williams, the red coat, the head of the horsemen, the Royal Canadian Mounted Police. The first body in the *Mummy Boys* case was found on Williams' turf. Mahoney fondly remembered Williams' chubby cheeks blazing red, his moustache twitching as he argued in the corner of the war room back home.

Williams had been hard to deal with, at first, but he'd come around. The head of Toronto Homicide, Sergeant Tomlinson, was a whole new can of trouble. He'd been a no-show at the airport, sending a taxi to take them to their hotel, along with a note ordering them to be at the Toronto Police Service headquarters bright and early the next morning.

Mahoney took a nice long sip of the rich dark roast and stared at the twitching moustache, then back at the hot-pink lips. This headquarters was full of characters. At least the coffee was decent. The brown water at the low-rate motel was almost undrinkable. His gut pulsed. How would this investigation go? Would it be a circus full of clowns? Would he be the bearded woman, not allowed to speak?

Circus music played in his head as Tomlinson's moustache twitched in time, his face spinning in circles, his grin wide and crazy. Hot-pink lips danced around beneath a red, bulbous nose. An oversized striped costume cloaked Barbie's body. Big red shoes flopped. He shook his head and took another sip of coffee. The chatter in the room was incessant. He wanted to get this show on the road, whatever kind of show it was.

He contemplated the mug he was holding. It was shiny, white, smooth and didn't have any chips. *Toronto Homicide* was painted across it in iridescent-blue lettering. The room was large, brightly lit, and had a huge window overlooking the vast Lake Ontario. The sun glowed hot rays through the window, bathing the room in a golden hue. White clouds painted the baby-blue walls in some sort of happy mural. The tiny, stuffy, body-odour-soaked war room back home flashed into his mind. How could he get a room like this? *Guess that's Sutton's problem now.*

The moustache halted as Tomlinson ordered everyone to be quiet. The room hushed. Mahoney settled against the back wall. Tomlinson, tall and lean, walked to the front of the room and hailed his audience with raised hands. His perfectly polished black shoes glimmered under the sunlight. His smooth, freshly shaven chin bobbed up and down as he walked them through a series of crime scene photos. The photos were lined up neatly on a massive blackboard held in place by round, glassy magnets. *Fancy war room, fancy board.*

"Sharin Lane. Sixteen years old. She went missing five and a half weeks ago. Lived in a foster care centre. It was concluded that she'd run away. Five foot five. Long, dark hair. The photos here show how she was left, in the park. As you can see, her, uh..." Tomlinson paused, clearing his throat. "She was slit from her heart down to the top of her pelvis. She bled to death." He paused again, grabbing for a shiny yellow mug and taking a long sip. A coffee droplet clung to his moustache. He put the mug down. "Only an animal would gut a girl like this. Appears to be a random act of violence. We have a man in custody. He was hovering around the scene."

Mahoney's mind buzzed to life. *Was she branded? What was her blood type?* He stared at his copy of the briefing, wondering if it was incomplete. It stated that the organs had been removed from the body. He shuddered. He didn't recall any missing organs on the bodies from the cold case.

A young detective with baby-smooth skin, wearing a crisp, slate-grey pinstripe suit spoke up. "Sergeant, you said she'd been missing for five and a half weeks?"

"Uh, I believe so."

"So, *if* this was a random act of crazed violence, then where was she all that time?"

"Well, Detective, we'll never know, will we? She can't exactly tell us." Tomlinson glared at Fancy Suit.

Snarky chuckles broke out through the room.

Fancy Suit spoke, "But Sergeant, if I may, isn't it our job to find out where she was?"

Tomlinson's moustache twitched madly. His face flushed. "It's our job to catch the sicko who did this. We've already brought in a prime suspect."

"But Sergeant, with all due respect, we haven't properly formulated a profile. We could be after the wrong type of suspect. Where was the girl, for five and a half weeks? And why wouldn't the killer flee the scene?"

"Detective Dixon, enough with the profiling. You are out of line." A bead of sweat trickled down Tomlinson's flushed cheek.

Mahoney took several strides toward the front of the room, abandoning the shiny mug along the way. "Sergeant, your detective has a point. Look at these photos." He walked up to the elaborate crime scene board and pointed at the sliced-open body. "The incision is precise. And all her organs are missing. This...-extraction...would have taken skill. Whoever did this needed the right tools, cutting skills, and patience. And where is all the blood? Not to mention her organs. The scene is too clean. The victim was clearly killed elsewhere and then staged. This looks planned, not an act of whim."

The moustache was out of control. The flush now blazed bright red. "*Detective.* We've got a direction here and have a suspect in custody. Developing dramatic theories is a waste of time and resources."

"What about the striking resemblance to the Susie Slaughters?"

Tomlinson stood and glared. His moustache twitched a couple of times.

"The Susie Slaughters. The reason I was brought in. Famous case. 1973. Named after the first victim. The similarities here are striking."

"Could be coincidence." Tomlinson swallowed. "And it wasn't *me* who brought you in."

"A coincidence?" Mahoney stepped toward Tomlinson.

"It would have to be one hell of a coincidence," Dixon said.

"Maybe it's one of those copycat things. The killer read the papers." Tomlinson cleared his throat.

"That would require a lot of preparation. Still doesn't look like a random act," Dixon said.

"Dixon. *Can it.* Like I said, we *have* a *suspect.* Fastest way to close this thing is to interview him. Get a confession." Tomlinson's voice rose as he glowered at Dixon.

Dixon smoothed his pant legs with his palms and stepped back.

"Was she branded, on her back?" Mahoney asked.

"Branded?"

"Yeah, a symbol. Circular. With an intersecting V. On the victim's back?"

"Not that I'm aware of."

"Has anyone followed up with the medical examiner?"

"Information comes to us as he finds it."

"This is critical. The three victims from the Susie Slaughters were sixteen-year-old girls with long, dark hair. All declared runaways from foster care centres. They were sliced open, bled out, and made up the same way as this new victim. The linkage here is undeniable."

Detective Tomlinson's voice dripped with sarcasm, "That case went cold. *You* should know. *You* were on it."

"Yeah. It did. And yeah, I was. Isn't that why I'm here?"

"You're here because one of my idiotic superiors likes to play politics with the senior citizens on city council. All I'm required to do is involve you. You can tag along on the suspect interviews, and file information as it comes in. Consider yourself *involved*."

What. The. Fuck. Sutton stood across the room, a look of bewilderment on his face. The green rabbit foot, Sutton's lucky charm that always hung from his belt, sat still against his jeans.

Mahoney scanned the crime scene photos. Was this guy for real? Did he really think the bizarre clues were only a coincidence? Or did he have some hidden agenda here? Whatever the case, the plan was sabotage right from the get-go. He and Sutton were never intended to be part of this investigation. His gut pulsed again. He wasn't going home on a cold case. *Not again.*

The moustache took up another round of erratic twitching as orders were barked. Tomlinson looked at two young clones of himself. "Myers and Biggs. You're with me. Let's interview the suspect." He smirked. "Detective Dixon, why don't you show our guests here around. Give them the rundown of how we do things. Then bring them in to observe the interview." Tomlinson trudged across the room and out the door. His clones followed.

Mahoney lunged for the door. "Sergeant," Mahoney called after Tomlinson as he rushed away.

Sergeant Tomlinson halted and spun. Annoyance washed over his face. "Yes, Detective."

"May I have a word?"

Tomlinson rolled his eyes. "Fine, my office."

Mahoney followed Tomlinson as he rushed down the corridor, as if trying to lose him.

They entered a huge corner space, glass walls letting in natural light. The view exposed the downtown core, tall glass buildings glimmering in the afternoon sun against a baby-blue sky. *Wow. Nice digs.*

Tomlinson shut the door hard, then yanked on a cord, closing the blinds and blocking out the inquiring eyes dotting the office space.

"What do you want, Mahoney?" Spit flew from Tomlinson's mouth.

Ignoring the speckles of saliva flying through the air, Mahoney stared hard at the sergeant. "There's been some miscommunication here. I'm here because I was on the original case. My team is to collaborate with yours. We're to be part of the investigation."

"You're here for show. To make the people who were around back then satisfied. To shut them up."

"That's not the impression Sergeant Jackson gave me."

"He's out of my jurisdiction. And this body is in *my* jurisdiction." The sergeant narrowed his eyes.

Mahoney walked up to Tomlinson, glowering back. "We need to meet with your superiors and conference in my sergeant. Get this cleared up. Now." He jabbed his pointer into the shiny, polished black desk lining the window.

"Detective. You're an old, washed-up has-been, slow to catch killers. We need to question our suspect, now. Do as you've been ordered, or I'll have you sent home."

"Go ahead. Question your makeshift suspect. You know as well as I do it won't get you anywhere."

"This is *my* investigation. It'll go however *I* want it to."

"It won't if another body turns up."

"That won't happen."

"Three girls were killed during the Susie Slaughters. *If* you don't have the killer in custody, which you don't, then we're looking at another dead body. *If* the killer follows the same pattern as before, another victim will be slaughtered. *In three days.*" Heat rushed up Mahoney's neck.

Tomlinson walked right up to him, pushing his red face a mere inch from Mahoney's. Hot breath blew from Tomlinson's nostrils. "We have the killer. There won't be another victim."

"I'll be talking to my sergeant." Mahoney spun, whipped the door open and stomped through.

Dozens of eyes stared. He paused. The eyes darted back to whatever work they were doing, files they were processing, reports they were typing. The room went back to work-level buzz. Mahoney strode through, back to the fancy war room.

Chapter 19

Calling Home

Mahoney flipped open his cell phone and yanked the antenna up. Perks of being back in homicide, he didn't have to deal with the plastic brick he'd been using. Pushing the buttons hard, he glared at the phone. *C'mon, c'mon. Answer.* Tomlinson's moustache twitched through his mind. His annoying voice followed, taunting Mahoney's nerves. *Washed out. Has-been detective. We'll see who's washed out.*

"Mahoney. You're early. You were supposed to call me later. At the end of your first full day out there."

"Yeah. You pulled me out of retirement for *this*? Tomlinson's a jackass. He doesn't want me here. He's a complete grade-A clown."

"Yeah. I pulled you out. Out of your self-loathing spiral. You *need* this. And you're telling me you haven't handled a couple clowns before?"

"Fine. But we're not getting anywhere. Tomlinson's fixed on arresting some random suspect. He's pushing me out of the investigation."

"Dammit. Constable Witton has assured me that Tomlinson would co-operate."

"He's not. He says that *he* didn't bring me out here." Mahoney sighed. "And, he refuses to admit linkage to the Susie Slaughters."

"What? His superior brought you in precisely because of the similarity."

"It's undeniable. There are some differences, but, the similarities are significant." Mahoney rubbed the bristle on his chin. "I can't get anything done like this."

"Can't, or won't?"

Mahoney sighed. "Sarge. You sent us here with a process heavier than an encyclopedia. Tomlinson is pushing me aside. Now you're telling me to get shit done. You can't have both."

"Can't I?" The sergeant's sigh vibrated through the phone. "Mahoney. You need to catch this guy. I know it's haunted you since the case went cold."

The pale faces of three girls rushed through his mind in a blurry white streak. He closed his eyes hard, slowing them down, looking into each pair of eyes, pleading with him to set them free.

"Mahoney. You with me?"

"Yeah. Sure. Whatever."

"Listen, leave the buy-the-book to Sutton. He's gotta learn how to cover the department's ass. I've kept his leash too tight. You worry about...being you."

A vision so clear rushed though Mahoney's mind. He could see himself, holding a hunting knife, sliding it into a man's stomach, then slicing him clean open. The man crumpled to the ground, clutching his cut flesh. A great wave of fresh blood tumbled toward them, washing them both away.

"Mahoney? You there?"

Mahoney jolted back to reality. A shot of tingles vibrated his gut. The wave of instinct rode up his insides. "Yeah. Sarge. Got it. Sutton by the book. Me be me. Catch the fucker."

"And, Mahoney, be careful. Be nice to the clowns. Join the circus. Give me some time to work this out with the ring master. I'll get you the support you need. But you gotta buy me some time."

"Yeah. Sure." He snapped the phone shut and dropped it on the table. It clattered across the crystal-clear glass.

He looked around the room. The sky-blue walls annoyed him. A war room for processing murder scenes wasn't supposed to be happy. The soft puffs of painted clouds annoyed him even more. Where the fuck did these clowns think they were? Heaven? This was a goddamned murder investigation. And they had no idea what kind of sick monster they were dealing with. He grabbed his derby and his phone, then went to play in the circus.

Chapter 20

Smooth Over Sutton

"Sutton. War room. We need to review the crime scene, now."

Sutton's soft brown curls floated as he spun around, "Hey, I was looking for you. Mahoney, we've got to join in the suspect interview."

Mahoney smirked. "Ah. I see you're getting used to being the boss. War room. Crime scene."

Sutton's brow furrowed. His mouth twisted. "We need to join the investigation."

"I know. I just talked to Sarge. We will. Give me ten minutes."

Sutton sighed, twisting his mouth in a contortion of annoyance. "You talked to Sarge? Thought we were doing that later. Together." The last word dripped a warning.

"Yeah. Things changed."

Sutton stared. The rabbit foot dangling from his belt swayed back and forth, bright-green fur and a gnarly claw.

"You still follow your gut. Or you wouldn't be carrying that ugly thing with you." Mahoney pointed at the scraggly green fuzz.

Sutton halted the dangling, stroking the fur. "Yeah, sure."

"So you must know this murder wasn't the work of some random guy strolling by."

"Yeah. But this isn't our case to lead."

"I get it." Mahoney clasped Sutton's shoulder with his hand and looked him in the eyes. "We play along with these clowns. But they won't get anywhere, and you know it."

"Yeah. But I gotta be by the book."

"Yeah you do, and we'll do these useless interrogations, just give me ten minutes. Hell. We could have been done by now if you would stop arguing with me."

"Fine. Five minutes. Then we join the detective twins."

Mahoney chuckled. "The detective twins. Good one. They are a pair of clones. Twitching moustache clones, minus the moustache."

Chapter 21

Side Circus

Mahoney stared at the deluxe crime scene board. He missed the chipped wall back home. A flaking, worn-out wall was a thorough one. Every picture was always included, no matter how gory.

The elaborate, glass-rimmed board with wheels and stoppers was nice to look at, but it was inadequate. It represented everything he hated about this place already. The mural of pretty blue paint and fake fluffy clouds, the view of the bay, the shiny coffee mugs. All of it for show. None of it to solve a murder case.

Mahoney stared at the photos of the girl, slit open, bled out, then made up like the devil's demon doll. "It's too organized. It wasn't random."

"To slice her...like *that*..." Sutton's eyes widened as he stroked the scraggly green fur of his rabbit foot lucky charm. "Wasn't a rush job."

"The killer would have needed a specialty knife. Something that can slice the membrane clean from the organs." Mahoney rubbed the bristle on his chin. He'd left his razor at home. The hotel probably had one. Or one of the dozens of high-end shops cluttering the streets of the downtown core. But then what would he rub while he was solving a murder?

Sutton piped in, "There's no blood at the scene. She was killed elsewhere, then placed. He'd need somewhere to do this. To *prepare* her."

"Yeah." Mahoney nodded.

"What kind of knife would leave an incision like that?" Sutton raised an eyebrow.

"Looks the same as the one on all the victims of the Susie Slaughters." Mahoney pointed at the long, precise cut running from the heart to the top of the pelvis. "My bet is it was made by the same killer. With the same knife." He sighed. "We never did find the knife. Examination of the incision pointed to a gut-hook hunting knife. For large game."

"The hooked curve at the bottom, near the stomach. Standard hunting knife? Or custom made?" Sutton screwed his mouth up and narrowed his eyes at the photos.

"I recall a close match on standard hunting knives. No exact matches. Distinct. Signature."

"You sound like Agent Quesnel."

"Yeah." Mahoney smiled. Quesnel. What *was* his favourite FBI agent up to these days?

"You mentioned a brand, in the group meeting."

"All the victims, from before, had a brand on their back. A symbol. A circle with an intersecting V."

"A message?"

"Don't know. It was never figured out."

Sutton turned, looking him straight in the eye. "Never figured out? Something that weird?"

"Yeah. Case was run by a bunch of yes-men." He returned Sutton's direct stare. "Wouldn't deviate from the orders they were given. Even when they didn't make sense."

Sutton swallowed.

The door swung open. Chattering trickled in.

They both turned. The young detective from the group meeting dressed in the pinstripe suit shot them a surprised look. "Oh, sorry, Detectives. Didn't mean to intrude." He turned to leave.

Mahoney stopped him. "Wait. Detective..."

Fancy Suit spun. "Yeah. Detective Matt Dixon." He extended his hand.

Mahoney shook it. "Join us. We're reviewing the photos a little closer. The meeting seemed...rushed."

The young detective's baby skin flushed pink. His eyes twinkled with excitement. "I agree. That's why I came back."

Mahoney probed further, "What do you make of the makeup on this girl? And the slit down her body?"

Dixon approached the crime scene board, adjusting his wire-framed spectacles. "Makeup is elaborate. Gives off a dark vibe. She was painted up for some...-*purpose.*" He hovered close to the board. "The incision is precise. There is no trace of all the blood, or the organs. She was bled out, cleaned up afterward, then dressed. The killer would need a *place* to pull this off without being seen. I don't see this as a spur of the moment kill." He pulled back.

"Go on," Mahoney encouraged.

"Well, it's too close...looks just like victims of the Susie Slaughters." He swallowed. "The only difference between the new body and the previous ones is the missing organs. It's not a copycat. It's the same killer. He's progressed."

"I think you're dead on," Mahoney said.

"You were on the Susie Slaughters case, but...you weren't leading it, were you?" Dixon asked.

"What do you know about that?" Mahoney smirked.

"Well, based on your recent cases...I think you wanted to go in another direction. Not the way the investigation was taken. I think it was out of your hands." Dixon shot Mahoney a nervous smile.

Mahoney looked down at his hands, then back into the young detective's eyes. "Well, kid, sometimes a man's hands are tied. But sometimes they aren't."

"I can't say mine aren't, now."

"You might be right. May not stop you from helping. Without the wrong people knowing about it."

Detective Dixon's smile relaxed as his eyes lit up.

Mahoney continued, "Who does the medical examinations?"

"Used to be Doctor Woodson. Tomlinson had an arrangement with him. The guy's a dinosaur. Word is he retired."

"He did what Tomlinson asked?" Sutton remarked.

"Yeah," Dixon confirmed with a smirk.

"You said *used* to. Who does them now?" Mahoney asked.

Detective Dixon narrowed his eyes. "Not sure. I heard there was a sudden change in personnel. Don't know the details. It all seems very hush-hush." He shook his head. "That seems to happen a lot around here."

Mahoney nodded. "I understand. Seems like there may be a lot of *arrangements* going on around here. Sometimes arrangements can be *undone*."

The young detective smiled slyly. He looked back at the photos. "I have a suspicion not all the photos are here."

"They're not." Mahoney nodded. "Why do you say that?"

"I read all the files, from before."

Sutton whistled. "Nice light reading."

"One of the highest profile cases to ever hit here. It was before my time. When I was in training, I read all the info I could get my hands on." Dixon pointed at the photos lined up on the board.

"So, where do they keep case files? Cold and fresh?"

"Tomlinson keeps a tight hold on those."

"You've got access?"

"All detectives on a case have access. Until you *misbehave.* My access seems to have vanished."

Sutton chimed in, "How convenient."

"Yeah."

Sutton fidgeted with the dangling green fur, stroking the contorted claw.

Mahoney said, "Leave it to me. We'll get those files."

"Detective, would I be out of line to ask you a question, about your serial killer cases...the Glam Boys and the Mummy Boys?" The young detective's eyes sparkled. He swallowed, eagerness washing over his face.

"Shoot."

"You had an FBI agent, from the criminal profiling unit, helping you out?"

"Yeah."

"How did you get the go-ahead to bring her on?"

"Didn't. I brought her in. Then I got approval."

Sutton shifted from one foot to the other. His fingers grasped at the messy green fur.

A smiled stretched across the young detective's face. "The clues. We need to focus on the bizarre clues. Then blend in the behaviour that would drive someone to focus on such weirdo things."

"I concur." Mahoney nodded. "What else do you see here?"

"I think a wide search perimeter should have been in place, and all the surrounding woods should have been scoured for hidden items. Any sort of message. The killer spent a lot of time on staging the body. He might want credit of some kind."

Mahoney smirked. The young detective sounded like Agent Quesnel. "Do you know how wide the search zone was?"

"Yeah. Not wide enough."

Sutton piped in, "There could still be items out there? Is the crime scene still closed?"

"Nope. Tomlinson had it processed and reopened. Fast. He likes to solve it and move on. Forward progress is his motto."

Beads of sweat trickled across Sutton's forehead. "Kids playing in the park could end up finding shit belonging to a sick murder scene."

"Scene will be tainted by now." Mahoney frowned. "OK. You two should get to the interrogations, keep Tomlinson happy. I'm gonna poke around, look for the missing crime scene photos."

Sutton shot him a glance.

"Don't look so nervous, Sutton. I'll be subtle." Mahoney smirked.

"I don't think you know the meaning of subtle," Sutton shot out, his face coated in sweat.

"You're a sweaty mess. Get yourself together."

Sutton nodded. He wiped his face with his sleeve, then took a deep breath.

The door swung open. Tomlinson stared them down. His moustache twitched as he barked at them. "Detectives, the interrogations have started. If I were you, I'd get over there. Unless you have more important things to do?" He glared at them.

"Sergeant, your detective here was kind enough to answer a few questions I had that weren't addressed during the briefing. You do want us informed so that we can fully collaborate, I assume?" Mahoney coated the sarcasm is his voice with a layer of sweet professionalism.

The sergeant narrowed his eyes. "Of course. Thank you, Detective Dixon. Shall we?"

He gestured out to the hallway.

Mahoney stole a quick glance at Sutton, then Dixon, then led the way in tow of the clown sergeant toward the fake interrogations.

Chapter 22

Doll Collection

A row of dolls, each with a pretty pink dress and long blonde hair, stood in a perfect line on a white wooden shelf. Their faces were a fake shade of human flesh, their eyes bright blue, and their lips a soft pink. Chester picked up the one on the very end, holding it in his palm. He felt sorry for it, in its current state. This is what the toy store corporation said a pretty girl looked like. He knew what true beauty was.

He walked over to a table across the room and set the doll down on the prepared workspace. Resting the doll on soft paper, he sat down in his plush, pleather work chair and stared at it. At *her*. The table housed the materials and tools he would need to bring her to life. Meticulously organized paints, powders, brushes, combs, and scissors lined the top of the table, above the resting place of the doll.

Chester leaned back against the pleather, looking at the doll. "Not yet, my dear. The mood must be right." He stood, walked over to the corner of the room, and perused a series of cassette cases lining a shelf. He chose the only one he ever listened to when he worked on his dolls. *Marilyn Manson & The Spooky Kids* was scrawled in crude black lettering across a white background.

The cover looked like a handmade ticket to a freak circus. It was a treasure. The first recordings of a metal god that couldn't be categorized. A serpent-like man who looked and sounded like no other. The first track was a tribute to one of the biggest metal bands of all time, *Black Sabbath*.

Chester opened the case, slid the tape out, eased it into the tape deck, and pressed play. A tinny drumbeat pierced the silence. Synthesized pulses ebbed through the room, creating a heavy, eerie vibe. A famous guitar riff, recognizable by most of the planet, ripped through the air. The voice followed. The deep hissing of the serpent-man metal god. Telling Chester that the time was here. That he could go forth without fear.

Energized for his special project, he walked back over to the table with slow steps, relishing the moment of delight before working on one of his treasures. It wasn't a hobby. No. More than a hobby. His life's work. His *vocation*.

Chester sat down in the chair. His back straight, he picked up a pair of thin plastic gloves and pulled one over each hand, snapping them into place. He smiled. He was ready. It was time for her transformation.

He looked at the fake flesh face of the doll. His heart skipped a beat. Turmoil swarmed in his stomach. The hardest part was forgetting. He didn't think he ever could. In a flash he was back in that bedroom, the one he dreaded, the one from so long ago that his mind took him back to—against his will. He was small and weak. His arms were skinny little chicken bones. His skin was pale. His lips were too red for a boy. They all called him a girl, all those kids at school.

His memory took him across his childhood bedroom over to the closet. He opened it, as if he were there again. He stepped inside, wedging himself behind the hanging clothes and into the back corner. The black box sat just where he had left it. Sitting down cross-legged, he sunk into the red shag carpet. Picking up the box, he slid has hand over the smooth, black top. Then he opened it.

They were all there. The dolls. The ones he had taken from his sister, one at a time, hoping she wouldn't notice. He just didn't understand why he wasn't allowed to have dolls. His mother wouldn't allow it. She had even told him not to ask her ever again. It was *inappropriate.* He needed to grow up and be a man.

It wasn't his fault his dad was gone. Why did he have to be a man? He wanted to be a child. He wanted to play with pretty dolls just like his sister did. He picked up a doll from inside the black box. Stroking her long, black hair, he touched her face. This was his favourite doll of them all. She looked like his sister. So pretty. So perfect. Just like Violet.

A loud ring pierced his ears. Chester jolted back to his work room and looked down at the doll on the white wooden table. Another ring shot through him. He stood and walked over to the ornate golden phone in the corner, perched on a small cherry wood table. He pulled his gloves off, threw them into the trash bin, and picked up the phone.

"Hello," Chester crooned in his outside-world voice.

"Chester. It's Dina."

"Hello, Dina. How are you today?" He layered another coat of sugar into his tone.

"I am wonderful, thank you for asking." Her voice rang with delight.

She bought it. He had become so good at turning on his public persona, even when he was interrupted. "How nice to hear. Now, what can I do for you, my dear?"

"Well, I'm having a few people over this Friday. And I wonder if you would do me a huge favour. Those macaroons...would you be able to make a batch for me? You see, I've been bragging about how delightful they are to my friends and they just have to try them for themselves. They won't shut up until they do."

Her chatter stabbed his ears. He blurred out her voice and stared across the room at his doll.

"Chester? Are you there?"

"Yes, Dina. I was just listening to your delightful story."

"So, the macaroons?"

"Of course." His shoulders tensed. He'd have to bake for the whole private cul-de-sac. Again. Rich buggers would gossip, especially Margery, and he needed to keep all four of his hoity-toity neighbours on his side. Equally. "I would love to. Friday, you say."

"Yes. Friday. Oh, thank you so much. How ever will I repay you?" Fake concern filtered from her voice.

"Oh, I'm sure we'll find a way." He thought of her long, blonde hair, rich and shiny just like the money she had poured into the products she bought at the high-end salon she went to bi-weekly, on the dot.

"OK, bye now," she chirped.

He replaced the shiny, golden receiver into the cradle of the phone.

Looking at the doll on the table, he walked across the room, sat down, and began his work.

He picked up the doll. "Now, where were we, my lovely?" He stroked her blonde hair.

He opened a small tube of black hair colouring and went to work streaking the golden blonde strands, turning them raven. The head covered, he massaged the dye into the scalp, then pulled the strands of hair straight, resting them around the head. She looked like a punk rocker. A temporary position until the darkness took and he could wash out the residue and brush her strands stark straight. No more golden. No more curls.

He opened a tube of white paint, picked up a small brush, and stroked her face, turning the fake fleshy colour to delightful cream. Happy with his streak-free work, he closed the tube and set it aside. He opened a small, glass jar of thick, flamenco paint. Choosing a small paint brush with tiny bristles, he dipped it into the thick red. He made cautious strokes around the doll eyes, creating blood-red circles. One tiny brush stroke at a time, the hours ticked away as he transformed the doll, helping her find her true beauty.

Satisfied with the eyes, he moved on to the lips. He chose a tiny brush, even tinier than the one he had used on the eyes. He dipped it into a midnight paint and, like a pencil, he used it to draw the lips she deserved to have. Once the sketch was complete, he filled them in with thick black.

He laid her down on the soft paper. Picking up a pair of long, thin scissors, he snipped up the length of her dress, then removed the hideous pink garment. He tossed it in the garbage can resting next to the work table. A purple box tied with a scarlet ribbon sat in the top right corner of his work space. He slid the box toward him, untied the ribbon, then lifted the lid.

A long, black-lace dress, the perfect size for the doll, lay on a red satin lining. He lifted the dress, then with delicate movements covered the naked doll with her new garment. She was perfect. She lay against the soft paper, looking at him through her blood-red circled eyes.

He left her to rest until she was set. Then it would be her time to join the collection of those that had already been transformed.

Chapter 23

Barbie

Mahoney huddled over his borrowed desk. Tomlinson had crammed him, along with Sutton, into a single, tiny desk with two cracking wooden chairs, one on each side. What a thrill this was. He sifted through a folder, pretending to examine the files within. Out of the corner of his eye he kept a watch on the twitching moustache. The sergeant concluded his directions, spun, and walked briskly from the room. The interview with the makeshift suspect had been a farce. The suspect denied any involvement. Tomlinson applied as much pressure as he could, dancing dangerously close to violating protocol. The suspect hadn't caved. Tomlinson stormed out without the prized confession he was after

Mahoney strode up to Barbie, Tomlinson's glorified secretary. Barbie's lips were ghastly hot pink, her bleached-blonde hair riddled with split ends and almost white from too many treatments. Her skin was over-cooked with a fake tan. She looked like she belonged on a Miami beach.

Mahoney shrugged off the slight repulsion and put on a smile.

"Analyst Tussly, is it?" He flashed a stunning smile.

She smiled back. "Yes, *Detective.*"

He didn't like the emphasis she put on detective.

"You can call me Barbie."

Is she for real?

"My friends do. And, well, the guys around here who know me well—they do, too." She smiled sheepishly.

"Well, Barbie..." The word tasted ill. Was he in some sort of strip joint? "I wonder if you could help me with something. You're the analyst on this case. I need some information."

She blushed a shade of pink almost as ghastly as her lips. "Well, sure, technically I guess I am the analyst, but..."

"But your boss has you doing simple work." He paused. "C'mon, Barbie, we both know the truth. You're smarter than your duties show."

She looked at the ground. "Well, sure. I did go to school."

"I saw your credentials. You're an *analyst.* I'm here, I'm from out of town, I'm trying to get some work done. I need some analysis. You're the analyst on this case. So, are you going to help me out?"

A tear escaped from the corner of her eye, trickling down her cheek and taking a line of black mascara with it.

Mahoney pulled his handkerchief from his jacket pocket and handed it to her. "I didn't mean to upset you."

"Oh no. I'm sorry. It's my fault."

"Let's go somewhere more private." He led her by the elbow into the fancy war room and closed the door. "Have a seat. No one will hear us in here."

"I'm sorry."

"Don't be." He sat across from her.

She recomposed herself. "You're right. I am the analyst. I can get you information."

"I knew it." He smiled.

She smiled back. "What do you need?"

"This case we're on...I was involved in something very similar sixteen years ago. Here."

"The Susie Slaughters."

"You know it."

"Yes. I hear the guys talking. They think I'm stupid. But I listen. And I remember. They think it's linked to the case you guys are on now."

"Yes, some would say there's a very strong resemblance between the current body and the bodies from that old case."

"I don't see how you could conclude otherwise. I read all the articles, in the paper, from back then."

"Well then, we're on the same page here."

"Yes." She looked at him. "You want to see all the old files?" Her eyes twinkled.

"I would. It would help to...refresh my memory. I'd also be interested in any *additional* photos of the new scene. Anything not included in the briefing."

"Those files are locked away."

"Who has access?"

"The sergeant. And his direct reports."

"Ah, yes, Tweedledee and Tweedledum..."

She giggled. "Yeah."

"What about Dixon?"

"No. His access card was taken away. He abused his privilege." She formed two sets of quotation marks with her pointer and middle fingers and smirked.

"Well now, have you ever abused your privileges?"

"No. I have access."

"You can get me those files then?"

"Well, technically, I am the liaison for information access to out-of-town collaborators on a case." She smiled at him. "According to my official job description."

"Really? So, there is a lot in the official job description that you aren't being used for."

"Yes."

"And, you would only be fulfilling your duties, according to your official job description, if you got me those files?"

"Yes." She smiled, lowering her hands to rest in her lap.

"Well then, let's put you to full use."

"Listen, I better get back. I'll get those files for you."

"Thank you, Barbie."

"Anytime, Detective."

He tipped his hat. She stood up and exited the room.

Chapter 24

Tiger's Eye

The staircase went down into a dark space.

Why does every door lead to darkness? Mahoney shook his head and proceeded down the stairs, stepping carefully from one to the next. He wasn't sure why he'd walked through the door of the shop. He'd slipped out of HQ and strolled down the streets of the downtown core, trying to clear his head. He'd been navigating his way back when the store name grabbed his attention. *Happy Soul.*

At the bottom of the stairs he found himself staring at a bright-blue door. The handle was silver. He turned it. The door opened and a flood of light welcomed him. He could have sworn there would be a chorus of angels on the other side singing in songbird voices. There wasn't. There were rows upon rows of polished stones and sparkling gems. The room was vast. He could barely see the back wall. Along the walls were shelves housing a plethora of spectacular items.

One wall housed stacks of sapphire and emerald pillows, the material looking soft and satiny. Another wall housed lines of bowls. Some were gold metal, others looked like pottery in earthy tones, and others were glass or crystal, light bouncing off them from the bright tubed lights overhead. Wooden and metal mallets sat in the bowls and beside them.

The last time he was in a store like this, he was focused on finding a gem left at a crime scene. He wondered if the store back home had bowls and pillows like this one.

A melodic tinkling erupted from the front of the room and echoed back to him. A man floated from behind a curtain of long strings of beads. The metal tubes of a wind chime responded as the beaded curtain made contact. It was as if the man didn't have feet. He glided on air up to the counter and greeted Mahoney.

His songbird voice filled the room. "Welcome to Happy Soul. May I help you?"

"Yes." He slipped his hand into his tweed coat pocket, retrieving a polished, pink stone and placing it on the glass counter. "I need an upgrade." His heart swelled as he thought of the woman in flowing green-and-blue scarves drifting around the gem-cluttered store, reading his emotions, insisting he take the rose quartz. She had been right. The stone had done him good. Even if only to remind him to ease up on himself, once in a while. Now, he had a need for something more potent.

"Lovely stone. A reminder of self-care and love. Are you, shall we say, needing a different energy?"

"Uh, well, I don't know. I need something...stronger." He slipped the stone back into his pocket.

The man's blue eyes found his. Their gazes held for several moments.

The man said, "I see. I am feeling a bit of desperation coming from you. You were in a dark place. You found some light. You worry it is temporary. You are afraid the darkness that you fear is ahead."

Mahoney cleared his throat. It astounded him that this man could know so much. "Yes. That's it."

"I believe I have a gem for you. A special gem." The man broke his gaze and floated around the counter, then across the room.

Mahoney followed, his shiny black shoes clicking along the linoleum floor. The occasional blotch of rust on the otherwise polished floor caught his eye.

The man halted. Mahoney followed suit.

The man picked up a gem gingerly, resting it in his palm, and presenting it like an offering. Golden and chocolate stripes wove through the rich, tawny, polished stone. "Tiger's Eye. The stone of the mind. The nurturing bodyguard of perception and insight. I think you will find this quite satisfactory."

Mahoney opened his palms and received the gem. As it touched his rough skin, an unexplained rush of energy jolted through him. Was he going crazy? *Perhaps.* But this had to be better than pills and booze. *Right?*

The energy subsided and eased into a gentle ebb of warm tingling that pulsated through him rhythmically. He followed the floating man up to the counter to make his purchase.

"I get the sense you are from out of town."

"How'd you know?"

"This is the largest gem store in the city. And the closest to the downtown core. People in suits don't come in often. The ones who do are usually regulars."

Mahoney smirked.

"You get the visitor's discount." The man punched the buttons on the cash register. He re-inspected Mahoney. "I get the sense that you are in dire need of this stone."

"Yeah. I guess so." Doctor Sherry's pill bottle drifted across his thoughts.

"Then you get the special customer discount." The man's delicate fingers tapped the buttons on the register. He looked up. "That will be the special price of four ninety-nine." He smiled.

Mahoney dug his tattered wallet from his inside coat pocket and rustled through it. Sliding a bill across the glass counter, he waited as the man entered the purchase. "Uh, those pillows—what are they for?"

The man looked across the room. "Meditation pillows. They help one to focus when practising the art of stilling the mind."

"Oh. And, the bowls, what are they for?"

"Singing bowls. They emit vibrations when played. The vibrations are of different frequencies, ones that help heal the soul and calm the mind."

"Oh."

"Here you go." The man handed him a small bag, the gem inside. "Thank you for your business. I hope you will love the gem."

"I'm sure I will." He turned and walked past the meditation pillows, the singing bowls, and rows and rows of sparkling stones toward the bright-blue door.

Chapter 25

Cold Case Files

Mahoney plunked his derby onto his borrowed desk. He looked at the mug, shiny and new, but empty. He grabbed it by the handle. His eye caught two folders sitting on the desk. They weren't labelled. He swore they weren't there before. He flipped the top one open. The scent of rose floated through the air. A note on pink paper, in beautiful penmanship, sat on top of a stack of files and photos.

Detective. The files you requested.

Your case analyst - B

His gut tingled. *Well, B. You came through.* He closed the folder, grabbed his tattered briefcase and slid the folder inside, looking around the room to see if anyone noticed. The few officers still around at this hour were engrossed in their own duties. He abandoned the mug. *Coffee won't do for this review. Where's Sutton?*

He scanned the room. Sutton was over in the corner, talking to Dixon. Maybe Sutton was warming up to a side investigation. He walked up to them.

"Sutton. It's getting late. Let's grab a drink."

"OK, sure."

"Hey, Dixon, you should join us for a nightcap. I have some interesting reading material that we could review."

Dixon raised an eyebrow. "The missing photos, from the scene?"

"Yeah. And files, from the old case."

"How'd you get those?"

"You have a good analyst on your team." Mahoney shot his eyes over toward Barbie's desk.

"Well, well, someone's got some charm." Dixon winked.

"Only using the personnel around here for the duties they're qualified for and assigned to."

Sutton jabbed him in the ribs. "Boss. Keeping it by the books. Nice."

"Pipe down. And I thought you'd stopped with that *boss* shit." Mahoney rolled his eyes. He looked at Dixon. "He's gotta get it through his thick skull he's the head honcho now."

Dixon smirked. "Where're you staying?"

"Meet us at the Toronto Hilton."

"Sure thing."

Mahoney nudged Sutton. "C'mon, *boss.*"

Chapter 26

Bourbon-Laced Cold Case

A waitress in a skin-tight, black cocktail dress walked toward them. Her lean legs conquered the distance quickly, her red high heels clicking against the black tiles.

"Good evening, fellas. What can I get you?" Her peach lips parted in a smile.

Haven't had fruit in a while. "Bourbon. Double. Straight up."

Sutton hesitated. "Ah...I guess I'll just have a beer."

"We have Bud, Coors, and Keith's on tap."

Sutton frowned.

"If you prefer, we have a list of bottles." She opened a small leather-bound menu and turned it to Sutton.

Sutton glanced at the menu. "Stella, please." He smiled sheepishly.

Mahoney smirked. "Fancy."

The waitress winked at Sutton, then snapped the menu shut. Mahoney watched her turn and walk away. The muscles in the backs of her legs rippled as her red high heels clicked across the floor.

"You should go easy, boss."

Mahoney snapped his gaze on Sutton. "Stop calling me boss."

"Fine. I mean it. Go easy."

"The bourbon? Or the waitress?"

"Both."

"Can it. And I'm *not* the boss here. If you're gonna get any respect, you need to start by believing that *you* are the boss."

"Yeah, yeah. It's just...I'm not used to this...with you."

"I know." Mahoney leaned back in the black leather chair. "Nice lounge. Wish we were staying here." A flash of pinstripe caught his eye. "Aaah. Look who's here." He motioned with a hand wave.

Detective Dixon walked over to their table. "Detectives."

"So, how much trouble will you get in by being here?" Mahoney inquired.

Dixon took a seat. "I don't know. But I need to see those files. Besides, Sergeant's already gone home for the night. He doesn't like long shifts."

Mahoney grinned. "You got the bug, so to speak. A passion for psycho killers."

"I guess." Dixon leaned back against the leather, crossing his foot over his knee. "I've seen the way Tomlinson runs cases. I think we need a different approach on this one. It's unique."

"You got that right."

The waitress placed their drinks on the table. Her peach lips parted into a smile.

"Can I get you a drink?" she asked Dixon.

"Sure. I'll have a bourbon, single shot, straight up."

"Look at this." Mahoney knocked Sutton's knee. "He's got good taste. Just needs to up his dose."

Sutton glared.

Dixon scanned the lounge. "Nice hotel."

Mahoney smirked. "Yeah. Wish we were staying here."

"You're not?" Dixon raised an eyebrow.

Sutton frowned. "Nope. No budget for this. We're at the good ol' *Hav-A-Nap* on motel strip."

Dixon whistled. "Wow. Crack town. With a side of prostitutes."

Mahoney shook his head. "It wasn't that way last time I was out here. It was booming with tourists. Don't think our *booking agent* knew that."

Sutton's frowned deepened. "Yeah. Wish we had a booking agent."

Dixon chuckled.

Mahoney sat up in his chair. "Well, Detectives, we have a thick stack of files here. We need to dig in. Wouldn't want to be up all night, now would we?" Mahoney leaned over, extracted two folders from his briefcase, and snapped them onto the centre of the table. "Barbie dug up the cold case files. And a copy of what's filed away on our current case. Let's take a fresh look. Say, Dixon, what's with your boss anyway? Was he always a dick running a circus?"

Dixon chuckled. He leaned forward, pushing his wired spectacles up the bridge of his nose. "I've only been on his team about six months. I don't know what he was like before then. From the get-go, something was off. Things that should have been pursued weren't. He'd take them on, they'd vanish. It's gotten worse. He blocks access to things if you don't play along. There's got to be a reason."

"So, his resistance to link this victim to the Susie Slaughters, it's one of those things. But not so little."

"Yeah. I don't get it. It's so obvious that this case is linked." Dixon smoothed his pant legs with his palms. "I'm only speculating here, but, I think it either has to do with power or money. As much of a tyrant as he is, I've seen him a couple of times with his superiors. He's a real yes-man. Someone might be pulling his strings, promising him a solid future. And..." Dixon glanced around the lounge. "He just moved into this massive house in a ritzy area. Not sure if that's linked to a promise of a promotion with a bonus up front, or what. Where else would he be getting the money? Typical Sergeant wage doesn't land them in York Mills."

"Clear linkage to the Susie Slaughters, yet he's driving the investigation away from it," Mahoney said.

"Like I said before, I think we're dealing with the same killer here. Tomlinson is blocking the investigation from taking that path," Dixon said.

"I think I'm developing a crush on you, Dixon. Good taste in drinks, and you trust that feeling in your gut." Mahoney took a swig of bourbon.

Sutton narrowed his eyes and shook his head.

The waitress placed the single shot of bourbon on the table. "Anything else, fellas?"

"We're OK for now." Mahoney smiled. "Cheers, boys." He raised his glass. Sutton and Dixon followed. After a long sip of sweet bourbon, Mahoney set the glass down and looked at Dixon. "Well, let's keep this between us, for now, boys. Seems that Barbie's access to the old and current files wasn't revoked. Maybe we'll figure out what's holding your sergeant captive. For now, we need to focus on a killer with a passion for blood." He flipped open the folder housing the cold case files.

A girl with a ghastly face stared back at them. Red rings wove around her eyes, like circular smears of blood. Her vacant eyes stared at him. Her black lips threatened to whisper in his nightmares.

Mahoney extracted several photos and laid them out in a row.

The scene came to life. Black lace flowing down a still body. The face of the devil's demoness stared back at them. Black pupils pierced their souls. Blood-red smears circled her eyes. Her face was far too white to be natural. The shape of her lips, two points pulling her top lip into a sneer, her bottom lip full and pouty, looked fabricated. Thick black filled in the fake lip shape.

Chills ran up Mahoney's back and crawled over his skull.

They stared at the photos, reliving the scene in their minds, searching for something. A tidbit that didn't fit in, that would tell them something about how this girl got to her grassy bed and who laid her there.

Sutton said, "Looks exactly the same as this fresh case. If this is someone following in the footsteps of the guy from sixteen years ago, he did his homework."

Dixon nodded. Mahoney took a sip of sweetness, letting it burn down his throat.

He pulled out two more sets of photos, laying them in separate rows. An ice wave sliced through his gut. The same face stared back at them. The same eyes stared vacantly. The bloody and black makeup was exact down to the last red swirl. The dresses were identical. The grassy beds could have all been in the exact spot in the same park. Except they weren't.

Mahoney said, "There're three dead girls here, from the cold case. I could swear we were looking at the same girl, at the same crime scene, in the same park."

Sutton and Dixon, entranced in their search, scanned the photos.

Dixon said, "Let's look at the new scene."

Mahoney flipped through the second folder, retrieving a set of photos and adding them to the crime scene collage on the table.

The girl, now de-robed, lay on a steel slab bed, pale and lifeless. An incision sliced her flesh from her heart to the tip of her pelvis. Her body looked sunken, empty. Not only was her blood drained, but her organs had been removed too. The paint cleaned from her face, youth and innocence washed her features. A photo, one that wasn't lined up on the black crime scene board with a glassy magnet, caught his eye.

Mahoney's gut throbbed. He coated it with a swig of bourbon. "Look at this. The symbol."

Dixon and Sutton leaned in toward the photo.

Sutton said, "A brand. On her back. This photo wasn't on that fancy blackboard during the briefing."

Dixon agreed, "No. It wasn't. And when you asked about a brand, he acted like he had no clue what you were talking about." He looked at Mahoney.

Mahoney flipped through the cold case folder, puling out the remaining photos. He lined them up on the table. Three circles, each intersected with a V, branded into the backs of three different girls. "What did I tell ya? The victims from the cold case, they all have the symbol. On their backs. So does our new victim here." Relief washed through him. His memory hadn't failed him. The symbol he recalled from the cold case did indeed exist.

Dixon pulled at his chin with his pointer and thumb. "Dammit. It's gotta be Tomlinson. I knew he'd blocked access to the cold case files. It must be him hiding photos from the new case."

Mahoney said, "The symbol amplifies the linkage to the Susie Slaughters. Whatever's driving him, he's trying to cover up any connection."

They all turned back to the photos.

Dixon asked, "What does the symbol mean?"

Mahoney responded, "Good question. It was a dead end on the cold case. Not even a hint."

"It's gotta mean *something*. It looks burned into their skin." Sutton swallowed.

The symbol. It was there. On all of them. Mahoney sifted through several files in the cold case folder, scanning the information. Words jumped off the page, then flew from his mouth. "Type O negative." He sifted through the same files of the new case. "They all had type O negative blood. All four of them." He took a swig of bourbon. *He wasn't crazy. His memory hadn't failed him.*

"Wow." Sutton sat back in his chair. "He's after a specific blood type. That's...chilling."

"Was a match found on the knife used to slice them open?" Dixon asked.

"There's nothing conclusive here." He pointed at the files now resting on the table. "I recall it being identified as a gut-hook hunting knife, for large game. Exact match wasn't found. The search dwindled off when the bodies stopped coming." Mahoney sifted through the photos on the table. "None of these photos magnify anything."

Dixon said, "Lab probably has better technology now."

Mahoney sat up. "Yeah. I bet our medical examiner could help with that."

"If you can get access to him...or her." Dixon frowned.

"I'll get access," Mahoney said.

"Wow. I need to learn a thing or two about human relations," Dixon commented.

"You need to be careful," Mahoney responded. "You're at the beginning of your career. I'm washed up and old. Doesn't matter if I get in trouble."

Sutton nodded, sipping his beer. He looked much more relaxed than he had, all coated in sweat, back at the foreign HQ. Maybe he believed he could put on the front of playing by the book while his old boss broke all the rules.

Mahoney turned his attention back to the photos now covering most of the table. His gut pulsed. He picked up a photo of the newest body. He narrowed his gaze. "Look at her neck. You see that?"

Dixon leaned in close to the photo. "Is that a puncture?"

"What?" Sutton leaned in. "Wow."

Mahoney looked again at each of the victims, inspecting their necks. "They all have it. Even with my old-man eyes, I can see that."

Dixon said, "Let's walk through all the files, again. Let's see if there's anything about this."

"Yeah. And if we missed any other details." Sutton took a swig of beer.

"Sounds good, boys." Mahoney waved at the waitress. "Hope you don't mind late nights." He looked at Dixon.

"Not when I'm on a real investigation." Dixon smoothed his pant legs with his palms. "I just hope this killer doesn't stick to the same timeline as last time."

Black lips whispered through Mahoney's mind, reminding him that another kill could be scheduled in three days. If they were, indeed, facing the same killer from the Susie Slaughters. "Yeah. I hope so, too. Unless we get a real lead here, there's not a fucking thing we can do." Mahoney took a swig of bourbon and led them through a detailed scour of all the information they had their hands on.

Chapter 27

Black Out

The pounding in Chester's head vibrated through every corner of his brain. Pain thrashed his temples.

Time. He needed time.

The room spun. Slowly at first, then gaining speed. His motions beyond his control, he reached out an arm and steadied himself into an armchair. He closed his eyes and leaned back. The velour soft against his skin, his insides settled into a makeshift calm.

Time. He needed time.

His skull seized with every throb.

Time with his girls would help. Maybe a feeding. It wasn't time for a feeding. He'd already fed too early. He'd hung onto his source for much longer than usual, feeding slowly, small tastes, trying to satisfy his cravings. He'd made it to the New Moon, only by force.

Relief had washed through his entire being when he was able to perform the sacrifice, and the full feeding, on the intended night.

The pain pounded against his skull. He opened his eyes just a slit. The room darkened around him, sunlight turning to a forced night. The blackout wasn't far away.

He needed something more dramatic. He needed to hunt. *It isn't time to hunt.*

The word *hunt* floated through his thoughts. His body relaxed against the soft velour of the chair. The spinning slowed.

No. The cycle had not entered the next hunt yet. *How is this happening?* The cycle worked. Every time. The perfect balance of hunting, feeding, ritual, and sacrifice. It kept the pain, the blackouts, at bay. It was a controlled way to live. In his circumstances, it was the only way to live.

The pain pounded against the back of his head, reaching sharp tendrils over his skull.

He closed his eyes hard and moved into an imaginary hunt. Slipping into a window, in the middle of the night, unheard, unknown, like a ghost. Looking down at a perfect specimen, a valid candidate to join his collection. Sleeping, lost in her own dreams, unaware of the opportunity looming over her.

The pain eased. The buzzing dimmed.

He would tilt her head, and feed her freedom. It only took the briefest of moments.

She would wake, in a haze, in her new world. She would look at him. He would speak the words that would change her forever.

He mouthed the words now, his lips moving in a slow, dramatic dance. The pain ceased. The throbbing stopped. The tendrils slithered away.

She would look at him with those eyes—full of adoration, full of hope, full of dedication. He would know he had chosen well.

Electric vibes hummed through him.

He would take her small hand in his, and she would rise according to his lead.

He took a long, slow, deep breath. Every tiny prickle of pain disintegrated. His body relaxed against the soft velour. Stroking the soft arms of the chair, he opened his eyes.

The room was bright, sun pouring in through the windows. A warmth wrapped around him.

He had to hang on. The full moon was almost here. He couldn't afford another episode. A wooden cuckoo poked its beak out of a hand-crafted clock on the wall and chirped five times. Sundown was only hours away. He had to hang on. It was almost time to prepare. It was almost time for the full moon ritual.

DEMON
CORPSE

Chapter 28

Another Demon Corpse

Mahoney punched a button on the car radio. The annoying voice vanished. His makeshift rogue team had spun their wheels for four days, during the little time they weren't under Tomlinson's watch. They'd been unable to prevent another kill. Now, here he was, driving to another corpse. He'd expected them to discover another body yesterday, if the killer was sticking to the same pattern as before. Was the kill a day late? Or had he hidden the body well?

"Whoa. You don't like the radio here, boss?" Sutton chuckled.

"No. I like my blues." He missed his collection of albums, lined up in a row in his car. He pulled the black Sedan into an open slot. "I hate this rental."

Sutton raised an eyebrow. "You miss your ancient rust bucket?"

Mahoney glared. "It's *vintage*. '69 Pony. Citrus 12. A gem. Hard to come by."

"Yeah. Cause they're out of date, boss." Sutton laughed.

"*Whatever*," Mahoney barked. "And quit calling me *boss*. *You're* the boss now."

"Give me a break. Old habits die hard. Isn't that what they say?" Sutton shot a full smile across the car. "Or, can't teach an old dog new tricks?"

"Can it." Mahoney eased the car off High Park Boulevard and through an entrance marked with two elaborate pillars. A metal sign swung overhead in the breeze, declaring their entry into *High Park*. He followed a sign pointing to *Centre Road.*

Mahoney glowered at the sign. "*Centre Road.* In the centre of the park. Real genius."

"Hey, you OK? You seem grouchy."

Mahoney rubbed the bristle on his chin. "Yeah. I'm fine. Hotel bed sucks." *Nice excuse, Bug. When you've got Doctor Sherry's sleep remedy, you don't even notice the bed.* Maybe he shouldn't have left the pill bottle at home.

Sutton snorted. "Yeah. The pillows are pathetic, too. Why so thin?"

Mahoney nodded. He wondered if Sutton could see through his excuses.

They followed the road through the belly of a deserted park. Well-groomed grass stretched out on either side of them. An empty playground perched off to the right. A swing swayed back and forth in the breeze, waiting for an occupant. Like a flashbulb camera in action, an image lit up Mahoney's mind. *Flash.* Caleb. On a swing. The night that he disappeared. *Flash.* Caleb, the first body in the Mummy Boys case. The last case he would ever lead.

He shook his head. *Put it to bed, Bug.*

A wall of trees lined either side of the road like tall, grey skeletons, reaching their bony fingers over them.

Another forest full of death. Another flash of the camera. An image of Frog Lake was there, then it was gone. Frog Lake. The beautiful park on the outskirts of his home city. He could still see the body, deep in the forest, laid carefully on a bed of leaves, dressed up like a glam doll, crude lyrics carved into flesh.

He shook his head, hard. *Put it to bed, Bug. Now.* He had to stop the constant barrage of images from all the past cases that refused to leave him alone. Here, out of his element, he was lost. *You aren't lost. You don't have your toxic cocktail. You aren't in charge. Deal with it.*

Sutton halted. "Hey, you OK? You look...pale."

"Yeah, yeah. Fine. Like I said. Lack of sleep."

Sutton shook his head.

Mahoney looked down the path, through the trees. The familiar bright-yellow tape quarantined off an area of the park, warning of the gruesome scene. His stomach churned. A slight pang throbbed deep in his gut. He slipped his hand into the pocket of his tweed coat. His fingers ran along the smooth, polished stone. His new stone. The Tiger's Eye. A familiar warmth rushed through him. He took a deep breath. *You got this, Bug.*

The yellow tape led them along the road, a turn to the left, and a sign marking the *Hillside Gardens.* The road came to an abrupt end.

"Guess we walk from here." Mahoney eased the car into park and opened the door. It was silent. He missed the creak of the door on his vintage Pony. It somehow soothed him as he was about to enter a scene of death.

Mahoney led the way along a series of paths into the heart of the *Hillside Gardens.* Sutton followed close behind, his shoes clicking through the silence.

After a few moments, they reached a fenced-off area bustling with activity. Several men, white fluorescent letters, *CST,* flashing across the back of their jackets, moved around the perimeter, taking photos and collecting items in plastic bags. *They got half a dozen techies on this. Not bad.* Ample budget. Ample techies.

Mahoney scanned the area. Then he saw it.

A patch of green grass stretched out ahead, sloping downward to the central piece of the gardens. A series of circular pathways, one ring inside the next, cut a walkway for perusing a sculpted garden. Tall, bare trees hovered around the circle, like skeletal figures on watch. The crisp air caught in Mahoney's throat as he looked into the heart of the carved pathway. The garden had been morphed into an offering table for the girl with long, dark hair displayed in the dead centre.

In the middle of it all, a petite woman stood, looking down at the ground. Black cargo pants fit snugly against her muscular legs, a skin-tight black turtleneck revealed her sculpted, yet feminine, contour. Her feet were well equipped with heavy hiking boots. She looked ready for combat. Her dark hair was tied back neatly in a small knot at the nape of her neck. She adjusted her thick black glasses over the bridge of her small nose. Snapping a notebook shut, she crouched down and bent over the lifeless form.

He snuck another peek at her hiking boots. *Easy, Bug. She isn't Blackwood.* He had been so used to his old team, it was hard to imagine anyone else on a scene with him.

"Get on it, now," a loud voice barked.

At the edge of the walkway leading to the crime scene stood Sergeant Tomlinson, moustache twitching erratically, face flushed, belting out orders like a drill sergeant. *Dick. Can't he cool it for one second?* Maybe his over-the-top instruction would result in a thorough search. *Yeah, right. Clown.*

"Not quite like home," Sutton whispered.

"It'll be fine. Let's go." Mahoney marched past Sergeant Tomlinson, toward the body. Tomlinson was too busy barking out orders to notice him.

As he approached the small woman leaning over the still body, his mind played another film, frame by frame. Each flash was an image he didn't want. The movie didn't care. It played despite his internal protests.

Flash. He saw Blackwood leaning over a body with a glimmering black cloak and long tassels.

Flash. He saw pink lips, dramatically poised on a pallid face.

Flash. He saw Blackwood crouched in the back of a cave, leaning over a coffin.

Flash. He saw a small figure wrapped like a mummy.

Flash. He saw black, nothing eyes.

Flash. He saw blood-red lips whispering to him in his mind.

Flash. He looked down at the present body. His gut throbbed. His fingers grasped the smooth stone in his pocket. His new gem, providing him a fresh wave of guidance.

A young woman lay still, her face painted white, blood-red circles weaving around her closed eyes. Her lips were slightly parted, sketched and filled in with thick black. Her body was clothed in a black dress flowing down her legs and arms, covering the horror he was sure was underneath. Mahoney crouched down, across from the woman attending to the body. He choked on a thick cloud of decay. Swallowing the stench down, he stared at the face.

"This is a real doozy," a sweet voice rang in his ears.

He looked across at the woman.

Her chocolate-brown eyes stared back at him through her thick glasses. "Medical Examiner Halley Winter. I'd shake your hand, but I'm gloved and processing."

Sweet Jesus. She reminded him of Blackwood. Maybe that was a good thing. Maybe it wasn't. His mind swirled.

"You're here from out west, right? The detective from the case of the past." She smiled.

He cleared his throat. "Detective Mahoney. Yes."

"Well, I'd love to pick your brain on this. There's some weird shit here. But right now you gotta scram. Let me process her." Chocolate eyes pierced him. "I can't afford any distractions."

"Of course. You may want to be careful when you remove the dress. I suspect the body is..." He stopped. Another flash. Another image. A young woman, sliced open, gutted, and bled out.

"Spit it out." She pressed the middle of her glasses against the bridge of her nose with a gloved finger.

"What the hell is going on here?" Tomlinson's voice intruded.

"Pipe down, Tomlinson. I was just introducing myself to Detective Mahoney here." She cranked her neck and glared up at the red face staring down at them.

"Intros can wait. Get the processing done." The moustache bobbed.

"Yes, sir," she responded. Mahoney could swear there was a slight twinge of sarcasm to her voice.

"Sergeant. You need to see this." A tall techie with a buzzcut approached.

"You heard me. Processing." The moustache made a rash movement. The sergeant turned and followed the crime scene tech.

Mahoney rose.

"Wait. Detective." Her sweet voice halted him.

"You heard Sergeant Moustache. And you told me to scram."

"He's occupied. What were you going to say...about removing the dress?"

He rubbed the bristle on his chin. "When you remove it, be careful. The body might be drained and in delicate condition."

"I suspected. Looking her over, she looks...sunken."

"She's probably empty inside. Empty and drained."

"What do you mean, empty?"

"No blood. Organs removed. Empty inside."

She stared at him. "Well, that'd be a doozy."

Doozy. Ha. What was that Blackwood used to say? "Yeah. Real humdinger."

A half smile appeared as she looked at him. "Funny. I was planning to de-robe at the lab."

"You should. I mean...the body."

The half smile turned to a full smile. "Will you be dropping by my lab later? I could use your take when I process the layers on this."

"What about Sergeant Moustache? Not sure he'd like me poking my nose in."

"That's your problem. You decide. I'm open to your input."

"Speak of the moustache, here he comes. I gotta scram, like you wanted." He turned and rejoined Sutton.

Sergeant Tomlinson barked another order, "Everyone. Gather, now."

Tweedledee and Tweedledum jaunted over, side by side. Dixon joined at his own pace. The half-dozen crime scene techs left their processing and made their way over. Forming a large circle around Tomlinson, the group waited for him to speak. Sutton hung at the back of the formation. Mahoney sidled up next to him.

Geez. Like some sort of investigative cult. Mahoney rubbed the bristle on his chin with one hand, stroking the smooth stone in his pocket with the other.

"Techs have done several rounds of photos and are well into processing. So far, nothing. No blood. No prints. No hair. Seems to be no trace of this guy. Rescan then widen and scan again."

The techies all nodded in unison.

"There's got to be something here. Something that will lead us to this guy."

There won't be. Mahoney's gut pulsed. *He didn't leave a trace.* The stone was smooth against his fingers.

"Processing of the body is in the hands of the ME. She'll have the body transported and keep us updated."

I'll get my own update.

"Let's move this show back to HQ. Meet up in thirty. Come prepared. We'll camp till we go through everything."

Or just what you want us to know.

The detective twins nodded, their heads bobbing in sync.

Geez. Were they attached at the hip at birth?

Dixon stared, his eyes narrowed in contemplation.

Need to find out what he's thinking.

The group dispersed. Waiting for enough distance between him, Tomlinson, and the detective twins, Mahoney approached Dixon.

"Dixon, wait up." He raised his voice just enough to get the detective's attention.

Dixon halted and turned. "What's up, Detective?"

"Want to join me on a side jaunt, after Sergeant Moustache's big meeting?

"What're you up to, boss?" Sutton had snuck up behind them.

"Medical examiner, she and I had a chat. You worked with her before?" Mahoney looked at Dixon.

"No. The new personnel I'd mentioned. Word is, we're lucky to have her. She's got quite a track record."

"I suspected." Mahoney scanned the scene. Only the techies and the examiner remained. The lemmings had followed their leader. "She wants my eyes on the body."

Sutton shook his head. "Tomlinson will freak."

"Not if he doesn't know," Mahoney responded.

Dixon shifted, hooking his thumbs into his belt. "He doesn't have to."

"You want to come?"

"I do. But it'd be less conspicuous if you go alone," Dixon directed. "Besides, you're the one with the background on this one."

Mahoney nodded.

Sutton shook his head. "Don't like it, boss."

"I know you don't. I'm not your *boss.*"

"What about Sarge? He needs us in line." Sutton's eyebrows pointed down in a worried v-shape.

"I got Sarge. Do what you need to. Go by the book."

Sutton pursed his lips. His forehead wrinkled, taking away his good-looking charm.

"Don't worry. Doesn't look good on you." Mahoney rubbed the bristle on his chin. "You two get to the meeting of the lemmings before Sergeant Moustache busts a lung."

Dixon smirked. "Got it, *boss.*"

Chapter 29

Science Lab

The long hallway seemed to go on forever. White walls, white ceiling, white floor—it reminded Mahoney of the institute he had paid more than one visit to during the Glam Boys case. The place where Doris had locked up her only son, Seth. Finally, he reached the end. He shook off the memory and pushed his weight against the heavy door. He almost expected to see Blackwood on the other side, her almond eyes greeting him from behind big plastic goggles.

The bright room knocked him into reality. The petite medical examiner from the crime scene in the park stood at the far end, bathed in fluorescent light streaming from the buzzing tubes overhead. She was engrossed in her task. Her black cargoes had been replaced with an exact replica, in army green. A tight, long-sleeved, dark-green shirt clung to her muscular contour. A white lab coat hung loosely open, exposing a thick belt with several pouches attached, circling her small waist. Each pouch bulged against a snap. He wondered what was in them.

He walked across the room. As he approached the examination in progress, he noticed the back wall behind her lined with glass flasks, beakers, plastic tubing coiled neatly, and racked test tubes. It looked more like a science lab than a back examination room in a morgue.

He announced his arrival, "Examiner Winter."

She looked up from her work. Chocolate-brown eyes peered from behind oversized, circular goggles. Space-aged frames hooked around glassy lenses.

"Detective Mahoney. You made it. Hope you didn't have any trouble at the front."

"Not at all."

"You're just in time. I've completed the initial detailed scan, and was just about to de-robe. The victim, that is." She smirked.

Witty. "Don't let me interrupt you."

She turned back to the victim. The young, lifeless girl lay on a steel-slab bed. The thick, white mask had been removed. Her doughy skin puffed out over her face. Mahoney wondered what she really looked like, before she had started to bloat and decompose. Before she had met the hands of the monster who did this to her.

"As you can see, I've removed the white substance from her face. I've sent several samples off for analysis. It was quite thick. It seemed to have been applied in layers, as if whoever applied it wanted to achieve a smooth surface."

"Like a mask."

"Yes. Like a mask. Very strange."

"He was treating her like a doll. Making her up. Objectifying her."

She raised an eyebrow. "Well, hopefully the chemical analysis will provide some useful results. As you can also see, the skin is starting to puff out. She's on the brink of bloat. Glad we found her before she filled up with gases. You can see here..."—she pointed to a spot on the face—"some of the skin is just starting to fill up."

"Yeah. I've seen this before."

"Of course. I'm sure you don't need all this detail."

"Give me every tidbit you've got, no matter how tiny."

She raised her eyebrow again. "You're thorough."

"Thought it was standard procedure."

"It should be. But, in my experience, it isn't. Depends on who you are working with."

How thorough—or lack of thorough—was Sergeant Moustache? "I got in here. Let's be as thorough as possible."

"Got it." She turned back to the body. "I've found very little on the body. No blood. No prints. No fibres. I did find a couple of tiny hairs, lodged into the white makeup on her face."

"Hairs?"

"Yeah. I sent them off for processing."

Mahoney rubbed the bristle on his chin. "We can't be that lucky, can we?"

"Don't know. Given how DNA-clean the rest of the body is, I doubt it." She moved closer to the body, pulling a silver tool from a pouch in her belt. "I'm going to remove the dress now."

Mahoney stood, off to the side, watching.

Winter snapped the silver tool twice, forming a pair of scissors. The scissors clipped the dress in rugged slices. Winter peeled away the black lace in strips, following the cuts she had made. The body was an empty cavern. The skin fell in against the frame of bones. A slice ran down the body, starting at the heart, and ending just above the pelvis.

"Just as you suspected. She looks…empty." She picked up a camera and took several shots from different angles, capturing the long slice. She clicked a recorder on, made several technical vocal notes, then clicked it back off.

Winter snapped open one of the pouches attached to her belt. She pulled out another silver tool and unfolded it several times, creating a large set of forceps. She turned back to the body. Sliding a prong into the slit in the body, she clamped the tool onto one of the skin flaps and pulled it back. Her eyes widened for a split second, then returned to normal size.

Mahoney dared to walk up closer.

"Let's take a deeper look inside." With slow movements, she meticulously pulled back the skin, away from the slit, and clamped it in several places. She paused again to take more photos of the horrific examination unfolding before them.

As the empty body was opened up, Mahoney's suspicions were confirmed. He peered into the woman. His imaginary spider friend returned, crawling up his insides, creating a slow tingle that made Mahoney cringe. She had been slit open and bled out, like an animal. There was no blood. Her organs were gone. She was an empty carcass encased in a skin suit.

He rubbed the back of his neck, watching the horrific image unfold. He knew it would find its way into the never-ending scrapbook in his mind that came to life every night.

"You were dead-on, Detective. She's empty. Where is all the blood? In a body of this size, there should be about four quarts."

He shook his head. "I don't like being right."

"But you were." She stared at the body. "I wish I'd don't the autopsy on the first victim. I'd have more information for you. It's strange...I've had trouble getting access to the files. Anyways, that's a lot of blood. Only one, long incision. No other cuts. No bruising. No sign of...*struggle*." She twisted her mouth up. "I'd say she died of exsanguination. Bled to death. I'll have to confirm, of course."

"Of course." Mahoney nodded. *Gutted and bled out. Like an animal.*

Winter looked up from the body. "You've linked this...to the past, haven't you?" She paused. "I've read all the articles, from the Susie Slaughters. I wanted to be informed. I am new here, didn't want to miss a beat on my first gig."

"Then you know how that case ended."

Her eyes met his. "It went cold. The worst kind."

A chill rushed through him, chilling his fingers and toes. "You've been on a cold case?"

"Yes." Her lips formed a thin line. "You should tap into what you know from that cold case, Detective." She snapped her gaze away and turned back to the body. "Let's get moving. The white face paint is in processing. This slice, it's a doozy. We've got to be able to get something about the knife that made it. It can't be your normal household item."

"Probably a hunting knife."

"You hunt, Detective?"

"No. We had the incisions on the victims from the Susie Slaughters analyzed. Type of knife was nailed down to a gut hook hunting knife, for large game. Exact match was never made."

"Didn't see that in the articles."

"It wasn't." He held back. His gut told him he could trust her. But he needed to figure out the team dynamics before sharing too much.

"We'll try and get a match on it this time. The lack of blood concerns me. What I can do is a thorough exam of her insides, look for the minute details." She picked up a clipboard and scanned a sheet. "Look at this." She walked up the body, put her gloved hands on the head and turned it, exposing one side of the neck. One hand on the head, the other hand grasping for a tool from inside one of her belt pouches. She put a magnifying glass up to the skin. "See here?"

Mahoney walked up beside and leaned into the magnifying glass. Two tiny, circular dots punctured the pallid skin. Tingling surged in his gut. "Two punctures."

"I don't recall reading anything about punctures, either, in that cold case of yours."

"Never heard of any punctures when I was on the case. But..." He reached into his coat pocket and pulled out several photos. "Got my hands on some photos from the cold case. Looks like the victims from before had similar punctures." He set the photos down on a table for her to inspect.

"I could try and get those magnified."

"I was hoping you'd say that."

"Based on the puncture wounds of this gal"—she nodded at the fresh body—"a toxicology scan is warranted. We need to know if anything was injected into her. I got the ball rolling, as soon as I found the punctures. Put a rush on it."

Thorough. Efficient. He was impressed. He got a kick out of her scientific setup and handy tool belt. She was quirky. His gut told him to trust her. Yet, something held him back. She was new in town. She seemed to be playing nice while doing her own thing.

"That's all I have for now." Her warm russet eyes stared at him. "Listen. I'll be straight with you. I need your help. Like I said, I'm new in town. I've heard this Tomlinson guy is a real jerk. Not sure I'll get much collaboration from him, but if I screw up he'll make a big stink about it. You know the cold case. This one has got to be linked. I need to make sure I don't miss anything."

His gut told him to spill it. He cleared his throat. "Like I said, the punctures, never reported on the cold case bodies. As far as I know. When you flip her over, I suspect you'll find a symbol, branded into her skin. All the cold case bodies had them. The first victim, you said you didn't process her, and you haven't seen the report?"

"No. Why?" Her forehead sprouted a series of wrinkles.

"She had the same brand. The photos weren't included in Tomlinson's briefing at Homicide HQ."

"Really? That's odd."

"Yeah. Odd is right. Something doesn't smell right around here."

"Were the other victims empty?"

"The cold case victims were drained of blood, but their organs were intact. We never figured out where all the blood went. First body in this new case, also drained, and the organs were removed." He rubbed the bristle on his chin.

She shook her head. "Drained. Taken or disposed of who knows where. Freaky."

"Yeah. Do you know her blood type?" Mahoney pointed at the body.

"Not yet. It's important?"

"The other victims were all Type O Negative."

"Wow. I still have a lot of processing to do. Hopefully I'll find a trace of whoever did this. Back then, there wasn't much to go on?"

"We had no real evidence of anyone being there. Without evidence, there were no trails to follow."

"Doozy."

He couldn't help but smirk to himself. He loved her quirky choice of words.

Intensity washed her chocolate eyes. "Listen. I'm with you. There's clear linkage here. All the victims were missing for weeks. Then, boom, slaughtered and left on display. This one..."—she glanced over at the lifeless girl on the steel slab—"I'm betting she fits the profile perfectly. Sixteen. Deemed a run-a-way. A search for missing girls is already underway. Standard procedure to obtain an ID."

Perfect. "Swell. Like I said, I don't like being right, but..."

"I have a hunch she fits the pattern."

He nodded. "Yeah."

"Listen." She looked at him hard. "Let's keep this to ourselves. And let's keep each other informed. Give me your cell number." She grabbed a notebook, ripped off a page and handed it to him.

"Swell." He laid the paper against the steel table and scribbled his number. "I'd love to know her blood type. And anything else strange that comes up." He handed the paper back to her.

"I've got to get on with this examination. You need to scram back to your investigation. I'll keep you up to date."

"Sounds good." He adjusted his derby, nodded, turned, and walked out of the morgue.

Chapter 30

Locked Up

Chester never understood how a mother could lock up a child. His mother had made it clear that it wasn't her decision, although she thought he was imperfect—broken. He stared at the face of the doll lying in his hands. The doll had perfect milky skin and long, dark hair. Chester had brushed the hair a hundred times and massaged lavender and vanilla oils into it. It had belonged to his sister Violet. Violet had been the only one in the world who had ever looked at him with love. Mother had ripped him away from her, locked him up, and thrown away the key.

How could a child be declared to be deviant, a menace to society? How could a child be locked up in a juvenile prison and forgotten? How could a child be left in the hands of uniform-clad generic faces pretending to care about his wellbeing?

The long, lonely nights in a foreign bed with a single thin sheet and flat pillow. The haunting cries that echoed through the empty halls, seeping from the mouths of tormented children, alone and afraid. Calls that went unanswered for hours upon hours.

The only thing that had made his time in detention bearable was Harold. Chester's ability to put on the required persona had helped him to behave the way they wanted him to. Thus, Chester had been granted a double room with a roommate. The stars had shone down on him in his pathetic state the day he was assigned to be in the same room as Harold. Harold was...like him. They had the same skills. They had the same interests.

When Chester woke up sobbing, Harold would be sitting there, staring at him. Harold's eyes would bore right through Chester, into him. Harold was always ready to listen. Harold kept all of Chester's secrets. And Chester kept Harold's.

Together, they strategized to survive. The more they were willing to face their pain and anguish head on, and the more they were able to act like normal children, the less they were drugged up, and the more access they got to the tiny bits of almost-paradise in the otherwise hell. The burst of fresh air in his lungs and the warmth of the sun on his face had been worth all the faking the day that he got to go into the tiny park.

The park was boxed with steel bars in the middle of the compound. But if Chester closed his eyes, breathed the air, and smelled the tiny bit of pine floating off the few trees, he could pretend he was in the park with Violet.

Chester opened his eyes, back in his house, in his purple-velour armchair. He looked at the doll shaking in his hands. His cheeks wet with tears, his lips quivered in tiny convulsions. Placing the doll on the matching purple-velour ottoman, his body slid off the chair, and crumpled onto the carpet. He curled into a ball. A heavy weight of grief dragged through him, landing in the pit of his stomach. It pulsed, releasing strings of sorrow that wove within him, eating at his insides, chewing their way out of his flesh.

Violet's face flashed in his mind. He reached his arm out, grasping for her, only to claw at empty air.

Harold's face floated from his memories, into his present moment. "Harold. Help me," Chester cried.

It hurt. The pit of loss in the bottom of his gut throbbed.

All his gifts. All his talents. They had brought him here.

The truth was, despite his girls, he felt alone. No Violet. No Harold.

The first two years in the prison, while his mother was still alive, she'd never come to see him. At eighteen, his adulthood fresh, he was declared rehabilitated. With a clean slate, he walked away from the cage into a big, wide world. Alone. Until he'd started collecting Violets.

His girls loved him. But not the way his true Violet had. He'd taken his girls and preyed upon their vulnerability. They felt unloved, unwanted, and discarded. He swooped them up, gave them the love they needed, and plunged them into structured lessons. They ate up his words. His lies. Each of them believed that he loved her and only her. He'd moulded their minds. They were eternally loyal to him.

Chester pulled his arms to his chest. He curled into the tightest ball he could muster. The world moved around him in a fast circle. He let it take him. The darkness came, as it always did, washing over him, clouding his mind. He let it take him. The spinning blackness cloaked his mind, his body, his soul. He let it take him.

Chapter 31

Barbie

Mahoney scanned the Toronto Homicide HQ for any signs of Tomlinson and his moustache twins. The room appeared clear of clutter. He strolled over to Barbie's desk. She'd done a stand-up job on getting him the cold case files and the additional photos on the fresh case.

"Barbie." He smiled.

She looked up from her typewriter, her cheeks flushed. "Detective. I hope the folders I left you were satisfactory."

"More than satisfactory." He glanced around the room. Still clear. "I need some real analyst work done. You up to it?"

"Definitely." Her voice had a new, confident shine to it.

Mahoney popped his notebook from his coat pocket, clicked open a pen, flipped to a clean page, and jotted down a series of numbers. Tearing the page clean, he handed it her. "Call Dara. She's my analyst back home. Top notch. She'll get you set up with some serious database access. I'd try to explain it all, but computer terms aren't in my vocabulary."

Taking the paper, she looked around the room and slid it under a notepad.

"You call her. Get hooked up. I need searches, but first you need computer power."

"Great." Her cheeks glowed.

He turned and took a few steps.

"Detective?"

He spun on his heels, holding his derby to his head. "Yeah?"

"Thanks."

"I'll be the one thanking you once you get me some answers." He tipped his hat, turned, and walked away. He could feel the warmth from her glow and her smile as he headed across the room.

Chapter 32

Circus Declutter

Mahoney opened the door to the fancy war room. The smell of a dickhead sergeant and his clone sidekicks wafted from the room. Mahoney nodded at the twitching moustache. Sergeant Tomlinson glared back in return.

Mahoney joined Sutton and Dixon in the back corner.

Sutton swallowed. Sweat covered his face.

Mahoney smirked. "Sutton. You look terrible."

"Yeah, thanks."

Mahoney inquired, "What's going on?"

"I don't like this. Any of this. You going off on your own sideshow. Tomlinson's gotta know."

He had lingered at the murder scene, in the shadows of the techies, scouring for any missed tidbits. Then he'd spent a lot of time at the morgue. Wouldn't Tomlinson be relieved he wasn't getting in his way? Mahoney jabbed Sutton in the ribs. "Chill out. He doesn't give a flying fuck what an old, washed-out detective is doing. You're the boss on our team. You represent us. You play by the book. Get along with Sergeant Clown. He'll keep his eye on you, and away from me."

Sutton swallowed again. He managed a slight smile. "All right."

"What, you don't trust me?"

"I do, boss."

"Sutton. You're the boss."

"I know."

Mahoney tipped his derby at Sutton, then settled against the back wall, waiting for the show to begin.

Sergeant Tomlinson barked at the room, shutting everyone up. Feet shuffled as everyone turned to face their leader. Tomlinson walked up to the magnificent crime scene board.

"All right. Let's recap our progress for the day. We've got a second body. Appears the suspect we had in custody may not be the right one."

Mahoney stifled a snicker. *Got that right.*

Tomlinson continued, "Doesn't mean we're on the wrong path."

Sure you aren't.

"We'll take the same approach. You've all been busy, at the scene, interviewing witnesses, processing files. Thanks to your hard work, we've got a couple suspects from the new scene in custody. We'll question them. We'll determine if they know about the first scene. It's gotta be one of these tough guys. Looking for trouble in our parks."

Heat blazed up Mahoney's back. Why did he have to stand here?

"Write up everything you've found today. We'll proceed with the interrogations first thing tomorrow." The moustache bobbed.

Tomorrow? This case was moving slower than he could handle. Mahoney snuck a glance at Sutton. He stood at attention.

Sergeant Tomlinson barked more orders. Mahoney watched him, his mouth moving, his words fading into a muffled, garbled mess.

Mahoney pulled a filter over the world around him. Just like he did way back when he was a teenager in his friend John's car, giggling as they divvied up the bag of 'shrooms they'd gotten their hands on. He remembered sitting there, in the car, the mushroom cloud filtering their world.

He looked at Sergeant Tomlinson. He pictured him in long, striped pants, with a red bobble nose and big floppy shoes. His hair replaced by curly, red, erratic curls blasting in all directions. He was a clown, leading a circus. Clown Tomlinson held a bunch of bright-red balloons. Too many balloons...he couldn't stay grounded. Clown Tomlinson floated up and away. His clown clone sidekicks floated away with him. The room cleared of clutter. The circus departed.

Mahoney looked back at Sutton. He wasn't a clown. He wasn't part of the circus. He floated somewhere in between reality and the mushroom-filtered show. The bridge between where the investigation was going and where Mahoney needed to take it.

Mahoney scanned the room. Barbie, seated at the front, typed away. Detective Dixon, along a side wall, arms crossed, scrutinized the show playing out in front of him. None of them floated away with the departing circus. They all remained. His rogue team. They hadn't gotten anywhere with the strange clues. Yet. Tomorrow would be a new day.

Barbie would be hooked up with computer power. They'd have more autopsy results. He knew it. For now, he'd play along with the circus. Then he'd have a cheap, warm bourbon in his shitty motel room. Tomorrow would be a fresh start. It had to be.

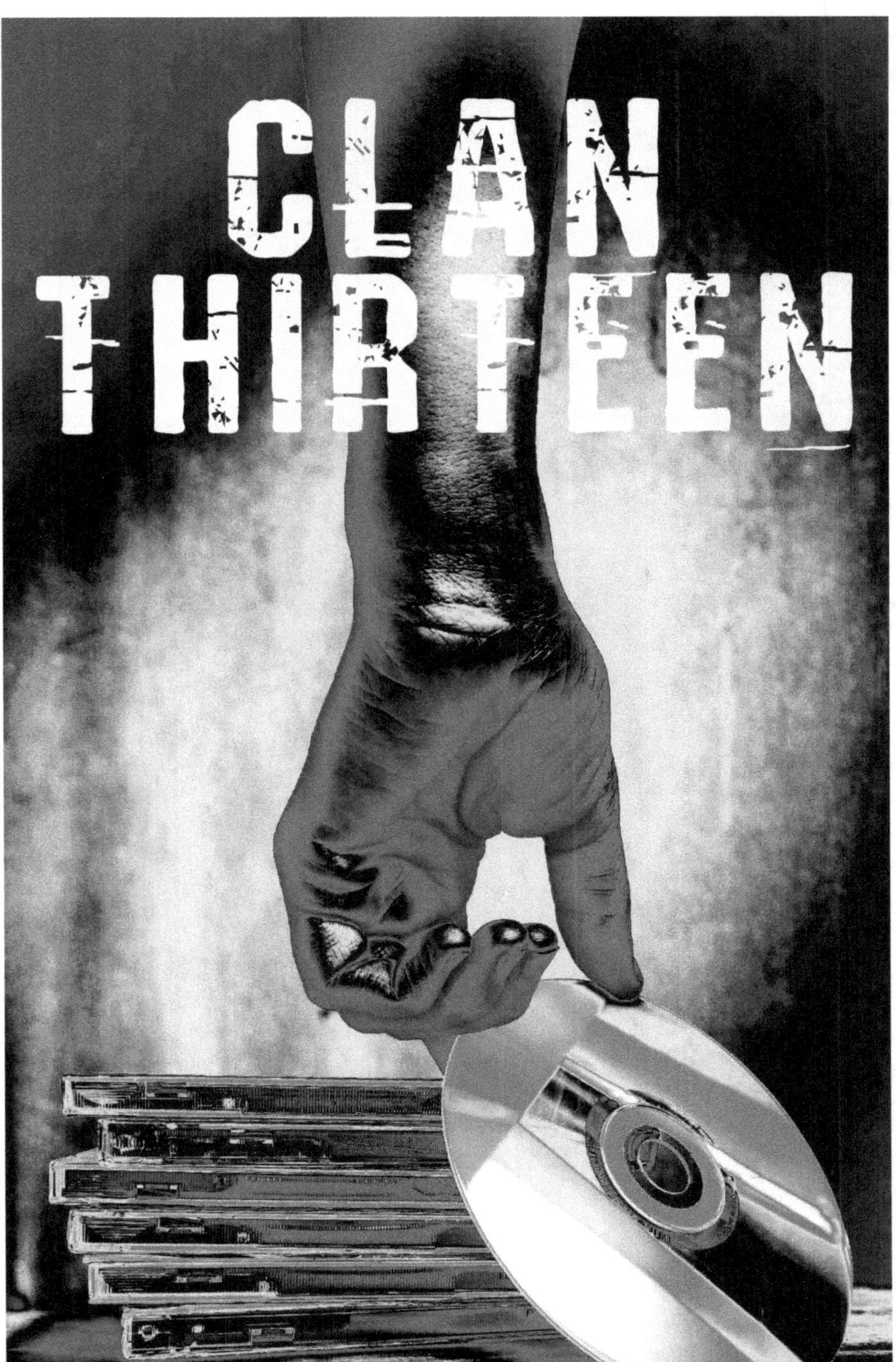

CLAN
THIRTEEN

Chapter 33

Condolences

Mahoney slammed the black door on the shiny Sedan. He missed the creak of his vintage Pony.

"Can't believe Tomlinson dumped this on us," Sutton pouted.

"I know. It's *his* jurisdiction. The one victim that had found a new home." Mahoney rubbed the bristle on his chin.

"File said she'd only been adopted six months before she disappeared."

"Yeah. It's a shame. And we're the jackasses who get to inform the new parents. Geez. Tomlinson keeps the prime tasks for himself," Mahoney said. They'd attended Tomlinson's morning meeting of the lemmings, bright and early. He'd tasked the out-of-towner detectives with informing a family that their two-month wait was over, and that their new daughter would never be coming home.

Sutton sighed.

"At least we can be sure to make this delicate," Mahoney coaxed.

"True." Sutton nodded as he opened the passenger door.

Mahoney departed the rental and followed Sutton up to the front door of a small house. Rows of perfectly groomed peonies, geraniums, and roses lined the walkway. He pushed a button. Bells chimed on the other side of the door. Soft footsteps approached. The door opened. A short, round woman stood, staring at them.

"Good morning, ma'am. Are you Gloria Easton?" Mahoney inquired.

Her eyes widened. Her voice was barely audible. "Yes. I am."

"I'm Detective Mahoney. This is Detective Sutton. Ma'am, may we come in for a moment?"

The woman nodded, the dazed look on her face deepening. She turned, walking down the hallway. Her square-shaped fluorescent frock bobbed back and forth with her hips.

She led them into a cozy living space and motioned toward a floral-patterned matching sofa and chair set. Mahoney sat down on the couch. Sutton settled in next to him. The woman sat hesitantly on the edge of a wooden rocking chair, her pale knees peeking from the bright frock.

"Ma'am, we are here about Trina."

The dazed looked vanished. That knowing look—the one in which one's world all becomes clear—flashed across her eyes. Unwanted knowledge flushed through her. The fluorescent frock quivered.

"She's not..."—she swallowed—"she's not OK, is she?"

"I'm sorry, ma'am, but no. We found Trina's body." Black lace cloaked Mahoney's mind. A cold bead of sweat trickled down the back of his neck.

"Sh-sh-she's dead?" Full convulsions took over Gloria's body. Her broken words rushed from her mouth. Tears flowed down her puffy cheeks. The tight curls of her perm clung close to her head as she quivered.

Sutton handed her his handkerchief. She buried her face in the handkerchief, crumpling it into a wad. Mahoney exchanged a glance with Sutton, then sat back into the couch. He closed his eyes, facing the flowing black lace clouding his thoughts. Trina's face flashed, pale. Her dark eyes peered at him amid blood-red swirls, turning her innocent eyes into horrific demon globes.

Sutton nudged him. His mind jolted back to the grieving woman.

The bright frock stopped pulsing. Gloria dabbed the wadded-up kerchief against her moist cheeks. She swallowed, then released a loud exhale. "I'm sorry. You'd think after all this time, I wouldn't react this way. I mean, it's been *two months*. The chances of finding her alive..."

"No need to apologize, ma'am. Take your time," Mahoney coaxed.

"I knew. I didn't want to. But I knew. If a missing child isn't found within the first few days, the chances are poor." She breathed in, then out. "I had a feeling, too. You know? I know I sound crazy. Trina wasn't actually *mine*. Not by blood. But, I'd wanted a child for so long, and when we finally got her, well, I felt like she *was* mine. God, I sound like a cuckoo." Gloria shook her head and looked at her hands.

"Not at all," Mahoney said.

"Thank you." Gloria swallowed. "Like I said, I had this feeling. This sick hurt, deep in the pit of my stomach. In the middle of the night, last Wednesday. I woke up suddenly. I sat straight up in bed. The feeling throbbed inside of me. I saw her face, as if she were right there beside me. I heard her voice." Gloria's voice broke. Tears flowed down her face. She gulped against them. "Thomas, my husband, told me I was imagining it. But I swear, I heard her voice. She whispered to me. 'Mommy, I love you.'" Her lips pressed into a thin line.

Mahoney saw Trina again. Her black lips moving, eerie whispers escaping, wafting through his mind. *Mommy. I love you.*

"It's crazy. She never called me mommy. I just wanted her to. I wanted so badly for her to be *mine.*" Gloria wiped at her eyes.

Sutton snapped open his notebook. "Ma'am, you don't sound crazy. You loved her. I know this is hard. But do you think we can ask you a few questions about when you last saw her?"

"Of course. I...I want to *get him*. The person who did this." Her teeth clenched, her lips curling around them. The look in her eyes changed. A fire glimmered in her dark pupils.

Get him. Mahoney wanted to *get him,* too. He leaned in toward Gloria. "We intend to do just that." Gloria returned his gaze with equal intensity. "I know this is difficult. Trust me, I've seen this one too many times. Anything you can tell us, ma'am, could be very helpful."

Gloria nodded. She wiped her nose with the balled-up kerchief. It was no longer a borrowed item, but hers to keep. Mahoney didn't know how many he'd been through. Sutton would learn it was part of the gig.

"I don't know where to start." The focus in her eyes faded.

"Think of the last time you saw Trina. Anything you can remember at all, no matter how small or insignificant it may seem." Mahoney grabbed her gaze again. The fire returned.

"She went missing on February 15. I'll never forget that day. She'd been at her choir practice. She always had choir practice on Wednesday. It was the one activity that she agreed to. She was quite rebellious, given her lack of parenting until she came here. But she loved choir." Gloria smiled. "Anyways, she would stay after school, then walk home. She always walked home with Lisa and Lauren. They're twins. They live on the end of the street. She never walked home alone."

"What time would choir practice end?"

"Four o'clock in the afternoon. They usually left the school right away. I wanted her home in plenty of time for dinner. It was important to me—that we have family dinner."

"So, they would leave the school a few minutes after four? How long would it take for them to walk home?"

"About twenty minutes. Unless they got caught up chatting and giggling. You know how girls are." She looked down at her hands. "Or, maybe you don't. I don't know why I said that."

Sutton responded, "Oh, I know. I have a daughter. Teenager."

Gloria smiled. "Well, Trina's sixteen...or, she *was.*" She looked at her hands folded in her lap. "Detective, do you have a daughter?" She looked at Mahoney.

"I do. She's twelve." His mind bolted back to the beach. A little girl running along, giggling. It seemed like just yesterday that Stella was a little girl.

"Well, then, you both know girls can get carried away when they're together. So, usually it took them twenty minutes. Sometimes thirty. But she was always home by four-thirty. She knew the rules. She didn't adhere to them at first. But, the last couple of months, she was coming around. I think she was craving structure."

Mahoney asked, "Did she arrive at her usual time, that day?"

Gloria looked up to the ceiling, searching her brain. "Yes, she did. She had a big exam the next day. I'd made it clear good marks on exams would result in more privileges."

"What type of exam?"

"Chemistry. I think she enjoyed chemistry. Mrs. Charney was the one teacher she didn't despise." Gloria smiled. "I think she was smarter than she let on."

Mahoney thought of his own daughter and how she always talked about finding the cure for the world's diseases, or travelling halfway around the world to treat sick and malnourished kids. Ambitious for a kid. Just like Trina. "Was there anything unusual about the evening?"

"Well, not at first. She came home, said hello, then went up to her room to study. I sent her up with a glass of milk and a plate of cookies. I was roasting a chicken. I stayed in the kitchen to tend to the dinner. I had the TV on in the other room. I like to listen to something while I cook."

"Did anything happen between her arrival and dinner?"

"No. My husband got home at about five-thirty, as usual. He went into the other room. He changed the channel—his has a distaste for my shows. At about six o'clock, I called Trina down and we ate dinner."

"In the kitchen?"

"Yes. We had a small table in there. Less formal than the dining room."

"What did Trina do after dinner?"

"She went back upstairs to study. Usually, we would allow her watch TV with us. But, because of the exam, we required her to study."

"You said nothing unusual happened, at first. What was it that you remember?"

"Around eight o'clock, I heard a bang, from upstairs. I went up, knocked on Trina's door, and opened it. She was just sitting there, studying. I asked her what the noise was. She said she didn't know."

"Did you figure out what it was?"

"No. She said she hadn't heard anything. But it was strange. We heard it all the way downstairs. And, well, she had this strange look on her face. I chalked it up to her being tired and her mind full of chemistry equations. But when she was gone in the morning..."

"You wondered what that noise was," Sutton confirmed.

"Yeah. I should have known something wasn't right. I had my husband search the whole house. He didn't find anything. He said it was probably something outside, blown over by the wind." Fresh tears sprang free from her eyes. She dabbed at them, then continued, "But now I'll never know."

Mahoney flipped through his notebook. "The last day you saw her, that was Wednesday, February 15?"

"Yes." Her voice flooded with confidence. "You don't forget the date on something like that. After the first day, I tried to keep up hope. But I had this feeling. It was hard to convince myself that I would see her again. But, inside of me, there was this warmth, this feeling, like I knew she was still alive. Still out there. And then, last Wednesday, like I said, I woke up in the night. I knew she wasn't coming home." She wrenched the ball of kerchief in her hands. "I wish I could tell you more. This all sounds so hokey. A noise. Then she's gone. I still don't believe it myself. She was in her room when we said goodnight. The next morning, poof, she was gone."

"Ma'am, you've been very helpful," Sutton said.

Gloria nodded. "Of course." She looked at her hands. "You know, I haven't been able to go in her room. For *two months*. Not once. My husband couldn't, either. And now...well...he doesn't live here anymore. It took a toll on him when we adopted Trina. I think he would have been happy without children, but I wanted them badly enough that he conceded. It wasn't easy with Trina when she first got here. My husband fought with her a lot. A few months in, he took more of a back seat to his new parenting role, and I took over. I think when she disappeared, he blamed himself. He believed she had run away. It was too much for him. We grew apart. The whole ordeal was a wedge between us."

"I'm sorry," Mahoney said. "So, Trina was the last one in her room, except for the police?"

"Yes. A couple officers did a quick scan. In my opinion, they didn't seem to be very thorough. I think they had already decided she ran away, given her circumstances and that she hadn't been here very long."

"Do you think it's possible that she did run away?" Mahoney asked.

"It is a logical explanation, given how difficult it seemed for her to adjust here. But, like I said, the last couple months that she was here, she seemed to be coming around. She was following the rules more, and she was opening up to me, at least a little."

"Would you mind if we took a look in her room?" Mahoney asked.

Gloria nodded. "Of course. If you think it would help."

Gloria stood, smoothed out her frock with both hands, then turned and waved them to follow her.

Chapter 34

Clan 13

Gloria walked across the room, her bright frock swaying with her hips. Mahoney nudged Sutton ahead, then followed in tow. There was a possibility that the killer had touched this room, if Trina hadn't run away. If the police had indeed done as light of a dusting as Gloria had indicated, there might be a shred of evidence. Lots of possibility. One minute she was there, then, poof, the next minute she was gone. The empty ball in the pit of his stomach grew every time he chose a corpse over his own daughter. He couldn't imagine what that ball would feel like if she disappeared forever.

They followed Gloria up the stairs. Their socked feet sunk into the soft, blue carpet. Gloria led them down a small hallway, two doors on the left, two on the right. At the second door on the left, she stopped and stared into the room.

Mahoney touched her elbow. "Ma'am, may we?"

Gloria shook her head. "Of course." She stepped back.

Mahoney entered the room. The small bed, in the righthand corner diagonal to the door, was covered in a pink bedspread. Teddy bears were clustered around the pillows, staring at him with their fake black eyes. A small bookshelf was against the wall, on the opposite corner. A window, between the bed and the bookshelf, was adorned with lacy white curtains. The sun filtered through in an orange glow.

He slid his hand into his pocket and rubbed the polished Tiger's Eye. There had to be something here. Sutton took the other side of the room, examining a desk in the corner, against the wall. Mahoney walked over to the bed. It was made. The teddy bears sat up against the pillows. Their black, glassy eyes explored him.

"Sutton. She did say only the police had been in here, right?"

"Yeah."

"Then why's the bed made?"

"Good question. Maybe she never slept in it," Sutton said.

"Maybe Barbie can find the file on this, see if any photos were taken." He wasn't counting on it.

Mahoney rubbed the bristle on his chin. A small tape deck sat perched on a white nightstand, next to the bed. He walked up to it. He wasn't sure what he was looking for, but a pulsing sensation took over his gut. A stack of cassettes in cracked, plastic cases sat next to the player. The one on the top caught his eye. Electric-red lettering dripped in flames down the front of the case. *Clan 13*.

Retrieving a fresh pair of latex gloves from inside his tweed coat, he snapped them on. He lifted the case and opened it. Swallowing hard against the cold creeping up his throat, he stared at the inside cover of the cassette. A crude circle, intersected with a V, a slash mark on each of the arms, grasped his gaze. His body froze.

Blinking hard, he shook his head, then reached out and pushed the play button on the tape deck. Little plastic wheels spun. A dark voice vibrated through the quiet room, followed by an electric riff. The voice sung of clans of ancient beings making their marks.

Sutton shuffled up behind him. "Holy Shit. Is that what I think it is?"

Mahoney swallowed. His parched throat devoured the few drops of saliva he could muster. "The symbol. On the bodies."

His mind raced. Puncture wounds. Drained of blood. Now this. What the *hell* was *Clan 13?* What horrific fantasy had he stepped into?

Chapter 35

Symbols and Teeth Marks

Mahoney pushed hard against the heavy morgue door. It opened with a whoosh.

His cell phone buzzed. He halted, unholstered his phone and flipped it open. "Mahoney." His gruff voice echoed through the quiet space.

"Ha. It's me. Over here."

A hand waved, pulling his gaze across the dim room. Examiner Winter, chocolate eyes peering through thick lenses, waved at him. She set the lab phone back on its cradle. She giggled.

He walked over to the science lab corner lined with glass beakers and flasks. "That was you?"

"Yeah. Perfect timing. There's something you have to see."

"I have something to show you, too."

"Perfect." She smiled.

"You first."

"OK." Her lips turned down. She took a few steps over to a steel slab. The cold bed of the latest victim. The young, lifeless girl had been turned over, exposing her back. As the white cloth covering her skin was peeled away, Mahoney watched what he already knew would appear.

The symbol. It was on her back. A crude circle. Jagged slashes on either arm of the deep V intersecting the circle. Branded into her flesh. Representing something unknown to anyone other than the psycho who had imprinted it into her flesh. The symbol called to Mahoney. It pulled him in. He stepped toward the body. His mind buzzed. The symbol emanated a dark vibe. It was...*hypnotizing*.

"The symbol. I feel cold looking at it," Winter said.

Mahoney shook himself back to reality. "Yeah. The same as on the cold case girls."

"They looked just like this?"

He glanced again. "Yeah. Identical. " He scratched the bristle on his chin.

They stood, entranced by the strange, hypnotic symbol.

Whoosh. The heavy examination room door swung open, breaking the spell. A man in a lab coat entered, nodded from across the room, and proceeded over to the opposite corner.

"Listen. Were there any leads on this symbol, before the case went cold?" she asked.

"Nope. It was all manual searching. Library archives, books, that sort of thing. Back then, no computer power."

"Right. I've seen a lot of cases. I've never seen anything like this."

"I need photos."

"Will Sergeant Tomlinson pursue a search?"

"He's not interested in looking into anything that links this to the cold case."

"But we've got two fresh bodies, both with this symbol branded on their backs." She twisted her mouth into contorted pout. "Doesn't he have that bleached-blonde sidekick analyst?"

"Turns out the bleached-blonde sidekick has analyst skills. I've hooked her up with my analyst back home. We'll beef up her database access and searching power."

"Wow. You have quite the influence."

"I want information."

"Yeah. Me, too." She looked back at the symbol. "You see why I needed you to *see* for yourself?"

"Yeah. Pictures don't do it justice."

"It doesn't *seep* cold in the pictures."

"No, it doesn't."

"Real doozy."

A slight smirk crept across his lips. "I can top your doozy."

"Really?" She raised an eyebrow.

"Yeah. Just came from the victim's house. Met with her foster mom. We were able to look through her bedroom. The last place she was seen. Apparently, neither of the foster parents have been in the room since Trina went missing. And the police only did a quick scan. So far, no file can be found related to her disappearance." He dug into his tweed coat pocket and pulled out a small plastic bag. "I found this on the nightstand." He placed the bag on the steel slab. Red, flaming letters dripped down a plastic cassette case, declaring the masterpiece of *Clan 13.*

"A cassette? Clan 13?" She narrowed her goggled eyes.

"Yeah. Open it." Mahoney watched as Winter opened the bag with her gloved hands.

She pulled the cassette case out and opened it. Her chocolate eyes bulged from behind the round lenses of the goggles. "Double doozy is right. The symbol." She looked up from the case. "But what does it *mean?*"

"Don't know. But I'm gonna find out. I'll make some stops after I leave here. And we'll start using that database power, get the analyst doing some searches."

She nodded. "Before you go, I have another doozy for you."

"What's that?"

"The punctures. They weren't used to inject anything into the victim."

"What?"

"Her tox scan came back clean."

A tingling took over his gut. *Dammit.* "Clean?"

"Yeah. The puncture wound looks more like a bite than a needle entry. There're two punctures. And they're jagged. They look more like teeth marks."

"So, not needle marks. And not to inject. What fresh hell is this?"

"It doesn't add up. I re-examined the openings. I did a swab analysis. The wound culture indicates both openings are clean. No traces of anything inside of them. No substances. Nothing was injected into these punctures. I wonder if something other than a needle made these marks." She narrowed her eyes and screwed her mouth up. "Oh, I got the photos of the necks from the cold case victims amplified." She walked over to a side table, returning with a folder. Pulling out several photos, she shuffled through them. "Here." She snapped the photos onto the steel slab, next to the body. "These are magnified."

He looked at the photos. The two circular injections were no longer smooth circles. They were jagged punctures. Too thick to be made with a needle. He stood up. "They don't look like needle injections."

"No. And they're jagged. They look like the one on our victim here."

"Was she bitten? What kind of freakshow are we in?"

She shook her head. "I don't know. But something tells me you're going to find out. I got one more thing for you. If you didn't think this was weird enough already, the two hairs stuck in the makeup on her face...they're not human."

"What?" *Bites on the necks. No blood. Animal hair. Fresh hell.*

"Animal hairs. Of some sort. Lab is trying to pin it down."

He pictured a half monster, half man with fangs biting into a helpless victim.

She gathered the photos and slid them back into the folder. She leaned against the table. "I pushed them. They'll notify me as soon as they identify what the hairs are. I'll call you."

Mahoney nodded. "Swell. I gotta go. Need to follow this symbol." He tipped his hat and turned to the door.

"Later, Detective," her sweet voice followed him out of the morgue.

Chapter 36

Violet Sixteen

Violet Sixteen lay limp against Chester's arm. Her long, dark hair, spread out like a shawl, shone under the blue-purple pot lights. Chester stared at her pale face. The blood circles around her eyes faded to a soft orange. Her eyes were closed. Black lipstick smeared around her lip line in a dark, thick mess. Streaks of black mixed with white in cosmic swirls across her chin and cheeks. She was a mess. And she was dead in his arms.

No. It wasn't her time.

Violet Sixteen had joined his collection of Violets eight years ago. He'd almost passed her by, but there was something in her eyes. Something that said she didn't want to be where she was. Something that said she needed him.

He'd had real hope for her. She'd shown such promise. She had the potential to be perfect. Like Violet, the original.

Sweat drizzled down Chester's cheeks, smearing the white makeup, exposing the flesh underneath. He'd planned to spend time with his Violets. He'd descended into the basement. As they arose from their rest, Violet Sixteen continued to lay still. He racked his brain, but couldn't recall seeing any signs of her demise.

Chester ran his hand along the slivers of cuts behind her ear. *Had he been too eager? Had he taken too much blood from her?* He thought he had perfected his system. Every girl that he took had the type of life liquid he needed to thrive. Type O Negative. Just like Violet. Every orphaned girl was given a full medical rundown before admittance to her new institution-like home. A government admin, glorified data filer, wasn't paid much. After he'd delivered the first money-filled envelope, along with clear instructions, copies of the required files were left, on time, every year. At first, he'd only extracted the life liquid he needed when it was time to sacrifice. As his hunger grew, he found a way, using an ancient tool left by his grandfather in a chest in the attic, to bleed out small amounts, from his live Violets. Looking at Violet Sixteen now, he wondered if his process was flawed. It was too late now.

No. It was too soon. His heart thumped.

She wasn't supposed to be in *this* cycle of sacrifice. His nostrils flared.

She wasn't meant to leave him until *he* decided it was time. His brain throbbed.

He didn't want to purge her. His lip twitched. Twice.

He wanted to keep her. She had been promising. Eight years of work. Gone. A wild twitch pulled at his lips.

He shook her. Limp and unresponsive, her blood-circled eyes remained closed. He blinked hard against the twitch seizing the right side of his face.

He had planned on keeping her. To give her a chance to reach her full potential. His gut seized. Pain rippled through his insides and down his arms.

Violet Sixteen lay lifeless in his arms. Chester grasped her tighter. He shook her hard. "Violet." His cries, drenched in anguish, shot through the air. "Why did you leave me?" His cries were stifled by the silence cloaking the room, suffocating him.

He imagined Violet Sixteen opening her eyes slowly, looking up at him. Her weak, raspy pleas barely audible. "Saul. I am here."

Chester stroked her dark hair. He ran his fingers along her black-smeared lips. He slid two fingers into her mouth and spread them open, parting her bite. He reached over and grasped a heavy goblet dotted in red gems. Tilting the goblet toward her open mouth, red liquid poured over her tongue, drizzling down the sides of her face. Scarlet poured down the sides of her mouth, landing on Chester's chest. He tilted the goblet upright then placed it on the floor beside him. Violet Sixteen couldn't swallow back the life-giving red liquid. She was gone.

Chester stroked her hair. "If only you could feed. Your strength would return."

Violet Sixteen lay frozen. Her eyes closed. Her body heavy against him.

A pain throbbed in his gut, reaching its tentacles up through him, wrapping around each and every one of his internal organs and squeezing hard. Pain pierced all his limbs.

He leaned his head back and howled. His cries impaled every corner of the silent room. No one was there to hear him. Savage sounds rumbled inside of him, crawling up his throat, and escaping his mouth as primal screams. Hope drained from him, swirling into a ball of energy then disintegrating into thin air.

He gritted his teeth together and clung to Violet Sixteen, squeezing her lifeless body against him. He buried his smeared white face into her pale neck. Loud sobs shook him.

What will I do? It's not her time. Her salvation was mine to give.

How could he let her go before her time? How could he purge a Violet that he had not chosen to sacrifice? He had to do something to honour her. He couldn't put her with the others. The ones that had been part of his planned cycle.

His mind swirled. His thoughts descended upon him, filling him with dread. He shivered. He pulled Violet Sixteen closer in a suffocating death hug, the cold from her lifeless body seeping into his pores.

Chapter 37

Pink Pad and Feathers

Mahoney strode across the main Toronto Police Headquarters room, scanning the light scatter of remaining personnel. It seemed most of the homicide unit checked out before sundown.

Barbie looked up from her typing, making eye contact with him.

He approached. "Tomlinson and his crew have split?"

She exhaled a laugh. "Yeah. He rounded up a handful of suspects. I think he was about halfway through the interrogations when he departed, crew in tow, for the corner pub." She shook her head. "I hate to say it, but he prioritized a pint over catching a killer."

Impressive. She was embracing the side investigation like a star. With Sergeant Moustache gone for the night, they might get somewhere. "You up to putting in a few more hours?"

Barbie nodded, her eyes lighting up. "Of course, Detective. Dara got me all hooked up, and I think I'm getting the hang of running searches." She smiled wide.

"Perfect." Mahoney slid a slit of paper onto her desk. "A list of searches."

Barbie covered the paper with a tanned hand, spreading her pink-tipped fingers over the desk. She slid it discreetly into a stack of files and winked at him.

"You have any trouble, lean on Dara. Plenty of daylight left back home."

"You got it." Barbie folded her hands together and rested them on her desk.

Mahoney made a second scan of the room. Half a dozen detectives sat scattered at desks, engrossed in files or typing reports. "The list is ordered. We've got a slew of weird things. Start at the top. The symbol. It looks like it was burned into the backs of the victims. Like a brand."

Barbie stared at him intently, jotting down notes on a bright-pink pad of paper. Pink feathers bobbed from the end of her pen.

"Look for places someone could have a custom brand made."

Barbie scribbled furiously, pink feathers bobbing erratically.

"And find out anything you can on a band called *Clan 13*, and where their music is sold. Same symbol is plastered on their album. We found it in the last victim's bedroom. It's one hell of a coincidence." Mahoney snapped his notebook shut.

"You got it, Detective." The pen halted; the feathers settled.

Detective Dixon walked through the door, clutching dinner to-go in a paper bag.

Mahoney tapped the corner of Barbie's desk. "You need anything, you call me."

Barbie nodded.

Mahoney walked over to Dixon's desk. The smell of grease wafted from the spotted bag settled in the corner. "Dixon, you got a minute?"

"Sure thing. Just settling in for the night."

"You always work late?"

"Let's just say I find it easier to wade through the bullshit when the circus isn't in town." Dixon smirked.

"Meet me in that fancy meeting room of yours." Mahoney walked over to his borrowed desk and snatched up his briefcase.

Chapter 38

Unofficial Meeting

A purple-blue hue glowed through the large window overlooking the lake. The first appearances of stars glimmered in the darkening sky. Mahoney sat down in one of the plush chairs and set his briefcase and derby on the long table running down the centre of the room. He looked out over the tall, glass buildings cluttering the downtown core. It had looked quite different sixteen years ago.

"Detective," Dixon called as he walked through the door.

"Dixon."

Dixon sat down across from Mahoney and leaned over the table.

Mahoney inquired, "Anything new?"

"Nah." Dixon shook his head and frowned. "Sergeant's been chasing random suspects. Had me tagging along, doing meaningless tasks all day. I was just about to crack open the files on the fresh scene." He rubbed his smooth chin with his pointer and thumb. "You made real progress, didn't you?"

"Maybe."

"Give me the run down."

"Medical examiner is top notch. She found a couple hairs lodged into the makeup on the face. They're not human. Some kind of animal. The new victim has the same punctures as the ones we found in the photos from the cold case. Tox scan is clean. Punctures don't appear to be from a needle. Look more like teeth marks. And..." Mahoney leaned toward the table, opened his briefcase, and pulled out a photo. He slid it over to Dixon. "We found this in the bedroom of our latest victim."

Dixon peered at the photo. His eyes widened. "Hot damn." He looked at Mahoney. "Same symbol branded on the victims. Can't be a coincidence. But what does it *mean?*"

"I don't know yet. Stopped at a couple of record shops. None of them sell this. They told me to try Sunrise, but they were closed by the time I got there."

Dixon nodded. "Animal hair. Punctures...or bite marks in the neck. This killer thinks he's some sort of beast?"

"And all the blood, missing. Again." Mahoney leaned back into the soft chair and rubbed the bristle on his chin.

"Like some sort of vampire tale."

"It's weird. All the victims from before, and from now, dark hair, similar builds. Killed at sixteen."

Dixon leaned into the table and ran his hand through his smooth hair. "Victim type."

"What do you know about victim types?"

"It's part of building a profile of the killer. His victim type."

Mahoney chuckled. "You sound like someone I know."

"Your FBI agent, the profiler." Dixon smiled. He looked far too fresh and excited.

"Yeah. Think it's time I give her a call."

"You can do that?"

"I suspect she'll be as excited as you are about this."

Dixon slid a small notepad from the pocket in his pinstripe vest and flipped it open. "I've been looking closer at the timeline. The cold case. First victim was killed on April 3, 1973. The second victim was killed six days later, on April 9. The last victim was killed eight days later, on April 17. Two weeks. Three bodies. New case. Skip forward to sixteen years. First victim was killed on April 5. Second victim was killed seven days later, on April 12. I think this killer is on some sort of cycle." He pulled at his smooth chin with his pointer and thumb. "But then why not start on the same day? Why April 5 instead of April 3? And why a day late on the second kill?" Dixon's baby skin wrinkled across his forehead. "If it is a cycle, it's slightly off. And did this killer really have a sixteen-year dry spell?" He looked up from the notebook.

Mahoney smiled wide. His shoulders relaxed. The young detective was good. Real good. "I think you're on to something here. I've hooked Barbie up with some database power. She's working some searches, starting with possible sources of the symbol. You follow that gut of yours, look into this *cycle* concept."

"Sure thing." Dixon looked across the table, eyes washed with worry. "If this killer *is* following the same cycle..."

Mahoney stood. "Then we have six days until the next kill."

Dixon nodded, running both hands through his smooth, dark hair.

"You get on that cycle. Profile as much as you can." He grabbed his derby and briefcase. "I've gotta get in touch with my FBI profiler."

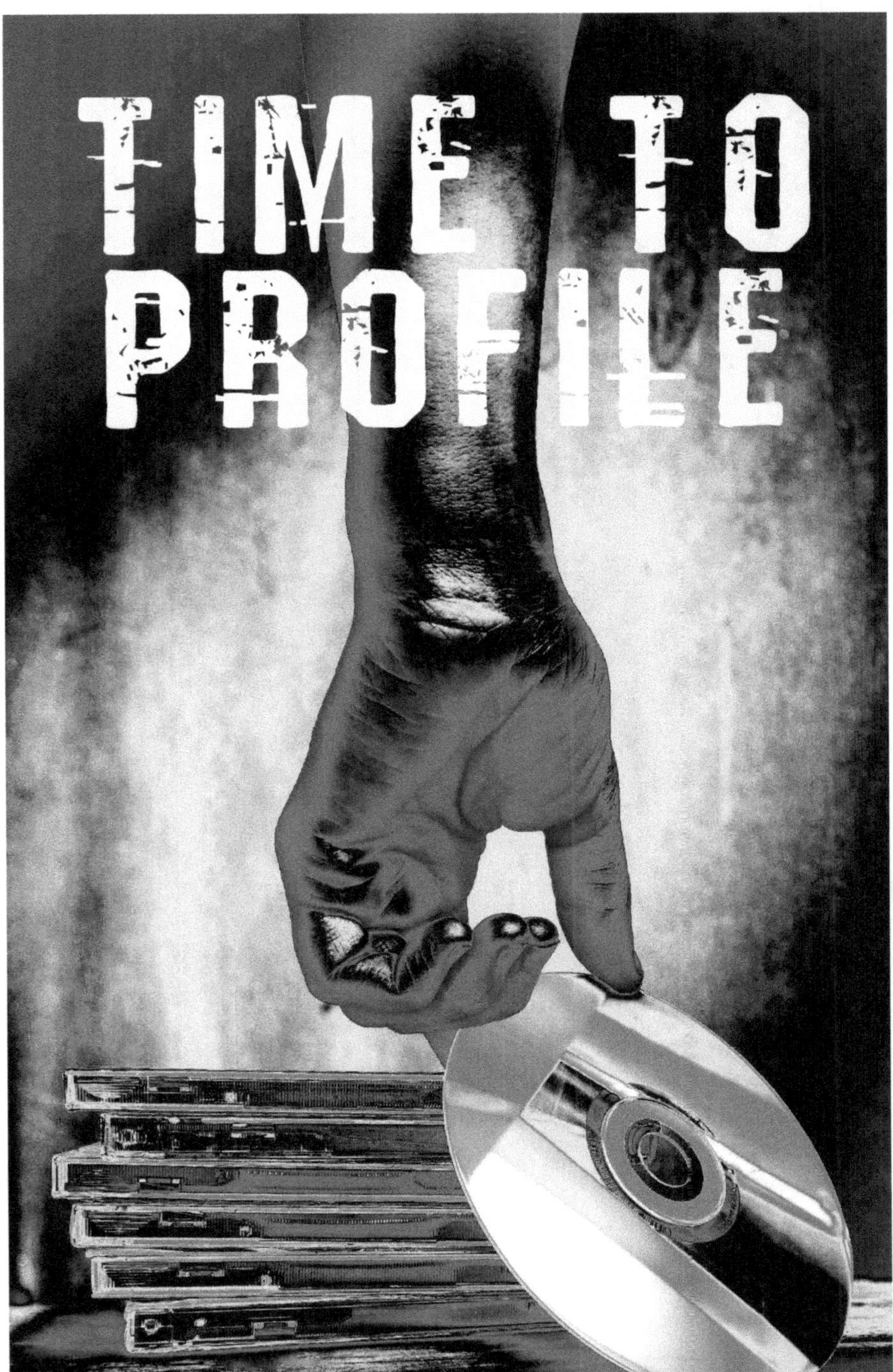
TIME TO
PROFILE

Chapter 39

In Trouble

A buzzing sound invaded Mahoney's troubled sleep. He opened one eye. His cell phone jumped around on the nightstand. He reached for it and snapped it open. "Mahoney."

"What the hell are you doing to me here?" Sergeant Jackson's voice nearly came right out of the ear piece and bit him in the face.

Mahoney opened his other eye and sat up in the hotel bed. "Solving a murder." How late had they stayed at the Homicide HQ? What time had he finally made it back to the Hav-A-Nap motel?

"You're goddam snapping every tiny shred of collaboration we had. You've *got to* make it look like you're working with Tomlinson. He's in charge."

"Tomlinson has his head up his ass." Mahoney slid out of the bed and shuffled across the room.

"Maybe. But you have to at least *give* the impression that you are working with him." Sergeant Jackson huffed. "Sutton says you disappeared yesterday. I told you, be you, but play along. Go to Tomlinson's meetings. Or at least stay in touch with Sutton for fuck's sake."

"I don't have *time*." Mahoney grabbed the chipped glass coffee pot, then sauntered over to the bathroom.

Sergeant Jackson's heavy breath pulsed in Mahoney's ear. "Make time."

"Tomlinson is trying to force a confession out of makeshift suspects. The only *involvement* he is allowing me is to watch from the sidelines, and file papers. Is there some kind of political bullshit side game going on here?" Mahoney asked. He turned on the bathroom tap and slipped the coffee pot underneath.

More breathing. Then a short, raspy snort. "What? Constable Wittman assured me that things were inline. You were closing in on a prime suspect. And *you* and Sutton were integrated into the investigation." He sighed. "I didn't peg

Wittman as a man without ethics. I still don't. He's tough. Requires obedience. Follows the law enforcement code. My guess is Tomlinson's putting on a show, convincing his boss that he's inline. I need to talk to Witton. Now. This is a delicate game, Mahoney. You can't just go blowing shit up."

"We need to get this guy." He yanked the tap off, grabbed the full coffee pot and made his way back to the main room. His bare foot caught on something crusty. His stomach cringed as he inspected the tattered carpet.

"I understand that. And I understand you're hot under the collar for this one. It's been itching at you for sixteen years."

"There were three victims last time. *Three*. Before it stopped."

"Yeah. I know."

"I won't let that happen again." Mahoney plunked the coffee pot down. Water splashed over his hand.

"Yeah. I know that, too." Sergeant Jackson sighed. "Listen. This Tomlinson, I don't know what's up with him. Like I said, I was assured he was inline."

"He isn't. He clearly doesn't want a link to the cold case."

"I don't know how he's getting away with this. They're mirror images of the girls from before." He eyeballed the collection of Hav-A-Nap motel coffees. The choices were limited—water coffee, water coffee, or water coffee.

"OK." Sargent Jackson sighed. "I'll call Wittman. Right now.

"Look, I've got an analyst and a detective out here, working *with* me. That's how sick of Sergeant Clown's bullshit they are. They want to solve this case." Mahoney swallowed.

Sergeant Jackson sighed. "Fine. Do what you do. But *get along* with Tomlinson. Don't piss him off. Do what he asks—even if you don't want to."

"I'll try."

"Do it. Use Sutton as your buffer. He can play by the rules. You go along with his direction. I'll deal whatever bullshit is going on here."

Silence hung across the invisible cell phone wires.

"Mahoney. Take it easy. You'll get him."

"Yeah. I will." Mahoney snapped his phone shut and shoved the antenna down. He tossed his phone onto the table, yanked open a packet of water coffee, and poured it into the coffee maker. *Yeah. I will.*

Chapter 40

Bug, Are You OK?

Mahoney sat down on the thin motel bed. The mattress caved in, the springs poking into his skin. He took a sip of water coffee from a chipped mug plastered in a cheap Hav-A-Nap motel logo and stared at his cell phone. He wanted to hear Stella's voice. Should he call her? Would she want to talk to him?

He plunked the coffee mug onto the night stand and flipped his phone open. Punching in the numbers, he plunged himself into the call before he could change his mind.

"Hello?" Her voice sounded so far away. She was far away. Why wasn't he with her?

"Stella. It's Dad."

"Dad." The smile seeped from her voice.

"I just wanted to say hello." He shifted on the bed, trying to escape the sharp poke of the mattress springs.

"You're still on that case? In Toronto?"

"Yes, I am. I'm sorry I can't be there." He grabbed the mug and took a swig of water coffee.

"It's OK. I know you can't come right now."

His voice shook. A tear trickled down his cheek. "Stella. I've...I've wasted so much time."

"Dad. You don't have to cry."

Dammit. Why was she so perceptive? He stared into the chipped, white mug, watching the thin, brown liquid swirl.

"I know...about the case you're on. All of it."

"What? How?" His gut wrenched.

"I read it. The library...they have old papers."

"*Christ*. Stella. Does your mother know?" He plunked the white mug back onto the nightstand. Hot droplets landed on his hand.

"Yes."

Fuck. "What did she say?" He shook his hand. The water coffee dripped free.

"She understands. I wanted to know. I *needed* to know. To know why you aren't here. And, Dad, I understand. I do."

"Jesus, Stella." He shook his head.

"You don't have to shield me anymore. I'm not a little girl."

Mahoney swallowed hard. In his mind, she *was* still a little girl. Why was she so goddamned smart?

"Dad. I can handle this. It's better this way. I see why...why you had to go back there. I mean...someone has to stop this killer. And what if some of those missing girls are still alive?"

Yeah. What if. "Stella, you can't get wrapped up in this."

"I won't. You had to go back there. You...you might be their only hope."

His heart pulsed three quick pumps. "Stella, you listen to your mother."

"I will. I do. It makes things easier." She let out a small laugh. "You know, she has me visiting this doctor. Like a shrink."

"Oh? Does it help?" He looked out the window of the motel room, eyeballing the empty parking lot for any late-morning movement.

"Yeah. It does. She's pretty cool. Lets me talk about what I want to talk about."

"Do you talk about...this case?"

"Yeah. A bit. But mostly I talk about you. I want you to be okay, Dad." She sighed softly into the phone.

He closed his eyes and smiled. A little hand wrapped its soft, warm palm around his heart and squeezed. "I'm fine. You just keep listening to your mom. And stop reading the paper."

"I can do one of those things."

He sighed. "Stella, I'm coming to see you. As soon as this is over."

"Dad...will this be your last case?"

Hell yeah. This was it. "Yeah. I know I said that before."

"But this is different."

"Yeah." He clenched his jaw. She was too perceptive for his comfort. He hadn't passed on his damn intuition to her, had he? "Listen, you just focus on school."

"Of course."

"I'll see you soon."

"I know."

He could see her emerald gaze piercing into him, even from thousands of miles away.

"Dad. I love you."

The warm hand squeezed harder; his heart felt like mush. "I love you, too."

Chapter 41

Sunrise Records

Detective Mahoney stood at the edge of the doorway, peering into the brightly lit store. To his right, rows upon rows of crime and horror movies filled tall shelves, strategically organized from A to Z by movie title. To his left, rows upon rows of cassettes, equally well organized, lined several shelves, promising to take even the most eclectic customer down a satisfying journey. At the back corner, a smaller section was lined with LPs for those clinging to the record, unsure of embracing the cassette. Near the front of the store another smaller section housed rows of compact discs for those living on the edge, embracing new listening technology.

He stepped into the store and wove his way through several circular racks of t-shirts plastered in band names. *Guns 'n' Roses, Poison,* and *Bon Jovi* plastered their names across cotton t-shirts in heavy lettering.

He made his way to the counter.

A young man with a lean, muscular build, wearing tight black jeans and a tattered t-shirt looked up from the *Rolling Stone* magazine he was perusing. "Watcha looking for?" The young man's voice was much deeper than Mahoney had expected.

The chains hanging from his belt loops jingled as he stood and walked up to the counter.

Mahoney retrieved the Clan 13 cassette from his coat pocket and snapped it onto the counter. "Do you carry this?"

The young man inspected the plastic-wrapped cassette. The severe scene on his t-shirt came alive across the counter—a dark night streaked with jolts of lightning, a metal god with long, dark hair, rough lettering declaring *Black Sabbath.*

"No way. Can't buy that in stores." The young man tossed his own dark hair over his shoulder. "Why's it in a plastic bag?"

"I'm Detective Mahoney." He flashed his badge. "It's a piece of evidence."

"Evidence?" The young man's eyes twinkled with excitement. "Someone who owned this committed a crime? Did they drop it when they fled the scene?"

"Not quite. You said this album isn't for sale in stores?"

"No. Clan 13 was an experimental Gothic metal band. Way ahead of their time. One album. Self-recorded. Sound was nasty. But they pushed the limits of metal." The young man raised his pointer and pinky and pumped a head bang.

"You know what this means?" Mahoney snapped a photo of the cassette cover onto the counter, revealing the symbol plastered inside the case sleeve.

"Yeah, dude. Symbol of the ancient vampire." The kid nodded as he smiled.

"Why would a band be associated with a vampire symbol?"

"It's a play on the band name. Clan 13. The symbol is a clan symbol of the ancient vampire. Symbolic of the stories that feed Gothic metal. It's far out, dude."

"What stories feed this...Gothic metal?"

"The stories of vampires. The romance. The sorrow. The idea of being some sort of human-animal."

"These band members, they think they're vampires?" Mahoney rubbed the bristle on his chin.

The young man snorted. "Nah, man. Just adds a deep layer to metal. Combines the raw edge of pure metal with a slower, deeper tone. Sure, some of the lyrics are about vampires, but it just adds an animalistic tone to it."

"Are there other...Gothic metal bands?"

"A few. Danzig. One album. Atrocity. Just released their debut. Type O Negative, but they haven't released an album yet. Word is they self-recorded some rough tracks."

Type O Negative? Wasn't that a rare blood type? "Not for sale?"

"Nope. Some believe the massive metal gods themselves played Gothic metal first." Chains jingled as he pointed to his t-shirt.

Mahoney scoured his brain. *What next?* "OK. This, Clan 13, are they a local band?"

The kid shook his head. "Nope. Minneapolis. Rad music scene there."

"How would one of their albums get here?"

"Like I said, self-recorded. Only way to get one would be at a show." The clerk narrowed his eyes. "I think they did one big tour." He leaned over, grabbed a stack of magazines, plunked them on the counter and shuffled through them. "Yeah. Here." Flipping through the pages of a magazine, he spread it open and spun it around for Mahoney to see. "One big tour. They travelled in a junky old van. Sold their tapes and t-shirts out of the back. It was far out, dude." His eyes widened with excitement. "They made one stop here."

Mahoney scanned the article. "You didn't go?"

"No." The clerk pouted. "They played at Lee's Palace. Wasn't old enough. Didn't have proper ID. Sucked."

"Say, can I take this magazine?" Mahoney asked.

The clerk twisted his mouth. "Can't get this issue anymore."

"Got a photocopier?"

"Yeah."

"Swell. Make me a copy of the article."

"You got it, dude." Chains swayed as the kid darted to the back of the store and disappeared into a room. He returned moments later, photocopies in hand.

"Thanks, for your help, kid."

"Anytime, dude."

Mahoney turned and walked back through the racks of t-shirts. The symbol, finally demystified, and all it did was solidify the killer's vampiric beliefs. It didn't give Mahoney any clue to who he was hunting. Time was ticking, and he wasn't any closer to stopping the next slaughter.

Chapter 42

Big-City Drink

The bright-blue strobe light electrified Mahoney's eyes. Deep bass boomed, shaking his entire body. *What the hell is this place?* Mahoney stepped a shiny black shoe onto the polished, silver floor of the *Sparkles* dance club. His foot slipped, and his leg clenched. He chuckled. He stood tall, scanned the crowded room, and spotted two open chairs up at the bar. He'd made his way to the top of Toronto's shining glory, the CN Tower. He'd assumed there'd be a cozy lounge up here. He'd been wrong.

He made his way through tightly packed partygoers, done up in sequined, strapped tops, high heels, and shiny pants. His nose stung against the clouds of conflicting perfumes fighting with each other. The music boomed louder. Purple smoke filled the stage up front. A sick sweetness permeated his nose. The purple haze cleared, revealing several high-booted girls encased in golden-barred cages. The music thumped. The dancers jerked and shook in time.

He reached the bar. His shoulders relaxed as he plunked himself down onto the high chair. Setting his briefcase on the chair next to him, a whiff of citrus grabbed his attention.

"Hey there, sweet stuff. What can I get ya?" Hot-pink lips flashed under the blue strobe light.

"Sorry?" He leaned over the bar.

"What can I get for ya, sweet stuff?"

Sweet stuff. That was a new one. "Bourbon. Straight up."

"What's your preference?"

"Maker's Mark."

"Perfect." She winked at him, her silver eyelid shimmering in the blue light. Her long, pink-streaked blonde hair flew as she spun toward the centre of the bar.

He looked around at the ridiculous dance scene. He'd avoided the Toronto Homicide HQ all day, checking in with Barbie and Dixon by phone. Seemed Tomlinson was keen on interviewing his makeshift suspects, trying to pin the murders on one of them.

The corner pub hadn't lured him away as usual. Barbie hadn't made much progress on her searches with Tomlinson breathing down her neck, ordering her to type up notes from the fake interviews. Dixon had been forced to tag along with Tomlinson. It seemed the sergeant wanted to keep a close watch on him. The day had slipped through Mahoney's fingers, the night was descending, and the next kill was predicted in four days. *If* the killer stuck to the cycle from the cold case. So far, he'd been close. He swallowed the ball of fear and bile building in his throat.

A finger tapped his shoulder. "Mahoney." FBI Agent Quesnel shot him a cherry smile.

He grabbed his briefcase, set it on the bar, and motioned for her to sit down.

She hoisted herself up onto the high chair. Her fire hair gleamed under the blue strobe light. "This is quite the place."

"Yeah. I'm not up to speed on the local bars. Things have changed since I was last here."

"A decade will do that."

"I thought there'd be a lounge up here. Didn't expect *Sparkles* the dance club."

She looked around. "This place is ridiculous. Tall building. Tall hair. Wonder what the cocktails are like."

"Yeah." He chuckled.

Pink-blonde hair caught his eye. The waitress set a plastic coaster on the counter, a crystal glass on top, then slid it over to him. "That'll be eight-fifty."

"Sorry?"

"Eight-fifty. Would you like to start a tab?"

Eight-fifty. Jeebus. He pulled out his wallet and slid a credit card over to the waitress. "You can put her drinks on here, too." He nodded at Agent Quesnel.

"I'll have a martini. Classic. Lemon twist," Quesnel said.

The waitress smiled, her hot-pink lips shimmering silver under the blue strobe light.

"Thought you were a rum-and-coke girl," Mahoney said.

"I am. Just thought, when in Rome..." She waved her hand around the room. "Besides, you're paying." She smiled.

He chuckled. "This place is gonna break my budget."

"I examined everything you sent me, on the plane. It's spotty—there's stuff missing...isn't there?"

"Yeah."

A strobe flash caught the rhinestone-studded bracelets weaving around her wrist. Pink streaks flashed under the light. The waitress placed a coaster in front of Agent Quesnel, then topped it with a fancy martini glass brimming with clear vodka and a curl of lemon peel.

Mahoney nodded his thanks. He didn't want to yell over the booming bass.

Quesnel dipped her cherry lips into the translucent alcohol and sipped. She licked her lips. "Delicious. So...the missing cold case items?"

Grabbing his tattered briefcase, he pulled out a folder, snapped it onto the bar, and opened it. Rummaging through the photos, he spread them out in front of her. "From the cold case files. They were under lock and key." He laid them out in sequence.

She picked up each photo in turn, one by one, examining the face looking back at her. "These weren't in the official case files?"

"No. I had to convince Sergeant Moustache's bombshell secretary to get them for me."

"Sergeant Moustache?" Her cherry lips twisted into a delicious smirk.

He smirked back. "Yeah. Sergeant Tomlinson. The head honcho around here. Leading the investigation. He has a tight hold on information from the cold case. Refuses to discuss any linkage."

"What? That's ridiculous. Three victims, sixteen-year-olds, all slit and bled out, all dressed in black gowns, and all painted with bloody circles around their eyes and thick black enunciated lip lines. Two more fresh ones, exactly the same—down to the brand of eyeliner." She sat back in her chair, crossing her arms.

"An idiot can see the resemblance. Tomlinson can't—or refuses to."

"I'd place a bet on power or politics." She clicked her tongue.

"One of his detectives thinks it's power or money. My Sarge says to sit tight, he'll get Tomlinson in line. I don't have time for this shit. It's a huge block."

"These photos you uncovered, they all show the brand. Any leads?"

"Nothing concrete. Dara set up the local analyst with database power. She's digging into a slew of searches I gave her, when Tomlinson isn't breathing down her neck." He pulled a photo from his inside pocket and snapped it on the bar. The symbol plastered on the *Clan 13* cassette case insert glowed an eerie red under the overhead lighting. "It's a cassette insert. Found it on the nightstand in the bedroom of the last victim. Apparently, the police barely scanned her bedroom when she went missing. Neither of the parents have been in it since."

Quesnel peered at the photo. "Weird. And unlikely a coincidence. Did the parents know anything about their daughter's taste in music?"

"No. They only adopted her six months before she went missing. Mom was shocked when we showed her the case. The others, on the nightstand, typical bubble-gum pop you'd expect a girl that age to be listening to." Mahoney rubbed the back of his neck.

"Ha." Agent Quesnel smirked. "A girl that age, especially one this rebellious, may not stick to *bubble-gum pop*. Still, it could have been left there by whoever took her."

"Yeah. No way to know. I've been to half the record shops in the city. Only one of them ever heard of this band. Apparently, it was a self-recorded tape. Not for sale."

Quesnel narrowed her eyes. "Any lead on what the symbol *means?*"

"Metal kid working the counter said it's a clan symbol of the ancient vampire. Whatever the fuck that means. Kid said it was just a play on the band name and the concept behind the Gothic metal they play. Lyrics of vampire tales. Nothing more." Mahoney took a swig of his drink. "The band isn't local. They played here once, over a year ago. Only way to get a copy of this tape was from them."

"So either the girl went the show, or whoever left the cassette in her room did."

"Yeah. Doubt she went to the show. The music store clerk said he didn't go 'cause he was underage and valid ID was required. I need to go check out the joint where the show was."

Quesnel whistled. "Quite the brand he's leaving on his victims."

Mahoney nodded. "Yeah. Now we know what it *means*. But that doesn't give us any leads on who he is."

Quesnel took a sip of her martini. "They were all slit from the heart down to the start of the pelvis—but nothing was revealed about why they were bled out? And these new victims, their organs are removed."

"Yeah."

"What about these punctures. The medical examiner did a tox scan?"

"Yeah. Tox scan was clean. So was a swab analysis. The punctures weren't used to inject anything. They aren't circular, like a needle. Plus, there are two. She says they look more like bite marks than needle punctures."

Quesnel clicked her tongue. "Slit open. Bled out. Missing blood. Bite marks."

"Yeah. That's not the weirdest part. There was animal hair found lodged in the makeup on the face of the newest victim."

Agent Quesnel crawled her fingers over the table and leaned in toward him. "Vampirism."

A tingle seized his brain and crept through his skull. "What?"

"It's a paraphilia. Remember? Our bona fide serial killers, they have severe sexual fixations. More than one. At least four on average, probably more, woven together in layers of lustful fantasies that control their lives."

"I remember."

She leaned in over the table, her cherry lips flashing under the blue strobe. "Vampirism. It's a paraphilia."

"Is it what it sounds like?"

"Drinking the victim's blood. Pre or post mortem. Or both." She took a hefty swig of her martini.

Mahoney shuddered. "So, the puncture wounds, they were made by teeth?"

"Not necessarily. I'm not implying we have a Dracula on our hands, but someone who thinks they are. The punctures could be from some sort of makeshift teeth to act out the fantasy of being a vampire. The bulk of the blood could have been drained from the body, saved for later consumption. Or he could have been drinking it during the kill. But that's a lot of blood for one sitting. Thirsty vampire." She smirked. "And now, he could be progressing."

He rubbed the bristle on his chin. *Did she ever get creeped out?* He sure as fuck was. "Progressing?"

"Yeah. This almost reminds of me Jack the Ripper. He started with cuts, then took a single organ, eventually emptied the abdomen and even took the heart."

"Why the fuck do these sickos have to come into my life?"

"Because you can handle it."

He stared at her.

"You don't believe the universe gives you what you can handle?"

He snorted. "I don't know about that. But tell me more about this vampirism."

"It has come up in serial killer cases. One of the most prolific was the Vampire of Sacramento. He killed six people in a month, drank the blood of the victims and cannibalized their remains. His modus operandi was to capture, kill, disembowel, devour raw." She paused and took a long sip of her martini. "Point is, sounds like we have a case of vampirism on our hands. And more *evolved* than the cases I know of. This killer, he's doing *something* with all that blood. He's also got a clear victim type, and he's killing according to some sort of cycle."

Mahoney's friendly daddy long legs walked through his brain. "We're heavy on fantasy. Light on evidence." The tingle in his skull crept down his neck, stepping over his spine one vertebrae at a time. "And according to this *cycle*, another kill could happen in four days. Maybe sooner."

"I know. But if we continue to unravel the fantasy, maybe we'll uncover a physical trail. The punctures, the lack of blood, the animal hair, this weird symbol. If we understand his ultimate goal, we might uncover something concrete along the way. Something to lead us to him."

Mahoney shook his head. He looked at the photos amplifying the punctures, or teeth marks, or whatever the hell they were.

"So, you've got this analyst on your side. Anyone else?"

"Yeah. One of Tomlinson's detectives. Dixon. He seems to have a natural profiling ability."

"I like him already." She shot back the rest of the martini. "Looks like you're buying me another."

"Sure. Why not." He shot back the rest of the bourbon.

"What about Sutton? He's out here with you?"

"He's uncomfortable. First lead away from home. I told him to play by the book."

She clicked her tongue against the inside of her cheek. "That's a tough one."

"You've had resistance. A lot, right? I mean, with all your new-age behaviour profiling."

"Yeah. Big time. What I wouldn't do for a dick and an old-man face. I'm young, fresh. Look at me. Men don't take me seriously. And this is a man's world, you know."

"Right. So what do I do here?"

"Well, you got the dick. And the old-man face...meh...you're not quite there yet, but close enough."

"Funny."

"We've got to crack the code on this top security that Tomlinson has on this old case. We might need to profile him, find out why he's afraid to link this to the Susie Slaughters."

"Profile him. Not bad."

"Yeah. I can work on it. And I'll put my feelers out on any cases with even the slightest trace of vampirism. I'll reach out to my profiling colleagues. If anything with any sort of resemblance is out there, they might know about it."

"Great. Thanks." Pounds of weight lifted from his shoulders. "You're gonna love the circus they call an investigation around here."

"Won't be my first one. And that's quite a name—Susie Slaughters."

"Yeah. It was named after the first victim." His shoulders dropped. Thank the homicide gods she was here. He didn't give a fuck what feathers he ruffled, he needed to find this blood-sucking vampire.

Chapter 43

The Original Violet

The track ended. *Click. Click. Click.* The wheel spun against the resistance of the stuck tape. Chester stood up, walked over to the sound system, and clicked open the cassette deck. He pulled the cassette out, a shimmering trail of black tape following. Using his finger, he spun the small plastic wheel until the tape tightened. He put the tape back in the player, closed the door and pushed play. He picked up the cassette case and stared at the dark letters—*Black Sabbath*—slithering down the paper insert. The leaders of his favourite sub-genre of metal. The group that had tinged their heavy music with a Gothic flair well before it became a musical movement.

Walking back to his chair, a click caught his ear. He halted. The clicking stopped. The track started. He continued walking, then settled back into his plush, velour armchair.

A heavy, slow guitar riff hammered through the room. The distinct voice of a man born to be a metal god wailed along. Chester pictured a dark sky, rain splats echoing over the silence, lightning jolting the night alive. The heavy drama of the track fit his mood. A sense of doom had washed over him last night, lingering into this day, like a thick black cloud. It had convoluted his judgment. In his doom-doused haze, his evening routine had faded into the back recesses of his memory.

The tune playing from the cassette seethed through the air, weaving into his ears. He jolted. Then froze. The very song that rang through his ears the last time he'd touched Violet. His stomach plunged. His hands shook. The room swirled around him.

He leaned back into the soft velour of the chair and closed his eyes. His memory had full control over his mind and his body. He let it take him.

He was there. In her bedroom. In their childhood home. She was smiling, playing with her dolls. He peeked in through the slightly open door. She beckoned him to come. She always let him play, even though *Mother* didn't allow him to touch dolls. Mother was out at the store. She'd never know.

He sat down on the plush carpet, close to her. Sweet lavender and vanilla drifted over him. Her hair always smelled delicious. He wanted to touch it. He reached out and slid his fingers over a long, dark lock. She looked at him, giggled, then pulled away. She gave him a doll and started the game of 'doing up' the doll in her own hands.

A ball of desire pulsed in the pit of his stomach. He wanted her. Every part of her. He wanted her all to himself. His fingers trembled as he tried not to touch her. They had a mind of their own.

His fingers crept up her arm.

Her dark eyes found his. "Saul." *Saul.* She was the last one to call him that. "You should brush your doll's hair."

"But I want to brush *your* hair."

"We should play with the dolls. I know we're kids, but, well, you shouldn't brush my hair."

"But..."

"Saul. I love you. Let's play with our dolls. You'll understand one day."

His hand slid into his pocket. His finger found the blade of the paring knife he had taken from the kitchen. Pain pierced his fingertip as the blade poked into his flesh. A burst of blood trickled over his finger.

He looked down at the doll he was holding. He tossed it aside. He looked at Violet. She stroked the doll's hair with a small, silver brush. He sat there, staring at her.

As he slid deeper into the memory, the music seeping through the present moment, from the tape deck perched in the corner of his room, played the perfect background. The electric guitar shot up several amps. The voice, dark and luring, told Chester that Satan was sitting and smiling while the flames got higher. The words seeped into his ears, weaving through his mind, shooting him back to that day, with Violet.

He continued to stare at his sister, Violet, as she brushed her doll's hair. The room tilted slightly. He pressed his finger harder against the tip of the paring knife.

It slid into his flesh. He stood and pulled the knife from his pocket. Blood trickled down his arm.

He loomed over her. The ball of desire swelled. It burst open, pouring hot lust through every molecule of his being. With a force he didn't know he had, he thrust himself on top of her. She fell back against the floor. The doll fell from her hand, rolling over the carpet.

"Saul!" she gasped.

The room spun. His arm plunged toward her. The knife sliced into her. She screamed.

His arm pulled up. The knife sliced a rough, zagged line up her body.

Her blood seeped over her, covering his arm with a warm, wet blanket. He raised his arm to his lips and licked her red life from his pale skin. Swallowing, licking, swallowing more, her essence flowed through him.

The copper taste tinged with lavender and vanilla trickled through him. The ball of anxious love in the pit of his stomach unfurled. Warm tingles probed their way through him, his heart, his arms, his fingers. The warm tingling reached his brain, wrapping around it. His mind throbbed.

Violet lay on her back, blood pouring out of her. Her head turned to the side, her dark locks were splayed out around her.

He bolted across the room, opened her closet, and fumbled through her dresses, smearing them with red streaks. At the back of the closet, he found her makeup kit. He pulled the rectangular, silver box from the floor and rushed back to her. Clicking open the buckle-style locks, he retrieved several plastic bottles.

She loved to mix her own makeup, experimenting with colours. He unscrewed a cap and held an empty vial up to her body, catching her red life liquid. He watched it seep down the sides of the plastic cylinder.

He kept his ear tuned to the doorway. Nothing. Mother hadn't come home yet. He continued to work on his life supply. After filling and securing a dozen vials, he rummaged through the makeup kit. He pulled the cap off a bright-red lipstick, twisted it open, and held it over Violet's face. Drawing savage circles around her eyes, he paused when she stirred.

A muffled sound escaped her lips. She went still.

Returning his attention to the makeup kit, he found a black eyeliner. He uncapped it and drew dramatic over-emphasized lines around her natural lips.

Filling in the black like he was colouring a picture, her bottom lip hung in a full pout, her top lip pointed up in a pair of peaks.

Makeup kit packed up and back in the closet, he returned to her. He leaned over, grabbed her doll, and stared down at it.

Her whisper grabbed at his ears. "Sssauuul. *Why?*"

He caved to his knees. He looked at her dark eyes, full of sorrow.

"We can be together," he spoke.

The room spun. Blackness washed over him. He laid down beside Violet, leaning into her, wrapping his arm around her. The warmth of her blood oozed over him. He closed his eyes.

DEMON
TWINS

Chapter 44

Demon Twins

Detective Mahoney parked the rental Sedan in an empty slot in the almost deserted lot. No techie truck with shiny letters—*CST*. No homicide squad cars. Even Sergeant Moustache hadn't arrived yet. Only a black pickup and a single police cruiser. His shoulders relaxed. He had really lucked out. It would just be him, the medical examiner, and some poor patrol officer sent to be first on the scene.

Sutton would be...what? *Angry? Furious?* No. *Miffed.* It had been a late night at the *Sparkles* dance bar with Quesnel, scouring and re-scouring files. The night had continued back in his shitty motel room at the Hav-A-Nap with a bottle of bourbon and cheap chips of motel ice. He'd ditched the motel early, before Sutton was up. Cruising the streets lining the massive parks of Toronto, trying to clear his mind, he'd re-routed the second the location crackled through the radio. Thank the homicide gods that Barbie had got him hooked into the radio system. Sutton would have to find his own ride.

The shiny black door on the rental car opened without a sound. He missed the soothing creak on the door of his vintage Pony when he arrived on scene. He shut it quietly, then walked briskly toward the cemetery entrance. The chill air sliced his face. A golden glow ebbed from the rising sun over a grey sky sketched in charcoal strings of clouds.

He walked under a stone arch housing a metal sign carved in black lettering: *Necropolis Cemetery.*

Cold trickled down his back. He proceeded to follow a cobblestone pathway lit with golden globes, paving the way along rows upon rows of graves. Bare trees, yet to be touched by the bloom of spring, hovered over him like black skeletons.

As he made his way into the belly of the beastly cemetery, the grave sites grew more elaborate. Mini castles with peaked roofs and stone archways protruded from the dark ground. Elaborately carved family trees declared the clumped clans of bodies that had been put to their final rest.

A shiver shook his bones. He tightened his tweed coat around his chest. Lengthening his stride, he hastily moved along the intricate pathway. He moved with ease over the cobbles, his hiking boots gripping loose dirt and pebbles. The cool air stung his throat. Sweat popped over his chest and back.

He secured his derby against his head and amped up the pace. The camera logging his life, with its bright flashing light, peeked into his mind, wanting to show him horrific images. He told it to fuck off. Sweat trickled down his back. The cold air in his throat and lungs warmed.

A flash of yellow tape caught his eye. A dark figure stood watch, donning a police cap, arms wrapped around his chest against the morning chill. On the other side of the yellow tape, Medical Examiner Winter stood, donned in cargo gear, a million pockets dotting her getup.

She stared straight up. He followed her gaze.

He gulped—two dark figures were stretched up in the trees. The world spun. The figures blurred.

That pesky spider, his imaginary friend, stepped a leg down his neck. The spider walked slowly, a tingling sensation trailing behind it, down Mahoney's neck, down his spine and the backs of his legs. Would he ever walk a path that didn't have a corpse at the other end?

Get moving. He didn't know how much time he had before Sergeant Moustache and his sidekicks would arrive. He approached the watchman.

"Detective. No one else has arrived yet." The young, fresh face was pale. His voice was fast, drenched in nerves.

Mahoney shook his head hard. *Get it together, Bug.* "Listen, I need you to go up to the cemetery entrance. Make sure no one comes in here unless they are authorized."

"Yes, Detective." He took three steps, then stopped and turned. "What do I say?"

"Just tell them the cemetery is closed until further notice."

"What if they ask why?"

"Tell them you have no further information at this time."

"Right. Thanks."

"You'll be fine."

The young officer nodded, then walked along the cobblestone path, heels clicking through the silence.

Mahoney blinked several times and shook the images out of his head before they could enter. Securing his derby, he ducked under the yellow tape and strode straight toward the pocket-dotted cargo pants. *What does she keep in there? Just like Blackwood's pack. I bet she could survive a whole night out here—or two.*

His thoughts could only distract him so long. The two dark figures came into focus. He slowed, paused, and looked up at them. Two human outlines, each dressed in long, black-lace gowns. The white of their faces was stark against the dark morning sky. Their black lips were forever poised. Blood-red circles wove around their eyes.

Two horror dolls, waiting for him to find out how they got here. They were launched, high up, attached somehow to two different trees. Their arms stretched out wide on either side of their bodies. They were dressed and displayed like demon corpses.

His imaginary spider friend now crawled up the front of his legs, into his gut, and up his insides. The camera flashed a bright light, capturing the new images to be added to his horrific scrapbook. His feet were glued to the dirt ground, his arms and hands numb.

"Detective." A sweet voice yanked him from the dark figures hovering from above.

"Winter." Mahoney nodded.

"Double doozy." She looked up at the hanging bodies.

"Yeah." He rubbed the bristle on his chin.

"How in the hell would someone get them up there? I've circled, several times, from different angles. I can't figure out how they are attached."

"They look like bloody demon corpses." He rubbed the back of his sticky neck.

She shuddered. "Yeah." She rubbed her arms with her hands. "Listen. I don't know how much time we have before—what did you call him? Sergeant Moustache?" She giggled. "Before he and his team arrive. I think we should take a close look before they get here."

"Yeah." He forced his feet to move and walked up to one of the trees. "How do we get closer?"

"I can climb. Just keep a look out. Warn me if you seen any movement on the trail."

"Sure thing." He stood at the base of the tree.

She pulled a pair of latex gloves from a pouch and snapped them on. She dug a boot into the tree trunk, clawed her hands into the bark, then launched herself up. Finding another hold with her other boot, she made her way up into the tree. The branches were bare, exposed. Pieces of bark crackled and fell to the ground. She climbed like a monkey. In no time she was at eye level with one of the corpses, from behind.

Retrieving a small, square black plastic tool from a pouch, she slid the square open, producing a magnification lens. She moved her gaze and the lens along the outstretched arm.

"Detective. Her arm is attached with several lengths of clear thread, maybe fishing line. From shoulder to wrist." She moved the glass along the back of the body. "And her neck. Several lengths of this clear thread is tied around her neck." She paused. "I want to get a look at her face, if I can."

Mahoney scanned the trail. "Still clear down here."

She strategically placed each of her boots into the crook of two separate branches, straddling the tree. She twisted and leaned around the tree. Almost face to face with the corpse, from a side view, she ran the magnifying glass along the pallid neck.

The spider crawled up Mahoney's face. Tingling crept along his cheeks, his nose, his forehead, and over his skull.

He waited. He stared at the blood-red circles weaving around the eye sockets, the pale white of the face, the black lips, parted and whispering to him, *"You were too late."*

"She's got crusted red splotches on the sides of her mouth. As if blood spilled out," Winter called down to him.

Flash. The camera went crazy. *Flash. Flash. Flash.* Now he had images that would forever be etched in his mind. The spider darted down his back. The tingling grew into a prickle, like pins poking him all down his spine. *What fresh hell is this?*

A rustle behind him made him jolt. He turned. Shiny platinum boots darted toward him. Fire hair spilled toward the ground as Agent Quesnel leaned and slid under the yellow tape.

"Mahoney." Her eyes darted up the tree. "Holy shit."

"Yeah. Vampire games."

"Your favourite sergeant is on the way in. Saw him pull up as I entered the trailhead. Wow, this is some cemetery." A slight smirk crept across her cherry lips.

"Got that right." He called up the tree, "Hey, Winter, Sergeant Moustache is on his way."

Winter stuck the magnifying glass back into a pocket. Like a fast little spider monkey, she crawled down the tree.

Mahoney pointed at Winter. "Medical Examiner Winter." He pointed at Quesnel. "FBI Agent Quesnel."

Winter nodded, then raised an eyebrow. "Tomlinson brought in the FBI?"

Quesnel clicked her tongue. "Not exactly. I'm here as a favour, for Mahoney."

Mahoney said, "Tomlinson doesn't know."

Winter shook her gloved hands; bits of bark dropped to the ground. "I need to proceed with an initial scan." In a slow circle, she walked around the tree she had disembarked, crouching and looking at the ground.

"She said the victim is tied to the tree with fishing wire, and has dried blood stains around her mouth." Mahoney looked at Agent Quesnel.

"Anything else?" Quesnel asked.

"No. Just what we can see from here." Mahoney looked back up at the dark, hovering figures.

"It's early. And two bodies. The timeline is off, and the killer is progressing." Quesnel clicked her tongue, staring up at the posed bodies.

Winter had halted, crouched down, and was peering at a spot in the dirt.

"Wonder if the victim was drinking blood," Quesnel pondered.

"Or the vampire killer fed it to her." Mahoney rubbed the bristle on his chin.

"*Vince the Vampire.* Self-given name. He wore teeth, bit into his victims—only for show. He had a photo album. The teeth left marks. He may have licked the blood from the wounds, but the real drinking came from the jars he collected after bleeding out a body."

What kind of sicko was he hunting?

"Hey, come look at this," Winter called to them.

They walked over. She pointed to the ground. Quesnel crouched, following Winter's pointed finger.

Quesnel peered into the dirt. "The symbol. Carved into the ground."

"Same one etched into the backs of the victims." Winter looked back up the tree housing one of the victims.

A voice barked from the trail. Tomlinson—mouth moving, moustache twitching, yelling orders—appeared at the yellow tape. He saw them. His faced flushed. He yanked the tape over his head and rushed toward them. "I see we have a party going here." He glared at Winter. "Has anything been touched?"

"Sergeant. I proceeded with an initial scan of the perimeter." Winter nodded, her lips a thin line, annoyance seeping from her chocolate eyes.

"That's all?" The sergeant glowered.

"Of course." Several CST coats trickled in toward the trees. "I need someone to photo this spot, here, before the dirt gets dislodged." She pointed at the symbol drawn into the dirt. She stood and stepped back, watching a techie execute the order. Two other techies, cameras in hand, went to work. Circling the trees, they took a montage of photos.

"Who the hell is this?" The Sergeant eyeballed Quesnel.

Quesnel extended her hand. "Agent Quesnel, FBI."

The Sergeant froze. "FBI? I didn't authorize you."

"No, you didn't. I'm a colleague of Detective Mahoney's. I've facilitated in past cases, out west."

"Don't get in my way." The Sergeant turned and raised his boom-box voice. "Everyone, gather here." He waved his hands toward him, summoning his crowd.

Mahoney found Winter's chocolate-brown eyes with his own. She rolled her eyes, smirked, then nudged his arm. "We better do as we're told."

Agent Quesnel looked amused. "Who is this clown?"

Mahoney took the bait. "Oh, you're in for a show. I just can't wait to see if he can handle you."

Mahoney stood next to Quesnel, at the back of the group, pretending to listen to the sergeant. He stared up at the trees, wondering why the sacrifice had doubled, hoping he could piece this together before the next kill.

Chapter 45

Sac of Critters

A chill washed through Mahoney as he walked into the back room at the morgue. A brightly lit corner intruded on the otherwise dim room. Glimmers glared off a row of glass beakers lining the wall. Examiner Winter was tucked away in her corner, scouring the face of a dead woman.

"Winter," Mahoney warned her of his impending approach.

"C'mere." Her chocolate eyes met his through her thick, round goggles.

He obeyed.

She motioned him over to the body covered in white cloth. "First body was easy to ID. Sixteen-year-old Tania Nash. She went missing February 25. ID of the other victim is a proving to be tricky. She seems to be older." She removed the white cloth, revealing the body. The body was spread open, the skin pulled apart in two flaps, away from the incision, held in place by clamps.

Mahoney regretted the mid-day meal he'd wolfed down on his way over. Burger in a box, with a side of grease. He swallowed against the foul taste stretching its fingers up his throat.

"Look at this." She leaned in toward the open body. She pointed with her gloved finger. He followed the direction. A massive cluster of larvae crawled inside the woman, their legs clinging to her skin and to each other. She grabbed a small flashlight, clicked it on, then hovered it over the open excavation. "That's quite a colony. Look. Here." She pointed with a long silver probe, revealing a small sac, nested inside the victim's ribcage, tucked under her heart.

"Eggs?"

"Yeah. Blowflies target dead bodies. A nice warm place to lay their eggs. Usually occurs during the active decay phase of decomp. You see here"—she pointed into the body—"her skin has started to liquefy and blacken. Active decay. We're looking at a minimum of eight days post mortem."

"What? She's been dead for at least a week?" Mahoney scratched the back of his neck, instantly regretting it. He wiped his sticky, sweat-coated hand on his pant leg.

"Active decay _usually_ starts at a _minimum_ of eight days in. Depends on the body and the conditions. Looks like several cycles of eggs were laid. At least one batch has hatched as indicated by our creepy crawlers here." She pointed at the batch of moving legs. "There are at least two other sacs here. One looks larger. I'll remove the sacs, get them to the lab, assign an entomologist. As they hatch, we can determine age. That'll indicate when they were laid, and give us a decent approximation of how long the victim has been dead," she stated matter-of-factly, adjusting her goggles.

Mahoney cleared his throat. "So in the realm of two weeks, but to be confirmed."

"Yup." She snapped the mini flashlight off and slid it into a pouch of the elaborate toolbelt fastened around her minuscule waist. "I'm just estimating. We need a proper timeline here. I'll collect samples and send them off for analysis." She popped open a snap on another pouch on her belt. Retrieving a small plastic vial and a set of tweezers, she plucked at least half a dozen of the little crawlers and placed them in the vial. She snapped the cap on, then lifted the vial up. "Hope you guys can give us a solid timeline." She placed the vial on a shelf of a steel box, along with other plastic bags and vials.

"I wonder where the body was...between death and display." Mahoney scribbled in his notepad.

She stood up, sliding the goggles on top of her head. "That is your department, Detective."

A shiver shook Mahoney's shoulders. "I don't get it. They've all been...fresh...so far."

"Yeah. Real doozy. The other one"—she nodded toward another steel slab, a couple feet away—"likely killed yesterday."

"One fresh, fits the pattern, except the timeline is early. A second one, had her for a while. Doesn't fit the pattern." What was the killer _doing_ with these girls? Why two? Why now?

"I'll get those crawlers processed. Secure you a timeline." Winter grabbed a clipboard off an adjacent steel counter and flipped through the pages. "Let's look at what else I've got for you."

"Sure." Mahoney flipped to a fresh page in his notebook. "Shoot."

"Let's talk makeup. As you can see, I've removed all the paint from both these girls. I've sent samples for processing. Didn't find anything unusual. No more animal hair." She paused, biting her lower lip. "Analysis came back on Trina—second victim in this case. Chemical makeup of all that paint on her face seems standard. Nothing sticks out."

Of course. "Standard makeup. Slip under the radar."

"But the hair on Trina's face, the full report came in. Get this…" She rescanned the page on the clipboard. "It's hair from a sable."

"What?"

She read from the page on her clipboard. "A sable. Species of marten. Small, omnivorous. Lives in the forests of Russia and the Ural Mountains of Siberia."

"What does that have to do with a make-believe vampire?"

She lowered the clipboard and smirked. "Hell if I know. Never was much of a vampire fan." She looked back at the clipboard. "Both these girls have puncture wounds. Look just like the ones on the last victim. I've started the tox scan, but…" She looked up from the clipboard.

"It'll come back clean."

"Probably. I did a swab of the open punctures. Clean." She looked back at the clipboard. "Tania is empty. No blood. No organs. The other one has lost some blood, but her organs are intact. She wasn't cut open."

"COD?"

"Preliminary look still points to blood loss. Look at this." Winters moved toward the unidentified body and moved the hair away from the neck with her gloved hand. "There are several slices, behind her ear. The only place I can find where she might have lost blood from. I need to examine her further." She released the hair.

"No blood at the scene. Again." Mahoney rubbed the bristle on his chin.

"Yeah. So, we're missing several quarts of blood. Again."

"It's possible he's drinking it."

"What? You mean real vampire shit?" Her chocolate eyes widened.

"Yeah. Agent Quesnel's input. Guess it's more common than you'd think."

"Or would want to know." She shuddered. "Eck. You know what that would do to your system?"

"No, I don't," he responded.

"Humans don't have the appropriate mechanisms to digest blood. Ingesting copious amounts can cause stomach issues. Even vomiting." She shook her head. "Enough of that. Let's talk incision."

"Let's." He flipped over the page in his notebook.

"I sent detailed photos over to the crime techs. Incisions on Tania are precise and match the ones on the previous two victims. Thin, yet deep. Hook at the bottom, near the stomach. Appears to be a gut hook hunting knife, as you suspected. It looks like the membrane was sliced clean from the organs before they were removed. So far, no exact match has been found. The jagged part on the hook seems to be the catch." She screwed her mouth up in contemplation.

"Custom knife. And the killer had practice using it."

"Likely. I'm hoping the techs can find a match. Using that strange bit of jaggedness, we might get lucky."

"Let's hope so." His gut told him they wouldn't. The jagged hooks, they were too *unique.* He suspected it was a one-of-a-kind custom-made weapon. Not the kind you bought over the counter in your standard hunting shop.

She flipped through several pages on the clipboard. Her chocolate eyes found his. "That's it. Wish I could give you more. I suspect the tox scans will be clean, the makeup is standard, over-the-counter product, and there's no trace of who did this left on either of the bodies."

He nodded, flipping his notebook shut.

"I'll focus on the larvae. A solid timeline might be our only big lead here."

He snapped his notebook shut and slid it into his pocket. "Do what you do. You're thorough. Precise. If there's anything here, you'll find it."

"I sure hope so." She nibbled on her bottom lip.

Chapter 46

Fire Power FBI Agent

Quesnel's heels clicked behind him. Mahoney had missed those platinum boots. They reached the war room door, and he pushed it open. Hot air clogged his nose. He flicked the switch. The fluorescent lights buzzed to life.

Agent Quesnel whistled. "This is fancy, Mahoney. I had my sights set on your stuffy little war room coated with Dara's mountain mist." She smirked.

"No, you didn't. But you did miss me." He shot her a wink.

She rolled her eyes. "Ha. Corduroy-clad men aren't my type."

"Very funny. Some women appreciate *vintage.*"

"Well, you let me know when you find one of those women." She wrinkled her nose.

He walked over to the fancy crime scene board, plastered with two separate collages. His face went grim. He turned to her. "Joking aside, I'm glad you're here."

"Me, too." She sat down in one of the plush leather chairs, leaning back and resting a boot on her knee. The fluorescent lighting glimmered off the platinum. "Wow. Sweet chairs. Beats that cheap, cracked plastic you got in your HQ."

"Yeah, well, our budget is tight."

She spun the chair slowly on its circular hinge, her fire hair gleaming under the bright lights. "Fresh paint, no chips. And look at that fancy board for the crime scene photos. Can't your HQ get in on some of this budget?"

"Doubt it. Not my problem anymore anyways."

"Oh yeah, your retirement. So much for that." She brought the chair to a halt, facing him. Folding her hands together, she placed them on the table. "You sure Sergeant Moustache won't bust in on us?"

"Nope. He's off trying to force confessions out of fake suspects. He didn't stay at the scene long. Pulled in anyone milling about that he claims looked suspicious.

Now that the bodies are building up, he's finding it harder and harder to prove his wonky theory that this is not linked to the Susie Slaughters. He doesn't want anyone saying the wrong thing."

"Good. He's out of our hair. While you were off at the morgue, I followed up with my colleagues. They've found other cases of killer vampires."

"Really? That was quick."

"Don't get too excited. They're all dead, or locked up. But, I'm hoping they'll find something soon. When you give a group of profilers something this juicy, they tend to stay up all night seeking out answers. Somewhat of an addiction."

"I get it." How many nights had he spent at his tiny kitchen table with a bottle of bourbon and a series of cryptic clues?

"The body count on your cold case, it was three?" She raised an eyebrow.

"Yeah." *Flash.* Blood-red circles dripped from eyes down a pallid face.

"And for this round, what, we've got four bodies so far?"

"Yeah." *Flash.* Two bodies hanging like demon corpses on nature's cross stared down at him. "Two singles and one double," he croaked out the words against his clenched throat.

"This is sixteen years later. The timeline is off. And he's doubled up on the kill."

"Yeah." *Flash.* He was back in the park, sixteen years ago. *Dammit.* He wished he could control the horror flick continuously playing in his mind. He had no hope it would go away. But if he could at least keep it to the present, he could focus. He shook his head, walked over to the crime scene board and stared at the photos.

"This killer has quite a *repertoire* built up. A well-evolved modus operandi. It's like magic how these girls vanish into thin air. He preys on potential runaways. Knows their situation. Knows their physical features, and their blood type. I think a child is given a full physical when placed in a foster centre. If he's planned out who and when, well in advance, then he's someone who figured out their blood types. We should look into the foster centres the victims disappeared from. Check out their process. And who has access to files." She placed her palms on the table and leaned over it.

"I'll get Barbie on it." Mahoney rubbed the bristle on his chin. "The ones who vanished from these places, I get it. Lots of kids. Only so much supervision. But,

Trina...how can a girl be taken from her bedroom, while her parents are home, and no one notices until she's long gone?" Mahoney asked.

"Elaborate preparation phase. Equally elaborate execution phase. Watching and planning. His meticulous process continues even after he's taken them. Bleeding them out and painting them. The icing on the cake is the elaborate display he leaves. One hell of a way to dispose of a body. This killer is the real deal. Where was he for sixteen years? Someone like this doesn't just *stop*."

"I concur. What was he doing? Did he go somewhere, then come back?" Mahoney's shoulders relaxed. Pieces clicked together in his brain.

"If he went somewhere, he may have left a trail." Quesnel licked her lips. "As I said, my colleagues, they've found a handful of other killer vampire cases. They're all dead, or behind bars. None of them were anywhere close to here."

"So now what?"

"More digging. Get my colleagues to amp up the parameters they're searching for. The vampiric serial killers we do know have liked to bite, even if it was just for show, and often some level of cannibalism was involved."

"Jeebus." Mahoney shuddered. Just when he thought it couldn't get any more horrific, it did.

"And our killer, he's progressed to taking the organs. What do you think he's doing with them?"

"I don't want to know."

"Well, we might have to focus on missing organs to find this killer. Layer on some cannibalism to our blood drinker. Don't you have a good rapport with the bleach-blonde tart who services Tomlinson?" Her cherry lips smirked.

"She's not what you'd expect. She's treated like...well, a tart. But she's got the makings of a solid analyst."

"Sorry." She bit her bottom lip. "Didn't mean to rub a tender spot."

"You didn't. I think she can help us."

"I appreciate your skills at human relations. Everyone seems to want to help you."

"Not everyone. Tomlinson's a real pain in my ass."

"Tomlinson's a dick. He's a pain in everyone's ass. His own team hates him. Sounds like this budding analyst is one of them. You say she can help. We'll need to dig back a ways. I think this guy's on a cycle."

"Yeah, I concur. Dixon was looking into it. He might have an update for us," Mahoney said.

"I'll throw that to my colleagues, too. Maybe this guy stuck to his cycle, even if his kills were in other cities and didn't look the same. It's a stretch, but I don't buy that this guy didn't kill anyone for sixteen years." Quesnel clicked her tongue. "Maybe I'll have a chat with Barbie. She hates Tomlinson. She's smart. She's our girl." Quesnel winked at him, her silver-blue eyelid shimmering. "You said you had Dara hook her up with her database access?"

"Yeah."

"Then we need to get this budding analyst on some searches."

"Scour the local scene for killer vampires."

"Precisely."

"I'll get her on this sable hair, too. I'm gonna head to that joint where Clan 13 played their show."

"Sounds good." She leaned back into the leather chair and folded her hands behind her head. Her fire hair glimmered under the bright lights against a baby-blue sky dotted with puffy clouds.

Chapter 47

Lee's Palace

Blasting through the intersection, the light flickering from yellow to red, Mahoney eased up on the gas as the black Sedan reached the other side. He glanced over at Dixon, clinging to the holy-shit handle, eyes darting around the street.

"You all right?" Mahoney snapped his gaze back through the front windshield.

"Yeah, fine." Dixon released the handlebar and smoothed his pinstriped pants with his palms.

Probably wiping the sweat off. Mahoney chuckled to himself. "The next right?"

Dixon checked the address Barbie had scribbled on the pink piece of paper that smelled like roses. "Yeah. Next right."

Dixon leaned into the door as Mahoney steered the car sharply to the right. This was the street. Somehow Barbie got a real boost in analyst capability with the flash of Dara's wand. He suspected Barbie was a lot smarter than she looked—or acted. He also suspected she was in survival mode with Sergeant Jackass watching over her shoulder. He'd left her deep in searches, working with Quesnel.

He pulled the black Sedan along a curbside, in front of a brick building plastered in neon graffiti. *Lee's Palace,* scrolled in bold weather-beaten lettering hovered high in the centre of the building.

Mahoney slid out of the Sedan and placed his derby on his head. As he sauntered over to the artistically decorated brick building, he wondered what this rundown palace would have to offer. He pushed open the creaky door, walked through, then held it open with one hand, waiting for Dixon to join him. Bright lights electrified his eyes. The space was tight and hot. The smell of booze and bad choices clouded the room.

Shiny, cracked wooden panelling lined an open space. A bar lined the right wall. A stage perched at the end of the room, a rectangular pedestal awaiting a metal god to screech to a wild crowd. An electric hum buzzed from somewhere at the back of the stage. A man was hunched over, up on the stage, examining a cluster of wires.

Mahoney walked down the wooden floor, Dixon in tow. Photos cluttered the walls, covering most of the chipped cherry paint, each one depicting tattooed men, sweat glistening on their shirtless, muscular chests, their hair hanging limp and tangled from a wild show.

"Must be the bands that played here." Mahoney nodded at the wall behind the bar as he sauntered along, inspecting each framed photo.

Dixon froze. Mahoney halted and twisted to see what had grabbed the detective's attention.

"I'll be damned." Dixon's voice was a raspy whisper as he stood, staring at a photo.

"What?" Mahoney sidled up next to him. A photo in an elaborate, golden frame worn with time grabbed his attention and refused to let go. A symbol. A circle, swirling over a slick, bulging bicep.

Flash. The pallid back of a young girl, covered in the same marking, swirling over her dead body, pulsed in Mahoney's mind.

Dixon intruded. "The symbol. On the girls. They look just like that." He leaned in closer to the photo. "Wonder if it's Clan 13."

Mahoney shook his head, tearing his gaze from the hypnotic symbol. The man with the symbol tattooed onto his upper arm was surrounded by three others, arms hung around each other, clinking the necks of their beer bottles. "Yeah. It's the same. Let's get some answers." He turned and walked toward the stage at the far end of the joint.

The man who was hunched over turned his head. "Be right there." His voice was deep.

Dixon snapped a photo of the picture of the muscular man with the symbol tattooed on his arm, then joined Mahoney at the counter.

Mahoney riffled through his inside coat pocket, retrieving a stack of photos.

A tall beast of a man thumped across the stage, towering over them, muscles rippling over his bare arms, a black leather vest covering what Mahoney was sure was a twelve pack of tight muscles. The man's shoulder-length hair was slicked back, his moustache groomed into two thick handlebars. He jumped down from the stage, his heavy boots hit the wood panelling with a thud.

"How can I help you?" the deep voice vibrated across the counter.

Mahoney's insides rumbled. "I'm Detective Mahoney." He flashed his badge. "This is Detective Dixon." He nodded his head toward Dixon. "We're looking for information about a band that played here." He laid the photos across the counter of the bar.

The man leaned over the photos. "Detective, you say?" He stared at Mahoney.

"Yeah."

"What's your interest in this band?" He looked at the photos.

"We're working a case. A homicide. The victims have this symbol branded on their backs. The same symbol is on the insert of this album by Clan 13." He pointed to the photo of the album cover.

The man raised his eyebrows. He blew a low whistle across the counter. "This is some weird shit."

"Yeah. This Clan 13, they played here, just over a year ago. You know anything about the show?"

The man placed both his massive hands on the counter, spreading his fingers out wide. "I don't recall."

"How long you have you been working here?" Mahoney asked.

"Ten years."

"Is the owner around?" Dixon asked.

"I am the owner."

"Lee?" Mahoney asked.

"Jim. Lee sold the place to me. Ten years ago."

"So, you would remember this show then?" Mahoney asked.

Muscle man looked him square in the eye. "We have a lot of shows here. I don't remember all of them, off hand."

Dixon piped in, "There's a photo on the wall of a band. One of them has this symbol tattooed on his arm." He pointed at the gold-framed photo on the wall.

Mahoney smirked. *Fancy Suit's got balls.* He glared at the massive man. "You said you're the owner of this place?"

Muscle Man pursed his lips, pulling the thick handlebars down his chin. "Yes. I am."

"Then you must know who took this photo? And be able to look up the shows that were booked here?" Dixon asked.

Muscle Man gritted his teeth against his words. "Fine. Yes. Clan 13 played here. Once."

Mahoney stood up taller. "You can tell us who worked that night?"

"You got paperwork?" The man glared.

Dammit. "It's in the works. You either give us the info *now* or we come back and intrude on your place a second time." Mahoney's gut pulsed. This wasn't going to work.

The man stared, his mouth screwed up in contemplation, the handlebars twisting along with it. "No. No way. I'm not giving out info unless you got the warrant for it. I don't want my staff *bothered*."

Mahoney leaned against the counter. Something sticky caught the elbow of his tweed coat. Sweat dripped down the back of neck. His blood boiled. "You're wasting our time. And yours. Might as well give it to us now."

Muscle Man leaned toward Mahoney, nostrils flaring. "Forget it, *pal.*"

"Who you calling pal? You lowlife." Spit flew from Mahoney's mouth.

Dixon grabbed Mahoney's shoulder and pulled him away from the counter. He looked at the Muscle Man. "Fine. We'll be back. It's a waste of your time, like my partner said."

The man paused, then shook his head. "Get out of here." He walked away and hoisted himself back up onto the stage. He stood and glowered down at them, his nostrils flaring.

"You need to cool it," Dixon hissed.

Mahoney glared at him and grabbed the photos scattered across the countertop. He shoved them into the inside pocket of his tweed coat and stomped across the palace and through the door. The cold air hit him with a dose of calm.

Dixon jogged up behind him. "I'll call Barbie. Get that warrant, pronto." He put a hand on Mahoney's shoulder. "I'm sorry."

Mahoney turned toward the baby face of the young detective.

Dixon continued, "Wasn't trying to step on your toes in there. Didn't want it to escalate. It's too good a lead. Besides, did you see his arms?" Dixon smiled.

"It's fine." Mahoney swallowed. "I get a little hot under the collar. I want to catch this vermin."

"So do I." Dixon nodded at the Sedan.

"Besides, I don't know how good of a lead it is. What? We're going to question a bunch of young punks that work at a dive joint about a show that happened over a year ago?" He walked toward the Sedan and tossed the keys to Dixon. "You drive. I'll call Barbie."

Dixon nodded. "You got it."

Chapter 48

Vampiric Nightcap

The hotel lobby of the Toronto Hilton glowed a soft orange. Mahoney slid a chair out from a round table, dropped his briefcase onto the floor, then plunked into soft leather. He set his derby on the table and leaned back into the chair. A wave of exhaustion pulled everything inside him down.

"Tough day?" a sweet voice trickled down to him.

He looked up. The same waitress from the other night stood over him, this time in a red dress snuggling close to her curves. He sat up straight. "Yeah, you could say that." He smirked.

"Bourbon. Double. Straight up," she said it more like a statement than a question.

"Perfect."

He watched the muscles in her legs ripple as she walked across the lounge, her red heels clicking across the polished floor.

A pinstripe suit caught his attention from across the room. Dixon approached, plunking into the chair across from him. "Detective."

"Dixon." Mahoney nodded.

"Glad to put some distance behind us and Jim's Palace."

"You got that right. What a bust."

"Yeah. Even if we get a warrant, what? We question a few employees that worked a crowded show over a year ago? I've already got Barbie buried in higher priority searches."

Citrus wafted over the table as the red-dressed waitress leaned over and set down a glass half full of amber liquid. She looked at Dixon. "Bourbon. Single." Another statement. She knew her clientele, even after a single visit.

Dixon nodded.

The waitress walked away.

"You boys having all the fun without me?" Fire hair greeted them with a smirk. Agent Quesnel reached out a hand toward Detective Dixon. "Agent Quesnel."

Dixon's eyes lit up like a kid in a candy store. He stood and pumped Agent Quesnel's hand with his own. "Agent. Pleasure to meet you. I'm a huge fan..." His baby face flushed. "Of your work, I mean."

Quesnel eased into a black leather chair and smiled. "You see this, Mahoney? True appreciation."

Mahoney snorted. "Don't let it go to your head. The kid's a newbie. Lacks experience." He shot Dixon a smirk.

Quesnel scanned the lounge. "This place is fancy. How can your low-budget operation afford this, Mahoney?" She clicked her tongue.

"This place would bust my budget. Sutton and I are tucked in at the *Hav-A-Nap* on motel strip."

"Motel strip?" She raised an eyebrow. "Isn't that place overrun with crack and cheap sex?"

Mahoney nodded. "Sure is. Didn't know that when we booked it."

"Oh yeah, sure you didn't." Quesnel winked at Mahoney. "Mahoney, you're buying me a drink."

Mahoney snorted. "Oh yeah?"

"Yeah. I found you something. Something good," Quesnel said.

The waitress interrupted their banter. "Excuse me." She settled Dixon's drink in front of him. "What can I get you?" she asked Quesnel.

"Rum and coke, please. Tall." Quesnel smiled at the waitress.

"Sure thing, sweetie." The waitress eyed Quesnel up and down, then turned and walked away.

"Well, look at you, being all charming." Mahoney narrowed his eyes at Quesnel. Dixon chuckled.

Mahoney asked, "So, what you got? Better be worth a fancy hotel-lobby cocktail."

"It is." She reached into her pleather bag and pulled out a folder, then snapped it onto the table. "Harold. Beheader of young girls."

"Great. Just my type of bedtime reading." Mahoney forced a chuckle as a chill crept down his insides. It was harder every night to scramble for a couple hours of sleep. He doubted Harold would be much help.

Dixon leaned over the table. "Harold?"

Quesnel leaned in to meet him. "Harold. He's holed up at the local lunatic asylum. Well, now it's been renamed. Queen Street Mental Health Centre." Quesnel pointed at the folder. "All his deets are in here." She paused. "Well, the details of his adult life. Need a bit more time to access his teenage years. Harold's got quite the elevator pitch. He has a thing for young girls. Especially their heads. All was well with Harold's adventures, until he was found with a set of heads, all lined up, staring back at him."

Mahoney shuddered. "Seriously?"

The waitress returned, set a tall glass in front of Quesnel, paused a moment to find Quesnel's gaze, then departed.

Quesnel looked at Mahoney. "Seriously. This Harold. When they took him away, they scoured his apartment. Everything matched his work, his fantasy. Except for one thing. A vial of blood."

Dixon raised an eyebrow. "What did that have to do with his murders?"

Quesnel answered, "Nothing. The blood didn't belong to any of his victims. It didn't match any part of his *work*. It was type O negative."

"Seems like something our current killer would have as a cocktail." Mahoney took a long sip of the sweet bourbon, willing the images of headless girls to stay away.

"Exactly," Quesnel said. She looked at Dixon. "Missing blood. Strange teeth-like punctures on the necks of the victims. Animal hair. I think we're dealing with a killer that is infested with vampirism."

Dixon leaned closer to Quesnel, his eyes widening. "One of his stacked paraphilias."

Quesnel nodded. "Exactly. I had my colleagues look for any such cases. Dead end. Nothing local. Any that did come up are either dead or locked up. I pushed it further. Added to our parameters. Anything to do with blood, teeth, and cannibalism. That's how I came across Harold. Apparently, Harold had acquired a certain *taste* for the heads of his victims. Chipped away at them slowly." She paused, taking a sip of her drink.

Mahoney swallowed against the swell of sick in his throat.

"It seems too coincidental to me that one of the most prolific murderers to ever be locked away in your sweet city just so happened to have in his possession a vial of type O negative blood that didn't belong to any of his victims. And that you are currently hunting a killer who is obsessed with precisely the same type of blood. Wouldn't you say?" She took a sip of the rum and coke.

"Can't argue with that." Mahoney took another long sip, dreading the night of reading ahead of him. Did he really need to add beheaded girls to the horror flick throbbing in the back of his mind?

Dixon sat back in his chair. "Brilliant."

Quesnel nodded at Mahoney. "You need to go see Harold first thing tomorrow. Use that charm of yours." She turned to Dixon. "He's quite the charmer. Especially with the criminally insane."

Dixon tipped his glass toward Mahoney. "Cheers to the charmer, then."

Mahoney glowered at them both.

Quesnel said, "I took another look at the timelines. The cold case. And the current one. The cold case killer left three bodies. The first one on April 3. The second one on April 8, six days later. The third one on April 17, another eight days later. Current killer is following a slightly adjusted timeline. April 5. Then seven days later, April 12. A day late. We weren't expecting a third body until April 20, if we adjust for the shift on the second one. But he doubles up and leaves us two bodies, four days early. I think he's escalating."

Dixon leaned in. "Something's happened. He's been triggered."

Quesnel smiled. "Yeah." She looked at Mahoney. "Hey, I like this guy."

Mahoney slid his notebook out of his pocket. "Medical examiner found larvae in the unidentified victim. Rough estimate, victim's been dead at least eight days. All the other victims were killed and displayed on the same night."

Dixon put his drink down. "Maybe she wasn't an intentional kill."

Quesnel joined in, "Maybe she died unexpectedly. He hung on to her, mourning, not wanting to purge outside of his cycle."

Dixon asked, "Then there's the misalignment of the start dates. Cold case, the first victim was killed on April 3. New case, first victim was killed on April 5."

Quesnel answered, "Yeah. Not exactly sixteen years later. Doesn't line up."

"I dug into this. First victim was killed on the *New Moon*." Dixon pulled at his chin with his pointer and thumb. "You know what the New Moon means to a vampire?"

Quesnel clicked her tongue. "Time to feed."

Mahoney took a swig of bourbon, looking back and forth between Dixon and Quesnel.

Dixon leaned back toward the table. "His victim type is well defined. Long, black hair. Five foot five. Thin build."

Quesnel took a swig of rum and coke, then clinked her glass onto the table. She leaned over, meeting Dixon halfway. "Exactly. These girls disappear, for weeks. Even months. What's he doing with them all this time? Grooming them? Training them? For what? Who is he modelling them after? I bet there is, or was, some dark-haired woman in his life."

"Before you two get too deep in this moon cycle thing, I got some updates." Mahoney intervened.

Dixon and Quesnel both looked at him.

"Winter got an ID on the second victim, at the last scene." Mahoney flipped through his notebook. "Keenan Kingsley. She was twenty-four. Went missing when she was sixteen."

"Eight years." Quesnel whistled. "Confirms our theory. He's keeping them. I doubt he intentionally killed this one. Did anything come up on the slices behind her ears?"

Mahoney flipped the page on his notebook. "Yeah. Winter had them analyzed, by the lab. They match something called a scarificator. Four bladed. Apparently they can have up to twelve." He snapped his notebook shut and grabbed for his drink.

"For bloodletting. To treat medical conditions. Wow. Maybe he was trying to take blood, without killing." Dixon ran his palms over his pants. "That's old school. Don't know where in the world you'd get one of those."

"I've got Barbie searching. Hasn't gotten anywhere yet. She's having trouble finding a custom made brand that matches the symbol." Mahoney clenched his jaw. "I wonder if he's making his own tools."

"Would be more *personal.* This bloodletting, it fits our theory. Taking girls. Keeping them. For their blood." Quesnel leaned forward, resting her elbows on her knees. "Part of his progression was taking their organs. For what, we don't know yet. Another part of his progression was getting their blood, but not having to kill them to do so. Feeding his addiction."

Dixon's eyes twinkled. "I wonder how many he's taken. This killer, he's pure, bona fide, serial breed." He took a swig of bourbon.

Quesnel dipped her cherry lips into her rum and coke, bumping the maraschino. "I've been studying this *breed* a long time. Never come across vampirism firsthand." She placed her drink on the table.

"I've got more," Mahoney said. "Barbie got a list of foster centres, on the outskirts of Toronto. There's over a dozen. Add in another two dozen in the Toronto core, and we've got a pool of hunting grounds." He took a sip of his drink, soothing his parched throat. "There's a bunch of smaller admin offices scattered, but appears to be one main admin office that services all the centres, in and outside of the core. Seems that the paperwork for every kid goes through this main office first. Not sure exactly what is included in that paperwork. Barbie couldn't access that info." He sat back in his chair.

"Wonder if blood type is on that paperwork," Quesnel said.

"And who has access," Dixon said.

"Dixon, can you follow up first thing tomorrow? Go to the admin office. I'd go, but I'll be chatting with Harold the beheader, apparently." Mahoney smirked while choking back a ball of sick swelling in the back of his throat.

"Got it." Dixon nodded.

"Good. Solid plan. Let's get back to moon cycles. Tell me everything you've been looking into. He might be slightly off on his timeline, but I doubt he'd miss the full moon. And what...that's in three days." Quesnel looked at Dixon, taking a long sip of her rum and coke.

Dixon's eyes lit up again as he launched into a ramble about moons—waxing, waning, and full, hunting and feeding, mapping the habits of a wild animal onto a human monster.

Mahoney took a long, slow sip of his drink, watching the profiling of a monster breed unfold before his eyes. He knew he was in deep. Deeper than ever before. He knew they'd find this killer vampire. With a budding analyst, a keen detective, and double profiling, there was no other way for this to end. He wanted—he *needed* to get this killer. Yet, tendrils of terror slithered through him at the thought of facing this monster head on. He didn't think it was the thought of facing the killer vampire, looking him in the eye, that caused tentacles of terror to sprout within him. He knew it was because he needed to put a real end to the adventures of a killer vampire.

Chapter 49

Spirit Wife

The room was dimly lit by six tall, black candles in ornate silver holders, circling a small cherry wood table. A coaster, with a picturesque mountain scene, sat in the middle of the table, atop it a crystal goblet half full of dark-red liquid.

Chester reclined in his favourite armchair, within reach of the table. The armchair had recently been upholstered in a dark-purple velour. He stroked the soft material along the contour of the chair's arm.

He reached over and lifted the crystal glass from the cherry table. Bringing it to his nose, he closed his eyes and breathed in long and deep. He loved a vintage...*Merlot.* It was...such a treat. Taking a long, slow sip, he swirled the liquid in his mouth, then let it run slowly down his throat. The smoky flavour with a hint of cherry and a dash of pepper was delightful to his palette.

He put the goblet back on the table and looked down at the photo album sitting on his lap. His long bathing routine over for the evening, he was dressed in red satin pyjamas, a matching robe, and slippers. Before he could allow himself to rest for the evening, he had to face his nightly torture. The task he dreaded, yet needed.

He couldn't sleep with it.

He couldn't sleep without it.

If he didn't face it, his dreams were filled with horrific images of Violet in his arms, a jagged cut up her torso, bleeding out. A reflection of what happened on the day she died.

If he did, his dreams were filled of images of her, gutted and bled out, her carcass neatly folded in a box for safekeeping, and her blood in a neat row of vials. A vision of what could have been, if he hadn't acted upon his emotions, taking her life without any forethought. When he would open his eyes from the dream, she would be hovering over him, her translucent, spirit body shimmering in the moonlight. She would be looking down at him, understanding and agreement bleeding from her ghost eyes.

Having absolutely no choice in the matter, he sighed, then opened the golden cover of the photo album.

He looked at the photo on the first page. Violet's milky face framed with long, dark hair, her black eyes staring into him, his insides quivered. She had just turned twelve when the photo was taken. Goosebumps sprouted down both his arms. He didn't want to continue looking at her. He had no choice. He let her eyes search him, asking him for answers. *Why, Saul? I could still be with you.*

"No. No, you couldn't. Mom wouldn't let you be with me. It was the *only* way." He grabbed the goblet and took a long, deep drink of the thick, red wine. Replacing it on the mountain view coaster, he turned his focus back on the photo.

Violet. Sixteen years old. The only sibling he'd ever had. He wished she were with him now.

He flipped the page. The day of her birthday party. A photo of Violet. A pink paper hat with yellow polka dots strapped to her head. She was blowing out the candles on a pink princess cake. How fun it had been…for the other kids. He had hidden in her closet and watched her play with all her friends. He didn't know why she wanted them. He could have been the only friend she needed. All those girls playing with all those dolls. Brushing their hair, changing their outfits. He wanted to play dolls with Violet. He wanted them to be his. His doll collection. But his mother would never allow it.

He flipped to the last photo that was ever taken of Violet. He remembered how she'd looked that day. She was all alone in her room, playing with her dolls. How she loved those dolls. Her door was slightly open. He peered at her through the small opening, just a crack. A slit of a view into her world. The world he so wanted to be part of.

He closed his eyes and exhaled. *Why, Violet? Why did you make me do it?*

He grabbed the goblet. He swallowed a massive swig of heavy liquid.

Opening his eyes, he looked back down at the photo. Electric tingles wove through his insides. He swallowed hard against the ball clawing up his throat.

Those eyes, looking at him, into him, asking him why. He could still hear her whispers as the life drained from her. *'Why? Why Saul?'*

He could still see the look of sadness in her dark eyes as she looked up him. *'Why? Why, Saul?'*

He could still feel her warm blood oozing over his hand as he slid the knife into her. He could still feel the pull of her skin against the blade as he slit her open. The copper tinge of her blood still lingered over his tongue. Her soft touch on his hand still made him shiver.

'Why? Why, Saul?'

Her whispers haunted his mind. He answered them. "It was the only way."

'The only way for what?'

"The only way for us to be together. Forever."

'I mean that much to you?'

"Always. Forever. You are my spirit wife now. No one can separate us." A tear escaped the corner of his eye and trickled down his pale cheek.

He looked at Violet. Violet looked at him. Just the way she was when her spirit became one with his. Long, shiny, dark hair. Perfect milky skin. Dark eyes. Pure.

The sadness poured out of him. Warmth rushed through him, reaching his fingers and his toes. The electric tingles surged, buzzing through him.

He picked up the goblet, brought it to his lips and titled his head back. Guzzling the remaining liquid, he swallowed the soothing drink. The warm fluid trickled down his throat, coating his insides with a rush of heat.

He stood, photo album open in his palms. He carried Violet over to his bed. It was time for them to retire for the evening. He and Violet, his spirit wife.

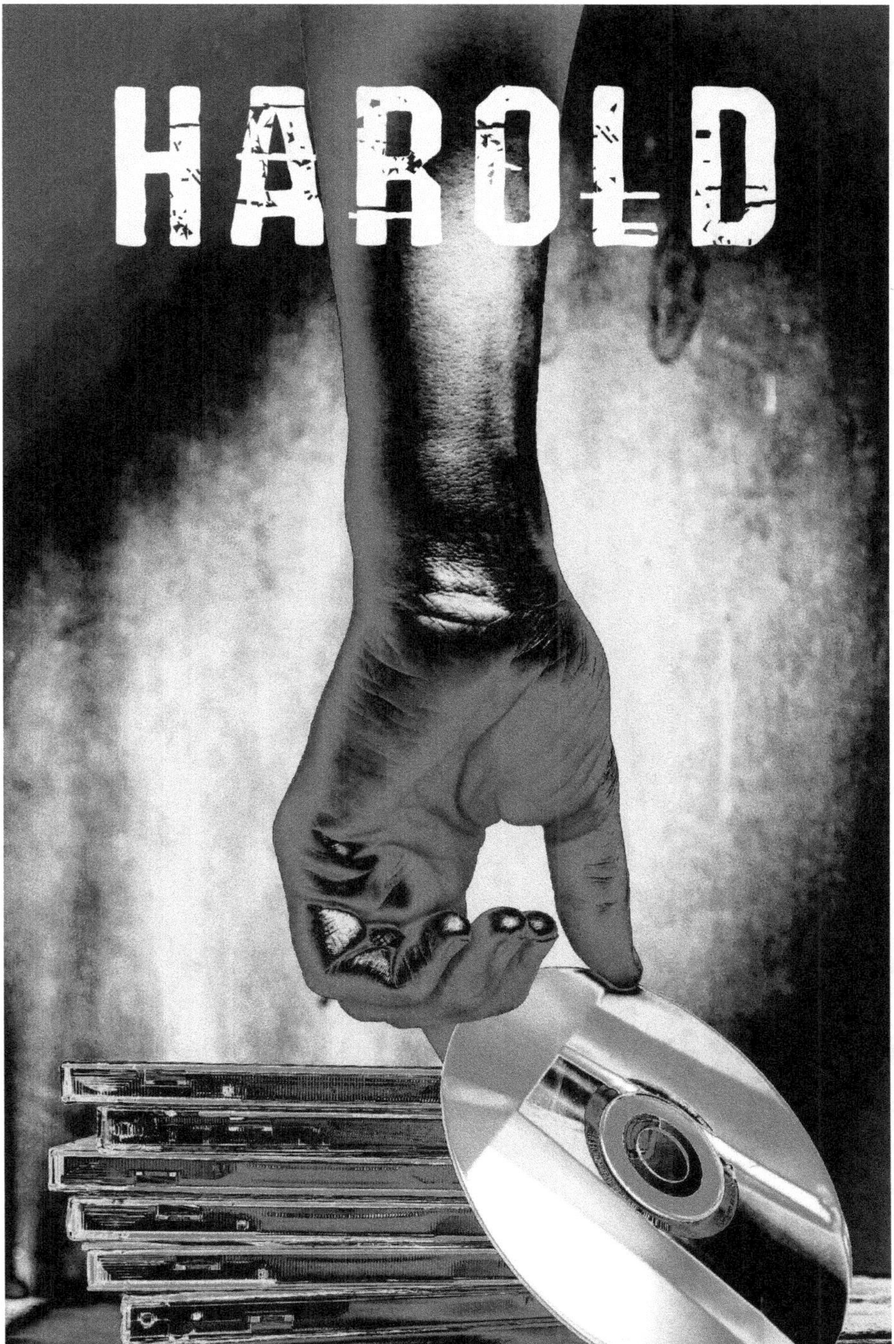

HAROLD

Chapter 50

Harold

Mahoney followed the attendant, staring at his bright-white shoes stepping quickly along. He hoped this wasn't a waste of time. The full moon was only two days away. The polished floor gleamed under the fluorescent lights running down the ceiling. The hallway plunged far ahead into luminescent nothingness. Mahoney picked up his pace, closing the gap between him and the young attendant, Todd. Heat swelled under his coat. They reached a T-intersection. Todd's shoes squeaked against the floor as he spun suddenly to the right. Mahoney wrenched his body and followed.

Todd halted. Mahoney dug his shiny black shoes into the floor, sliding to a halt, stopping a mere inch from the white coat.

Todd turned to a shiny steel desk. A woman with a tight bun and no makeup greeted them with a severe gaze.

"Margo. This is Detective Mahoney." Todd eyeballed Mahoney eagerly. "He's here to see *Harold*." The emphasis on the last word was strong, yet Todd almost whispered the name.

Margo raised an eyebrow. The rest of her face remained frozen. "Credentials?" Her stern gaze bore into Mahoney.

Mahoney slid his hand into the inside pocket of his tweed coat and pulled out his badge. He displayed it for Margo. She looked at it suspiciously for several moments.

Finally, she sighed. "Fine. You do realize who you are asking to visit?" She raised a thick eyebrow.

"Yes, ma'am."

She raised her other eyebrow, joining it with the first one, forming a broad unibrow. "Harold doesn't usually get visitors. His response to you and his resulting behaviour cannot be predicted."

"I understand, ma'am."

She sighed again. Her hefty unibrow lowered, then split into two again. "Fine, you'll need to fill this out." She snapped a clipboard onto the steel and slid it across toward him. She clicked a pen open with extra emphasis and clapped it onto the clipboard.

Mahoney scanned the sheet.

Queen Street Mental Health Centre and its personnel are not responsible for the safety of visitors to the criminal prisoners detained for treatment.

He chuckled. According to Quesnel, the Provincial Lunatic Asylum occupying the historic building on Queen Street had been renamed a mental health centre. Not all the wards, however, had been *upgraded* to modern standards. Harold's home was one of them.

After speedreading the form, he scribbled a signature and turned the clipboard back to Margo.

"Todd. Take him to the entrance. I'll notify Jim."

"Sure thing. Thanks, Margo." Todd's cheery voice clashed with the silence cloaking the room. "This way."

This kid is way too excited to be working here.

"So, you're here to visit Harold? Wow. I don't think he's had a visitor since...well...you probably know all about that."

"No, I don't. Indulge me, kid."

"Oh, wow. You don't know this story? Cool." Todd rubbed his hands together like he was at camp, sitting around a fire, about to tell his favourite ghost story in hopes of scaring his Boy Scout friends.

"Get on with it, kid."

"Elenoire was the last one to visit Harold. She was Deena's mom. Deena was Harold's last, you know, uh, victim. When Elenoire came here, well, they hadn't found Deena's, um, well, all her body parts yet. Elenoire wanted to know where they were. All her parts, that is. She didn't take any shit from Harold. I mean, she went in there on a rampage. She demanded Harold tell her where the rest of her little girl was. They had to drag her out."

"What did Harold do?"

"He had a hay day. Loved the attention. Played right along. He started giving her a detailed description of what he did to that little girl. It got real graphic. He got real emotional about it, too. All riled up. Then..." Todd looked back, slowing his pace.

"Go on, kid."

"He turned on her. Went on his own rampage. Demanded to know what right she had to be here making demands of him. It was bad. They had to...pull him off her."

"Off her?"

"Yeah, when he first started telling his story, he seemed pathetic. He was all calm and sweet and apologetic. He convinced this woman to come closer to him, to take his hand. Then, when he had her hand in his, he started to describe what he did and how much Deena enjoyed it. He grabbed harder and harder onto Elenoire's hand. That's when he got angry, stood up, banged the table, and started yelling at her. They had to go in and pull him off her." Todd's hands waved wildly as he spun the tale.

"And that was his last visitor?"

"Yeah. Police had enough to keep him locked up. No one needed to see him." Todd shook his head.

"Thanks for sharing."

"Of course. Is there anything else I can tell you?"

"No."

Todd stopped at another steel-coated kiosk. "This is it. Jim here will go over everything, let you in." A bald man with a severe black moustache nodded from behind a window.

"Thanks, kid."

"Good luck, Detective. Be careful." Todd looked sincerely concerned.

"I'll be fine." Mahoney nodded.

Todd turned and walked back down the white, sterile hallway.

Jim stood and walked around the kiosk. A long buzzing halted with a click. Jim walked through a steel-barred door.

"Detective, follow me," Jim instructed, his deep voice laced with confidence.

Jim proceeded down another white hallway. Mahoney followed, wondering if they'd ever considered adding some colour to the walls. The clicking of Jim's freshly polished black boots against the floor echoed. The fluorescent lighting glared down on them. Mahoney's collar stuck to his neck.

Jim tilted his head over his shoulder, passing his instructions back. "It's bright here. Once we get to the next door, the lighting is much dimmer. Harold, and his cellmates, need dark. They need humidity, so it's warmer in there, too. They need quiet, so keep your voice low."

Dark. Humid. Quiet. Geez. The...*residents*...sounded like a bunch of nocturnal animals.

Jim halted at the next steel-bar door. "You sure about this?" His eyes ran up and down Mahoney.

"Sure as I'm gonna get." Mahoney nodded.

Another long buzzing. Then a click. A steel-barred door, running from the floor to the ceiling, slid away, exposing a long, dark hallway.

"Walk down the hall, you'll see three cells. Harold is on the far right, against the wall. He likes walls. And, get a load of this," Jim chuckled, "Harold didn't want to be sandwiched in by the other two *beasts.*" Jim let out a full laugh, slapped his knee, then wiped the corner of his eye. "That's what he called them. His own cellmates. Beasts."

Mahoney wondered if Jim had always had such a sick sense of humour, or if being cooped up in a dark dungeon, guarding the criminally insane had made him this way.

"Thanks." Mahoney stepped through, out of the fluorescent lighting into the dimly lit space. Small pot lights glowed an orange hue from the ceiling above. The warm, moist air clung to his face. He squinted, adjusting to the change in environment. It was like walking into the night animal section of the zoo where they kept the bats, sloths, and reptiles.

Were nocturnal animals carnivores? He was sure an old, washed-up detective wouldn't be their meal of choice anyways.

He walked into the nocturnal den. A dark hallway gave way to an open space, like a cave. Three cells lined the back wall, side by side, separated by concrete walls.

Jim had said Harold was on the far right. Harold liked walls, and he didn't like being sandwiched between anything. Especially two beasts. *What the hell have I gotten myself into?*

A scrawny skeleton of a man scuttled across the floor in the middle cell. On all fours, like some sort of human spider, he scurried up to the steel bars.

The stuffy air closed in around Mahoney. He opened the top button of his shirt and tugged at his collar, pulling it away from his sticky skin.

Two eyes glowed back at him from the middle cell. A finger poked through the bars. The human-skeletal-spider hissed a welcome. "Hmm...vissitor. Sss."

Mahoney turned and walked over to the right. To Harold.

Ok, Bug. Play the freak's game. Get what you came here for.

The cell glowed golden. Along the back, a purple hue clung to the concrete wall. A row of green plants lined the right wall. A neatly made bed with floral pillows lined the left.

Geez. Who is this guy?

Then he saw him. Harold was sitting, cross-legged, on a circular, shiny purple cushion. A small table sat in front of him. In one of his wrinkly hands he held a golden bowl, in the other he held a wooden stick which he dragged along the perimeter of the bowl. A soft ringing vibrated through the air.

Mahoney's innards tingled.

Harold opened his eyes, lowered the mallet, and held up the bowl. Deep ringing vibes pulsed through the cell.

The tingling inside of Mahoney deepened.

Harold stared right at Mahoney. Mahoney stared back.

"Well, it seems I have a...visitor. I could feel you as soon as you entered the front door. Please, do sit." Harold gestured with his hand at a wooden chair perched close to the bars caging him in. "It's a shame we can't be in the same room. But apparently I was ill-behaved during the last encounter I had with someone from the outside world."

Mahoney sat down on the chair, staring at the scrawny little man hunched over on his purple pillow. Something seemed familiar about the scene. His mind flashed a memory of the gem store he had visited, just days before. He'd seen pillows like the one that Harold sat on, and bowls like the one he held. What had the store owner told him? Meditation pillows and singing bowls. *How the heck did Harold get this setup in here?*

Harold broke Mahoney's thoughts. "So, Detective, what can I do for you?"

Detective. Did someone tell Harold who was coming?

"Oh, the look of confusion. Your coat and hat are a dead giveaway. Not to mention the serious aura seeping from your veins. Is that...hmm...I'm detecting a special gem. Do you carry that everywhere?"

Play his game. He ran his fingers across the pair of polished stones in his pocket. He pulled out the pink one and held it up in his open palm. "Rose Quartz. It was a gift."

Harold's eyes opened wide. "Oh. I haven't seen a gem with that aura in a long time. Can I touch it?"

Mahoney stood and walked over to the bars. "Sure, why not." The instructions on the sheet he'd signed flashed in his mind. *Do not give the prisoner any items.* To hell with it. He needed Harold on his side. "You can have it. I got a new one." He slid his hand into the cell, holding the stone like an offering.

Harold licked his lips. He stood slowly, his skinny legs shaking. He shuffled across the cell, his slippers scraping along the floor. Harold couldn't have been more than five foot three. He looked like he had spent much more time on his meditation pillow than exercising any of his muscles. His skin hung from his arms as he held them out toward the pink stone. Harold curled his bony, wrinkled fingers over the rose stone, scraping his rough fingertips along Mahoney's skin.

Mahoney stood, staring at this frail figure.

Harold's beady little eyes met his. "You are not like the others. You aren't scared of me."

"I've seen a lot of things." Mahoney stared into Harold's eyes. A bubble of air caged them into the moment. The world ceased to exist.

Harold broke the spell. "Yes, you have, haven't you?" He took the stone, walked back to his meditation pillow, and lowered himself onto his crossed legs. He examined the stone with zest. "This is a real gem. Thank you. You know, I am sure we can help each other out. In more ways than you know." He held the polished, pink stone in his palm, stroking it with his wrinkled, bony fingers, like it was his pet. He licked his thin, cracked lips.

The wooden chair creaked as Mahoney sat back down. "I'm sure we can." The back of the chair buckled as he leaned into it and adjusted his derby.

"That's a swell hat, Detective. Always wanted to wear one of those. Don't have the head shape for it."

Mahoney chuckled.

Harold's thin lips stretched into a sick smile. "You see. You get me. So. Why are you here?"

"Susie Slaughters."

Harold snapped his gaze from the stone and stared through the bars. "Detective, you sure you want to go down that path?"

"Well, Harold, I'm already on it. There's no going back."

Harold stared. "What do you know about the Susie Slaughters? That case has been cold for a long time."

"Sixteen years. I was on it."

"Hmm." Harold stroked the stone. "But you weren't in charge." His pupils glowed in the orange hue as he peered across the cage, through the bars.

"Nope. I wasn't."

Harold closed his eyes and hummed. His humming faded away. He re-opened his eyes. "You weren't in charge. Your hands were tied, Detective. There was nothing you could do. Until now."

"You got that right, Harold." He didn't know what kind of game this freak was playing. He'd probably read every article that ever mentioned the Susie Slaughters. Now he was searching his memory, pretending to be a mind reader.

"Detective, you and I both know everything that was in the paper. We also know other stuff."

"What stuff do you know?"

"There's been a new development, hasn't there?"

"Yup."

"A new...kill?" Harold licked his dry, cracked lips with his lizard-like tongue.

"You got it."

"Black hair. Blood-red circles around the eyes. Black lips. Painted faces." Harold put the stone on the small table and rubbed his hands together. Flakes of skin fluttered, landing on the purple pillow.

"Bingo."

"He's back."

"We're on the same page here, Harold."

"Cut open, from heart to pelvis. Bled out, but no blood to be found."

"Yes."

"Did this new...victim...have the same puncture wounds?" Harold's dark eyes looked demonic.

The spider was back, creeping down Mahoney's spine. That was never printed. He had confirmed when he went through all the cold case files, and his old paper clippings.

"How do you know about that?"

"Did the new...victim...have the signature punctures...in her neck?"

"Yes." *How did Harold know this?*

"A long time ago, before I came here, I had...colleagues."

"Colleagues?"

"Yes. Others with special talents, like mine."

"You murdered young girls. You cut their heads off."

"Like I said. Special talents."

The spider crawled over each vertebrae lining Mahoney's spine. Its imaginary, long legs pricked his skin, chilling his core.

Play the freak's game. "All right. Your special skills allowed you to cut heads clean off bodies. Great."

"It *was* great. While it lasted." Harold ran his lizard-like tongue along his cracked upper lip.

"You know others who also had special skills?"

"Yes. Exsanguination. Takes skill. Takes *practisss.*" Harold hissed the last word. "Someone skilled enough to slice with such precision would apply the same level of skill to the extraction of the blood."

"What are you talking about?"

"The blood. The bodies were missing most of their blood. The blood was never found. The blood had been extracted. The blood had a *purposss.*" Harold narrowed his demon eyes as he hissed the last word.

"What purpose?"

"You know, my colleagues and I, we have special desires. I believe there's a term for them. Paraphilia. Yes. Such a child-like term. All you common people have one. Usually some stupid fixation with a toy or object or body part. My people, we...take them more seriously."

"Yes, Harold. I do know a little about your people. Your fixations are more serious. And you are special, you have multiple fixations that, shall we say, blend with each other." Mahoney adjusted his derby.

Harold's reptile-like eyes peered at Mahoney's hat.

Mahoney leaned toward the steel bars. "What does this have to do with the blood?"

Harold closed his eyes and picked up the golden bowl. He ran the mallet around the hand-beaten copper. A ringing vibrated through the room. "We are finished for today, Detective." Harold's wrinkled hand ran in circles around the bowl. The ringing grew louder. Harold hummed.

Mahoney walked up to the bars. "The blood. What about the vial they found when they caught you?"

Harold's eyes closed harder. His humming escalated.

Mahoney stood for several moments, watching the wrinkled reptile-like man humming and playing his golden singing bowl. *Dammit.* He thought he had this nocturnal creep talking. Why did he shut down?

He made one more attempt. "Harold. Why did you have a vial of blood?"

He stood. He watched Harold. Harold hummed louder, never opening his eyes.

Realizing his efforts were futile, Mahoney adjusted his derby, then turned toward the barred door.

Chapter 51

European Imports

Barbie ran up to him, her red pumps clicking fast against the floor. "Bug."

Mahoney halted, turned, and looked at her.

Her hand shot to her mouth. "Oh. I mean, *Detective.* Sorry. It's just that Dara calls you that all the time and it got in my head. I'm so sorry." Her face went pink.

"It's okay."

Her hand slid from her face. Her pink lips moved. "What does it mean?"

"Just a name my trusted team members call me."

"Oh." She looked down at her red pumps.

"Seems you're one of my trusted team members now, aren't you?" He smirked.

Her face flushed a red-pink glow. She looked at him. "I suppose, yes." She smiled.

"I'll make you a deal. Tell me your real name, and you can call me Bug." He rubbed the bristle on his chin.

Her cheeks shone pink. "It's Briar."

"Works better for me."

She smiled. The pink flush left her cheeks. "You got a deal, Bug."

"What you got for me, Briar?" he asked.

"Oh..." She looked at the paper in her hands. "The sable hair. It's used in several products. Including high-end makeup brushes." She looked up from the paper.

Mahoney raised an eyebrow. "Really? This killer takes his makeup artistry seriously. Sounds like something he might purchase. We need to find out where these high-end brushes can be purchased."

Briar smiled like a cat who just caught a fresh meal. "Already did." She handed him a sheet of paper—pink and smelling of roses. "List of stores here. The one on the top is known for it's high-end, imported products."

Mahoney took the paper. His shoulders relaxed. "You're one step ahead of me."

"Good." She slipped him another sheet of freshly pressed paper. "I also got you a warrant to search the sales records, for the first three stores on the list."

Mahoney smiled. "Your sergeant didn't protest?"

Barbie smiled. "Found a way to get it done discreetly. Didn't want you walking away with nothing, like at the dive palace."

"This is top-notch analyst work, Briar."

"Thanks. I gotta get back to those other searches you gave me. Try and make some more progress before the sergeant gets back."

"Keep me posted."

"Of course." She turned and pattered back to her desk. She sat down and started typing fast clicks over her keyboard.

It seemed there was a chance he might catch a killer after all. The day he removed himself from the circus act spinning around him, taking a few of the less loony participants with him, was the day they started moving forward. Whoever this human vampire was, he was going to find him.

Chapter 52

Katie's Kraft

Dance music pulsed through speakers mounted high in the corners of the massive space. Pot lights glowed purple, pink, yellow, and blue. It was more like a dance bar than a makeup store. In the downtown core of Toronto, nestled in the centre of a massive mall, *Katie's Kraft* housed rows upon rows of facial products, creams, perfumes, lipsticks, and more.

"Jeebus." Mahoney glanced at Dixon.

Dixon, eyes wide, stood at the edge of the store, taking it all in. "I've never seen anything like it."

"Let's get this over with."

"Yeah."

Mahoney took the first step into *Katie's Kraft*. Dixon followed with timid steps. The neon space swallowed them up. Two outsiders in a strange world of high-end makeup.

No more than three steps in, a woman in a fluorescent-pink getup, tight mini skirt, and matching jacket with round, puffed-up sleeves, approached. Her fuchsia lipstick matched her puffed-up suit.

"Can I help you?" a high-pitched voice with a thick coat of cheer asked. The woman continued to approach, closer than Mahoney would have liked.

A cloud of lily and musk devoured him as he coughed and attempted to answer. "Yeah. I'm Detective Mahoney. This is Detective Dixon. We need to talk to someone in charge here."

"Oh, well, I'm Katie." She fluttered her thick, black eyelashes.

Mahoney stared.

Katie continued, "Katie. *Katie's Kraft.*" She smiled, glaring at him like everyone knew who *Katie* was.

"Right. You run the place?"

"I do."

"I need to know about makeup brushes. Made with sable," Mahoney said.

Katie smiled, again. It seemed real this time. "The best ones. We've only been selling them for five years. We ship them in from Europe. Is it a gift? For your wife, or girlfriend?"

"Gift?" Mahoney shook his head.

Dixon intervened, "We're working on a case, miss. We need to see your sales records, for these brushes."

Mahoney nodded.

"Oh my. What would my imported brushes have to do with a...*crime.*" Her eyelashes fluttered.

"We need to see your sales records," Mahoney repeated Dixon's statement.

Katie frowned. "Do you have a warrant? That's personal information of my clients."

Dixon pulled a paper from his pinstripe suit pocket. "Yes, miss. Right here. We need records on all purchases." He handed it to her.

Mahoney watched Katie as she unfolded the paper, inspected it with painstaking scrutiny, then scrunched her mouth up in a less-than-flattering frown.

"I see." Katie turned, whipping her long, curly hair, tied with a hot-pink scrunchy, over her shoulder. "Follow me."

Mahoney shot a look at Dixon. Dixon shrugged. They followed Katie across the store, bright lights and music pulsing.

They met Katie up at a glass counter spanning the entire front end of the store. Katie typed furiously on a computer keyboard, then stared at the screen. "You need the records for all purchases of the sable brushes, since we started selling them?"

"Yes, miss," Dixon confirmed.

"That'll take a few minutes. You're welcome to browse while you wait." She looked at them while the computer whirred, chugging through sales records. "You never know. You might find a gift for your wife, or girlfriend."

Mahoney frowned. *What wife? What girlfriend?*

Dixon smiled. "Thank you, miss. We'll do that." He tapped Mahoney's shoulder, then signalled for him to follow. "This is quite the place," he whispered when they were out of earshot of Katie.

"Got that right."

"Good thing we got the warrant."

"Yeah. Barbie had it ready to go before we headed out the door at HQ. This is the only place that sells high-end imports. Her gut was right."

"Yeah. I had no idea she was..." Dixon paused.

"Smart? Helpful? Useful?" Mahoney smirked.

Dixon sighed. "Yeah. Guess I need to open my eyes. I could learn a thing or two from your *human relations* skills. Wonder if you could have charmed the guy at the foster care admin center better than I did.:

"A bust?"

"Yeah. The guy said they run a real tight ship. No-one gets any information about the kids coming in unless they are authorized. Wouldn't tell me what information is in those files. Said I needed a real special warrant to access government information on minors. I'll talk to Barbie when I get back to the office."

"Sounds good."

Mahoney stole a glance back at Katie. He willed the computer to search faster. He wanted to see how many brushes were in the claws of the people of Toronto. And how many names he'd have to search through to find the human vampire painting young girls, turning them into demon dolls.

Chapter 53

Dixon

The tires on the Sedan squealed, spewing gravel in all directions. Mahoney took a sharp right. He pulled up to the glass doors of the Toronto Police Service.

Dixon peered at him from the passenger side. "You're not coming in?"

Mahoney shook his head, scanning the parking. A shiny police vehicle occupied Tomlinson's spot. "Nope. I need to stay clear of your boss."

"What's the plan?"

Mahoney squinted into the bright sun glaring through the windshield as it hovered low on the horizon. "You need to go in there and fit into Tomlinson's investigation. You've got a long career ahead of you."

"Fine." Dixon narrowed his eyes. "I'll pursue the names from the makeup store."

"Yeah. Give them to Barbie."

"There are hundreds. It'll take a while."

"Prune them. Start with the men. That's gotta narrow it down."

Dixon nodded. "Where are you going?"

"I'm meeting Quesnel."

"She's steering clear of here, too?"

"Yup. Your sergeant doesn't want her input."

"But you do."

"I do. We're meeting somewhere we won't be found. We need all the profiling power we can get. Seems you got a knack for it." Mahoney shot a smirk across the car. "Keep following your gut."

"Will do." Dixon opened the door and slid out.

Mahoney put the Sedan in drive, peeled out of the parking lot, and drove toward the downtown core, under the glow of the setting sun.

Chapter 54

Where's the Chicken?

Stale piss mixed with old sweat violated Mahoney's nostrils as he walked into the *Tasty Chicken House*. He scanned the joint. Dim pot lights fought against the dark vibe. The early evening, mid-week crowd you'd expect to be in this place was scattered, each of them nursing drinks alone.

Mahoney smirked. It was perfect. In a random location, between HQ and his motel, Tomlinson would never find him here. And he'd always loved this dive joint disguised as a chicken house. The warm air gushed over him as the door clanked shut behind him. He walked over to a corner table and plunked down in a cracking wooden chair.

A skinny, pale waitress with a tiny jean skirt and an even tinier tank top stomped up to him. "Drink?" She raised a dark, pierced eyebrow.

"Old Milwaukee and a plate of Doritos." He'd love a bourbon, but he knew better than to order that here.

The waitress turned and walked away.

His phone buzzed against his holster. He snapped it open. "Mahoney." His gruff voice broke the heavy silence of the room.

"Where are you?" Sutton's voice squeaked several octaves higher than usual.

"Taking a break." Mahoney shook his head and leaned against the cracking wood.

"You missed Tomlinson's meeting. Barbie and Dixon both claim they don't know where you are. I don't believe them. I don't believe *you*." Sutton's glare seeped through his voice into the phone.

Mahoney stifled a chuckle. "Told you. I'm taking a break. All this paper duty at the desk that Tomlinson has me doing is hard work."

Sutton sighed. "Look. Don't shut me out. I know, I'm supposed to do my play-by-the-book thing. You, well, you're supposed to be *you,* according to Sarge. Whatever that means."

"Yeah. Whatever that means."

The waitress returned and dropped a worn glass and a paper plate piled with orange chips on the table. No coaster. Cheap beer splashed onto the chipped table.

Silence seeped through the phone. Had he gone too far? He wanted to protect Sutton. His gut told him to cut him out of the path he'd chosen. Would Sutton understand?

"Mahoney. You still there?" Sutton sighed.

"Listen...I'm just taking a break. You lead the show from our end." He rubbed the back of his neck.

"Fine." Sutton sighed again, deeper this time. "You OK?"

Flashes of dead boys with no eyes pulsed through Mahoney's mind. A stream of young corpses followed, their red demon eyes swirling through the crevices of his brain. He shook his head. "Yeah. I'm fine."

"OK. Take your break. Get back here later."

"Got it." Mahoney snapped the phone shut, wondering how long he could stave off Sutton and his stupid rabbit foot. Thing was, Mahoney knew Sutton had good instinct. It didn't matter if he had a gnarly claw with scraggly fur to remind him of it. He slid his hand into his tweed coat pocket and pulled out the Tiger's Eye.

"What's that?" a sultry voice interrupted him.

He looked up. Fire hair welcomed him. He stuffed the stone back in his pocket. "Nothing."

Quesnel sat down in a wooden chair across from him. "What the flying freak *is* this place?"

"A hole in the wall. I came here a lot, last time I was hunting a murderer in this city."

"How's the chicken? I'm famished."

"They don't have chicken."

She clicked her tongue. "Of course they don't. What *do* they have?"

"Old Milwaukee. And Doritos."

"All right then. Guess I'm a beer girl for the moment." She paused. "How was your visit with Harold?"

Mahoney snorted. "Useless."

"What? He didn't want to talk?" She screwed her mouth up. "Thought he'd be lonely after all those years without a visit."

"Yeah. Well, he talked. Actually, he was quite chatty. Gave me nothing though." Mahoney rubbed the bristle on his chin, then took a swig of beer. The watery fluid was less than satisfying.

"Go back, see him again."

The skinny, pale waitress returned. She raised her pierced eyebrow at Quesnel. "Drink?"

"Old Milwaukee." Quesnel smiled.

The waitress rolled her dark eyes and walked away.

Quesnel chuckled. She looked back at Mahoney. "You need to go see Harold again."

"Why?" He frowned. "Don't have time for that."

"Sure you do. You want to get this killer, don't you?"

"Yeah." It was all he wanted.

"You got any better leads?"

"No." He shot a glare at her, then drank another ample sip of watery beer.

"He wants to talk. If he didn't, he wouldn't have talked to you at all."

The waitress hovered over them as she placed a coaster on the table in front of Quesnel, followed by a clear glass of bubbling beer.

"Thank you." Quesnel smiled at the waitress, then dipped her cherry lips into the glass.

The waitress half smiled, then walked away.

Mahoney chuckled. "Well, looks like you earned the royal treatment."

Quesnel eyeballed the pile of orange chips. "What? You didn't?"

"Nope." He took another pull from his drink. "Fine. How do I get Harold to talk?"

"You've warmed him. Now, give him something. What's most important to him?" She twisted her mouth into a contorted smile.

"His fantasy." He hated how much he'd learned about this breed of serial killers, as Quesnel referred to them.

"Feed him, like you fed Seth."

Seth. The killer he caught, then paid visits to regularly, learning more and more about the college kids he'd killed and painted up like Glam Rock Gods. He got things for Seth. And Seth told him things. He pictured Harold, scrawny, wrinkly, hunched over, hissing through the cell bars. Could he really get through to this weird nocturnal creature?

He looked at Quesnel. "You don't understand. Harold is not like Seth. Harold is...he lives in a fucking warm, dark cell like some sort of nocturnal animal at a zoo."

Quesnel took a long pull of beer. "I get it. He doesn't *look* like Seth. But he is like Seth. Seth had an obsession with college boys and rock gods. His fantasy was to become what he idolized. He used humans to create his fantasy." She leaned over the table. "Harold was, still is, obsessed with young girls. I'm not sure what Harold's full fantasy is, but the heads of his victims are at the root of it. Think about how you got Seth to open up."

Mahoney leaned back against the wooden chair and rubbed the bristle on his chin. "I listened to him talk about his glam dolls."

"Yeah. So do the same, with Harold."

He sighed. "Listen to him, talk about girls and their heads." He shook his head and leaned over the table. "Not my idea of a good time."

"Another?" The pale face of the waitress loomed over them.

"Yeah." Mahoney nodded.

The waitress spun and trudged across the room.

Quesnel looked right into Mahoney's eyes. "I get it. You don't *want* to hear it. But you *have to.* We still don't have any concrete leads telling us who our killer is. Harold didn't have the vial of blood by coincidence. He knows something. You can make him talk."

"By listening."

"Yeah. And take some leverage with you."

"Leverage?"

"Harold doesn't have access to his trophies anymore. At least share with him something about the trophies of the killer we're hunting. If Harold was connected to this guy, he could live vicariously through the trail he left."

The waitress plunked two more drinks on the table.

Mahoney stared into the hazy glass brimming with cheap beer and pondered Quesnel's words. A nocturnal human-like creature locked in a moist cave seemed to be his only lead in hunting down a human vampire. How the fuck had he gotten here?

Chapter 55

Saul the Slayer

Harold sat cross-legged on his purple meditation pillow. His back was straight, eyes closed, and hands resting on his knees palms up. A low hum rang in the background. From where, Mahoney couldn't tell.

Harold kept his eyes closed. "Detective. You've come to visit again, so soon. How nice."

Mahoney had barely made it before the institute closed to visitors for the night. He couldn't believe he was back here for a second visit with Harold in the same day.

"Hello, Harold." *Fucking lunatic.*

Harold opened his eyes, stretched his legs out and arched his back like a cat rising from a nap. He stood and walked over to the back corner of his cell.

Mahoney heard a click. The low hum stopped.

Harold walked over to a small desk and sat in the matching wooden chair. "They gave me a small CD player. I can't open it. Apparently a CD is sharp. Could be a weapon. The one album I can listen to is Buddhist chants. They say it keeps me calm. More *manageable.*" A creepy laugh curled around his cell. "I guess I'm something to manage. Now, what brings you by, *Detective?*" Harold leaned back against the chair. His mouth twisted into a sick grin. His eerie stare fixated straight ahead. He didn't blink.

Mahoney rubbed the bristle on his chin. Harold hadn't given him anything during their previous visit. He knew he had to throw him a gory tidbit if he was going to get this lunatic to talk. "You know about the Susie Slaughters."

"Yes, I do, Detective." Harold licked his cracked lips.

"You know there have been recent victims that resemble the young women from before."

Harold rubbed his scaly, thin hands together. "Yes. I do get news. But it's rather...delayed and incomplete. It appears our friend has left us two more *treats*, hmmm?" Harold's beady eyes peered from behind the bars.

"Yes. There's been another one. This time, two bodies. Tied up in trees."

Harold whistled. "Wow. That, I'd like to see. Sounds spectacular. More young, fresh *treats*, I presume?" His beady eyes took on a demonic hue.

"I can show you some pictures."

"Really?" Harold blinked several times.

"Yeah. But you gotta spill, give me whatever you know."

"Know?"

"Finish telling me about the blood. And the vial they found in your possession, when they locked you up."

Harold snorted.

Play his sick game. "Listen, I can walk right out of here. Not come back. Or I can show you what I have. Two more victims." Mahoney waved a folder in front of Harold's cell.

Harold's eyes followed the folder. "You show me. I tell you about the blood."

"Yes."

Harold's beady eyes bored into the folder. "Fine. I promise."

He better talk. Mahoney held the folder through the bars into the cell.

Harold stood and shuffled over to the bars. He took the folder and sprinted back to the desk.

As he opened the folder, his beady eyes glowed and his serpent-like tongue ran across his cracked upper lip. "This is quite ssspectacular."

Mahoney sat on the chair facing the cell, waiting in silence. *This place is gross. Sick freak better know something.* "Harold...what's going on over there?"

Harold raised a bony finger. "Patiensss. Plenty of details here."

There were. But none of them had led to anything.

"Well, well. Look at this." Harold stood, walked over to the bars, and held up a picture.

Mahoney stared back at a photo of a black-grey miniature castle in the heart of the Gothic cemetery. An elaborate family burial, perched in front of the two trees holding the victims on display. "What does this have to do with the vial of blood?"

"Detective, have you ever heard of Saul the Slayer? Saul was fourteen years old when he killed his sister. He cut her open. From heart to pelvis. It was crude. His first time. He took her blood."

"Saul the Slayer?"

"Yes, *Detective*. They never found his sister's blood. It was his little secret."

"How do you know about him?"

"He was my roommate. In the prison for juveniles. We were just children. Children with special skills. Living in our own world." Harold went back to his meditation pillow and sat down.

"What happened to the blood?"

"He stored it, for when he got out."

"He was released?"

"We all were. Declared rehabilitated. Given a clean slate. Fresh start. We weren't kids anymore. We were adults. Ready to manage ourselves."

"What happened to Saul?"

"Don't know. Lost track of him. We went our separate ways. But when the Susie Slaughters occurred, well, it sure looked like Saul the Slayer."

"Saul the Slayer," Mahoney repeated the gruesome words.

Harold stared at him. "You won't find anything on him, though. That was the name he gave himself. Since he was a minor at the time of his...*activities,* his full story was never printed. You have to be an adult in this world to get credit for your work." He licked his cracked upper lip.

Mahoney half expected the tip of Harold's tongue to split into a fork. His brain buzzed. He needed more. "He was your roommate?"

"Yes. He was."

"The vial of blood?"

"Type O negative. Rare." Harold closed his eyes.

Stay with me. "You took it, from this...Saul?"

"Yes." Harold started to hum.

No. Don't go. "Harold. Wait. What does this have to do with the cemetery?"

"I suggest you check into who is buried in that Gothic cemetery. It's been around a long time." Harold hummed louder.

"Harold, you promised. You'd tell me what you know."

Harold snapped his beady eyes open. "The blood was Saul's trophy. He was my only friend. I took it." He swallowed and licked his flaking lips. "I don't know where this Saul is now. I don't know if that was his real name. He talked about his sister constantly. She was buried in that cemetery. At least, that's what he said. But you never know if a lunatic is telling the truth, now do you?" His eyes snapped shut and his humming vibrated through the dark, moist cell.

Mahoney stood, staring at Harold. Was he telling him the truth? Was Saul the Slayer responsible for the Susie Slaughters? For the two bodies hanging from the trees in the Gothic cemetery? And who was Saul, really? More importantly, how would he find him? Before the next slaughter.

Harold refused to have his meditation interrupted. Mahoney stood and stared at him for several moments, then took his cue and stood. Time to get out of this disgusting place.

Chapter 56

Hallucinations of Violet

Chester walked down the stairs toward the black door. Stepping onto the pavement, he knocked on the door with his black-gloved hand. He waited. He raised his hand to knock again. A metal slit scraped open. A pair of eyes stared at him.

Chester spoke, "Death Love Trap."

The slit scraped closed. A chill crept up Chester's back.

The door opened. Spike stood, boots rooted into the pavement, sturdy frame casting a thick shadow.

"Chester." Spike reached out a fist.

Chester returned the greeting with a pump of his fisted hand. People were strange. They had all sorts of customs, protocols, and made-up rules you had to follow to fit in.

Spike turned and walked down a dark, concrete hallway. Chester followed.

"You here to see Mika?" Spike asked.

"Yes."

Chester followed Spike in silence for a few moments until they made a right turn down another dark, concrete hallway. He appreciated that Spike didn't chatter too much. He could always fit the bill, be who he needed to be, but right now it would be difficult. A dark cloud of a mood had fallen over him. His nightly routine walking down memory lane with the family photo album hadn't been working. He'd been having horrible nightmares. The cast of characters had grown. His mother had made multiple appearances, as if rising from her grave to come and tell him what a failure he'd been. And Violet—well, Violet was there, but she didn't whisper to him. She wasn't a floating spirit shape. She was all cut up and bleeding, and her soul slithered away to some dark corner of the ether that Chester couldn't access. She was off limits.

His stomach clenched. He blinked hard several times and wiped his moist forehead with the back of his gloved hand. *Hold it together. Mika's a few steps away.* Mika meant release.

Spike halted. Chester waited behind him. Chet rapped loudly on an indigo door. A buzz followed by a voice.

"Speak," a deep voice wafted from a small speaker mounted next to the door.

Spike pushed a button and leaned toward the speaker. "Spike. Chester to see you. Password successful."

"Enter."

A buzz and a click of a lock. Spike opened the door and waved for Chester to enter. He did.

The room glowed an orange-yellow hue from the candles circling the perimeter. The smooth, black, windowless walls shut out any outside interruption. Soothing electric guitar vibes seeped through the room, hypnotizing all who entered. Mika only played Gothic metal, and the least accessible recordings. Chester appreciated that.

A muscular figure, hidden beneath a cloak, emerged from across the room.

"Mika," Chester greeted.

"Chester. It's...been a while."

"Yes."

"You have been well?" Mika asked.

"Yes."

"Your routine has been working?"

"Yes."

"You need...replenishment?" Mika took a few steps closer.

"I do." Chester pressed his gloved hands together in a prayer position and bowed forward.

"Come." Mika gestured toward the far side of the room.

Chester followed the guidance, moving toward a large, emerald chaise. Azure high-backed armchairs formed a halfmoon across from the chaise. A round, glass table sat in the centre of the makeshift circle.

Chester settled himself on the chaise.

Mika lowered his hood, revealing his long, red hair. "The usual?"

"The usual." Chester nodded, removing his coat and setting it beside him.

"The dosage? You look...pale."

"Perhaps a little bump."

"Very good." Mika turned and walked over to a long table set along one of the walls. The table was curved to match the circular contour of the room. "It is good you have come. You will feel refreshed." Mika poured the ingredients to a concoction into a silver martini mixer. He shook the cocktail, his cloak falling away from his arms, his muscles pressing against his tight shirt. He removed the lid and tilted the mixer toward a silver goblet. Deep-purple liquid flowed from stainless steel into the cup.

Mika walked over to Chester and handed him the drink. "To calm you, while I fix your order."

"Thank you." Chester took a long sip. The sweet concoction slid over his tongue, trailing hints of lavender and vanilla. He took another long, slow sip, then placed the cup down on the table.

He watched Mika tend to the order. Mika's tall torso rippled with muscular contours, seething strength and sexuality. Chester had always felt a draw to Mika, even in the early days when he had to prove he was a loyal, discreet customer.

Mika brought a silver tray over and placed it on the table in front of Chester. "Your order. As usual, take your time."

The silver tray displayed two purple pills and two lines of white dust.

Chester unbuttoned his cuffs and the top three buttons of his black silk shirt. He loosened his collar and rolled his shoulders a few times. He closed his eyes, rested his hands on his knees and inhaled deeply. After several deep breaths, he opened his eyes and scanned his order.

It had been a while since he had allowed himself this luxury. He'd been...controlled. His routine had worked. *Maybe I should go. Finish my drink. Pay for my order. And leave.*

He pictured himself doing just that. Then he pictured himself slipping into bed later that evening.

No. He couldn't face the nightmares that would descend upon him. His head was cluttered. He was off kilter. His ghost mother would come in his dreams and haunt him. Tell him that he was a sick murderer. That he deserved to be locked up with all the other insane psychos. And Violet. Her chopped-up, bloody body would be spewed across his nightmares. Her vacant eyes wouldn't even recognize him.

He looked back at the pills and the powder. He needed this. Picking up the goblet, he swallowed most of the remaining concoction in several large gulps. The liquid swirled in his mouth, tantalizing his tastebuds, sliding down his throat. Numbing following, through his body, over his arms and hands.

Chester shook his hands several times, then picked up a thin, silver tube. He placed the end of the hollow tube at the base of the first line of white powder, the other end toward his right nostril. He inhaled hard.

Sweet relief washed over him. He leaned back in the chair, his neck rubbing against the chaise.

The room ebbed and flowed with the orange glow of the candle flames. Chester became lightheaded. His heavy thoughts evaporated, dissolving into nothing. He felt lighter. He indulged in the second line of magic powder, chasing it with a purple pill, washing it all down with the remaining vanilla-lavender liquid.

He settled in against the chaise, his heavy body sinking into the soft cushion. He ran his hands along the plush velour. The room spun slowly around him.

A thin outline of a woman hovered over him. He leaned his head back, deep into the soft material. He opened his eyes wide. Electric love pulsed through him. *It's her. At last.*

She looked down at him. Her figure floating, shimmering a foot above him. She leaned down, her black lips reaching for him, planting a soft kiss on his cheek.

She pulled back. Her dark eyes searched him, piercing through his flesh, into him, looking deep into his soul. She knew everything. He wanted her to.

Her whispers shivered through him, a tingling sexuality following her words, into him, through his body.

"Saul. I've missed you."

It was her. And he was...*himself,* again.

"I've missed you, too. All I ever wanted was you."

"I know, Sssauuul." Her whispers drew out his name like it meant something. Like he was something. He was Saul again.

"Good." His tongue heavy, he tried to move it. "I...I...looo..." His tongue fell against the bottom of his mouth.

She reached out her hand and pressed her finger against his lips. "Ssshhh. Don't speak," she whispered.

He let go. Every muscle in his body relented. All tension dissolved into the air, like water droplets evaporating in the heat of the sun. His bones disintegrated. His body became jello.

He smiled. Then giggled. He was Saul again. He was a boy again. Back in her room. With her.

Her wavering image of a body grew a shade darker. Her dress materializing before his eyes, the translucent image of her face became flesh. Her eyes darkened. The sketch of her became real. The dark lines alluding to hair became long, lush locks, falling over her, reaching for him.

He reached out and took a lock in his fingers, stroking it from root to tip. The smoothness tickled his fingertips, sending electric shocks through his body. His virility surged.

She leaned closer to him, still floating, a slight shimmer to the flesh that clung to her frame. Her lips found his. She kissed him long and hard. Her sweet juices slid into his mouth, and he swallowed them. The luscious concoction of *her* filled his body with the essence he desired.

She pulled away, breathing in a long, deep breath. Warm air sucked from him, leaving his open mouth, pouring into her. Her transformation complete, she fell from the air, landing softly in his lap. Her flesh against him jolted his extremities. She leaned over, pressing her breasts into his chest. Tingles shot through his veins.

"Violet," he gasped. "It's really you."

"I'm here. Let's feed."

She leaned over, reaching for the silver goblet. She poured the contents into his mouth. Warm liquid with a hint of copper slid over his tongue, reaching for his throat. The warmth oozed down into him, covering his internal organs with a life-giving coat.

He swallowed hard, leaned back against the chair, and exhaled.

Violet leaned over him, licking warm drizzles from the sides of his mouth, from his lips. She slid her tongue into his mouth and roamed, looking for every last scrap. Her exploration over, she sat up and took a long drink from the life-giving goblet.

She arched her back, her black dress stretching along her body, her breasts pressing hard against the lace, pulling at the seams. Placing the goblet on the table, she wrapped her arms around his neck and tickled his skin with her fingers.

"Saul. Let's be one."

The room spun around him. Her face tilted round and round. The swirling orange-yellow hue became a deep purple-blue. A cosmic pulse vibrated through the room, turning the swirl into a techno-coloured beat.

His fingers slithered. He stretched his arms out in front of him and looked at his hands. They were liquid hands, morphing into different shapes. Shining emerald mermaid fins wove over his fingers, eating them. Pale faces poked from the fins, white faces with red eyes and long, dark hair. Ten Violets replaced his fingertips, their black mouths moving, speaking to him in a chant.

"King Saul. Let us Feed. Let us Eat you. Let us Be you." They wavered back and forth in a trance-like state, chanting over and over.

He felt fingers running over him, his chest, his abs, his thighs. He felt a warmth wrap around him, sliding over him, eating him, sliding back and forth, swallowing him, then releasing him, then swallowing him again. His nerve endings twitched. He drowned in pleasure.

The Violet mermaids grew taller, stretching from his hands, towering over him. Whispering to him, goading him to take in the pleasure they offered him, their sacrifice for him.

The pleasure heightened beyond a peak. A hot rush shot through him. A million lights flashed, purple, blue, orange, yellow, dissolving into the soft orange-yellow glow of the candle flames.

Violet, on top of him, her dark eyes boring into him, whispered, "Saul. We are one."

Her flesh shimmered. Her body vanishing, he looked at her, the crystal table, the purple couch, the dark wall behind visible through her. She was a thin sheet. Black specks of glitter fluttered through the air, landing softly around him, on him. He inhaled. His body pulsed with the new life infused into his veins. The life Violet had given him. Her blood was his blood. He was whole again.

His body went limp against the plush chair. His heavy lids closed. His clear mind allowing him to rest, he fell into a deep sleep.

Chapter 57

Corpse of Corpses

Sweet caramel wove from a crystal glass, teasing Mahoney's nostrils. He downed the bourbon in a single foul shot. Sweetness lingered at the back of his tongue. The familiar burn followed, trickling down his throat. He leaned against a dust-coated, hole-infused chair, looking out the streaked window of his room in the *Hav-A-Nap* motel. His gaze blurred out the rundown parking lot littered with crack whores and scanned the glimmers of the moon over the dark ripples of Lake Ontario.

Dixon had tried to talk him into a nightcap in the fancy lobby of the Toronto Hilton. Quesnel had applied her own pressure as she handed him a folder filled with files telling the story of the roommate of Harold the Beheader. He couldn't. He needed to be alone. To fester in the slipping grip he had on Saul the Slayer. Or whoever the fuck he was.

His budding analyst wasn't getting anywhere with all the weird shit. The brand for sizzling a vampire clan symbol into the flesh of girls. A scarificator for extracting blood from live victims.

He stared at the bright moon. It was in the first quarter phase. Tomorrow it would be well into waxing gibbous. If this human vampire was sticking to his schedule, there'd be another kill, only two nights from now.

He poured another ample shot of bourbon and swallowed half of it in one gulp. His arms tingled. His brain buzzed. The dark skyline stared back at him, stars twinkling like all-knowing eyes. *Where are you, Saul?*

He yanked his stare from the moon and flipped open the folder, holding the story of Saul. The information was sparse. The words popped off the pages as he scanned.

Saul Ripper. Institutionalized at age fourteen after sliding a paring knife into his sixteen-year-old sister, Violet. Some of her blood, type O negative, had been missing. It was the photo of her that made the hot, bourbon-infused breath catch in Mahoney's throat.

Long, dark hair. Pale. Thin. The spitting image of the sixteen-year-old girls. A crude version of the demon doll paint job on the bodies at the crime scenes.

He'd checked in with examiner Winter by phone. What little blood remained in the four victims of the new slew of murders had been type O negative. It appeared that the profiling duo, Quesnel and Dixon, had been dead-on when they theorized that the killer had a strong victim type because he was trying to reproduce a particular woman—girl—of his past.

Ripper. Could that really be his last name? The files *claimed* his mother, Sylvia Ripper, had signed the papers sealing his fate in the institution. Yet, there was no record of a Sylvia Ripper. Was it a sick joke? His mother's way of formally disowning him?

Mahoney sighed, downing the rest of the pour. He'd read and re-read the files. The story was sketchy. It provided a glimpse of the events that had created the fantasy that drove Saul the Slayer, the *Ripper,* to take sixteen-year-old girls, slice them open and bleed them out. What was missing was any clear indication of where this Saul was right now, at this moment. There was no Saul, or Ripper, on the list of names from Katie's Kraft.

Initial searches of the family plots at the *Necropolis Cemetery* hadn't yielded any Violet Rippers. Tens of thousands of bodies were put to their final rest in the old plots. Results would take time, if they came at all. Quesnel and Barbie had still been huddled over Barbie's computer, trying to wade their way through the building searches and sea of names when Mahoney slipped out the door, clutching the folder in his hand.

Mahoney sighed, snapping the folder shut and pushing it away. Closing his eyes, he searched for warm memories. Wading through a sea of small faces, the innocence of young girls shining through pairs of dark eyes circled in blood red. Their long, dark hair waving through his mind. Their black lips whispering to him. He squeezed his eyes shut harder and willed himself through the sea, searching for the pearl at the bottom.

There it was. The image he wanted.

White waves crashed violently against the wet, hardpacked sand. Startled seagulls squealed, taking flight. A large, white wave met the beach and reached its long, trickling fingers toward the untouched, soft sand. Before it could settle, another rolling wave roiled over the deep-blue water, gaining height and tumbling toward the beach at an ungodly rate. More birds flocked, scrambling, flying, scattering.

Dark-grey clouds descended toward the building surf, creating a black, toiling backdrop for the ferocious ocean.

Mahoney blinked, hard. Wait. This was not how he remembered this. The claws of the memory grasped him, pulling him away from his two-star motel room, and back in time.

He looked around, scanning the vast expanse of beach. Not a single soul. Just him and the birds, the rolling, angry surf, and black clouds.

Something stirred at the water's edge. Bony fingers, flesh dripping from them, clawed into the wet sand, scraping their way along the hardpacked granules. The sand clumped into glops, sticking to the flesh, sticking to the bones.

An ice wave cut through Mahoney's gut. His insides flushed with cold. He blinked hard, three times. He shook his head. *Where the fuck was he?*

He stared back at the ocean's edge, not wanting to look but unable to look away.

He watched in horror.

The corpse of all corpses pulled itself out of the water. Flesh clung to its bones. Blood oozed from its eye sockets. Slimy green algae stuck to its face. The smell of rot cloaked the entire beach. Mahoney choked on the bile lurking in his throat. He swallowed hard, dug his boots into the sand, and stared into the blood-soaked empty eye sockets.

"Who are you?" he yelled. "What the *fuck* do you want?"

A sick laugh throttled over the crashing waves as the skeleton jaw cracked open.

"You know me, *Bug*. You know me, *Detective*. I'm all the corpses you failed." The skeleton jaw creaked shut.

Skeleton fingers gripped the hard beach, yanking the corpse to full height. The body wasn't just a skeleton body. It was bones, it was hunks of bloody flesh clinging to a carcass, throbbing in unison as if the fleshy clumps each had its own beating heart. It was a corpse composed of thousands of corpses, each with its own blood-dripping empty eye sockets and creaking jaw. The jaws opened and closed, thousands of haunting voices shimmering through the air, shattering Mahoney's insides.

The jaws creaked. The voices crawled over him. "We are all the corpses you failed. The carnage you left."

"Fuck you," Mahoney's lips trembled as he spat out the words. "Get the hell out of my life." He ran his hands through his hair. His face dripped with sweat. "Leave me alone," he yelled so loudly his throat went raw.

He fell to his knees. Wet sand clung to his pants, soaking his skin. He screamed. The world spun around him.

An eerie croak of echoing ghost voices filled his ears.

"Bug, Bug, Bug..." The last word was a raspy whisper.

"You, you, you..." Dozens of skeleton jaws creaked.

"Failed, failed, failed..." Dozens of bloody eyes peered at him.

Each word echoed, spilling into each other, cluttering the next word.

He shut his eyes and yelled against it, "Leave me alone."

He curled into a ball, sinking into the wet sand. He squeezed his eyes shut. He clamped his arms against his ears.

The skeleton face, sticky with rotting flesh, forced its way in, prying into his mind, ripping his eyelids open. He couldn't fight it. He stared at the blood oozing from the empty eye sockets.

"I stopped it," Mahoney whimpered.

The voice creaked from the skeleton jaw, "After the carnage."

"I stopped it."

Beetles crawled their shiny black bodies over the clumps of flesh, gooey with blood, skittering over charcoal bones.

"Not the carnage, Bug."

"I stopped it, you *motherfucker*." His voice cracked and gave way. He crumpled into himself, hugging his knees against his chest.

He pictured Stella. Perfect. Innocent. Full of sunshine. Blonde and strawberry flowing curls. He squeezed his eyes shut and slammed a wall between his brain and the world. His mind swirled. He funnelled down into himself, into the blackness. Ice waves washed through him.

The crashing surf went quiet. The squealing of the birds vanished. Creaking bones halted. Whispering skeleton jaws went silent.

He hugged his knees harder into his chest and squeezed his eyelids together. He waited. Silence.

He opened his eyes. The corpse of all corpses was gone. The dark skyline of Lake Ontario splashed across the horizon. The first quarter moon glared. The all-knowing, twinkling eyes beckoned him. He'd lost all the warm memories of the beach, warmed by the sun, soothed by the soft waves. Of her. His only daughter. The one person he didn't want to fail.

He *should* walk away from this mad hunt for a human vampire. He *couldn't.* What if one of those girls were Stella? He couldn't face her, his angel, his Stella, knowing he'd let a monster walk the earth, hurting other girls. Girls just like her.

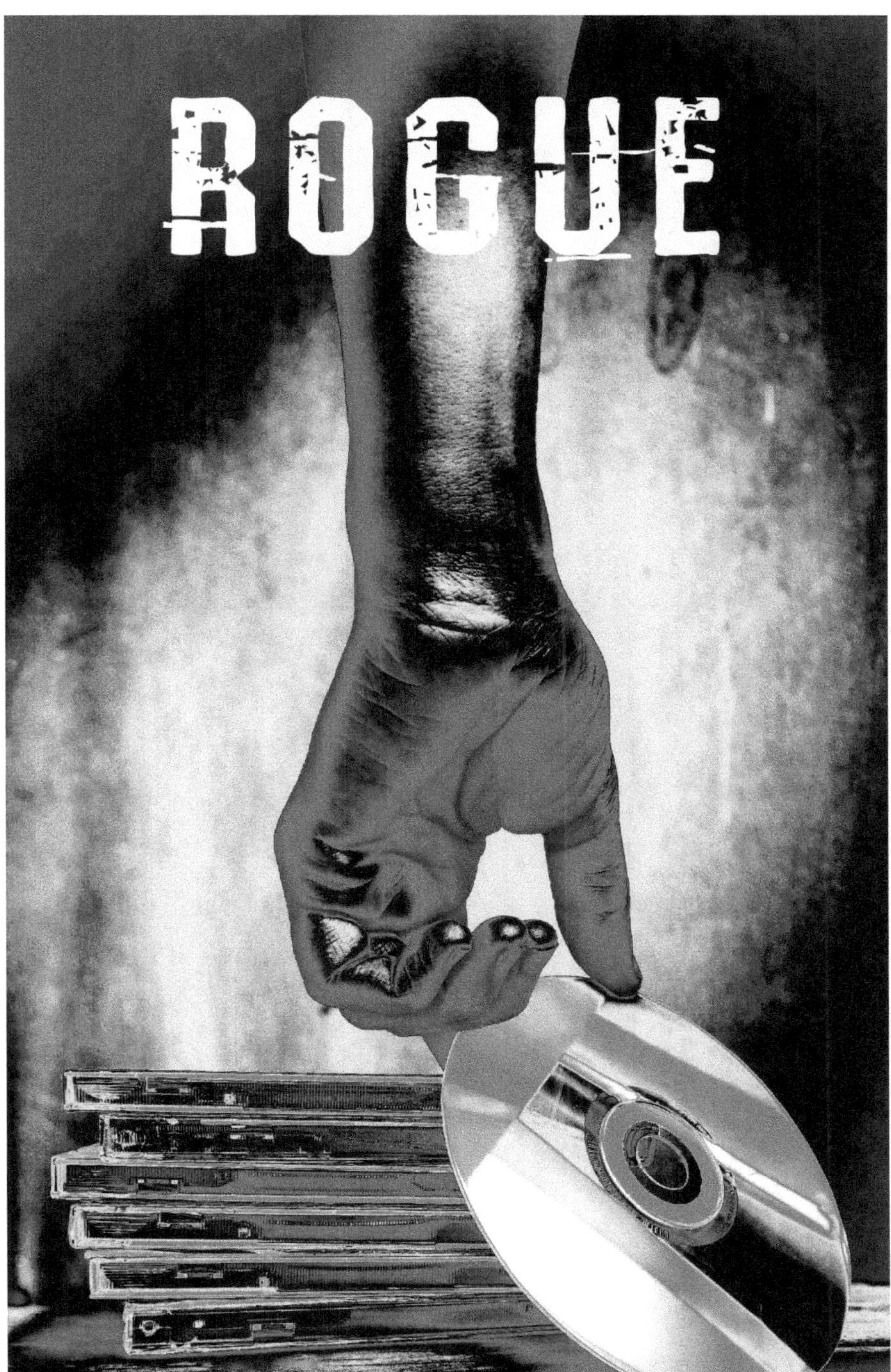

ROGUE

Chapter 58

Budding Analyst

The main room to the homicide HQ was quiet. A single light shone from a desk in front of Tomlinson's office. Bleached-blonde hair glowed under the light.

Mahoney walked across the room, up to Barbie's desk. "Good morning."

Barbie looked up. "Detective." Dark shadows hung under her eyes.

"You pulled an all-nighter," Mahoney stated.

"I did." Her eyes lit up. "I got somewhere." She frowned. "It's not all the way, but close. I did what you said. Filtered that list you gave me from Katie's Kraft. Confirmed there is no Saul, and no Ripper. Then I focused on the men. I had to do this manually. There are more gender neutral names than you would think. I'm down to a dozen."

She'd worked fast. Yet, the speed he needed was impossible. He cleared his throat. "The list had hundreds of names. That's top-notch work."

Barbie blushed. She shuffled papers, and pulled one out. "I got addresses for you." Her mouth twisted in contemplation. "It'll take time to follow up on all those."

Mahoney took the paper and scanned the names. "I'll take a copy of this. When Dixon gets in, see if he can follow up on any of them. If Tomlinson doesn't trap him into useless tasks."

"You got it. I'm still trying to make progress on the cemetery. It's taking time." Her pink lips turned down into a frown. "I'm still not getting anywhere with this brand or the scarificator."

Mahoney rubbed the back of his neck, contemplating how to speed things up, and what his next move should be. His gut throbbed. "Listen...can you get a copy of everything you've found—make that two copies. One for Dixon. One for Quesnel."

Briar's pink lips broke out into a wide smile. "You got it, Bug."

"Thanks, Briar." He tipped his hat, then turned toward his borrowed desk. He needed to get out of here before the circus returned. It was time for another visit to his nocturnal friend.

"Hey, Mahoney." Sutton's voice cut through Mahoney's train of thought and halted him in his tracks.

"Sutton. You're here early." Mahoney cleared his throat.

"Yeah. Hoping to find you here." Sutton approached, glaring, sweat sprouting across his forehead. "We need to talk. War room. Now."

Sutton stomped across the room.

Barbie looked up and shrugged. "Good luck." She grabbed a neon-pink coffee mug and walked away from her desk, toward the corner of the room.

Chapter 59

Rabbit Foot Attack

The gnarly, pickle-shaded rabbit's foot dangled from Sutton's belt, swinging back and forth. Little claws reached from the end of the green fur, taunting Mahoney. He wanted to rip it from Sutton's belt and toss it in the garbage. *Sutton and his goddamned lucky charm.* His gut throbbed, instinctual tingles swelling within it, migrating through him, up his stomach, toward his heart, reaching for his throat. Wasn't he the one who had told Sutton to follow his instincts? That they would guide him to become a Prime Investigator? *Fuck.*

The ridiculous baby-blue sky mural closed in around him, the puffy white clouds suffocating him.

Sutton's eyes narrowed. "Mahoney. Where have you *been?*"

Mahoney swallowed hard against the bile rising in his throat. "Following up on some leads."

Sutton shook his head. "You've been skipping out on Tomlinson's meetings. Hell, you haven't been picking up when I call." He ran his hand through his silky, brown curls. "I can't put on a front if I don't know what the hell you're up to."

Mahoney took a deep breath, walked up to Sutton, and put a hand on his shoulder. "Listen. You don't want to be part of my sideshow. I get it. You play by the rules. You've got a long career ahead of you." Mahoney released his hand from Sutton's shoulder. "I don't. I've got a killer to catch."

"Do you? You've shared *nothing.*" Sweat sprouted across Sutton's brow. His eyebrows leaned in toward each other, forming a V. "You're off the rails. I get it, you need to get this killer. It's been haunting you a long time. Do you really have any leads here?"

Mahoney rubbed the bristle on his chin. His neck flushed with heat. "Yeah. I do. You know this whole thing stinks. You know Tomlinson's compromising this whole investigation. His motives are pumped full of something. Power. Maybe greed. He has no interest in catching the killer."

Sutton took several strides across the room. The rabbit foot swaying erratically. "You *might* be right. Sarge told you to play along. Give him time to work with Tomlinson's superior. Sarge has made progress. But, you'd know that if you'd pick up your goddamn phone."

Mahoney clenched his jaw and stared Sutton down.

The rabbit foot swung back and forth.

"Turns out Tomlinson's been feeding his Constable false reports. Making it look like he's got a prime suspect, things are lining up, and you and I are involved. Constable Witton didn't believe it, at first. Sarge pushed. Witton had someone watch Tomlinson. An internal investigation of Tomlinson has been initiated. It'll take time. They'll crack this open. In the mean time, we are *supposed* to focus on being part of the investigation."

Mahoney jaunted toward him, his blood boiling, his face flushed. "While you're playing along with Tomlinson's game of an investigation, waiting for his superiors to get him in line, I'm getting closer to the killer."

Sutton walked right up to Mahoney. Their faces a mere inch apart, Sutton's hot breath clouded Mahoney's face. "Listen, *boss*. You're out of line. Sarge told you to play along, be part of Tomlinson's show. Any liberties you were taking were not to compromise the investigation. You're off the rails. You don't show up. You don't answer your phone. You're out of line."

Mahoney spat his words, "Back off."

Sutton refused to budge. "No. It's over. I have my instructions. I need your badge and your gun."

An ice wave cut through Mahoney. Sweat trickled down his back. His nostrils flared. He took several steps, backing away from Sutton's hot breath and bulging eyes.

Sutton remained frozen. The rabbit foot settled. "Your heard me, Mahoney. Badge and gun."

Mahoney's brain buzzed. The baby-blue sky and puffy white clouds swirled around him.

Sutton approached. "This is *your* doing. And you know it." His expression changed from hot to sad.

Mahoney slid his hand inside his tweed coat, pulling out his badge. He took several steps over to the long table running down the centre of the room. He snapped the badge onto the table, then unholstered his gun and set it down with a clank.

Avoiding further eye contact with Sutton, he turned, re-settled his derby on his head, and walked through the door.

The office was empty. Sutton lingered back in the room. Barbie had left her desk. Her access badge sat next to her keyboard. Mahoney walked over to her desk, scanning the room to make sure he was alone. A stack of mail, the top letter addressed to Tomlinson, caught his attention. He scanned the room, again. Still no sign of Barbie. He shuffled through the letters. They were all for Tomlinson. He halted on a thick, purple envelope. It was simply addressed to Sergeant Tomlinson, handwritten, no return address. Mahoney picked it up. It was thick, yet not heavy. He ripped it open. A stack of bills were wrapped neatly with a single sheet of purple paper. He slid the paper from the money, and scanned the letter, written in perfect penmanship, instructing Tomlinson to drive the investigation of the Susie Slaughters to a close before the moon fell from full to waning. It was signed by *Saul the Slayer.*

He left the envelope open, exposing the bribe, with the letter neatly position on top, in the centre of Barbie's desk. He shoved the access badge into his tweed coat pocket and made for the exit.

Chapter 60

Nocturnal Pressure

An eerie orange glow ebbed through the dark, moist cave-like enclosure. The first two cells were dark, the occupants still and quiet. The glow was coming from Harold's cell.

Mahoney approached, his black shoes clicking against the hard floor. Feeling naked without his gun and his badge, he'd been relieved when Margo, with her tight bun and stern expression, had waved him in, bypassing the usual procedure. Harold's wiry frame slouched over a desk, perched in the centre of the cell. A small lamp provided a bright burst of light. Harold fixated on an open book, reading along as he moved his bony finger across the page.

Mahoney took a few more steps. Harold raised his gaze, his beady eyes imploring Mahoney before he could utter a single word. A chill trickled down Mahoney's back. His collar stuck to the back of his neck. Harold didn't scare him. Hell, being in this dungeon didn't make him twitch. It was what was in Harold's mind that created the cold chill sticking to his skin despite the moist heat of the room.

Harold spoke, his voice raspy, "Detective. So good to see you again. I didn't expect another visit so soon."

"Pleasure is all mine." Mahoney sat down in the wooden chair still facing Harold's cell from their last visit.

"Oh no, Detective, I assure you, the pleasure is equal." Harold's cracked lips broke into a sick smile. "What can I do for you today?"

"Well, it seems I need a little help with the search I'm on."

"For the human vampire." Harold licked his dry upper lip.

"Yes. That's the one." Mahoney paused. "I need to know where he's living. I know you can help me."

Harold's beady eyes darted back and forth.

Mahoney leaned toward the cell. "You had that vial of his sister's blood. You *knew* him, didn't you?"

Harold's eyes halted, fixating on Mahoney. "I already told you, he was my roommate."

"Yeah. But you *knew* him. Well. He was more than a roommate to you. You admired him. You still do. That blood was his trophy. You took it because you thought having his trophy would make you closer to him. I know how much trophies mean to you, Harold." Mahoney stood and walked up to the cell, facing Harold's black, beady stare straight on. "It's a shame you don't have access to *your own* trophies anymore."

Harold sat up straight, spreading his skeletal fingers over the desk in front of him.

Mahoney slid his hand into his tweed coat and pulled out an envelope and a small, plastic bag. He held them out in front of the bars. "*You* may not have access to your trophies, but *I do.*" The back wall of the evidence room at the Homicide HQ flashed into his mind. He'd been quick. He'd left Barbie's badge on the floor by the coffee maker, as if she'd dropped it. Her head had been buried in her searches as he'd slipped out the door.

Harold shot up, knocking the chair over with a clank. "What is that?" His eyes widened. He rubbed his hands together. Flakes of skin fluttered to the ground.

"Something special. For you. From your past." Mahoney waved the envelope and the bag back and forth. "If you help me, you can have it."

"Are those...picturesss?" Harold hissed.

"Yes. Photos. Of the *trophies* you collected."

Harold swallowed. His Adam's apple pulled at his wrinkly neck as it bobbed. "What's in the bag?"

Mahoney opened the bag and pulled out a lock of shiny, golden hair. He held it up for Harold to see.

Harold's eyes bulged. His hands trembled. "It can't be."

"I assure you, it is."

Harold closed his eyes and took a deep breath.

Mahoney slid the lock of hair back into the bag and stood, staring in the cell at Harold.

Harold's eyes popped open. A glow overtook his gaze. His bony shoulders lowered. "Fine. You want to find *Saul the Slayer*."

"Yes. I do."

"And, if I tell you…more…about him, then you will give me those?"

"Yes, Harold. But you have to tell me something *useful*. No cryptic messages. Tell me where he is."

Harold narrowed his beady eyes. He shook his head, then shot his gaze back to the plastic bag. His shoulders shook. "Fine." His hands trembled as he stared at the lock of hair, licking his scaly lips.

Mahoney waited. "Well, what are you waiting for? Spill it."

"There's a house. Up on a hill. An old mansion he inherited while we were roommates. He told me about it. Said it was a Gothic mansion. It was his grandfather's."

Mahoney's gut trembled. A jolt of adrenaline rushed through his veins. He ground his teeth, listening to the words seeping from his nocturnal friend's mouth. "Where, Harold? *Where?*"

Harold squinted. "He said it was by a lake…" He rubbed his flaking hands over his wrinkly face.

Mahoney swung the plastic bag in front of the bars. "Think, Harold. *Think.*"

Harold's beady eyes clung nervously to the plastic bag. "Gothic mansion. Overlooking a lake. I swear. That's all he said."

Better not be making this shit up. "OK, Harold. Come get your prize."

Harold skittered across the hard floor and approached. His beady eyes fixated on Mahoney as he reached out a gnarly hand and took the envelope and the bag. He stood, staring at Mahoney.

"You might need a special *tool*. If you're planning a visit." The words dripped from Harold's mouth.

"Tool?" Mahoney asked.

"We all have something we like to hunt, *Detective*. You seem…on the prowl. If you are, you might want to be…*equipped*. There's a hidden gem in the basement of *Sneaky-Dees*. If it's still there. Follow the *Silver Strand*. Find the man with the classy hat, behind the black door." Harold turned and scuttled back to his desk.

Mahoney's brain buzzed. *Hunt. Tool.* How different was he from Harold? *Sneaky-Dees?* What the hell was Harold talking about? "What are you talking about?"

"We are done, here, Detective." Harold stared at the envelope and bag now laid out on the desk.

Not wanting to be part of Harold's fantasy, Mahoney turned and left the dark, moist cave.

Chapter 61

Knife For Gutting

High voltage music pumped through the hot room. College kids clumped together, close to the stage, jumping in a spasmic dance to the punk beat. Mahoney snaked his way along the perimeter of the mob of party-hards. The less enthusiastic sat at scratched tables, devouring towers of nachos and chugging pitchers of beer. Sneaky-Dees was exactly what Mahoney had expected.

Mahoney had left Harold to live out his fantasy in his nocturnal cave. He'd called Barbie. There was no hint of a gothic mansion on a lake area on the short list. She went to work rescanning the hundreds of names.

He manoeuvred to the far corner of the room and found a black door. He knocked on it and waited.

A silver steel silt in the black door opened with a whoosh followed by a click. Two eyes peered at him. "Password."

Password? What had Harold said…follow the Silver Strand. "Silver Strand," he managed meekly. Sweat trickled down his neck. Cold jolted through him.

The slit slammed shut. Silence. He waited. The sweat trickled down his back, soaking his shirt.

Dammit, Harold. You didn't play me, did you?

A buzz, followed by a click, and the black door opened.

A large man with broad shoulders glared down at him, then pointed.

Mahoney nodded, then followed the thick finger sticking into the darkness, down a staircase.

The remains of light vanished as the door slammed shut. He shuffled his feet along the damp floor. Staring at the outline of the wall, he shuffled down the stairs, gripping the railing like an old man until his eyes adjusted. The room below became clear. A bar lined with bottles to his left. A woman with ample breasts leaned over the countertop. Another counter to his right, a glass counter, locked, its contents wrapped in black cloth. Two men sat in the corner, a line of shots on the table, as they talked in deep voices.

One of them wore a black felt Fedora. Harold had said find the man with the classy hat.

The man looked up, halting his conversation with his hand. "Please, help yourself to a drink." He waved at the bar. "Felicia, help this man." He looked at the bartender. "Have a drink, then we talk."

Mahoney made his way over to the bar.

A sickly-sweet smell rose from the counter. The ample-breasted waitress eyeballed him suspiciously. "Well, what do you want? You're new here. I don't know your order."

"Bourbon."

She rolled her eyes, turned, and grabbed a bottle. She looked at him while she poured. "Really, bourbon? Are you as predictable as your drink? And your hat and coat to match."

She slid him the drink. He slid her a couple of bills.

She pushed the money back. "Nope. Your money's no good here. That's what I'm supposed to say." She pasted a fake smile on her face.

He sat down on a round, wooden stool perched beside the bar and took a sip of bourbon. Eyeballing the two men in the corner, he took another swig. The alcohol burned the back of his throat, leaving a less-than-desirable aftertaste. Not his usual choice, but what was he going to do?

The music boomed from above. The noise and the crowd was a perfect cover for whatever went on down here. He sat, perched by the bar, taking long draws of the cheap bourbon. A mere second after he polished off the last swig, the man from the corner summoned him with a wave of his hand.

Mahoney abandoned the empty glass and the unpleasant bartender and walked over to the corner of the dark room. He sat down as the other man rose and walked away. The man who summoned him stared him squarely in the eyes.

"You are looking for a special tool, I assume." The man's voice dripped darkness and confidence.

"Yeah," Mahoney gruffly retorted.

"The kind of tool that is used for hunting dangerous...*vermin.*"

"Yeah." The image of his own hand sliding into a man's torso popped into his mind. "You could say that."

The man with the hat continued, "I am sure I have what you are seeking." He waved a hand toward the glass case against the wall, housing cloth-covered items. "Hunting such vermin can be dangerous." The man stood and motioned to the glass case. "Shall we choose your weapon for your hunt?"

Mahoney nodded, then followed the man over to the case. He watched as the man unlocked the glass housing, reached a hand inside and removed several black cloths.

A jolt of cold froze Mahoney the second he saw it. Ivory handle. Long, precise blade. A jagged hook on the tip. He pointed. "That one."

The man stopped and looked at him. "Solid choice. A hunter with a strong sense of his tool will succeed in capturing his prey." The man turned to summon Felicia.

Mahoney reached into the case and picked up the knife. The intricately-carved ivory handle was heavy against his gloved hand. He turned the blade over, catching a glint off a pot light overhead. A flash of thick scarlet drizzled down the blade, then vanished. He would succeed. He knew it.

Chapter 62

Night Creature

It was time for transformation. His girls, his *Violets,* would be expecting him. Chester could slip out of his public-world persona, hang it up for the night, and step into the comfort of his doll-master cloak. It would take time, but it was time that he relished in. Every step of the transformation took him deeper into himself. His *true* self.

Creeping along the top floor of the spectacular Gothic mansion his grandfather had gifted him, he found his way to a circular room nestled at the centre. He entered the room, closed the door behind him, and clicked a button on the remote in his hand. The electronic system moved into lockdown. Doors clicked and silence followed.

His secret room at the core of the great house, perched on the top floor. The only other place he enjoyed more was the chamber that held his collection of Violets.

He'd be there soon enough. First, his transformation.

A soft, orange glow welcomed him, cast by candles set in heavy silver holders lining the walls. Complete silence cloaked the round space. Everything was *in place.* Waiting. For him.

Chester walked over to the far-right portion of the circular wall, housing a plethora of shelves and a shiny hi-fi compact disc player. He stood still, scanning neat rows of albums. Everything was in place, organized according to his system. He slid a black-gloved finger along the plastic casings, slowing, then halting on the perfect choice for the evening.

He removed his gloves, and slid the plastic case out from the tightly packed row. He held it. He ran his fingers over it, along the rough letters dripping with blood, declaring the album to be the work of *Type O Negative.* Yet to release a formal studio album, Chester had come across the crude live recording. Mika had slipped it to him during one of his visits seeking release.

Tingling anticipation crawled through him. He opened the case, removed a shiny disc from the plastic clamps holding it in place, and inserted it into the player.

He picked up the remote, adjusted the equalizer settings to be appropriate for the musical choice, then clicked the play button. Music wafted from the shiny speakers. He set down the remote, closed his eyes, and let the deep, soothing voice wander into him and seep into his soul.

The guttural vibes of a slow, dramatic guitar riff wove along with the voice, seeping into Chester's ears and seething through his veins. He took a long, deep breath, tilted his head back, and exhaled. He let the lyrics infuse him, convincing him that survival meant letting his grotesque actions surface.

The words dripped from the speakers, wafting into his being, and infusing him with new life.

Black lipstick stains on a goblet of scarlet.
Your midnight lips move.
I can feel your words.

The black lips of a thousand Violets seeped through his mind. He could feel their words whispering through his soul. Calling to him. To come. To find the one true Violet who would replace the one he could never get back.

Chester's body vibrated with electric energy as he walked across the plush carpet over to the vanity and sat down. Slipping his hand into his pocket, he pulled out a set of keys. He selected a key, and unlocked the door on the front of an ornate, silver stand perched on the vanity. As he opened the door, he eyeballed the plethora of selections.

Foundations in creamy tones, others stark white. Eye shadows in dark blues, purples, and reds. Lipsticks and glosses in severe tones of red and black. It was the paint palette of a night creature.

The rich voice reached across the room, weaving through him.

Close your eyes. Let me love you. Now. And in death.
Am I pure enough for you?
Let me love you till blood seeps from your veins.

If only he'd been pure enough for Violet. The one Violet. The real Violet.

He sighed. It was too late for the real Violet. His only salvation could come with the perfect replica. Tonight would be another evening filled with longing, feeding, and searching for the one. The one who could replace *her*.

The track ended. The silence between songs quieted the room. He looked into the mirror at the image of the public-world Chester. His lips curled into a twisted grin. He couldn't wait to rid his face of this disgusting fake being. Reminding himself it was a necessary disguise to accomplish his life's work, he proceeded with his transformation into his true being.

A new track began. A savage beat of drums pounded at the walls. Electric vibrations wove through the air. The primal screams of a goth metal god blasted through the space. A dark vibe crawled over the room, its claws clutching the ceiling, the walls, the air, and Chester's skin.

Wake up. It is time.

Those I loved. Long gone.

Six feet beneath me.

Violet's face shimmered in his mind. Seething in the vibrations clawing through him, Chester chose a delicate brush. He dipped it into a thick, black paint, and sketched the outline for his masterpiece. The brush barely touched his face as he drew thin, slight lines over his cheeks, chin, and forehead, outlining his plan. Putting the brush down, he evaluated his work. The sketch was good. The sultry curves put a dramatic spin on his delicate features.

The transformation stepped up a notch. He picked up a full brush composed of fine sable hair. He doused the fine bristles in a thick coating of white powder and began his work. Sweeping the soft hairs over his face, his pale flesh turned a creamy ashen. The hairs tickled his skin, sending a tingling sensation through his face and over his skull.

He imagined his Violets running their delicate fingers over him, massaging his face, his head, his arms, crawling their way over his physical body, finding their way into his soul. He would give them what they wanted tonight. A sultry leader seething with sexuality. It would be the gathering of all gatherings.

Satisfied with the smooth white mask that cloaked his face, he moved on to the deep dramatic colours of the night creature he would become. Switching the brush for an equally rare yet smaller version, he dusted his eyelids with a deep purple that sparkled under the bright vanity lights. The song continued, the dark electric vibes blending with the orange-yellow hue of the candle flames, the room pulsating with a romantic yet haunting aura.

Each layer of his work added a new dimension to his masterpiece. White face, purple-shimmer lids, black liner enunciating the oval shape of his eyes, and deep rouge heightening his already high cheekbones. He picked up a medium-sized brush, dipped it in blood-red cream and swept circles around his eyes. The untouched deep-purple shimmer now encased in blood circles turned him into a glamorous, savage being.

The final touches were aching to come to life. Chester plucked a tiny brush from the eclectic collection and drew his lips in black. His bottom lip became full and pouty, his upper lip crested in two pointy peaks. Chester picked up a lipstick labelled *Black Night*. Slipping off the shiny silver top, he touched the tip to his lips, pressed, and moved it along the contour of his mouth—his new mouth, the one he had drawn. Pale pink skin turned to slick midnight oil.

The facial mask portion of his transformation was complete.

The track clicked to a stop. Silence hung around him. The first strums of the next song hovered over the room. Dark. Deep. Dramatic. A gritty guitar riff clawed through the room. The whisper of the goth metal god clung close to the climbing vibes. The raspy whisper turned to a gut-clenching deep growl, shooting words into the room. Into Chester.

She floats away
Like a bird
Chasing her dreams
I miss her
If only she would
Die with me

Chester stood and moved to the music over to a massive closet housing hundreds of costumes. His naked, lean, tight body slithered like a standing serpent across the room. His hips swaying to the rhythm, his arms raised overhead. A fiery red tattoo covered his upper back, forming a circle, intersected with a sharp V. Rugged lines slashed both arms of the V. The signal of the ancient vampire that his soul told him he was, ever since he had tasted Violet's blood. In death, she was his spirit wife. A bond unbroken for all time.

Tonight, he might find another one. Another Violet. As pure as the first.

He pressed a button on the wall outside the closet. A strobe light pulsed rhythmically, casting a soul-stirring aura over the orange-yellow glow of the candles. He pressed another button on the wall of the closet, causing the ring of costumes to turn slowly. One by one they passed by his scrutinizing eye. None of them were a match for his evening. Until a glimmer caught his eye. He halted the spinner, reached out a hand, and caressed the shiny sequins running down the length of the arms and legs of the silky material. Soft, yet textured. He stroked the scintillating garment.

Trickles of excitement ran through his fingers and up his arms. He unclasped the shimmering black delight and walked over to a full-length, oval mirror perched in an ornate golden frame. Holding the special costume like a second skin against his body, he smiled.

He stepped one leg into the dark glam suit, then another. Pulling it over his body, he zipped it all the way up. The obsidian sequined satin clung to his tight body, transforming him into a juxtaposition of seduction and gore.

It was time for his crown. He walked over to the closet again, pushed the button, and watched the plethora of costumes shimmer by. The wig stand came into view. He pushed a button, halting the machine. There it was, on top of the stand, his crown.

The tone of the song changed. From hope and love to dark death. The voice plunged deeper. The grit of the guitar heightened in raw pulses.

Chester looked back at his crown. The hair had been washed with the highest quality European shampoo, ordered from his favourite salon—more of a specialty boutique. The hair had been brushed with one hundred strokes—he had counted them one slow stroke at a time. The brush he used was made with boar bristles. Guaranteed forever shine.

The hair now hung, spread in a perfect flow around a glass bust. He'd had the glass bust made to mimic his own delicate features, so he could achieve an accurate visual of what the styled hair would look like once the wig was placed on his head. The hair had been Violet's. The original Violet's. He'd cut long, luscious locks, one by one, while she slept, collecting them over time. He'd placed them in a satin bag and taken them to a secret underground specialty shop. A place where discretion was top priority.

He picked up the wig and walked back over to the vanity. He placed dark hair on his own head and looked in the mirror. A rush of electricity sparked through him, from head to fingertips, to toes. His body vibrated with life.

It was time to perfect his crown. He picked up the special brush and touched up the wig to perfection. No longer a wig, but a crown of his own DNA springing from his own head the way it was meant to. The long, dark hair framed his pale face. The red blood rings around his eyes popped against the dark hair. He fluttered his eyes, specks of glimmer catching the overhead pot light, sparkling against the deep-purple shadow streaked over his eyelids.

Stretching his arms wide, long flowing streams of glimmering black trailed from the long sleeves, touching the soft carpet. His body weaved back and forth in time with the primal rhythm blasting from the speakers in each corner of the room. The entire room filled with savage screams echoed by raspy whispers—filling him with hope. Telling him he had to do certain things to reunite, in life or in death, with his one true love.

The last step, the signature piece, the final bit that would declare him the night creature, was ready for him. He sat back down at the vanity, unlocked a drawer, and pulled out a purple box.

Placing the purple box on the vanity, he stared at it. After a few moments, he opened it. A pair of long, white fangs sat perched on a purple satin lining. The treasure he had obtained when he lost the one he had loved the most. He had kept them for so long. He cleaned and polished them after every evening event. He kept them hidden and locked, and only allowed himself to look at them, to touch them, to use them at an evening event.

He took them now, in his hand, and slid his thumb along the smooth polished surface. Picking one of them up with a thumb and forefinger, he stretched his mouth back wide and secured it on his third tooth from the centre, on the left side. He secured the second one, then looked at himself in the mirror.

Anyone who knew him in his public life wouldn't know it was Chester. No. They wouldn't know who he was. He was no longer Chester. He was Saul. *Saul the Slayer.*

Moments from now, he would be the ultimate doll master. His Violets would desire his touch, long for it, beg for it. Together, they would blend their physical and spiritual beings. Together they would feed. Together they would move toward the ultimate place, seeking the one who would go with him to the ultimate place.

Chapter 63

Dive-Bar Bourbon

Beer and body odour engulfed Mahoney as he walked into the *Swan Dive*. He didn't spot a swan. But it *was* a dive. Three patrons were the only souls in the dingy room. Two tucked away in a corner, solving the world's problems over a pitcher of beer and a pack of Lucky Strikes. A loner hunched over the far end of the counter, nursing a pint. A line of empty shot glasses cluttered next to a brown wallet that had seen better days.

Perched at the outskirts of the Toronto core, in quick reach of each of the highways shooting out to the various lake areas, he figured this would be the best place to wait until Barbie called him with the address he needed.

Mahoney removed his derby and shuffled across the room toward the bar. Slick, wet slops seeped from his shoes as they stuck against the gooey carpet. He smirked.

He approached the bar, taking the seat at the vacant end. He wanted to be alone.

The bartender—his chiselled back leaning against the bar, his muscular arms crossed—looked his way and raised a thick salt-and-pepper eyebrow. He greeted Mahoney with a gruff voice. "What's your poison?"

Mahoney plunked into the seat and managed a meek answer, "Bourbon. Double. Straight up."

The muscular bartender went to work. As he slid a short, half-full glass across the bar, the sweet caramel-infused alcohol pulled at Mahoney, luring him in. He was finished trying. Trying to avoid the things that numbed the pain. Trying to pretend to play a political game of bullshit, when all he wanted was to hunt a hunter. If there was one thing he could do, it would be to stop the slaughter of the next young woman.

The bartender's gruff voice snapped Mahoney from his reflection. "Cash? Or open a tab?"

Mahoney fished his tattered wallet from the inside pocket of his tweed coat. "Cash." He pulled out a couple of crumpled bills and slid them over the bar. The bartender took them, turned his broad, rippled back, and walked away.

Sweet fingers of bourbon seeped up Mahoney's nose. He took a long, slow swig and let the alcohol linger at the back of his tongue. Numbing tendrils wove down his throat, over his arms, and down his insides. He was ready to succumb to the one path he knew was left for him. He checked his phone again, to make sure the volume was turned up. He willed it to ring, to hear Barbie's voice on the other end. A drink would calm his nerves. Time was ticking. The moon was nearly full. Would he get to the Gothic mansion before Saul the Slayer killed again?

The bartender returned, snapped Mahoney's credit card on the bar, then turned to tend to the other patron at the far end of the bar. On his way, he clicked a remote, changing the channel on the TV. Electric letters declaring that they had tuned into *MTV* shot across the hazy screen. An electric vibe swept through the room as a rock god took the stage, his long, golden hair shining under the lights. His eyes oozing an aura of mystery.

The Cult - Sun King flashed across the screen as a guitar beast blasted out the opening riff. The violent strums crackled through old speakers perched above on either end of the bar.

Mahoney took another luxurious swig of his drink and stared at the rock god as he took his place on stage. His voice, strong and soothing, seeped from the speakers, drowning out the crackles of the dated system and telling Mahoney that this is where it all ends.

Mahoney downed the remaining bourbon. The liquid slipped over his tongue and slithered down his throat, soothing his senses. He set the glass back on the counter with a clink.

The bartender returned. "Another?"

Mahoney nodded. Placing two fingers on each of his temples, he rubbed circles into his throbbing head. He closed his eyes and listened to the smooth voice laced with grit.

Mahoney pictured the beer-soaked Don's Joint, the leather-clad, blood-lipped waitress, and a glass of bourbon. He created a mini-movie within his mind, moving through the scenes, replaying them, wishing he were back there now. Blood-red lips spinning sweet words. Red-tipped fingernails wrapped around a glass of bourbon. A tall man standing at the centre of the stage, embracing the microphone in an eccentric dance. The man's hands stroking the metal bulb, his mouth opening, his soothing voice seeping from his black lips. Long, dark strands of hair flowing over his shoulders. The man's eyes closing, silver shadow streaking his eyelids, shimmering against the purple lights shining down on him. The story he told building momentum, his voice growing deeper, darker.

The man's words wove through Mahoney, down his insides, into his soul. Mahoney stared at the image of the glam demon, still vivid in his mind, watching black lips enunciating each syllable. The man opened his eyes. Dark spheres stared right into Mahoney's soul. He stared back at the dark eyes piercing him. He let them in. Their searching, probing gaze. What would they see? Deep down inside him.

Mahoney squeezed his eyes shut harder and rubbed his temples with vigour. He stared into the crevices of his mind. He found a dark tunnel. It opened before him. He stared down the tunnel, into the darkness. He knew this tunnel. He knew the circular openings dug into dirt walls where white corpse faces and black nothing eyes resided, staring at him, willing him to look. He wouldn't. Taking slow steps further into the hidden memory, he made his way over the cold, hard ground and through the tunnel. Voices called to him, labelling him *Bug* and pleading with him to save them.

A clink of a glass against the counter. The images vanished. Mahoney snapped his eyes open and stared at the glass of bourbon that had been delivered. He lifted it to his lips and gulped half of it in a single swallow.

The throbbing pain that had hijacked his gut for the last several weeks subsided. He reached inside his pocket, finding the smooth stone with his fingers. Retrieving the *Tiger's Eye* from its home, he placed it on the counter and stared at it. Golden and chocolate contours wove over the polished rock. A warmth washed through him, leaving a pulsing glow that swelled within him. At this moment, he knew his own true intentions. He wouldn't back away.

The rock god screeched to a climax, vibrating the small speakers. The next video flashed its beginning. *The Scorpions - Always Somewhere* scrolled over the screen. Acoustic guitar strums wept from the speakers. An electric layer joined in, crying. A new rock god took the stage. His rough voice wailed in pleas, telling Mahoney he had no time to call today. That he'd be going back to the hotel again.

Mahoney shook his head, staring into the bourbon. He had time to call. But he couldn't do it. He couldn't imagine coating his voice with a cloak of lies that Stella would see right through.

The rock voice heightened, pushing from the speakers, down to Mahoney, swirling around him, seeping into his pores, telling him he'd be back to love her again. He couldn't fathom staring into Stella's eyes and convincing her he had love to give. Not after this was all over. He could feel the rage boiling his blood and broiling his skin.

The riff squealed sorrowful bursts through the speakers, vibrating through the room.

His phone buzzed, snatching his attention from the rock show.

"Mahoney." His voice was gruff.

"It's Barbie. I got you an address."

"Nice work." He pulled out his notebook, eager to hear the location of the man he was ready to hunt.

"I had help. Called in Quesnel."

He clenched his jaw. "What?" He lowered his voice. "I told you *not* to involve Dixon or Quesnel until I confirm this isn't some trick. I got the tip from a crazy man who got locked away for beheading girls."

"I know. I'm sorry. But it was taking me too long. Dixon is fresh, young, I get why you don't want to tarnish his career. But Quesnel, I get a feeling she can handle herself."

Quesnel's smirk flashed through his mind. He couldn't argue with Briar's logic. "You got a point. Give me the address."

"317 Bouchier St, Roches Point. Name on the title is Sylvia Artemis. She's deceased. The name on her death certificate is Sylvia Ripper. Had a daughter, Violet, also deceased, and a son, Saul, apparently still alive. Saul Chester Ripper. We, Quesnel and I, think he's in the house, left it in his mother's name, somehow."

Mahoney scribbled the address on his notepad. "Tell Quesnel to hold off until I can confirm he's actually there."

Briar snorted. "I'll try. But she's a bit of a firecracker."

"Do your best."

"One more thing. Old houses like that, sometimes they have these smaller doors on the back of the house, or on the side. They were used for staff entrance. Might be a less-watched entryway."

"Thanks, Briar."

"Be careful."

"I will." He snapped his phone shut, gulped back the remaining bourbon, then signalled the bartender over. He needed to leave. Now. It was time to hunt a human vampire under a full moon.

Chapter 64

Glass Pedestal

Chester took twelve steps forward. He looked down at the peaceful scene. Six perfect rows of six cylindrical, glass enclosures, fanning out into a circle, meeting in a vortex. At the epicentre, an ancient symbol of the vampire. A circle—made of glass, lit up with glowing, red light—connected the ends of each row. Two arms intersected the circle, forming a V. A jagged slash crossed each arm. The entire symbol glowed orange-red.

Thirty-six homes for potential Violets. Eighteen of them occupied. Twelve years ago, once he had his process evolved enough, he'd found three new Violets every year. He kept the two best candidates, and sacrificed one. This year, sixteen years after he'd been released from his cage, sixteen years after he'd honoured the authentic Violet with a trio of sacrifices, he'd had an overwhelming urge to repeat the ode to his beloved sister. When Violet Sixteen had perished unexpectedly, his emotions took over. He sacrificed a Violet too soon, and left both of them on display. Four Violets gone. Leaving him with only twenty. Tonight, on the full moon, he had to follow the planned sacrifice in Violet's honour. He'd awakened the chosen one early and prepared her for her fate. Thus, leaving nineteen Violets. Eighteen of them occupied the glass homes. The most special Violet, the one who served him in ways none of the others would, was resting in another part of the house. She hadn't been feeling up to the festivities.

As he took inventory, grief swelled within him like a great wave rushing toward the shore of a deserted beach. He couldn't let it win. Grief. Sadness. *No.* He had his Violets. Perhaps the unplanned outcome of this current cycle of sacrifice was meant to be. Perhaps it was a sign that he should purge those that he'd had for too long. *Yes.* He was in control. He had to be. His Violets *needed* him.

He looked down upon his resting Violets. The electric being from within him burst from its cage.

The silence in the room clung to the air like a thick cloak. They slept inside their glass homes. Every day he rose them from their quiet rest for lessons, feeding, and cleaning. When he was unavailable to tend to them, they rested quietly in their glass cages, equipped with oxygen and filtration systems.

He relished in the moment.

Then he clicked a button. A strobe light pulsed through the room, their first signal that it was time to rise.

A daunting sound echoed through the vast space. An alarm clock from a horror film, echoing through the darkness like a primal scream.

Chester clicked another button. A savage beat echoed through the vast space. A slow, dramatic guitar riff wove through the beat. Then a whisper, blowing words into Chester's ears. Reminding him that he did love himself and that he liked the dark. Telling him to make his devil's mark on the milky white necks of his Violets.

He clicked a third button. Glass lids opened from the glass coffins. The bodies lay still. Their long, luscious dark hair framed their faces. Their long, dark dresses clung to their beautiful figures. A primal urge thrust through Chester's insides. His virility surged.

The riff climbed to new heights, filling the room with wild electric vibes. The whisper morphed into a savage ritualistic chant, speaking of apparitions, moonlight, and wind. Reminding Chester that her voice was beckoning. Violet's voice. Always there. His nocturnal mistress. His spirit lover.

His Violets opened their eyes. Their bodies stirred. Their eyes opened. They rose in their glass beds. Their eyes wandered, seeking the target of their desire. Their eyes came to rest on the figure with the long, midnight hair and the shimmering sleeves hanging from his raised arms as he stood on the balcony over them. He walked to the edge of the balcony, gripping the railing with his black-gloved hands, and addressed his Violets.

"Violets. Arise."

They rose from their glass coffins in unison. Like an army of dolls, they floated out of their glass houses and moved in a slow trance toward the vortex of the glowing red symbol. Chester walked down a winding staircase, one careful step at a time, in sync with the savage beat blasting through the room. He drifted along a walkway, over the demon symbol, to the vortex—a glass pedestal above the rows of glass coffins. Above the lines of floating figures in dresses.

He ascended the pedestal. They halted in perfect rows, protruding out like human spikes on rows of glass.

"Violets. It is time to be filled with my soul."

He stepped down from the pedestal, leading them toward a stage at the front of the room. The stage glowed a deep purple-blue. The savage tune continued pulsing a beastly vibe through the room. Upon reaching the stage, Chester stepped up onto it, and offered two hands. The first two Violets in the line reached their hands out and took his. They followed his lead onto the stage, over to a mahogany velour crescent sofa. It was the place for those who gave themselves to be fed by the soul of their leader.

Rows of figures stood with vacant stares, eyes fixated on the stage show. Fixated on him. Chester. Saul the Slayer. The saviour of their souls.

The first two Violets lay on either side of Chester. They ran their hands over his body, his chest, his legs. His head arched back as he accepted their probing hands.

The music pulsed. The beat grew more savage, stabbing the air. The voice increased in intensity, primal cries of lust and burning hell and salvation engulfing the room.

His shimmering sleeves spread over the mahogany velour. Small, soft hands unbuttoned the sequined costume. The hands ran up and down his tight, muscular torso. Their fingers crawled over the rippling contours of his abs. Chester moaned in pleasure, encouraging their exploration.

White, delicate fingers slid down his body. He moaned louder. They grew more eager in response. A flame flickered behind their vacant eyes as the praise they desired came through the cries of their demonic leader. Two pairs of hands pulled down his glamorous garment. Two pairs of hands worked on his exposed body. They used their black lips to heighten the intensity of the response.

The two Violets paused and looked at each other. The first Violet took her rightful position. She slid her black panties off from beneath her dress and over her boots. She mounted her demonic leader and slid him inside of her. She moved in perfect rhythm to the primal screams and the savage beat, washing pleasure over her face and tilting her head back at the right moments. She played the role to perfection.

Whoever she had been had vanished a long time ago. No trace of a little girl. No trace of virgin-like behaviour. Only sheer lustful pleasure washed over her face. There was a reason she was Violet 1.

His demonic soul drained his life seed into her.

She licked her black lips with lust. She'd earned her position as Violet 1. She was the most promising of his collection to carry on his legacy. The release purged any traces of the fake being he'd been wearing all day. Fully immersed into his world, his true being, his calling, he caressed Violet 1's hair as she lay down next him. He readied himself for Violet 2 as she rekindled him with her soft hands. He summoned Violet 3. She proceeded across the stage, over to the crescent couch and perched next to Violet 2.

He waved his hand. Violet 3 kissed Violet 2. A long lingering kiss, black lips on black lips. Violet 2 continued to prepare him as Violet 3 pulled her dress down her shoulders and kissed her milky skin.

The mass entourage of Violets came as summoned. Some of them were passed over for the night, left yearning for the next feeding. The next time they may be chosen by their demonic leader. To those he chose, he transferred them a piece of his soul. So they could feed. So they could thrive. So they each had an equal chance to become as perfect as Violet, the original. So he had the chance of being reunited with her again, flesh to flesh. So she could be more to him than his spirit wife.

GLASS
COFFIN
CULT

Chapter 65

Live Demon Doll

The spectacular Gothic mansion that Saul's grandfather had gifted him was perched up on a hill, in a gated community, overlooking Lake Simcoe. Mahoney had parked the rental Sedan a few blocks back, behind a deserted park. Sweat stuck his shirt to his back and his collar to his neck as he trudged up the hill, toward Saul's fancy home. The pack slung across his back seemed to get heavier as he climbed.

Mahoney was deep into the hunt, and there was no turning back now. His fists clenched into tight balls, stretching his black gloves over his whitening knuckles. The blood running through his veins boiled with adrenaline. The scent of prey prickled his nostrils.

He was going to get Saul the Slayer, Chester the Ripper, whoever this human vampire was.

He had planned to somehow get into the house, confirm there was indeed a Saul Ripper, then get Briar to pull the trigger on his backup. The last thing he wanted to do was pull Quesnel and Dixon into this hunt until he knew it was legit. Since Quesnel was already pulled in, and most likely on her way, he didn't have much time. Something nagged in the pit of his belly, telling him that he'd intended to deal with the killer himself. From the get-go.

He turned the corner, amped up his pace, and closed the final distance between him and Saul.

There it was. Mahoney cranked his neck back and looked up. The monstrous dwelling loomed over him from the perfect perch at the top of the cul-de-sac. He scanned the dark street. Several ornate lamp posts dotted the street, the small, individual glows blending into a single bright orb, exposing any intruder in an instant flash. He stuck to the treeline bordering the far side of the sidewalk, hiding under thick canopies of black-green. His hiking boots dug snuggly into the moist grass. Like a cat, he made a stealthy crawl, keeping close to the trees and away from the light.

He took another look at Saul's abode. Massive. Looming. Two houses up. A mini-castle from a past century. Carved stones spiralled into the denim sky like watchtowers. Massive windows stared down at him like black eyes under peaked grey-black stone archways. Closed in by a gate. An acre of land behind it. There had to be a way in.

He couldn't exactly walk up to the front gate and asked to be buzzed in. He smirked. No. He'd prowl behind and find a way onto the vast plot of land behind the house.

Half a house away, he slowed. The wrought-iron gate loomed over him. The long, winding prongs of the gate ended in sharp spikes. Before he reached the gate, he beelined sharply to the right, following a stretch of grass marking the property line behind Saul's mansion and the neighbouring monstrosity. The chill air stung his cheeks.

He pulled his tweed coat tighter around his chest. Keeping his eyes peeled, continuously scanning the horizon, he took quiet steps around the house. He reached the back. The vast acreage stretched out before him, a juniper blanket dotted with silhouettes of trees against the black sky. A tall, iron fence lined the acreage. He walked along it, slowly, examining the fence for any indication of a way in. Finally, a gate. And a heavy padlock. Nothing he couldn't handle. He slid the pack off his back and retrieved a hefty bolt cutter. The lock snapped, echoing through the silence.

Mahoney froze. His skull seized. He waited several moments. No indication that his lock breaking had alerted anyone. He slid the lock off and set it on the cold grass sweating with late-night dew. He slid the bolt cutter back into his pack, slung the pack over his shoulder, then eased the gate open with extreme care. No creaks. His shoulders relaxed.

He slipped through the gate. Hugging the fence line, away from any light glowing from the house, he crept along, close to the left-hand side of the dwelling. A dwarf-like iron door was carved into the side of the stone wall. His heart thumped as he approached it. Could it be that staff entrance Briar mentioned? As he leaned over to examine the door, it opened. He jolted. His brain buzzed.

Standing in the doorway was a young woman with long, dark hair. Her face was painted white. Blood-red circles wove around her eyes. Her enunciated lips were the colour of midnight.

Mahoney blinked several times, confirming that it wasn't another ghost face haunting his mind.

The live demon doll jerked her head and looked behind her, then stared at him. "Who are you?"

"I'm a detective. I can help you." He tried to see into the house, but the darkness was too thick.

She narrowed her eyes at him. "Help? Me?" She jerked her neck again, checking behind her, then returned her suspicious stare back to him. "Who are you?" She hissed her words.

Mahoney raised his hands and backed up a couple of steps. "I'm a detective. I work with Toronto Homicide."

"Show me your badge."

"I don't have it."

"Why not?"

"The investigation was going too slow. I wanted to stop whatever is happening in this house. Now. Didn't follow protocol."

"Why the hell should I believe you?"

"I can prove it." He slid his hand into the inside pocket of his tweed coat and pulled out his wallet. He took out his police photo ID and showed it to her.

"This could be fake."

"It's not." He turned the ID back and forth. The police department emblem shimmered, changing from one image to another. "You see?" He paused. "I have more." He dug back into his pocket and pulled out a series of photos from the cold case and fresh crime scenes. He handed them to her.

She hesitated, then snatched them from him. She shuffled through them, scrutinizing each one in turn.

"See? Those are from the cold case file. They're stamped, by Toronto Homicide, and have the case number." Sweat trickled down his back. "How would I get those if I didn't have access to the case files?"

"Fine." She thrust the photos back at him. "How the hell did you get in here?"

"I cut the lock on the gate." He slid his pack off his back, opened it, and pulled out the cutters.

She nodded. "What the hell do you want here?" Her blood-circled black orbs implored him.

"To help. What's your name?" he asked.

"Violet Thirteen." She spat the words out.

Violet Thirteen? How many copies of Violet did Saul the Slayer have? "Are you being kept against your will?"

She snorted. "What do you think?"

"I think that the man who owns this house kidnapped you and is holding you captive, along with other girls." He zipped his pack and slung it back over his shoulder.

"How can you help?" She crossed her arms. The blood rings around her dark eyes sent a chill down his spine.

"I can get you out of here."

She laughed. "Right. I'm already out." She advanced, brushing his shoulder and pushing past him.

"Wait," he pleaded.

She halted, spun on her heel, and stared him down with her dark orbs. "What?"

"Where will you go? What will you do? Don't you need help? Food, money?" he asked.

She twisted her thick midnight lips. "Look at me. I need to get the fuck away from here. I don't care what happens after that."

"Well I do. I want you to be OK."

"You don't even know me, *Detective.*"

"No, I don't." He sighed. "But I suspect you've been a slave to this man. For who knows how long. No one except you can truly comprehend what you have been through. But I assure you, I want to help. If you walk away alone, it's you against a cold, harsh world."

Her black lips turned down into a slight frown. "Fine. *If* I help you, right here, right now, then I want a fresh start. You give me money. I leave. I don't want any part of any this, ever again."

"Done." He rubbed the bristle on his chin. "How did you get out here?"

She released a sick laugh. "Played him. Before my *mother* dumped me on the front step of the local fire department with a note filled with lies, she played a lot of people. Always got what she wanted. I learned that *my master* would give me certain liberties if I dished out certain favours. I kept up the act for a fucking long time. Took me years to get this opportunity. Feigned illness. Convinced him to let me rest while he performs his sick ritual with the others. So, you better not fuck this up for me."

"I won't. He's in there now?"

"Yes. In the basement, tending to *them.*"

"Them?"

"His Violets."

A chill shot through Mahoney's core. "Lead me to him. Then come back out here. Go down the hill, turn left. My car is two blocks down. Wait there. My team is on their way. They will help you."

She fixed her eyes on him. The blood rings pulsed. The black orbs clouded with suspicion. After several moments of silence, she spoke. "Fine." She lunged through the door and walked down the hall. "Hurry up," she called back. "I just want to get the fuck out of here."

Chapter 66

Feeding

The pedestal rose high in the room, towering over the rows of glass coffins. Chester stood tall, perched above his demon doll army. He raised his arms above his head, his black sleeves flowing around him. Long, dark strands of hair fell around his shoulders and down his back, shining under the purple-blue hue of the pot lights dotting the ceiling. He closed his eyes. The blood-red circles around the deep-purple shimmer of his eyelids was striking against the perfect mask of creamy white covering his face. He pursed his black lips, the two peaks reaching for his nose, the perfect, full pout of his bottom lip dramatic and daring.

He loomed over the room, looking down on his Violet collection.

Like a well-trained army, they stood on glass planks lining their beds, waiting. Puppets attached to invisible strings, being pulled by a master. Chester again raised his arms high in the air and spoke to them.

"It is time to sacrifice, my Violets. Come forth," his raspy voice vibrated through the dungeon with a demonic hiss.

The young beings marched as if one along the glass planks in rows toward the vortex of the room. Toward their master on a pedestal. Chester, Saul the Slayer, examined them, each of their faces, looking for flaws. Creamy, white faces, smooth complexions, deep-red circles, dark pupils, and black lips. One by one, he searched their faces for the slightest smear or miscolour.

They are all perfect. All my Violets.

He was pleased. Tonight was meant to be special. He didn't want any mishaps.

The marching halted. They stood, lined up in their six rows, shooting out from the centre of the room. Their heads turned, as if by some magic cue, and they all looked up him with their blood-red-circled black eyes. They waited for him to speak.

"Tonight is special. We feed. We shall have fresh food. First, we sacrifice."

Gasps whispered through the dungeon. Pairs of black eyes remained fixed on him.

Chester picked up the remote control. The buttons glowed. He pushed one. A whirring noise echoed from the ceiling over the waiting faces. A pair of pale feet appeared, tied at the ankles with rope. The whirring increased in volume.

The feet lowered. A pair of pallid legs were revealed. A young woman, a newly acquired Violet, fresh and young, hung by her bound wrists, her arms stretching high overhead. Her eyes were closed. Her naked, white flesh glowed under the purple-blue hue of the overhead lighting.

A weak moan drifted from her parted, black-painted lips. Her eyelids fluttered, but remained closed.

Chester tilted her head back with one gloved hand, opened her lips with the other, and poured a rich, scarlet liquid into her mouth from a thin tube. She swallowed the special drink. The fluttering behind her eyelids rested. Her moaning ceased.

The physically-transformed Chester—now fully immersed into his true being of Saul the Slayer, dressed as the night creature—pulled a knife from a sheath hanging from his belt. The weight of the intricate ivory handle pressed against his leather glove. He flared his nostrils and took a deep breath. *It is time.*

He turned to face his dolls.

His voice boomed over them, "It is time."

Saul turned to his human sacrifice

He lifted his arm and ran his gloved fingers through her raven locks, down the side of her creamy cheek. He caressed her curves with his cupped hand, sliding his leather-clad fingers down her body. He leaned in close to her face and tilted her head, exposing her neck. His lips curled back. White fangs glimmered, then sank into flesh. Scarlet oozed over pale skin. He licked the life liquid, quivering as he swallowed.

She was perfect. He'd put effort into finding her. He'd groomed her. She hadn't grown into the one Violet he needed her to be. She would become a life source for the other flourishing Violets. His temples pulsed, reminding of the throbbing pain that threatened to take him to blackness as he'd staved off his needs, waiting for the full moon.

He lifted the knife. The blade shone under the orange-yellow hue of the candles circling his pedestal. He slid the blade into her flesh, just above her pelvis. The steel sliced into her as if he were cutting soft butter. Red trickled down her body. He kneeled and licked it away. The warmth against his tongue made him tremble.

He slid the blade up her body.

Without a sound, without any resistance at all, it slid easily through her. Keeping the blade in motion, he stood and slid it up to her neck. A stream of red dripped down her body, landing with splats in a large, silver goblet. The pit-pat of the dropping blood quickened. The droplets became a thin, steady stream of red, flowing into the heavy cup.

The cup filled, Saul replaced it with a large, silver bowl, empty and ready to collect the expired Violet's life source. He raised the goblet over his head and declared to his Violets that it was time to feed.

Placing the goblet to his black lips, steam kissing his smooth skin, he closed his eyes. His purple-brushed eyelids shimmered under the glow of the room. He drank a low, slow, satisfying portion from the cup of life. He opened his eyes, looking at the first Violet in line. "Come. It is time for you to feed."

Chapter 67

Live Demon Doll

Mahoney had followed the live demon doll, Violet Thirteen, down dark hallways, weaving through the belly of Saul's mansion. Finally they reached a door. Eerie music seeped through from the other side.

The demon doll turned and looked at him, black orbs pulsing from the centre of blood swirls. "In there. Performing his ritual with all his Violets."

"OK. You get out of here."

Without a word, she took off back down the hallway, into the darkness.

He took a deep breath, sliding his hand over the hunting knife. He doubted Briar would have been able to hold off Quesnel. She was probably on her way here now. He'd had enough of a head start to buy him some time. He was sick of makeshift investigations with disappointing outcomes. He wanted this fucking vampire dead. He wanted him to feel what all of his Violets felt when he slit them open.

Mahoney turned the knob on the door and eased it open in silence. The room opened up before him. A vast space.

He looked down from the ledge he teetered on. He stuck close to the wall, scanning the scene. The vast space below the balcony on which he perched opened up before him like a scene out of an old horror flick. Candles lined the walls, casting an eerie glow over the dungeon.

Glass coffin-like structures lined the floor below in an intricate pattern, circling their way around the perimeter, shooting in straight lines into a vortex marked with a symbol. A circle, glowing red, with a sharp V intersecting it. Ragged edges sliced the arms of the V. The same symbol on each of the victims. The ancient symbol of the vampire.

From the symbol sprouted a tall pedestal, launching toward the ceiling. The circular top provided the perfect platform for viewing the entire room.

On top of the clear pedestal stood a figure outlined with a fire glow. His head was bowed, his arms raised in front of him. Long sleeves flowed from his arms, glimmering under the purple-blue hue of the overhead pot lights.

Hell. I'm in hell.

Mahoney looked up, past the figure, the cult leader, the killer he was hunting. Behind him, a young woman hung.

Am I too late?

The imaginary spider that had been crawling up Mahoney's back sprouted into a full-sized tarantula. Hairy legs walked up his back. Fuzzy insect feet pricked his spine, inching up to his neck. The sticky feet clung to his flesh, walking their way around his neck, up his face, across his cheek toward his eye. The tingling prickle escalated. Tiny stabs of pain inched their way into his eye sockets and across his skull.

The young woman hung limp, her arms stretched over her head, her wrists tied. Her naked body was red from the blood bath that had poured from inside her when she'd been sliced open. Her insides had spilled out from her freshly gutted flesh, her organs stacked in a silver bucket. Droplets of blood trickled from her body, landing in a silver bowl, full to the brim with blood. Her blood.

He was too late. The kill had been completed. Sick swirled in his bowels. Acid gurgled in the back of his throat. Fury seared his pores. His blood boiled. This had to stop. He had to stop it.

The leader, Saul the Slayer, Chester the Ripper, raised his head slowly. The sequins of the black sleeves glimmered as he raised his arms, his hands reaching for the ceiling. He brought a silver goblet to his lips, drinking from it. Scarlet liquid drizzled down the sides of his black mouth, landing on the floor with wet splats.

I need to kill him.

Saul the Slayer motioned to the girls standing in their dark dresses waiting to be called. Like a series of haunted shells, the girls shifted forward. Every single one of them stared at the pedestal vortex. They moved as a single mass, their bodies floating into motion toward their leader.

Holy fuck. The tarantula crept across Mahoney's skull, digging sticky insect feet into his brain. His shoulders seized.

A deep voice vibrated from the pedestal over the dark-haired girls. "Violets. It is time to feed."

Violets. Replications of the sister he had crudely slaughtered at the young age of sixteen.

In unison, the girls walked toward the pedestal, their black dresses flowing over their feet. An army of white faces with vacant eyes stared into the distance.

The man spoke again, "Come, Violets. Feed."

The vacant-eyed, haunted beings, in a trance-like state, stepped in unison to a driving beat, floating in a smooth motion toward their leader.

The tarantula dug his way into Mahoney's brain. Sticky fuzz clouded his mind. He couldn't comprehend the scene before him. He didn't want to. Not hell. This was beyond hell. This was the hell after hell.

The sea of white faces moved in sync, their black lips weaving rehearsed words. A haunting whisper echoed through the glowing room. "We are hungry, master. We welcome your gift." Scarlet-swirled eyes focused on their leader as they chanted, over and over.

The haunting whisper seeped into Mahoney's ears, wove through his ear canals and into his brain.

The first girl reached the leader. The leader, Saul, held the goblet to her lips as she drank. Red seeped from the sides of her painted, soiled mouth, drizzling down her chin and over her pale neck.

The master of the cult of Violets lifted his hands again. His voice boomed over the chant, "Feed, my Violets, feed. Take your life source."

Mahoney watched, stuck to the wall beneath the shadows as one by one the girls of various ages approached their master and received their gruesome gift. The first Violets appeared older. As the line continued, they looked younger.

He swallowed hard every time blood trickled over a pale neck, gagging back his nausea. Some of the girls looked young. Other looked like they had grown into young women. He counted. He could have sworn he reached eighteen as the ritual came to a halt.

The cult leader stood tall and set the goblet down. A tight, black-sequined garment clung to his body, catching glimmers off the orange-red of the candle flames and purple-blue of the pot lights. He raised his head. His white face was striking against the dark background. He curled his midnight lips back in a demonic grin.

A white, jagged fang poked from each corner of his mouth, droplets of red sliding down the polished white gleam. His eyes glowed a demon red as he scoured the white-faced clan marching toward him.

Separate streams of black-laced girls merged into one winding swirl, circling around their master. Their white faces leaned up toward him. Their vacant eyes stared into nothing. They didn't see him. His words were all they needed. His orders moving their limbs for them. His words coming from their lips.

They were vacant beings, white-faced puppets. All control over their bodies, their minds, their mouths, came from him.

A chill pulsed through Mahoney's insides. It was ice cold. His hands numb, he grasped at his mind, trying to gain control. Trying to determine what the hell to do.

The vampiric master walked along the top of a row of glass coffins, toward a stage at the front of the room. The swirling circle of empty beings uncurled and followed him in a single line, like a giant, black centipede.

He stepped up onto the stage. They lined up in rows, his audience, leaning their faces up to him, closing their eyes, waiting for his next command.

Mahoney's brain buzzed. Hot rage simmered through his veins. *Fuck it. I need to kill this monster. Now.* He was done with locking up human monsters. He knew why he came here. To kill Saul the Slayer before he could kill another innocent girl.

Mahoney scanned the perimeter of the room. The ledge he was on followed the walls, on either side. If he were stealthy, maybe he could make it to the front of the room and sneak up behind this human vampire. He crouched down, behind the small balcony wall, moving like a bug behind it.

His knees cried out with each crouched step. This was no time for his old-man joints. Grinding his teeth against the pain, he crept along till he reached the corner of the room. He spun on his toes and inched along the side of the room. The red-orange glow from the flames lining the wall hot against his head and his cheeks, he swallowed hard and focused on the end of the walkway.

He reached the front corner of the room. Raising himself slowly, he peeked over the balcony ledge.

The draculian cult leader was engrossed in his ritual. He raised his arms, his black-sequined sleeves like wings around his muscular body. His voice slithered through the room. "You have received my life seed, some of you."

What? Life seed? What was he doing to these girls?

"You have all fed. You shall all have your opportunity to become the one you were meant to be." He took another drink from the goblet. Thick red trickled down the sides of his face as he took several gulps. Lowering the goblet, his white face was streaked in red, white fangs clawing out the sides of his black mouth.

The haunted beings inched toward him as one. Each in turn, they took their place in a new formation. Somehow, they knew exactly what to do, where to be. How to be. They all turned their faces toward their master, waiting for his orders.

Mahoney shook his head hard. *C'mon, Bug.* He looked ahead. The red-orange glow revealed a staircase in front of him, the stairs descending into darkness. He stretched out each leg, then walked over to the stairs. A board creaked. He froze.

The deep voice drifted up from the stage. Loud, commanding, telling the girls their time had come.

Mahoney continued his stealth walk to the stairs. He took one slow, cautious step at a time, descending into the darkness, blinking hard to make out each step down. At the bottom, he scanned for his next move. A small door in the corner called to him. He walked up to it, turned the knob, and pushed it open. The draculian cult leader stood, back to him, facing the room. The clan now looked toward him. He had the same view as the manic master.

Engrossed in his ritual, Saul the Slayer, Chester the Ripper, seemed unaware of the intrusion.

Mahoney slid his hand down the ivory handle of the gut hook hunting knife attached to his belt. The tarantula crept across his brain. He mentally kicked it in its fuzzy gut. He slid the knife out of its sheath. A flash intruded his thoughts. He gripped the handle of the knife hard, his white knuckles protesting. He flung the imaginary camera from his mind into the abyss. No more fucking pictures.

The knife shone back at him. Time to gut an animal.

Chapter 68

Saul the Ripper

The only sound was the loud *thump-thump* of Mahoney's heart against his chest. Tiptoeing cautiously across a hardpacked dirt floor, every step was a careful placing of his toe to the ground followed by the easing of his heel to follow suit. Mahoney gripped the beast of a knife hard, his fingers shaking, his knuckles white. The leather handle dug into the flesh of his fingers as he crept toward his prey.

The killer. Saul the Ripper. A glam Dracula night creature stood a mere few feet away, looming over his followers. White faces stared up at him vacantly, awaiting his order. Black-sequined satin clung to the demon leader's tight body. His long, dark hair glistened under the purple-blue pot lights. He spoke to his set of homemade Violets, even though he didn't need to. They followed a script that had been drilled into their souls. They knew what he wanted. He had branded his instructions into their minds.

Rows and rows of girls stood facing him, walking in a trance-like state, repeating their oath of devotion in unison. Well rehearsed, none of them missed a syllable or a beat.

The sequined sleeves slipped over muscular shoulders again, catching a glimmer from an overhead beam of light. The leader held his hands high, then pointed a finger and signalled his troop to continue.

En masse, again, the words flowed in a creepy, monotone flow, as if timed by a metronome. The voices in sync formed one voice, filling the dark, closed-in space with an eerie vibe.

Mahoney's hand shook. He gripped the heavy handle harder, slowing the shaking. The heel of his shoe lowered and he sunk his foot against the moist dirt. He fought against the urge to clear his throat. He couldn't afford to alert the glam Dracula.

If he died, it wouldn't matter. But if he failed, any one of these young girls could become the next human sacrifice. Past ghost faces already filled Mahoney's brain to the brim, spilling over the sides. There wasn't any more room for another corpse.

He lifted his foot and continued his slow creep toward the sequined creature. Feeling his way along the wall, he kept in the shadows, avoiding the patches of light hitting the floor. He stared at the spotlights, following their beams to the floor, examining the pattern of light cast and avoiding any contact.

As long as the glam Dracula didn't turn around, he would remain undetected by his prey. He had no idea, however, what the reaction would be if one of the Violets spotted a stranger. Their minds were moulded into a shape undiscovered by humanity. It was impossible to say what the mass would do. He didn't want to find out.

Closer and closer he crept, staying in the side shadows. He was a few feet from glam Dracula. Strong musk wafted off the man, sticking in Mahoney's throat. He almost gagged, but swallowed against it, silencing the intrusion. Two more tiptoed steps and he could almost reach out and touch the end of one of the flowing sleeves.

His hand re-adjusted around the heavy handle. A bead of sweat trickled down the side of his face. The chill migrated, trickling down his spine and into his gut where it swelled in a mass of tingles. His molars ground against each other, the back of his jaw clenched tight.

He took another step. He swallowed hard. Then he thrust himself toward the glimmer of the sequins in one final powerful stride, no longer worried about alerting his prey.

His shoe plunked to the ground, dislodging a pebble. The small stone clicked across the ground. The entranced mass of faces all stared at him in a single, simultaneous jolt, their empty eyes looking past him.

The sequined sleeves flared as the glam Dracula spun around, his chiselled body clenched, his eyes alert. His hand wrapped around the handle of a large knife. Saul thrust his arm toward Mahoney.

The blade slid into Mahoney, the tip slicing into him as if his flesh were butter. He jerked back, the silver tip releasing from his skin. His lower abdomen warmed as blood oozed from the fresh slice.

Fuck.

It didn't matter if he died. *No more human sacrifices, you sick vampire.*

He lunged forward, gripping the heavy ivory handle hard, staring his prey in the eyes. Saul lifted his arm, knife in hand, raising it high.

Mahoney lowered his hand, gripping the heavy handle even harder. He thrust the blade into Saul.

The blade slid into Saul's flesh, entering his stomach.

Thick red gushed over Mahoney's hand.

The red bath coated his hand, sticking to his fingers. Saul's fingers released the knife from their grasp. It dropped to the floor with a heavy clank. Mahoney pushed his knife further into Saul's flesh.

The red stream flowed strong, drenching Mahoney's hand and forearm. Thick drops dripped to the ground, landing in splashes.

Saul stumbled forward.

Mahoney caught him by the chest with his free hand, shoving him backward. The knife released from Saul's body, taking chunks of flesh with it.

Saul fell onto his back with a deafening thump that echoed through the room.

The gasp of multiple voices in unison rang through the room. A sea of white ghostly faces stared, their mouths dropping open, their blood-circled eyes wide.

Mahoney lunged toward his fallen prey. Saul clasped his side with a blood-soaked hand. He reached his hand out toward Mahoney.

Mahoney landed beside Saul, crouching down. His eyes wild, his breathing loud and raspy, he plunged the knife back into Saul in the very spot that had critically wounded him.

Mahoney's hand trembled. He tightened his grip on the heavy handle. He twisted the knife inside of Saul, slicing his internals into a catastrophic mess. The handle turned toward Saul's neck, Mahoney pulled it all the way up Saul's body, slicing his flesh into one long incision from pelvis to heart, splitting him open.

Leaning over Saul, he peered into his half-closed eyes, his own eyes in a demon-like haze.

"How does it feel to be gutted like the animal you are?" Mahoney's words hissed from his mouth, spit flying along with them.

Mahoney pulled the knife out of the dying Saul. Saul gasped, his body trembling. Blood poured in thick streams from the slit, covering him, pooling around him, drenching the sequined sleeves. His lower lip quivered. Saul stretched his lips back in a sick smile, revealing two white fangs. Blood spilled out of the corner of his mouth.

His deep voice rich with passion despite his demise, he said, "Your...end...will...come."

The man narrowed his eyes. His head fell back against the ground. His raspy breath slowed. His throat gurgled. Blood spurted from his mouth, sliding down the fangs. His body convulsed, then stilled.

His eyes glazed. The raspy breaths halted.

A chorus of creepy voices raised through the room. "You have taken our leader. You have taken our salvation. You must die."

Pain sliced Mahoney's gut. He stared back at the dozens of eyes glaring him down. Their vacant stares were focused. Focused on him.

Chapter 69

Violet Army

Warm blood oozed over Mahoney's fingers. He looked at the knife shaking in his trembling hand. He looked at Saul, lying on his back, limp hands by his side, his body still.

What have I done? Mahoney took a deep breath, his eyes fixating on the knife. His knife. The knife that had been inside the dead man. Inside of Saul.

I did what I came to do.

His name is Saul Chester Ripper. And I killed him.

He grabbed his coat and wiped the sticky blood off the blade. Blotches of red soaked into the grey tweed. He knew it would never come out. He also knew it didn't matter.

He reholstered the knife into his belt. The room spun around him, creating a vacuum in which only he and gutted Saul existed. The concrete walls lined in candles whirled around him, forming a circular orange-yellow streak of colour. He shook his head and focused on Saul.

The spinning slowed in clicks, like gears grinding down, one notch at a time. It was like he was on a merry-go-round coming to the end of a ride, slowing in a way that its occupants wouldn't be jolted out of the merry place they'd been put in by the spinning and the music. The room stopped. Stillness and silence followed.

I did what I came to do. Mahoney forced confidence into his own internal thoughts. He was the only one he had to convince of anything anymore. The walls pulsed around him. The candle flames burned hot and red. Sweat poured over his forehead and down his cheeks.

Chanting wove over him. He pulled his gaze off Saul and looked out to the vast space filled with rows of glass coffins. Perfect lines of girls with vacant stares stood, their empty eyes turned on him. The blood circles around their black orbs amplified by the purple-blue light pulsating over the stage raising him above them.

Their black lips moved in unison. A raspy whisper shot from the moving mouths, across the room, aiming at him. He chose one girl to focus on, examining the movements of her lips, listening to the chant, trying to decipher the words.

"You have taken our leader."

"You have taken our salvation."

"You must die."

Like a broken record, their single unified voice repeated the words over and over.

Their leader. Their puppet master. A gruesome glam Dracula, lying crumpled on the ground, gutted, just like he would have gutted them. If someone hadn't stopped him.

It's done. I did what I came to do.

It was his own hand that had gutted their master. Now they wanted to take him. What damage could they do? An army of empty beings. They marched as they were told. They spoke as they had been wired to. What did they know of choosing their own way?

The ghost army marched toward him, their legs moving as one giant leg.

He stood tall and projected his voice through the dark room filled with glass death. "Listen. Girls. It's all right. He can't hurt you now."

His words vanished into the darkness, unheard by their closed ears.

Their chant grew louder.

"You have taken our leader."

"You have taken our salvation."

"You must die."

Their marched quickened. Black boots hit the ground with thuds that echoed as one loud boom through the vast space, filling the dark room with the thumping drumbeat of a marching ghost army.

He waved his hands. Their eyes remained glued to him.

"I'm a detective. I'm here to help. He can't hurt you now."

Their eyes looked through him.

Their chant grew louder.

"You have taken our leader."

"You have taken our salvation."

"You must die."

The marching quickened. The thumping grew louder. The room filled with an acoustic beat of heavy black boots.

He wasn't getting through. Their minds were moulded, shaped by the gutted man lying crumpled on the floor. Could they be re-programmed? Re-set? Back to who they were?

Not here. Not now.

The black boots of the ghost army tramped up the stairs onto the stage. The first row of ghost girls circled around him. The blood-red circles around their eyes glowed. Black pupils shot vacant stares at him. Their chanting quickened. Their voices heightened. An older Violet broke through the circle, raising her arm, clutching the blood-soaked knife of her master. She plunged the blade straight at Mahoney.

He jerked. He ducked. He thrust himself through the circle and across the stage, toward the door in the back corner. The circle of glowing red eyes turned to him and marched toward him. He opened the door, slammed it behind him, and bolted up the staircase that had brought him down from the balcony above.

He paused, looking down at the room, at the army. They had formed a long line, streaming toward the door at the back of the stage. The door opened. They snaked through, weaving their way up the stairs toward him. He lunged across the balcony, toward the exit that had been his entry way into this underground cemetery of lost girls.

He plunged through the door and slammed it behind him. Narrowing his eyes, he peered through the darkness, willing dark shadows to materialize into something useful. His eyes caught the outline of a chest. He ran over to it, heaved his weight against it, and slid it against the door.

He breathed a sigh of relief.

Wracking his brain, he attempted to retrace his steps as he'd followed the live demon doll.

Chapter 70

Tweed Wrap

Mahoney scanned the entire street. Empty. No demon doll. Where had she gone?

He eased himself into the Sedan, slammed the door shut, and flipped open his phone.

"Mahoney? Are you OK?" Briar's sweet voice shot him full of relief.

"Yeah. Quesnel on her way?"

"Yeah. Used her FBI clout. Called in a SWAT." She paused. "I couldn't hold her off."

Thank the homicide gods for Quesnel's no back down attitude. "Good."

"Is he there? Saul?" She asked.

"Yeah."

"Good. Are you safe?"

"Yeah."

"Good." She sighed into the phone.

"Get her a message. Tell her there's a bunch of girls, in the basement."

He flipped his phone shut and tossed it onto the passenger seat.

Pain sliced his gut. Opening both sides of his tweed coat, he peered down at the red blotches seeping through his shirt. He inhaled, held his breath, and leaned into the steering wheel. Hot pain seared his skin, fresh blood oozed from the open wound. He yanked off both sleeves of his coat then laid it beside him.

Easing back against the seat, he took a few breaths. His shoulders unclenched as the shots of pain eased.

He unsheathed the gut hook hunting knife from the holster in his belt. Puncturing the bottom of his beloved tweed coat with the silver blade, he pulled the knife through the heavy material, slicing free a rough strip of tweed.

As he leaned over the centre console, a fresh burst of pain rushed through him. He bit down on his lower lip against the hot slice searing his insides and opened the glove box with a trembling hand. The heavy ivory handle thudded against the inside of the glovebox. He snapped the plastic door shut, then sank back against the driver's seat.

He took hold of the rough strip of tweed, leaned forward again, biting against blazing needles of pain, and wrapped the strip around his back. As he sank back into the seat, he pulled both sides of the strip around his belly. He took a deep breath, then pulled tight, tying the strip at his side. Little specks of red popped through the tweed, but the thick material held up well against his life liquid.

He was sure it would hold for a while. He'd seen a movie once, an old gangster flick. One of the mobsters got shot right in the gut. The gangster had sprawled out on the floor for most of the movie, slowly bleeding out. The placement of the open gunshot seemed to align with the large gash in his own torso. He was sure he'd be fine. For a while.

He grabbed his now tattered tweed and pulled it back on. Closing his eyes, sinking his head into the headrest, he breathed deep and counted to ten. His heartbeat slowed. The sweat trickling down his face eased. Opening his eyes, he fished his phone out of his coat and dialled the only number he wanted to call.

It rang. He waited, picturing Stella on the other end. He prayed to God she would answer. It was a few hours earlier, way out on the Sunshine Coast, but it was still the middle of the night.

"Hello?" Stella's sweet, sleep-laced voice sounded far away.

"Stella."

"Dad?" Her voice jolted to attention. "What time is it?"

"It's late. I'm sorry I woke you."

"No, no. It's fine." She paused. He could see her mouth twisting as she put the pieces together. "Is it over? Are you coming home?"

Home. He wasn't sure where that was. "Yeah. It's over." He sighed, shifting in his seat. Pain sliced his gut. He winced.

"Dad? Are you OK?"

He gritted his teeth and swallowed. "Yeah. I'm great. Just, uh, wrapping up out here. Wanted to let you know."

Silence wafted over the phone waves. "Dad, you're not coming home yet, are you?"

"Not quite. Soon."

More silence. "I want to believe you." The tears in her voice shook his core.

"Stella, listen. You have to know I love you. More than anything."

Her voice quivered. "I do. I know. I've always known. But...you don't sound good."

"I'll be fine." *Would he?*

"Did you get him?"

"I did."

She sighed. "No more dead girls."

"No more dead girls. Stella, you listen to your mom, OK?"

"OK."

"Goodnight, Stella."

"Goodnight, Dad. I love you."

He clicked the phone shut just as the tears washed down his face over his trembling lip.

HEAVY
METAL
SPIRAL

Chapter 71

Heavy Metal Spiral

The black Sedan swerved erratically down the winding road as Mahoney pressed his foot to the pedal and made his escape from the Gothic mansion. Quesnel and her SWAT would take care of the girls he'd left in Saul's basement. He'd killed a man. He'd *chosen* to kill a man. He couldn't get Quesnel caught up in his mess. He needed to clear his head.

The darkness of the night descended over him. He put the pedal to the metal and made it to the downtown core in record time. Approaching the bright lights of the big city, he eased up on the gas. He didn't need any unwanted attention. Not now.

Cruising through the rundown streets on the outskirts of the belly of the big city, he looked for a place to go. He needed a stiff shot of something so he could figure out his next move.

A fluorescent purple sign pulsed an eerie welcome. *Siboney Club.*

Easing the car to a slow cruise, he scanned the dimly lit street housing the pulsing purple sign. The parking lot was littered with a collection of rundown vehicles. The rest of the street was deserted. He rolled the car to a stop behind a looming dumpster.

He opened the door and stepped out of the car. Night air chilled his cheeks. Moist rot floated from the dumpster. He approached the door to the night club. At first he thought it was purple. Then deep blue. But then it looked black. *Whoosh.* He pushed it open. He stepped through to the other side.

Bang. The mood door slammed behind him. He looked into a long, dark tunnel. A low vibration pulsed through the tunnel. The tunnel breathed in rhythm with each guttural wave. He shook his head hard, refocusing down the black tube. Sliding his tweed coat open, he wrenched on the tied ends of the strip of tweed around his gut.

A gasp escaped his lips. He clenched his jaw. Blood-soaked splotches seeped through the grey material.

Fuck it. He needed some substances to numb the pain. No one would find him here.

He pulled a paper bag from his tweed coat pocket and slipped a small plastic bag from within. He crumpled the paper, shoving it back into his pocket. He pulled open the small square of clear plastic, exposing a handful of white pills. The guy in the black hoodie that smelled of an unattended toilet had told him to take one at a time. He placed two on his tongue, then hesitated. He caught a whiff of his tweed sleeve. His own stale odour with a slight coating of Irish Spring hit his nose. Time for a dry clean. He wasn't so fresh either.

He swallowed back both pills then shoved the plastic bag into the inside pocket of his tweed coat. He adjusted his tattered derby, cleared his throat, and embarked on his dark path. The darkness engulfed him until he couldn't see. He followed the rhythmic, deep vibrating rumbling through the tunnel, through him. Like a nocturnal animal, he followed his instincts. He thought of Harold in his dark, moist cell.

His gut pulsed. Cold trickled through him. Dim light poked its way into a circular opening ahead. The deep, rhythmic pulsing grew louder. Voices clattered over the mess of sound.

A purple-blue hue met him on the other side. The guttural vibrations opened up into a full-out electric riff. Something hissed. He jolted. A woman in all black with cat ears perched on her head recoiled, holding her hands like paws. She meowed at him, then purred.

Placing her paw hands on the wooden stand hiding her body, her voice purred at him. "Sixteen-dollar cover."

There was a cover for this place? And why was the number sixteen so familiar?

Mahoney nodded, pulling his wallet from the inside pocket of his tweed coat. The small plastic bag dropped to the floor. The feline hostess bent over, picked it up with slender fingers tipped in black, then arched her back as she slicked her way to standing.

"Watch your goodies in here…" She licked her bright-pink lips as she handed him the bag.

He took it, replacing it with several wrinkled bills.

"You look clean...fresh," the feline hostess purred. "Like I said, watch your goodies in here." She licked him from head to toe with her eyes.

A tingle crept down his back, one tickling step at a time.

He nodded at the feline temptress then plunged himself into the room. It was like a cave. Circular, dark concrete walls painted like grey-brown rock.

Stainless-steel tables were scattered haphazardly around the cave bar. Tight leather clung to sleek, muscular bodies. Black-painted lips moved in conversation and sipped from glassware of ornate shapes. Chains jangled as bodies moved to the angry beat pulsating from the stage across the cave bar.

The stage displayed a performance beyond his comprehension. He gulped, then stared. A tall being, half-man half-woman slithered around the stage like a serpent. Sexuality seeped from the lean body. Black-blue lips wove over a silver bulb, deep, smooth tones seeping from the voice within. Long fingers caressed the mic stand, teasing every being entranced by their movement. Black hair slicked back, framing a white face. Topaz eyes pierced into Mahoney, looking down inside him, probing, exploring for his deepest, darkest secret.

Frozen, Mahoney's arms tingled. His feet went numb. He listened to the serpent being singing to him of people who wanted to abuse and those who wanted to be used.

He snapped his gaze from the serpent being. Scanning the purple-blue haze sphere, he found the bar. He wove through pleather, chains, piercings, and staring eyes. He was sure he'd been eye-raped a dozen times before reaching the bar. Feline hostess was right. He was fresh meat in his not-so-fresh tweed. He needed to up the dose on his toxic cocktail if he was going to do this. And he was—going to do this. There was nowhere else to go now.

Barely reaching the stainless-steel bar, a petite pale woman with perky breasts punched his way.

"What's your poison," steel-coloured lips asked.

"Bourbon. Double. Straight up."

A black-lined, silver-shimmer eyelid winked at him.

She was back in a flash with his sweet demise. She lurked, watching him as he downed the drink in three swallows.

"Another?" She curled her tongue over her top teeth, parting her steel-shimmer lips.

"Sure."

She was back and sliding the drink his way. He offered her a small stack of bills, sliding them over the smooth steel.

He stared at the counter.

"Stainless steel. Easy to clean. Splash proof." She sneered.

Her perky breasts poked hard against the thin layer of pleather stretched across her chest.

He nodded. The serpent voice slithered back into his mind, seeping an introduction to Cami.

Finding the stage with his eyes, he watched Cami join the band. Cami crawled her way across the stage like a savage huntress. Curling up beside a long silver pole rooted to the floor and the ceiling, a golden spotlight brought her to life. Her muscular leg slid up the pole, her silver thong caressing it. Her body moved in vicious thrusts to the heavy croonings and electric vibes created by the serpent singer and his body-builder guitarist.

Cami's emerald eyes made their way across the room. They found him. They stared into him, finishing the attempt to uncover his darkest secret. Emerald eyes, golden shimmer, and a silver spike-studded choker hypnotized him. She was a lion on a leash. A long chain hung from the back of the choker, down her spine, and coiled on the floor.

"Cami's got a free slot, right after her performance."

He turned. Shimmering silver lips greeted him. She nodded to the back of the cave bar. Several round doors lined the back wall.

She eyeballed his drink. "Another?"

He nodded. She returned.

"A round of Cami?"

He nodded.

"Kat told me you might like the full-meal deal."

Full-meal deal?

She toyed with the silver circle piercing her lip with the tip of her tongue. "Kat. The hostess. Cat ears. Likes to hiss. She helped you with your goodies."

Goodies? I didn't let her touch me, did I?

"You dropped them, from your coat pocket. You OK?"

"Yeah. Sorry."

"You're into, shall we say…a variety of treats. You might like the full-meal deal."

"Sure."

"She'll be done in twenty minutes." Her hand slid across the steel counter, leaving a shiny golden key. "Purple door." Her eyes pointed to the end of the room at the series of doors lining the cave wall.

He nodded.

"You can pay her when you're done."

He nodded again, then turned back to the serpent man sliding across the stage, words seeping from his black-silver mouth.

Downing half the bourbon in the glass he was holding, he turned his attention to Cami. She slithered up and down the pole with ease, her golden-pink shimmering eyes fixating him.

The serpent man slithered across the stage over to Cami. His white face didn't belong to his long, lean body. It was like it was pasted on. His black-purple lips wove an entrancing song. Cami curled around the pole, then slunk across the floor, wrapping around the serpent man's feet. The deep riff filling the room grew more intense. Heavy vibrations pulsed through the room, filling the entire space.

Cami crawled on her hands and knees, glitter shimmering over her body under the purple hue of the stage. She clawed her way up the serpent man's body as his mouth stretched wider and his voice plunged deeper.

Cami looked up into the serpent man's black eyes, her hands pawing his chest. Electric strings shot vibrations over the packed crowd. The serpent tilted his head back and wailed deep, hard, loud. Cami slunk to his feet and curled into a glimmering gold ball.

The stage went dark. Shouts echoed through the room. The vibe grew raw and primal. Mahoney shot back the rest of the bourbon, grabbed the golden key, and made his way to the purple door.

Chapter 72

Toxic Swirl

Mahoney stared at the purple door. It pulsed and swirled. He shook his head, inserting the golden key into the lock. He turned the key. It clicked. Twisting the golden knob, he stepped through, closed the door behind him, then walked into a hazy blue hallway.

Third door on the left, purple-shimmer lips whispered to him.

The hallway ebbed and flowed, turning pink, then red, then blue again. He blinked his eyes and seized his skull, grasping for his senses. The third door was a glimmering gold, just like Cami's eyes and her body crawling across the stage.

The door was locked. He tried the key. He went through. Stepping into another world.

"Lock the door behind you," purple-shimmer lips whispered. He did. Placing the key on the small table perched in the centre of the room, a plethora of treats waited for him. A glass, half full with sweet brown liquor sat beside a bottle labelled Maker's Mark. Four lines of white powder perfectly partitioned on a glass tablet grabbed his attention. Was this where he had come?

Heat rushed over his hand as the image of blood pouring from a man's body washed over his hand. Saul the Slayer. Chester the Ripper. A human monster.

Yes. This is where he was.

Slipping out of his tweed coat, he hung it over the back of a chair. Placing his tattered grey derby on the chair, he stared at the white powder.

Fuck it. All in.

He leaned over and sniffed a line, then another. Chasing it down with three long gulps of bourbon, he sat in the chair, resting his derby in his lap.

A spotlight shone to life, sending a beam down a pole and leaving a circle on a small, raised stage.

Sultry music seeped through the room. Cami appeared from a back door onto the stage. She spun on high golden heels. Her skin shimmered under the spotlight. Her leg stretched up against the pole. She rubbed herself against it. Placing her finger in her mouth, she pulled it out slowly, golden-glimmer goo seeping along it. She slid her finger into her silver thong, and along her pleasure spot. She gyrated against the pole, against the tip of her finger, and moved her head in circles to the smooth, sultry riff.

Moaning softly, she closed her eyes, her golden eyelids shimmering against the spotlight. She ran her tongue along her pink lips.

Mahoney's mind buzzed. His loins tingled. He downed the rest of the bourbon and poured another glass. She slinked up to him, picked up his derby and placed it over her blonde curls. He gave in to her guidance as she slithered around him.

She picked up his tweed coat, hanging on the back of the chair. She took her time with it. Sliding her arms into the sleeves, she swayed her hips back and forth, squatting in front of him, spreading her legs. She slid her hand into the inside pocket, pulling out his handcuffs. Light bounced off a shiny silver cuff as she slid it over her wrist. She pulled the other cuff with her free hand, the chain linking them expanding behind her head. Golden heels planted against the concrete floor, she gyrated her hips in a full circle, taunting him with the wet spot on her silver g-string.

Standing tall, Cami slid the cuffs into one hand, then took his empty glass with the other. Slithering over to the makeshift bar of treats, she poured him an ample drink. Handing him the glass, she leaned in close, then ran her tongue along his lips. The music pulsed hard. She spun, leaned over the table and pushed her ample, round ass cheeks toward him, then sniffed a line. Then another. Her blonde curls, streaked with silver and tipped in black, slid over her shoulders as she stood, leaning her head back and relishing in the jolt.

She turned to face him, hanging by the table. Preparing another four perfectly proportioned lines of white powder, she summoned him with her pointer finger. He did as he was told. He stood, walked up to the table, and looked at her. She pointed to the white lines. He stared at the thin, white lines. Black-sequined sleeves clouded his mind. Wet heat flushed over his hand. The feel of Chester's hot blood oozed through his fingers. He could see the knife sliding into flesh. He could feel his hand twisting, gutting the sadistic monster like a pig.

Sadistic monster. Was he any different? He didn't give a fuck. The psycho was dead. The girls would be found. But he wouldn't.

Fuck it. All in.

He leaned over, sniffed a line of powder. He exhaled loudly, then sniffed another line. His eyes bulged, trying to leap from their sockets. His brain buzzed. The riff echoing through the room grew angry, seeping through him, into his soul. His entire body pulsed.

Cami ran her tongue along his arm. A tingle followed the wet trail.

She dangled the cuffs, pulled him by the hand and led him to the stage. *Click.* His wrist was cuffed. Clank. The cuffs pulled around the pole. *Click.* His other wrist was cuffed, the connecting chain wrapped around the pole. He stood, attached to the pole of the lowest form of entertainment, naked and exposed. It felt good—to feel.

Cami's heels clicked against the concrete floor as she walked across the small room. Her back to him, he couldn't see what preparations she was making. She spun, facing him, walking toward him again.

Click, click. A lighter lit. A candle came to life. Mahoney stared into the blue centre of the flame, hypnotized by its glow.

A voice ripped from the speakers, then ripped through him. Angry and raw, the voice spoke of people who wanted to abuse. A chill jolted through him.

Fuck it. All in.

He focused on the orange-red heat of the flame.

Cami came right up to him. She yanked open the top three buttons of his shirt. One of the buttons shot across the room. She tilted the candle. Hot wax simmered his skin. He jolted. His back hit the cold pole hard. Burning flesh wove into his nostrils. His nipple tingled. The tingle migrated into him, down through him, and into the pit of his stomach.

Fuck it. All in.

He willed his brain to feel Chester's blood on his own hands. He forced his mind to see the look on the sick psycho's face. He dug deep for the images of the knife twisting into flesh, slicing up internal organs.

Sizzling ripped through his ears. Pain seared his other nipple.

Fuck it. All in.

Click. Cami flicked a switch with the tip of her golden shoe. A strobe light came to life, pulsing an aggressive vibe into him.

She undid his belt, and yanked it from him like a wild whip. She grabbed his pants, then froze, staring at the blood-soaked tweed strip.

Her sultry voice seeped into him, "Shall I continue?"

He nodded.

She pulled his pants down to his knees and crouched in front of him. Hot-pink lips lined in black wrapped around his hard cock. They slid, back and forth, following the aggressive rhythm of the pulsing light and the rough beat. His entire body tensed. The room spun, purple, red, blue light whirling around in a theatrical circle. The buzzing in his brain took over his neck and buzzed down his spine.

She released him, leaving a glittering golden goo.

Another visit to her prep corner and she returned, sliding a black whip through her fingertips. Crack. His skin split. Pain pierced him. His body seized. Blood trickled down his chest. That was it. The answer. The pain. He could feel, again.

Fuck it. All in.

Crack. Another split. Another piercing pain. Another trickle of blood.

He stared deep into the spinning hue of colour. An electric energy ripped through him.

Fuck it. All in.

Several cracks later, Cami abandoned the whip. She slid her silver thong down her shimmering legs and kicked it away with a golden heel. She crawled up to him like a wild animal. Mounting him, she wrapped her legs around his torso. Muscles rippled as her legs grasped him and latched on to the pole. She rode him raw. Hot juices plunged through him and shot from his body. The ultimate purge followed.

Images of the corpse of corpses, a million little faces turned into one horrific skeleton, clawing its way from the ocean, chunks of flesh clinging to its bones, shot from his mind into the swirling mix of coloured light. Black-sequined sleeves, a tight body cut open like a pig, blood pouring, organs and flesh mixed in a gruesome display.

Cami slid off him. She bent over, giving him a full view, and retrieved her silver thong. Snapping it into place, she walked up to him and whispered, "You sure you don't want some...*help?*"

Cami's eyes pleaded with him as she eyeballed the strip of tweed blotched with blood.

He licked his parched lips, focused on her mouth, and croaked the words, "No. I'm fine."

She froze. Her eyes pierced into him. "Well, customer is always right." She shot him a glimmering golden smile.

"Yes."

"You take care of yourself, honey."

She walked over to the prep table one last time.

She walked up to him, pressing her breasts against his bare chest, she brushed her lips against his, then slid her hands up his arms. *Click. Clank.* The cuffs released the pressure hold they had on his wrists. She stepped back, placing them neatly on the table of treats. She poured him a drink, prepped him two more lines, then placed a small, purple box on the table, beside his farewell treats.

She placed his derby on her head, tipped it with her fingers, then spun on a golden heel, walking toward the door.

Chapter 73

The Other Side

Cami slipped through the door, taking every trace of glimmering gold with her.

Mahoney poured one last bourbon and raised it in a lonely toast. He leaned back into the chair and sipped the soothing liquid. The room ebbed a strange purple, pulsing like it was alive. He ran his hand over his bristly chin and waited for the room to settle around him.

Glass empty, he planted his palms onto the table and pushed himself to standing. The purple, pulsing room swayed. He leaned into the table and took a few deep breaths. Settling his derby in place, he slipped his arms into his tweed coat. He looked down at the rough-cut edge running along the bottom of his beloved coat. The red splotches on the length of tweed around his midriff had grown and deepened. The thick material barely held him together.

He turned and slipped through the purple door.

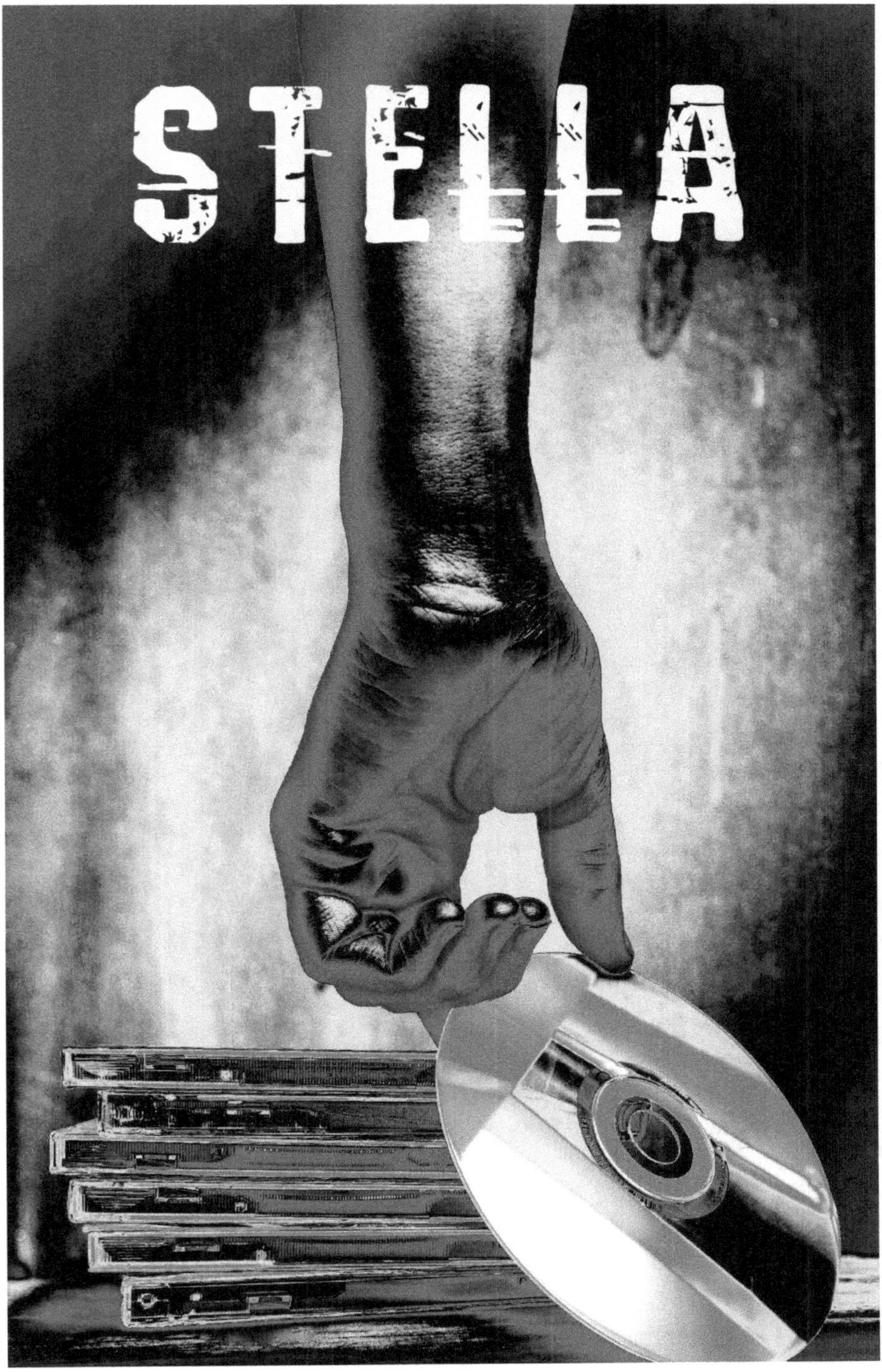

STELLA

Chapter 74

Stella

October 13, 1989

Stella flung the door open, slammed it behind her, and ran up the stairs. Her mother wouldn't be home for at least another hour. Yanking her black boots off, one at a time, she dropped them onto the plush blue rug. She flung her pack onto her bed and walked over to her hot-pink boom box. She pressed play and turned up the volume.

The manic vocals of Black Sabbath blasted through the bedroom.

She peeled off the constricting blouse and plaid skirt, the freshly pressed outfit that met school standards, and left them crumpled in a pile on the floor. She slid into a pair of tattered jean shorts and her cozy Ozzy t-shirt.

Raw raspy vocals seeped through the room.

Banging her head to the savage beat, her strawberry-blonde hair flew wildly and her legs made spasmic dance movements over to the bed. Purging the confines of her school-girl persona, releasing the Stella within. She zipped her pack open. Retrieving a stack of newspapers, she set them on the bed, then sat down cross-legged next to the stack. She hoped with all her might that there was a pearl of information in the sea of words. For months, ever since her father's death, she'd been hunting down copies of newspapers from all the stands she could get to. He died on the other side of the country, in the big city of Toronto. She was all the way out here, on the west coast. Her mother had fed her a nice story about how he'd died stopping a killer, saving a bunch of girls.

She wanted more. She wanted all of it. The grit. The raw truth. She *needed* to know what it was like for him when he died. And exactly *how* it had happened.

Time passed as she flipped through papers. Her mother would be home soon. She couldn't be caught reading what was inappropriate for a twelve-year-old.

A headline caught her eye. She halted and stared. She took a deep breath, then read the article with painstaking slowness, taking in every word, creating a vision of her father's last day on earth.

West Coast Star

Oct 13, 1989

SUSIE SLAUGHTERS – A COLD CASE BROILS ANEW

After a six-month investigation into the grisly details of the Susie Slaughters, a case gone cold then reopened sixteen years later, the full picture is finally coming together.

The original case, deemed the Susie Slaughters, was named after the first of three victims. Three sixteen-year-old girls were killed in April of 1973 in Toronto. The case went cold, and the killer was never caught.

Sixteen years later, the body of a sixteen-year-old girl was found in Toronto on April 6.

Detective Mahoney, of the Calgary homicide department, had been on the original case in 1973. Detective Mahoney and his colleague Detective Sutton had joined the reopened investigation led by Sergeant Tomlinson of Toronto Homicide.

Stella gritted her teeth. This was all old information, regurgitated for the millionth time. She glanced at the clock across the room on the baby-blue wall, then returned her focus to the article, praying to the homicide gods for even a small morsel of fresh news.

After the bodies of three more girls were found, the second killing spree was put to a stop.

Saul Chester Ripper, deemed by the press to be the Killer Vampire and the Blood Demon, was killed in the basement of his home in Roches Point at 1:45 a.m. on April 21. Nineteen young women were recovered alive. They had been kidnapped over the last 12 years and held captive in Ripper's basement. One woman was found dead at the scene, the other eighteen were extracted from the basement dungeon and placed in safety until they are properly transitioned into new homes. Buried in the plot of land behind the residence, the bodies of another twelve young women were recovered. The ages of the young women ranged from sixteen to twenty-six. The oldest of them was taken by Saul twelve years ago. The victims who did survive were kept captive in Saul's underground dungeon the entire time. All of the surviving victims had been sterilized. The full extent of the acts performed by Saul on these young women may never be known.

Detective Jagger Mahoney was found dead in his car two blocks from the home of Saul Ripper. Det. Mahoney had a stab wound to his abdomen, which caused him to bleed to death. After an extensive investigation into the details of the events of the evening of April 21, it has been officially declared that Det. Mahoney was following a solid lead and had called for backup. It was Det. Mahoney's intention to question Ripper, to determine if he was a prime suspect. When he entered the residence, he was attacked by Ripper. In self-defence, Det. Mahoney inflicted critical injuries on Ripper. Det. Mahoney was able to escape the residence and make his way to his vehicle. He immediately called for help, at which time he was informed that FBI Agent Quesnel, who had been collaborating with Toronto Homicide on the case, was on her way to the scene with SWAT.

After an extensive investigation into the evening of April 21, it has been officially declared that if Det. Mahoney had not entered the residence of Saul Ripper, the lives of more innocent girls could have been taken, and Ripper could have escaped.

When interviewed, FBI Agent Quesnel provided the following information. "A detailed sweep of the entire mansion answered a lot of questions. All the bodies recovered, within the mansion and from the plot of land behind the mansion, were drained of blood and missing organs. We discovered a small room, attached to the kitchen. Some of the organs belonging to the victims were recovered from a freezer. Vacuum sealed and labelled. Vials of blood, also belonging to some of the victims, were stored in a refrigerated unit in the same room. An autopsy performed on Saul Ripper has led us to conclude that he was consuming both the organs and the blood. He suffered from vampirism, an extreme addiction to the consumption of human blood and body parts. As every victim was a replica of his deceased sister, Violet, we have concluded that his fantasy was to consume what he saw as her life source. The girls that survived are brain washed. It will take time to rewrite the script wired into their minds."

Sergeant Tomlinson, who had been leading the case, was not on scene, due to removal. An internal investigation against Sergeant Tomlinson with regards to his conduct of the Susie Slaughters case has finally been closed. It has been officially declared that Sergeant Tomlinson received monetary bribes directly from Saul Ripper, in return for diverting the investigation by focusing on false suspects. It is further suspected that if Sergeant Tomlinson had not created such diversions in the investigation then law enforcement may not have had to suffer the loss of a stand-up detective.

Sergeant Tomlinson's home in York Mills has been sieged until such time that the funds he received can be retrieved, and an internal investigation into his conduct on previous cases can be concluded. Criminal charges against the sergeant are pending.

Stella swallowed hard as she stared at the words…*may not have had to suffer the loss…*

A photo of Tomlinson was embedded within the article. His slick smile made her stomach churn. Her blood boiled as it pumped through her veins.

Acknowledgments

Writing a book is not a solo effort. If you helped me out in any way at all, with a glass of wine, a head bang, a hug, a dance party, some honest feedback, thank you from the bottom of my heart.

A special thank you to Taija Morgan for continuing to wave her magic wand over my stories. Her scrutiny, her keen eye, her masterful mind, and her dedication to making my books as much of a masterpiece as they can be, are all crucial to my success as a writer.

A special thank you to Sarah Johnson for wearing golden pants, hitting the dance floor, providing a warm hug, and for her guidance on my writing journey.

A special thank you to Dave Sweet who never hesitates to provide his expertise regardless of how much is going on for him.

A special thank you to Cami Schulte for blasting through an early copy and providing honest feedback. Cami has been a star reader for this entire series, and her input has been crucial.

A special thank you to the Activated Authors Master Mind group. You provided me the support I needed to embrace my voice and let it shine. Without you, I would not have surged forward on my path in my way at the right time. You will all be in my heart forever.

A special thank you to James Hiner for setting an example for me in how to chase my dreams, and how to dig deep and never give up. He is a shining star in my life every single day.

A special thank you to all of you who plunged into the depths of Vern's on an icy cold night, danced your hearts out, and grabbed one of the first copies of Final

Track to enter the world. A special thank you to all of you who stuck around, joined a virtual party when a real one was impossible, and supported the release of Acid Track. A special thank you to all of you who are holding a copy of Back Track now. Your support will warm my heart forever.

About Author

Julie Hiner spent endless hours during her childhood lost in the pages of books. The only thing that took precedence over a book was her Walkman. To this day, Julie is a hardcore 80s rocker at heart.

After securing a solid education in computer science at the University of Calgary, Julie spent over a decade working on large scale network systems. On a break between contracts, Julie followed her longing to finish a book she had started, a work of non-fiction portraying her personal story of facing fear and anxiety on a bicycle in the European mountains. After some deep soul searching, she decided to write a novel.

Following her fascination of the dark mind of the serial killer, and finding inspiration at a talk given by a local homicide detective, Julie surged down her new path to writing a dark, serial killer novel. She now writes dark crime and horror. She loves detailed research, creating in depth character, and unleashing her inner artist on photos to create the cover and marketing material.

Also By

Final Track – Detective Mahoney Series, Book 1: books2read.com/finaltrack

Acid Track – Detective Mahoney Series, Book 2: books2read.com/acidtrack

Soil Solo – Detective Mahoney Newsletter Exclusive: killersanddemons.com

Owen's Terrarium – books2read.com/owen

The Omens Call – Horror Anthology, Edited by Hiner and Willcocks, Featuring 'Room Thirteen' by Julie Hiner, DevilsRockPublishing.com
'Hallowed Killer', featured in Pulp Harvest – BloodRitesHorror.com
'Corpse Forest', featured in The Other Side: Horror Anthology – DevilsRockPublishing.com
'Tuny', featured in Terrace VI: Forbidden Fruit - TheSeventhTerrace.com

If you enjoyed Back Track, please consider leaving a review Goodreads(.com), or Bookbub(.com), or your retailer of choice. A review is worth a lot to an author.
Come visit @ KillersAndDemons.com